MIRRORS

Or do they…?

Disappointed to find out the pr
incarceration had already been
Morelli stepped out from prison. It didn't take long to realise that
what he'd been told of the death of the man who had set him up
was a lie.

A lie told by Zane's own firm.
A firm who had already overstepped the mark during his absence
by scarring his face in retribution for their wrongful belief that he
had betrayed them.

But the truth was now loud and clear. The man who had succeeded
in getting Zane banged up was alive and so therefore, would be
paying for what he did.

This should be easy for someone like Zane, but there is another
person with a grudge. Not only with Zane, but with his target.
And Zane hadn't thought Erin Langley would prove such a thorn
in his side.

What readers are saying about *Mirrors Never Lie*:

- "Fabulous book. Didn't want it to end…"
- "Gripped with this book from the very start…"
- "If you're looking for a new series, this must be the one…"
- "Proper gritty gangland, Edie is one of the best writers around in this
genre…"

MIRRORS NEVER LIE

SCARRED #1

EDIE BAYLIS

ATHAME
press
· LONDON ·

First published in Great Britain in 2023 by Athame Press.
This paperback edition published in 2023 by Athame Press.

Front cover photography: kriscole/depositphotos.com;
stetsik/depositphotos.com

Paperback ISBN 978-1-7398114-8-8
Hardback ISBN 978-1-7393009-4-4
Large Print ISBN 978-1-7393009-2-0
e-ISBN 978-1-7398114-6-4

Athame Press
Unit 13230 - PO Box 6945 – London – W1A 6US

PROLOGUE

1996

I KNOW MY FACE is set with a cold, unreadable expression. I know because I've spent years perfecting it.

Give nothing away. Don't let anyone read you. Let no one into your mind. Let no one into your heart.

That's what my father told me. He told my brother, Marco, the same thing. He told us lots of other things too, but that was the first I distinctly remember being drilled into us.

The first memory of those words was after me and Marco were accused of pinching from the local shop and we were subsequently dragged home to face our parents' wrath.

I glance around the courtroom, waiting patiently for the jury to return, my mind desperate to focus on something other than what will happen before the day is out and find myself thinking back to that day in 1973.

I was six years old; everything about it crystal clear, like it was yesterday.

As our mother ushered Mr Gopal into the sitting room of

our house in Battersea, our father pulled us roughly to one side. Towering over us, he hissed those very same words before dragging us back in front of the irate shopkeeper to apologise. After that, we were instructed to empty our money boxes and pay Mr Gopal back for the stolen sweets.

Except we hadn't stolen them. Our mate Micky Flowers had, but we took the blame. My father knew it but we had to silently accept whatever was said.

Because you don't drop your mates in it. Ever.

As we'd grown up, following in our father's footsteps to take our expected place in his London firm, this advice remained the same.

Loyalty above everything was the key to success.

Let no one under your skin. Take the rough with the smooth. Give nothing away. Take everything on the chin and never betray your own. Disloyalty is always repaid four-fold.

I'm doing the same now. For the firm and for the cause. I can't and won't let the others down. And if that means I take the rap, then so be it. We all know it's a risk in this life.

Tommo assured me the brief has swung it so that I'll get the minimum sentence or walk completely. There's no proof I was behind any of it. Everything they have on me is purely circumstantial, he said.

He'd repeated the exact thing again during the quick meeting we'd just had before court resumed. But it still stings standing here like an animal being judged for something I did not do. Something none *of us did.*

I have to walk from here. Even a short sentence is too much. After my father's death six months ago, I should be at the helm of the firm. It was what he'd wanted and expected.

But the entire time I've been stuck on remand in nick, refused bail whilst waiting for this trial, Marco has taken my place.

But now I'm going to be free, at least I can get on with what I was raised to do.

The nerve in my neck twitches. If I think too much about the irony, it winds me up. I can't let anything wind me up. Especially as I'm being watched.

My eyes move to the members of the jury filing back into the room. I don't make a big deal of looking at them - I merely give them the impression that I'm acknowledging them making their way back to their seats.

Some of them glance in my direction - the man with the bald spot, resembling a doctor is looking condescendingly down his long nose at me. I can see his disdain because he can't hide it. He doesn't even try. Neither does that ugly old woman with the Play-Doh hair. She's staring at me like I'm something she trod in.

But why would they hide their contempt when they have perfectly fucking straightforward lives?

They must now know the evidence isn't enough to prove it was me who did this and it's pissed them off. Faces like slapped haddocks, the lot of them. Whether they believe I'm guilty or not, and I suspect they all think I'm guilty, they're gutted to be able to do sod all about it.

I stop my lips from twitching into a smirk, although I want to laugh in their faces.

I reposition my feet. The shoes I'm wearing are Marco's, not mine. My feet are bigger than his and a toe on my right foot is crushed to fuck. I want to rip the shoe off and smash it in that Doctor bloke's mug, but I won't. I'll stand here, unmoving and wait until I walk out of this place as planned. Once I'm in the pub sinking a whisky, I'll take the fucking shoes off and keep them to shove down the throat of whoever pulled the hit that we'd being expressly instructed not to undertake.

Someone *had done it, but that person was not me. Nor any of our firm.*

My gaze drifts back to the gallery where I spot Marco, Bill and Sonny - the three representatives from the Morelli firm. The others aren't here, I realise it wouldn't look good.

These fuckers from the Crown would love to pin something on one of us. They've been waiting for years, but they've got no chance. Another reason why I've said absolutely nothing in my defence, short of "not guilty".

I will say nothing to implicate any members of the firm into anything - no matter how small. Anything I say could be used against one of them and, like I said, where I come from, loyalty is everything.

'All rise.'

I barely notice the wizened old man they call 'Judge' making his way to his perceived throne at the head of the courtroom. I swallow down my irritation.

Catching my brief's eyes, he gives me a slight nod. It will soon be over. The time is here.

'Members of the jury - have you reached a verdict?' the judge asks.

I ignore the sweat forming on the back of my neck. This is just a formality.

The voice continues and I realise I'm thinking about the pub; about the fag I'm desperate to smoke; about that barmaid that I know will be more than happy to relieve me of my frustration, when audible gasps jerk me back to full alertness.

A creeping dread races up my spine and my posture tenses. The nerve in my neck twitches again as I hone my concentration on the nasally voice of the judge who is still speaking, presumably to me.

Somewhere I hear the words, "in the light of this new evidence…"

My eyes lock on to his.

What new evidence? What the fuck?

It's when I hear: 'Zane Morelli, I'm sentencing you to twelve years for aggravated burglary and the manslaughter of David Masters', that does it.

The second I feel the grip of the prison officers' hands around both of my arms, I cannot stop myself from lashing out.

I don't even notice my right arm breaking free and smashing into someone's nose. I hear splintering and I also hear commotion as other officers scramble towards me. People in the room are screaming and yelling, but they sound muffled, like they're underwater.

I'm underwater…

I'm still lashing out. There's no way I'm being banged up. They'll have to kill me first. This is a set up. I've been framed. Fucking framed!

Something is coming out of my mouth. I can hear myself roaring, but I'm not sure what I'm saying because the pounding adrenaline crashing through my veins deafens me.

All I can think of as I'm tackled to the ground by an unknown number of men, is that I will kill the cunt who set me up.

ONE

2001 - Six Years Later

ZANE MORELLI watched the clock on the small metal table by the side of his bed as it approached 5 a.m., every second taking the equivalent of a minute. As it moved, the second hand glowed a faint luminous green in the darkness.

The lights were still off, but they wouldn't be soon.

Zane had been awake for hours, promising himself that whatever happened, he would not grant *anyone* the satisfaction of knowing he'd been up all night, his mind churning. No one would know exactly how much he couldn't wait to get out of here and that this day had been etched in the back of his mind as he'd mentally chalked off each second, minute, hour, day, week, month and year that passed with excruciating slowness.

He'd found the slowness was made worse by sitting on his hands, playing the system, keeping schtum, keeping himself to himself. Not to mention keeping his temper firmly under wraps - all to ensure this day took no longer to arrive than it should.

And he'd done it. *Somehow*.

It had taken every ounce of willpower not to react to the shit thrown in his direction. Countless times he could have happily ripped the faces off the bastard screws or the have-a-go fuckheads desperate to prove their place in this shithole. But he hadn't.

In the darkness, Zane frowned. He'd done whatever necessary whilst in here. He'd taken no unplanned risks. Prolonging his incarceration was not worth anything. *Nothing that couldn't wait, anyway.*

Even after what had happened two nights after first being banged up…

His fingers traced the scar on his face, like they did every morning, familiar with each part of the jagged, raised line trailing down his right cheek.

A smile formed.

This would be paid back today. His next move was planned with utmost precision. It wasn't like he hadn't had time to look forward to getting compensation.

The message that was sent, courtesy of the people he'd classed as family - the people he *still* classed as family, whose initial belief, thanks to the bullshit evidence appearing at last knockings, that it was *him* responsible for the murder and robbery of David Masters, had been their justification for okaying the message.

For a short time, they'd actually believed for a short time, that he'd gone against orders and ploughed ahead with the hit himself – the one which every single member of the firm had clear instructions not to undertake. And because this evidence suggested otherwise, they thought he'd betrayed them. The short amount of time before discovering otherwise was enough to put the order in motion.

And the only person who could have sanctioned that order, was Marco.

His brother.

And that had hurt more than *anything.*

His own brother's lack of belief in thinking he couldn't be trusted hurt more than the gopher who'd jumped on his bed, slashing his face to mark him with the seal of disapproval.

Marco may have apologised time and time again for it. He may have explained that once he and the firm realised their mistake, and that they wanted to make amends and put things right. That they'd take revenge on the person they now knew to be the culprit, but it wasn't as simple as that.

It still wasn't.

Zane's famed temper spiked.

It shouldn't have taken until the firm's trusted bean counter disappeared for alarm bells to ring. There should have been trust from the *start*. Zane Morelli was his father's son. Giuseppe would turn in his grave, knowing what his youngest son and the firm he'd founded, had done to his heir.

The expensive brief Marco employed may have got his sentence cut in half, but it didn't delete the knowledge that for a short time, they'd all believed Zane had betrayed them.

And it never would.

He'd never betrayed his own and neither would he. They should have known that.

Zane moved his fingers away from the scar. It only wound him up and he did not need help in that department. He also refused to think about the bastard who *had* betrayed him. Betrayed the entire firm.

But choosing not to think of this didn't alter that he'd been robbed of the only thing keeping him focused – the driving force behind retaining his sanity - revenge on the wanker who'd organised the fake evidence to be delivered to the court. The traitor in their midst.

Flame.

Zane scowled. He'd promised himself he wouldn't think of that name today, even in his own head, but it was there regardless.

As much as he struggled to comprehend what had happened, he'd finally justified Marco's lack of belief into a liveable level, if not a forgiven one. Unlike him, Marco wasn't raised to take the reins; he'd never been instilled with the same discipline their father had insisted for *him*. Marco was green in that respect.

As the elder brother, Zane had always stepped in to protect Marco and steer him in the direction needed. He'd forgiven Marco for his many fuckups over the years and made excuses when his actions or behaviour was below par.

And he was *still* doing it, even after the gross unfairness and bad call Marco had made by believing *he'd* betrayed the one thing which had always been most important – the *firm*.

But his brother had done one thing right. He'd kept the knowledge that justice had been meted out to himself for the best part of Zane's sentence.

Had Zane discovered the true culprit had already been offed as retribution sooner, it would have finished him. The promise of personally undertaking that revenge was all which had kept him going. Without that, coupled with his firm's betrayal, he would have lost it.

But last week he'd finally discovered the truth that his target was no more. Surprisingly, he'd been grateful, no matter how grating it was. Sure, he'd been angry – devastated even, but uncovering the truth on the day of his release would have been even more unbearable.

Shaking his head to rid his brain of the man who was the first and last thing he thought of every single day, Zane pulled himself up in the bed, the springs making that strange clunking sound he'd got used to and in a strange way, would probably miss at first.

He rolled his large shoulders to lessen the building tension and listened to the darkness. The silence was punctuated only by occasional yelling from the stupid fucker down the corridor who did the same thing every bloody night. Over the years he'd lost count of how many times he'd wanted to smash that man's face in, but this was the last night he'd have to put up with it. Plus, for once, the howling and shouting had failed to wake him because he'd been wide awake for hours.

Like an automaton, Zane watched the second-hand approach the hour and mentally counted down for the usual scenario to unfold.

Predictably, it played out bang on time.

His smile widened when the lights in the small space he'd called his own burst into life. Hopping out of bed, Zane moved to the toilet in the corner and sighing with relief, took a long piss.

Deciding to have a proper wash when he arrived at wherever he'd stay for the next few days, he turned on the tap and sluiced his face with freezing cold water. The coldness stung, but it also refreshed him.

A sliver of annoyance resurfaced. Although he would soon be free, he wouldn't be really. Not *completely*. But he'd pick up where he left off and return to his old life. There he was owed plenty. He had a lot to make up for and a lot to reclaim.

Finishing brushing his teeth, Zane pulled on his jeans and slipped on a black T-shirt. His own clothes felt strange after all this time. Strange, but nice and with the bang on the door, along with the usual jangle of keys, he shoved the few knickknacks he owned into his bag.

He was used to this part of the morning's ritual, but today it was different.

Zane's heart thumped as the door opened but he masked his relief seeing the screw he'd made arrangements with.

Everything was in place.

Without a word, Zane picked up his bag and walked from his cell for the final time. He didn't look back. He'd already scrutinised every millimetre enough for it to be indelibly etched in his mind - just like the scar was forever etched onto his face.

I wonder what they'll think now? he thought, musing how the rest of the firm would react to seeing his face for the first time in six years? To see the result of when mistrust clouded judgement.

Would they look at the floor and pretend the scar wasn't there?

Zane walked down the landing, his eyes fixed ahead and purposely ignored the banging of other doors and the shouted well-wishes for his release.

The other prisoners resented his leaving. They wished they could murder him and go in his place. Not that he cared. It wasn't like he'd spoken to any of them. No friends had been made, so there was no one to say goodbye to.

Apart from one…

That man was no friend but would receive a special parting gift.

On the way down the corridor towards freedom, Zane glanced at the screw by his side and as the sick bay approached, the man gave an imperceptible nod.

The wanted man was in here - Zane had made sure of that. Last night's poisoned food wasn't enough to kill. He wasn't stupid. He didn't want *that* to be what killed this bastard. It was imperative the loser realised who killed him. And why.

Leaving the screw outside, Zane slipped into the sick bay. The other beds were empty and the nurse was, as planned, taking an important phone call in the office. She thought her mother had died.

She hadn't.

At least, if she had, it was nothing to do with him. But by the time the nurse returned, he'd have succeeded with what he came to do and be long gone.

Zane stepped behind the curtain of the only occupied bed and shined the bright torch he'd kept hidden in Sam Fennell's face. He smiled with growing satisfaction as the man's eyes flashed open. 'Good morning,' he growled, the urge to scream the words, strong.

Do what you planned. No more, no less.

Zane saw Fennell scramble from the blue bedsheet to reach for the panic button. He knew what the man was trying to do. He'd expected it. But this waster would achieve nothing. *There was no chance.*

He gripped Fennell's wrist. 'Dodgy burger last night?' Zane's eyes shone in the torchlight. He knew he looked scary. He always did – especially when on a mission. And this was no different. It would also be every bit as gratifying as he wanted it to be - *needed* it to be.

It wouldn't remove the scar, but it would offset a percentage of the accrued interest.

'Morelli,' Fennell spluttered. 'You can't... I...'

'Shut it,' Zane spat. 'You know why I'm here.' He didn't want excuses. The man would bleat he'd only followed orders; that he'd had no choice; that he'd been paid, so had to deliver.

Maybe. But it wasn't good enough. It would *never* be good enough. 'You shouldn't have been greedy,' Zane hissed, the words rushing like steam through his clenched teeth.

He pulled the razor from his pocket and used his teeth to rip away the protective cap he'd fashioned to stop it cutting through his pocket.

The razor blade was attached to a toothbrush shaft. The little weapon may not look fancy, and perhaps the most basic one he'd ever used to do something like this, but it would do the job.

Catching the glint of metal, Fennel's eyes widened and he flailed fruitlessly around in his sickbed.

Zane laughed coldly at the pointless struggle and gripped hold of Fennell's wrist so tightly even his own hand ached. The pain was enjoyable because this bastard was going nowhere. And he was *loving* the fear.

There was a lot he wanted to say to this prick, but there wasn't time. And, in all truth, no point. The man was fucked. Finished. And he knew it.

Zane suddenly caught sight of a blue biro on the bedstand next to the medical notes. The nurse must have left it behind in her haste to take the unexpected phone call. The pen wasn't part of his plan, but it presented such an excellent opportunity, it would be rude not to utilise it effectively.

Clamping the handle of the toothbrush in his teeth, he grabbed the pen with his free hand. He smiled down at Fennell. Whichever way the man looked at it, he would fail. Even more so in around two seconds from now...

'Life dictates that you should never act on anything, unless you've seen it with your own eyes.' Zane's voice was low, calm.

'What? I...'

Zane grinned. Fennel didn't quite get it yet, nor did he need to. He would soon understand everything. 'Lesson one. Use the gift of sight wisely...'

Without another word, he plunged the pen deep into the centre of Fennel's right eyeball. The pointed biro top made its journey pleasingly effortless. Fennell's face contorted in agony; his eyeball rendered permanently useless.

A random thought flashed into Zane's mind as to what an artistic, yet grotesque photograph this would make - a pen wedged through the pupil - only the bloodied white of the eyeball visible.

It was Fennell's gaping mouth, set to roar with pain which snapped Zane back to the now. Noise would ruin his plan. He should not have diverted.

Plucking the makeshift weapon from his mouth, he sliced left to right across Fennel's neck, then jumped back to avoid being splattered with blood spurting from the hairline slit stretching from windpipe to jugular.

He only spent a matter of seconds watching Fennel's one remaining eye darting around, bulging as shocked disbelief sank in. His other eye remained held in place for eternity.

Fennell's hands, now free, flailed around to grasp at the slit in his throat, now widening into a gaping chasm. Bubbles from his slashed windpipe mixed with purple blood and a strange gurgling noise came from his throat, whilst his mouth flapped silently up and down.

Turning, Zane capped his makeshift weapon and shoved it down the back of his boot, a low noise coming from his own mouth - the beginning of a laugh.

Quickly leaving the room, he closed the door behind him. He could laugh out loud at the screw's unwillingness to meet his eyes, knowing the accepted wad of cash sitting heavily in the officer's back pocket was what had made this small act of retribution possible.

Flanked by the screw, Zane continued up the corridor towards the room where his possessions were first taken when entering Winson Green prison would be returned.

By the time Fennell was discovered, Zane would be long gone and there would be nothing to link him to that man's demise.

Hiding his rising anticipation, Zane watched the screw punch in the code for the release room and ignoring the scowl on the release officer's face, he stepped forward to sign the waiting documentation.

He was now free.

Two

ERIN LANGLEY watched her fiancé fussing with his hair in the bathroom mirror, her jaw clenching behind her well-practised smile. Moving closer, she wrapped her arms around Anthony's waist, even though she didn't want to be anywhere near him.

She wanted him dead.

But she had to bide her time. She had a plan and must stick to it.

'Are you nearly ready?' Erin asked, noticing Anthony's concentration fully on his own reflection. She swallowed the brewing irritation. Anthony's concentration should be on *her* because however much it stuck in her throat, she'd done everything to dance to his tune. Still, he would shortly regret everything.

Erin studied Anthony's brown eyes in the mirror. They were like dead fish. They blinked like a normal person's, but that was that extent of it.

Not that she knew much about anything normal. But she played the part well. *Sort of.*

'I'd be quicker if you'd let me get on with things,' Anthony snapped, his mouth twisting into his default expression - a contemptuous snarl. 'My contact lens is uncomfortable.'

Erin inwardly sighed as Anthony glared at her in the mirror's reflection and wondered why, if contact lenses irritated him so much, he didn't just wear glasses?

She knew why. It was because he was too vain and would prefer to walk around blind, rather than wear specs, the prick.

'Erin!' Anthony shrugged out of her embrace. 'Give me space, for fuck's sake!'

Erin retreated from the bathroom, the door shutting firmly behind her. No doubt Anthony was now rummaging around in the silver monogrammed contact lens case which took pride of place in his mirrored bathroom cabinet.

Yes, his *own* cabinet. God forbid he should share his available space with her. It would dramatically cut down the room for his preening equipment.

Okay, with his deep brown eyes, chiselled face and neat, dark hair, the top locked into place with a host of different styling products, she supposed by many people's standards, Anthony was a decent-looking bloke, but that was of little consequence.

With the time and money he spent in tanning studios, hairdressers, on contact lenses and clothes, it was hardly surprising. But aside from the weird, obsessional way he dealt with every facet of his life, she also knew the *other* reason why he was so vigilant over his appearance. Oh yes, she knew *exactly* why that was so important.

He was never seen in anything without an expensive designer logo or tag either. He knew how to dress and didn't mind paying for the privilege.

A sneer crept across Erin's lips. His obsession with nice *expensive* things extended to her.

She glanced at the deep pink nails at the end of each of her fingers. These were kept in shape weekly, courtesy of Anthony - one thing of many he had no issue funding. He liked her to look perfect. Hair extensions, eyebrow shaping, massages, personal shoppers, as much money as she wanted...

Yes, she looked perfect. *Anthony's* version of perfect. And that wasn't her choice. In fact, she hated it.

A bit like this house.

Living in Solihull – or rather, not far from it, wouldn't have been her first choice of location to ensure she was in the correct vicinity. But Anthony wouldn't have accepted living in Birmingham. Oh no, that was *unthinkable*.

To him, Solihull was different. There, people refused to class themselves under the Midlands banner, let alone anything to do with Birmingham, but siting his new business and buying a house in Knowle was ideal for him.

The large, but leafy affluent village with its self-professed grandeur, fancy properties and equally fancy people were just up Anthony's street. Yet it was close enough to rub shoulders with the money and Birmingham's financial district, meaning he could play his game just perfectly.

As could she...

Erin's eyes moved around the massive master bedroom with velvet cushions lined against the headboard of the super king bed, just the way Anthony insisted. She knew just which cushions Anthony insisted went with which linen set. Attention to detail was vital.

But when all was said and done, and no matter how straightforward her plan seemed at its conception, no amount of money, trinkets or luxury made up for living with this man.

The only thing being around Anthony holding any clout was that it would eventually bring her what she wanted: what was hers in the first place. And his death...

She glanced at her diamond-encrusted Cartier watch – another gift from her 'devoted' fiancé. It was almost seven. They'd said they'd be at the wine bar by now, but as usual, Anthony's meeting in Birmingham was making them late. Would anyone have a problem with that? No, of course not. Anthony was fantastic with everyone he dealt with. Apart from *her*.

His popularity was only because his 'friends' were business

associates - or rather, people who, for a hefty sum, he advised over investments, mortgages and so on. Anything financial, he knew it. But Anthony's knowledge, his fancy life and decent looks could never be anything other to Erin than what *he* was.

What they *all* were...

Her eyes shone with ice. Anthony was a liar. A cold, control freak who gave a shit about no one but himself, the wiring in his head fucked.

Erin's soft hands curled into fists.

Anthony Walker had been part of *that* firm until he'd turned them over and done a runner. He may not have been the one to kill her father, but he'd been *involved*. He may have successfully reinvented himself, but he would pay when the time came.

Erin stared at the bathroom – the sound of a hissing aerosol loud from behind the closed door.

It was frustrating having to wait. And not just waiting for Anthony to finish getting ready, but waiting to remove him from the face of the planet. However, there was one benefit. The longer she waited for that golden time to arrive, the more her anger grew. It was that anger which would prove so rewarding when it was unleashed.

She twirled a glossy blonde curl around her finger. She preferred her hair straight, but Anthony wanted it wavy. It was the one and only reason he'd insisted on her having hair extensions. Extensions made from only the best human hair, of course...

Erin shrugged. She hated the bloody things. *Whatever.* It wasn't like she cared. Her hair made little difference. She had no need to cling to anything that made her who she was. Or *had* been. Being herself had brought nothing but misery.

Rubbing her lips together, she inspected her pout in the mirror. If Anthony took much longer, she'd need another coat of lipstick before they even got in the bloody cab. Long-lasting and expensive lipstick which stayed the distance, it may be, but everything had a time limit. *Again, like her.*

Her lips formed a thin line. She'd made her bed. In fact, she'd actively sought where she'd lain for the past six years.

She was fine when she didn't think about it. Reminding herself of her promises usually kept things at bay, but every so often something happened - a random thought; a smell, and against her will, the injustice rushed back.

Tugging open the top drawer of the dressing table, she snatched out a small, padded leather box and opened it to stare at the gold and sapphire bracelet inside. Another meaningless bauble, courtesy of Anthony. If she looked at it through anyone else's eyes, it was beautiful, but to her, beauty held no meaning any longer. Everything was for a purpose – at least that's what she'd trained herself to believe. And that worked well because it was the only way to bear this.

Draping the bracelet around her slender wrist, she struggled to do up the dainty clasp with her talon-like nails, then pulled a scrap of paper from underneath the box's velvet lining.

Unfolding it, she stared at the names written in her own hand several years ago. The ink might have faded, but what those words read, had not.

Her mouth twitched with the ghost of a smile. Every day she looked at this important list so that its power or the promised anticipation of what was to come didn't fade. Having those names in black and white enforced the ritual of what she'd promised to do.

Each day was a step further towards that ultimate prize.

As Anthony exited the en-suite bathroom, Erin tucked the paper back in its velvet hiding place, knowing he was about to scrutinise her to ensure she was up to par for leaving the house on his arm. *Another of his routines…*

Their life played out the same – day in, day out; their social calendar always full of networking drinks and dinners; meaningless hours spent with false people – all with their own agendas, whilst she and Anthony acted the part of the sickeningly happy and successful couple.

And that's all it was. Playing a part.

Erin popped her lipstick and eyeliner in her handbag. There were only two things she wanted. Money and revenge. Once she was married, everything of Anthony's would legally belong to her. Only then, once her financial security was assured, would she be free to complete her second objective.

The second that murderer stepped outside the prison it would be time to pick him off, along with Anthony and anyone else that new information proved should be added to the list. Anyone connected would be removed one by one.

Bang...

'Do you not think, considering the colour scheme, the purple dress would be more suitable?'

Anthony's voice grated in Erin's ears. *Colour scheme of the wine bar? Of course, how stupid of her...*

Without having to think about it, the smile materialised on her lips as she glided to the walk-in wardrobe. 'You're right, darling,' she purred in a fawning voice which sickened her. 'I don't know why I didn't think of that.'

Flicking through the colour coordinated dresses, suits, jackets and skirts - all lined in shade order on the rail, she lifted out a padded hanger holding a purple bandage dress.

This had been purchased after the Versace show in London. She'd enjoyed that show - not for the clothing, nor for the extra spending allowance Anthony transferred onto her card, but because it was one of the few places she'd gone without *him*.

He hadn't accompanied her, or rather, *wouldn't*. He didn't explain why and neither had she asked. She hadn't cared. It meant a night without him.

Anthony proudly inspected himself in the floor length mirror. 'You need to hasten, Erin. We're already late.'

Erin slipped off the dress to replace it with the one of Anthony's choice. Of course, it was *her* fault they were running late... Nothing to do with that he'd been delayed in Birmingham. He would do exactly the same tomorrow as well.

Whatever he wanted to believe was fine. The only relevant thing was that it was her choice to sell her body and soul in exchange for payback.

The man who'd murdered her parents would be released within the next few years and she would be waiting.

Unbeknown to Anthony, that was the only reason she was here; the reason she'd moved to this area and the reason she was with *him*.

She smiled. Anthony wouldn't be aware that bastard had been moved to a prison this side of the country. Neither did he know who she was or that she knew what he'd done. But she did know, because she'd made it her business to follow every single thing that went on where that subject was concerned.

She'd also followed *him*.

If Anthony *had* been aware of any of this, there was no way he would have had anything to do with her. Instead, he'd played into her hands and in return, she'd proved herself invaluable for making up for his failings in social etiquette. He wouldn't have gone with her suggestion to move here had she not manipulated things to look like the idea had been his and his alone.

He wouldn't have done any of it.

It was quite amusing really, but her work and patience had paid off. She was positioned in a close enough area, it was almost time and very soon she'd be married. Then, the moment she learnt of that murdering bastard's release she'd be ready. Ready for *all* of them.

Achieving her mission was becoming closer with every day that passed and if either of those bastards believed they would return to their lives, or even *have* a life, they were sadly mistaken.

Noticing Anthony impatiently tapping his foot over by the door, Erin smiled sweetly and rushed to grab her handbag.

• • • •

IN THE APARTMENT, Marco Morelli pulled open a desk drawer and rummaged for the folder he needed. He then pushed away the woman who'd been draping herself over him for the last ten minutes.

How was he supposed to think with her in here?

'Fuck off!' he snarled, the woman jumping away at his tone of voice. 'Don't pester me unless I *ask* you to!'

Marco glared at the woman's retreating back as she hurried from the room, her heels clicking on the thick wooden flooring, then turned his attention back to the desk drawer. Catching sight of a photograph at the back under a pile of paperwork, he scowled. He knew by its filigree silver frame exactly whose picture it contained.

And he knew because he'd shoved it there.

Marco didn't want the subject of that photograph scrutinising him all day, every day. Although it was only an image and no one was watching him in real life, it felt that way. The piercing eyes so similar to his own followed him around the room, judging, watching and making assumptions...

He didn't need that, nor did he want it.

Marco's heavy brows knitted. He'd meant to get rid of the picture, like the majority of the other things in this apartment. But out of sight meant out of mind and he'd forgotten about it. After all, he hadn't had cause to go into that particular drawer of what had been his brother's desk for a long time.

Not until now.

But much to his utter aggravation, it seemed that soon it might be time, so he needed to put some more things in place.

Since telling Zane that Flame had been dealt with, this scenario had played on his mind. He didn't know why he'd told his brother that Flame was dead, aside from he'd had to say *something*.

Having skirted around references to that subject in the past, he'd got away without answering directly. Actually, he'd done well in avoiding it until now, thanks to the sparse number of times he'd visited his brother since he'd been locked up.

What with Manchester being so far away from London, along with pretending he was up to his neck running the firm during Zane's unexpected absence, sufficed as valid reasons. After all, it wasn't like *he'd* been brought up as the son trained

26

in such things...

But since Zane had been transferred to Winson Green in Birmingham and several years had passed since he'd taken over running the firm, those previous reasons were not quite as valid or plausible for his absence. Hence, he'd had little choice but to act on many of Zane's recent visiting orders. It was during the last few visits it became apparent Zane was digging around, hellbent on retribution, so Marco had been forced to say revenge had already been carried out, rather than the truth being uncovered.

Surprisingly, Zane had taken the news better than Marco presumed. But he wouldn't take *this* well and that was a fact.

Marco's eyes moved around the room now resembling nothing of what Zane would hold in his memory.

Zane's reluctance to embellish on news of an impending release date bothered him immensely and if his brother didn't get collared for something else to add to his sentence soon, then he'd be out in a matter of months. That could not happen.

Marco had tried his upmost via orders on the inside for Zane to be dumped in situations to test his patience, giving his hot-headed older brother the excuse and impetus to lash out and earn extra time. But it hadn't worked.

That in itself was odd. It was unlike Zane to be so controlled. In fact, it was so unheard of, he'd even wondered whether his brother had found God during his absence from real life. But it wasn't that.

It was worse...

Zane was toeing the line until he stepped from behind those prison gates.

That wasn't how it was supposed to be. Zane should *never* be getting out.

Seeing *that* photograph of their father wasn't helping.

Slamming the drawer shut, Marco stared at the desk. It was the only piece of kit left of Zane's home office. The rest, Marco had got rid of at the first opportunity.

Who needed antique filing cabinets?

Not *him*.

He'd replaced all the tat with useful stuff - stuff akin to the way *he* worked and the way the *firm* now worked.

As his attention moved to the huge flat screen TV mounted on the wall and then over to the beer fridge, a grin formed on Marco's face.

Why not afford himself the option of watching the films he produced without bothering to move? As films were now the main part of the firm, it was reasonable to scrutinise the footage for approval from in here. The cinema complex he'd had installed in the living area was for the finished product and private screenings only.

Leaving the office, Marco moved down the marbled hallway into the open-plan living area and scowled at the woman he'd dismissed earlier lounging on a red leather sofa, waiting for his attention.

She'd get some, Marco thought, but all in good time.

First, he needed to call Bill and Sonny to tell them to touch base with one of their contacts in nick to get updates.

If there were any, he'd deal with them straight away because things were getting complicated.

THREE

ZANE SAT ON THE BED. The springs creaked, but they didn't make that clunking sound like the one he'd got used to in nick.

He glanced around the room, his attention drawn to a damp patch in the corner above the sink. Presumably a leak from the room above, but as long as the ceiling collapse on him during the night, he couldn't give a fuck.

He hadn't thought once he'd walked from those prison gates he'd opt to stay *anywhere* in the vicinity of the nick, but the minute he'd seen the light of day it had knocked him more than expected, so this B&B in Ladywood seemed the best thing to do in the short term.

He'd always believed the minute he was out, he'd be on the first train back to London, but as the date of his release neared, he'd decided it wise to stay around for a few days to get his head in gear. That had been a good call. He'd expected to feel disorientated, that's why he'd purposely kept his release date to himself. If he'd told Marco, his brother would have been waiting the minute he stepped through the gates.

Plus, Marco would have immediately realised he'd sacked the brief paid to deal with his case and hired another one.

And he'd want to know why.

Why? Because Zane had no longer trusted the brief had been working in his best interests. But on those suspicions, he needed to be sure before he did anything about it. And he wasn't. So, what he'd chosen as the alternative had been the best option for now.

But maybe he'd made the wrong decision? This B&B was not only a hovel of the highest order, but staying somewhere less than two miles from the place he'd been caged, felt *far* too close.

Zane picked up the plastic kettle from the dressing table and eyed the dusty foil caps of two small cartons of UHT milk. How long they'd been there was anyone's guess.

He could have stayed somewhere better than this. A *lot* better. It wasn't like he was broke. He had plenty of brass in his account - and it was still there, untouched. He knew this because he'd checked.

It was that experience which reinforced the decision to stay somewhere close and calm his head down before returning to London.

Going inside the bank today was dreadful. It had completely tripped him out. Standing in the queue, it felt like everyone was staring at him.

Zane shuddered, hating admitting to the panic which had brewed in the base of his stomach. He'd felt it churning, gradually gaining momentum. It took a lot of concentration not to run from the building, away from the fluorescent lights and scrutinising eyes of the bespectacled tellers.

Except no one had been actually looking at him. It was in his head.

Fixating on the tightly permed blue rinse of an old dear before him in the queue, he'd mentally calculating how many minutes it would take for her to locate her purse from the bottom of her handbag. This helped divert from the unfamiliar feelings of panic.

Moving his eyes to the scuffed dressing table mirror, Zane

stared blankly at his reflection.

He still looked like himself - apart from the scar.

The everlasting reminder of his firm's and his brother's betrayal.

Not that he needed one.

Zane chuckled, despite everything. He must have looked deranged when he'd eventually reached the front of the bank queue and explained his card had expired because the teller thought better of pressing the matter. After a short and whispered conversation with a colleague, she'd handed over the requested cash, saying a new card would be sent out within three working days.

And no, he hadn't explained *why* his card had expired.

He'd given this B&B address as a temporary measure. He could have given his London address, but something told him not to. Not yet.

He'd return to London when *he* was ready, not on the account of expecting fucking letters. And so, whether he liked it or not, he was stuck here for a few days longer.

The firm would find out of his release soon enough, even though they believed it to be months, perhaps *years* away. They might already know. They could be monitoring his bank account for movement. They probably were.

Tough shit.

Shrugging his leather jacket on, he ran his hand through his dark wavy hair. 'Zane Morelli, you're back,' he said aloud, his voice sounding overly loud in the otherwise empty room.

It was time to plan how and when he would return to step back into the position that was his. It *would* have been his for the last six years, had it not been for this unexpected time-out. Now Marco would have to accept the seat at the head of the table no longer belonged to him.

Zane scowled, his seething hatred for Flame escalating. Not personally eradicating the man who had got him sent down made the injustice ten times worse.

Feeling the usual surge of adrenaline rush through his veins,

31

he shook his head with irritation. At least he'd got revenge on one person left outstanding. Fennell's quick death this morning was cathartic.

There would be no repercussions for it either. Fennell was a nobody, doing the bidding of others.

Onwards and upwards.

Zane pulled the collar of his jacket higher. He would waste no more time on that. What mattered now was what went on from here.

Thanks to succeeding in withdrawing a big chunk of cash, he'd paid for a few nights in this dump, bought himself a mobile phone and sourced himself some transport. He'd also got himself a gun.

Not bad going for a few hours.

Getting details for these things for sale near to the nick was one of the few useful things that screw had done, apart from granting him access to the sick bay of course…

But the screw knew it was in his best interests to comply and then keep his mouth shut, if he wanted to continue spending life with his wife and kids.

Zane glanced out of the window down onto the road beneath where he'd parked his Yamaha FJ1200. Not a patch on what he owned back in London, but good enough for now.

He'd give it a proper run in the morning, but for now there was only one other thing to do: get his arse down the nearest pub and chuck several whiskies down his neck. And, he smiled, with any luck, a shag.

He was fairly sure he could find a willing recipient to ease his frustration. He'd had no problem in the past.

Peeling several twenties from the bankroll of cash, Zane shoved them in his pocket, then tugged the stiff top drawer of the dressing table open. He grimaced at the perfumed floral liner whose sole purpose was to hide the cheap wood. *It had failed.*

Thinking better of leaving a wad of cash in an unoccupied B&B room with an unsteady door, Zane stuffed all the money in his pocket. He knew better than to trust anyone.

For what it was worth, he locked the door behind him and shoved the key in his pocket. Loping down the creaky stairs, he nodded at the sour-faced landlady who eyed him suspiciously as she hovered at the bottom like a spider.

'The front door is locked at eleven.' The woman spoke to Zane's retreating back.

Zane ignored her. It wasn't like he couldn't get back in if he wanted. She may not realise it yet, but would soon enough if the need arose.

Grinning to himself, he slipped out into the night.

FOUR

BILL WAINWRIGHT stubbed his cigarette out in the heavy ashtray and grabbed a can of beer. Lounging back in the leather chair, he settled into his excellent vantage point and waited patiently for the scene to roll again.

Yeah, it was unnecessary to film this part for the third time, being as the last take was spot on, but with such a delectable view of this bird's arse, it was criminal not taking full advantage of his position.

Overseeing this part of the firm was a dream come true - much better than he could have dreamt of, and certainly a thousand times better than the daily grind of collecting and security which was his job in the Morelli firm before Marco took over.

He cracked his knuckles, mindlessly staring at the tattooed dots adorning his hands, then pulled another cigarette from his pocket and lit it with his initialled zippo. Eighteen carat gold, this was. Another perk of the job, thanks to Marco and his changes to the business. And Bill had been more than happy to take the offer of promotion to run *this* particular side of things.

Marco's previous position as head of the enforcement sector of the Morelli empire meant Bill had always been his right-hand man – running the boys who pulled in the readies from the many businesses on their payroll who happily shelled out for protection.

Well, perhaps not 'happily'... But by doing so, they escaped anything unfortunate happening to their premises. Or their families...

But how the Morelli firm operated now – or rather, *his* jump up the ladder, was something else. Bill was still Marco's right-hand man, but now on *every* facet of the empire - the main one being Marco's brainchild of jumping on the adult film industry.

Never short of try-outs with new girls vying for starring roles in their popular films was only one of the many bonuses Bill had benefitted from since Marco had taken the reins. It was a more than welcome change, as well as being a lucrative new offshoot of the firm. Gone were the days of concentrating solely on extortion and protection rackets. Moving with the times was the order of the day, so Marco said.

Bill's eyes centred on the peach-like buttocks of the slender girl kneeling on the bed, the lights from the set illuminating her perfectly rounded silicon breasts.

He scowled at the two men moving into position behind her. 'OIH!' he yelled, sweeping his meaty arm to the left. 'You're blocking my view! Take her from the other side and just move the fucking camera.'

'Yes, Mr Wainwright.' The cameraman dragged his wheeled trolley holding the large camera to one side and waited whilst the two men hastily changed position.

Bill smiled with gratification. If that chick was extra lucky, he'd give her a piece afterwards. She could stay exactly where she was too. It was perfect.

As the cameras began rolling and the action began, Bill grimaced when his mobile vibrated in his pocket. *For fuck's sake, what now?*

Dragging the phone from his jeans, he was all set to button the call, until he saw who it was.

Bollocks.

Begrudgingly getting to his feet, he quickly moved through the door to the corridor outside the set. 'Yes, boss? No, I'm at the studio… I'm overseeing the...' Pausing, he listened, concern brewing. 'Okay, I'll get onto it straight away.'

Ending the call, Bill shoved the phone back into his pocket, a frown creasing his pockmarked face. Well, that ballsed up his plans, but if Marco wanted an update, then that's what he'd have.

But he didn't like the sound of this because it seemed things might be about to change. And no one wanted that.

• • • •

OLIVES HAD NEVER BEEN one of Erin's favourites and these were no exception. She eyed the bowl of green objects floating in a sea of something putrid, accompanied by miniature cocktail sticks on a silver tray and wondered how many peoples' piss would be detected on the grotesque alien eyeballs. She'd once read an article about an experiment which discovered a huge amount of different peoples' urine in a bowl of nuts on a bar. Okay, so these weren't nuts, but it was the same difference, wasn't it?

To have these thoughts, rather than concentrating on the surroundings, underlined her boredom. She had to make an effort. She couldn't afford to get slack because Anthony watched everything she did to justify his incessant griping about how she'd 'let him down'.

He hadn't seen anything yet!

Erin stared at the dainty cocktail sticks. How she'd love to shove one in Anthony's eye. But she wouldn't. It was important to maintain the illusion of being a happy and successful couple, not the fractured pair entertaining this charade for reasons best not mentioned.

Inexplicably, the bowl of olives moved closer and Erin frowned, until she realised someone was holding them out to her.

Pulling her eyes from the offending bowl, she found the

olives in the hands of the wife of the man Anthony was hoping to gain further business from. She smiled at Jocelyn, avoiding staring at how the woman's teeth, despite being shiny and perfectly straight, hung over her bottom lip. If going to the expense of having teeth whitened to the point of brilliance, didn't it make sense to have them altered to look less rabbit-like?

Shaking away the thought, Erin instead concentrated on Jocelyn's oversized diamond earrings, which were slightly less offensive.

'I do hope you'll join us on Thursday afternoon while the boys do their thing at golf,' Jocelyn simpered. Getting the hint about the olives, she placed the bowl back onto the gleaming marble of the bar. 'Us girls are having drinks. Please say you'll come?'

'I'd love to,' Erin heard herself say, although she'd rather drown slowly in a pit of tar than partake in a mind-numbing afternoon of canapés and discussing hairstyles?

She ransacked her brain for something to say and focused on keeping her smile in place, knowing the minute she lost concentration, it would disappear. 'I love your dress. It's from the latest collection, isn't it?' Erin made sure to keep up with what was hot and what wasn't. She'd come too far not to keep up the act. 'It really suits you.'

'Oh! Do you think so?' Jocelyn flapped her hand, like she was surprised at the admiration, when clearly that's what she expected. 'By the way, myself and Jeffrey can't *wait* for your wedding.' She batted her spidery lashes. 'We were only discussing yesterday how wonderful your dress will be. We can't wait to see it!'

'It's just what I've always dreamed of,' Erin lied, the good-natured laugh escaping her mouth hurting her throat. It didn't sound like her, but then it didn't belong to her. *None of this did.*

'Anthony will be the envy of every bachelor in town.' Jocelyn made a strange hooting sound, like an owl with hiccups, her laugh falser than anyone's.

Erin couldn't bear thinking about the wedding. The dress was beautiful, it was just that she didn't want to be inside it.

You're doing what you set out to do, she told herself, as if that made it more acceptable.

It didn't.

'Come now.' Jocelyn nudged Erin. 'Can't you give me a teeny-weeny hint of what the dress is like?'

'I won't even tell Anthony, but you'll see soon enough.' Erin's gushing voice made out like she shared a secret with a friend, but Jocelyn wasn't a friend and never would be. She hated the woman almost as much as she hated Anthony.

It was true she hadn't said anything to Anthony about the dress, but that was because he hadn't asked. Nor would he. He was as interested in it as she was… His only comment was to point out it cost two grand more than the twenty he'd allotted for it.

Oh, well. Every point she scored against him counted.

Erin slipped gracefully from the leather-topped bar stool, the familiar sense of claustrophobia bearing down. 'If you'd excuse me.' She nodded in the direction of the ladies cloakroom, then tottered across the polished floor, hoping her Louboutins didn't slip on the shiny surface.

Her smile remained fixed as the door to escape drew nearer, hoping Jocelyn didn't follow to continue their 'chat'.

Refraining from breaking into a run, Erin rushed into the cloakroom, the gold fixtures and fittings making her queasy. The moment the door closed, her smile dropped and she thanked the nameless powers that be for allowing the toilets to be deserted.

Locking herself into a cubicle, she closed the toilet lid and sat down on the gold embossed wood, a layer of perspiration forming on her brow.

Putting her head in her hands, she closed her eyes to stop her breath from degenerating into ragged gasps. How much longer could she stand this half-life with a man who didn't like her and who she couldn't bear? How much bloody longer?

She already knew the answer. *Until her list was complete.*

Inhaling slowly, Erin pressed her hot forehead against the cool tiled wall. There wasn't long now. Once that ring was on her finger and the wedding certificate in her possession, she would no longer have to waste time being so bloody nice.

It would be easier just to kill Anthony and not bother with this charade and certainly not a wedding! She was confident she'd manage that perfectly, whilst avoiding being put in the in the frame for wrongdoing, but it was important to leave no stone unturned – no chance of being investigated or charged. With Anthony leaving her a grieving young widow, not only would her money be guaranteed, but her back covered for all eventualities.

Sickening or not, it was the sensible way of ensuring her innocence. *And payment...*

Her chin jutted determinedly. One way or another, she would reclaim some of what she'd lost. Not just financially. It just so happened that as well as paying for what Anthony had taken from her these past six years, he'd be picking up the fucking tab for what *they'd* done – the things propelling her towards this goal in the first place.

Happiness was irrelevant. She didn't require it. She hadn't had that for a very long time and no longer even *wanted* it. Following a defined set of actions whilst feeling nothing was the only way to survive.

A genuine smile slid onto Erin's face. It didn't happen very often. These days her smiles were made to order, but this one was real.

She was very nearly there.

Standing up, she walked from the cubicle, giving her hair a quick fluff in the ornate gold mirror's reflection. *You see, Erin? Keep things in perspective.*

Pulling the outer door, she moved back towards her drink, noticing it had been refilled in her absence.

Although she'd love to drink plenty, she wouldn't. It would be too easy to dull her feelings with alcohol and she needed them raw. Keeping the hatred fresh was the only thing driving her.

Sending a bright smile in Anthony's direction, Erin expected nothing other than a cold glance in return. Good job, because that's what she received. Unperturbed, she moved to join the coven of women at the bar waiting for her return.

FIVE

ZANE REALISED his forehead had creased to the point where his eyebrows almost tickled the bridge of his nose. As kids, Marco said he'd end up with a face like a concertina by the time he was forty from frowning so hard and he was probably right.

It wasn't like there was long to go until he reached the big four-zero either. Six years until that milestone. And what had he got to show for it, short of wasting the last part of his twenties and nearly half of his thirties banged up?

Besides, staring in mirrors had never been high on Zane's agenda. There were more important things to concentrate on. Mirrors were even less relevant since some fuck had ruined the good looks people once said he had.

Zane turned his pint around on the table. So much for the whisky. All they had in this pub was cheap shit and he wasn't drinking that.

He ignored the other drinkers who thought their stares went unnoticed. *He* noticed. He clocked *everything*. That's what made him so good at his game - apart from the royal fuck-up about failing to notice he was being set up by a member of his own firm.

Stupid. Stupid.

Anger bubbled as he took a long drink of his pint. To deflect from the intrusion, he thought about his apartment in Battersea. A beautiful and expensive penthouse within a complex formed during the regeneration of one of the old factories, it was literally a stone's throw from the Thames, boasted several balconies and a rooftop terrace. It was the dog's bollocks.

But he'd heard nothing of his apartment, short of Marco's report that it was fine and being managed in his absence.

Zane's hand brushed the inside pocket of his jacket which contained the keys to his apartment. He frowned. If he were to turn up there now, would they still fit the lock or had someone else been granted the use of his property during his long absence, his being consulted on this not deemed necessary?

Well, it was necessary. *He'd* purchased that flat with *his* money, not the firm's and the thought of someone else benefitting from the spoils of his hard work and spilt blood boiled Zane's piss more than it should.

How he'd longed for the bed he'd spent ages choosing. Having a mattress fit for a king, he'd spent *months* dreaming of its comfort. He'd also dreamt of the open plan space the place offered, as well as the swimming pool housed underneath the complex.

After a while even those things ceased to be important because he'd got used to sleeping on little better than a plank of wood and not having room to swing a cat.

But things like that mattered now because he was out and he wanted his fucking life back.

He ran his hand over the stubble on his chin. His mind was spiralling and he could not allow that to happen. It would divert his concentration. He had to walk back into his life and pick up where he'd left off, without chafing invisible wounds.

A couple of days, tops, and he'd be ready.

Standing up, Zane made his way to the bar. 'Another pint, please,' he mumbled, his concentration half on the barmaid, the rest on the mobile phone he'd purchased from a supermarket on the way.

Mobiles weren't commonplace at the time he'd gone inside, but just about everybody had one now - including Marco. He'd also learnt that contract phones could be tracked and traced, but off the shelf ones couldn't.

All that was left now was to work out how the fuck to use the bloody thing.

Placing a fresh pint down, the barmaid leant over the bar, her cleavage lined up perfectly in the handsome stranger's field of vision. 'You new around here?'

A half-smile moved onto Zane's lips as he picked up the pint. 'I guess you could say that.' New in as much as wandering around amid the human race, but new to the area, no. Not that he'd seen any of it until today.

His eyes studied the woman. *A nice-looking piece*, he thought, his cock twitching on cue. At least that still worked. After so long he'd feared it had forgotten how to react.

The woman played suggestively with her hair, ignoring an old man waiting to be served. 'Here for work?'

'Just having a few days break.' *That much was true.*

Disappointment flashed in the barmaid's big blue eyes. 'Oh? You're not stopping around?'

'It depends if there's anything to stop around for.' Zane grinned, not having lost the ability to turn on the charm. He was glad about that, thinking perhaps there was nothing left of that part of him either.

But he was lying. *Nothing* would make him hang around here longer than needs be. Not her, not *anyone*.

The moment his new bank card arrived, he'd go back to London and reclaim his life. In the interim, there was no harm in sampling the local cuisine...

'What is it you do?'

Zane's full lips curled. This woman didn't want to know that. Nor could he tell her even if he wanted to. *Which he didn't.* He nodded in the direction of the old man tapping his lighter on the bar top impatiently. 'You've got a customer.'

The barmaid reluctantly pulled herself off the bar and

glanced over her shoulder. 'By the way, I finish at 11.30...'

Zane didn't bother replying. *Maybe he'd take her up on that, maybe he wouldn't...*

Picking up his pint, he moved back to his table, stopping along the way to stare at a tired-looking cork board on the wall. He scanned the pinned cards offering plastering services, building work, babysitters, window fitting, car boot sales... *Blah, blah...*

Hold on...

A gym. First three sessions free? That might be worth a punt. Something to fill the time and keep his mind occupied over the next couple of days.

Making a mental note of the address, he returned to his table and pulled his new mobile from his pocket.

• • • •

ANTHONY'S GRUNTS WERE LOUD, but Erin found by concentrating hard she could go to a place far away from this - from *him*.

Usually, anyway.

Other times, like now, she failed to deflect the revulsion.

As Anthony slammed into her, her annoyance increased. It wasn't like she cared. Her body was a vessel to serve a greater good – to use as necessary to acquire what was important. But each time she failed to fully blank Anthony from her mind, she found herself all too aware of him, which allowed her to centre on how much she hated him.

And the more she allowed that to happen, the higher the percentage she'd snap before it was time...

Listening to his staccato grunting, all Erin could think about was killing him. If she did that before ensuring the rest was in place, then all of this, *everything*, was for nothing.

That, she could not allow. She *wouldn't* allow.

But she couldn't stop the vivid thoughts of what it would be like to crush Anthony's skull; to stab him through the heart; to watch every last drop of his fucked up, grasping blood leak out, spilling his life over the pristine polished floor.

It was a nice thought.

Erin didn't flinch, neither did she resist as Anthony pushed her legs towards her chest, shoving himself deeper, his grunts matching each thrust.

Her veins thrummed with hate. Anthony thought her incapable of doing anything other than his bidding.

How wrong he was.

She could be whatever he wanted her to be – what *anyone* wanted her to be. She could even cry on cue when required.

She bit back the urge to giggle. It wasn't funny. But what *was* amusing, was that this disgusting bastard would pay for both his deeds and the rest of his kind's sins.

And she couldn't wait.

Yes, Anthony could provide and give her everything. He kept telling her this, so she acted like he was her God.

Always grateful, Erin. Always grateful…

She winced as Anthony slammed her wrists against the headboard, holding them tightly in place.

That hurt more than it should. The yelping which escaped from her mouth was worse. She hated it because it was real. But she knew what to do next.

Throwing her head back as far as she could from her contorted position, Erin groaned just the way Anthony liked. She sounded like a mewling cat. It sickened her, but it would hurry him up, which was the main thing.

Her eyelids fluttered open seeing his expressionless eyes and the taut sinews in his neck.

Sensing the light at the end of the tunnel, Erin cried out in a pseudo combination of pleasure and pain. It never failed to bring him off.

As Anthony unloaded into her, Erin smugly chalked off another day from the calendar in her head which counted down to the time of reckoning.

SIX

AS ZANE'S EYES OPENED, a snapshot of his surroundings came into focus. It wasn't pitch black and when he turned to peer at the clock, the bed didn't clunk.

Shit! Almost eleven? He couldn't remember the last time he'd slept past five, or rather, that he was *allowed* to sleep past five.

With difficulty, he ran his tongue over his teeth, his mouth like the bottom of a birdcage. *Where was he?*

Stiffening at movement on the mattress next to him, Zane readied to place his big hands around the neck of whoever had snuck into his room. He hadn't yet failed to throttle the life from whoever he chose.

Freezing mid-pounce as his memory caught up with his lagging consciousness, he almost chuckled at the close call.

He was out!

Propping up himself up on an elbow, he spied the mussed tangle of dark blonde hair on the pillow next to his own. *The bird from the pub.*

Grabbing his cigarettes, he sparked one up and scowled at the 'no smoking' sign peeling from the damp wallpaper. He'd had enough of being told what he could and couldn't do. The landlady could bill him for a can of air freshener if she wished, but she could fuck right off if she thought he'd refrain from smoking!

The girl in the bed stirred, a smile spreading over her face. 'Morning, handsome,' she murmured, her hand finding its way under the duvet to wrap around Zane's hardness ready and waiting for her attention.

Zane grinned. *And why not?* He'd been in a drought long enough and last night had brought much needed replenishment. Closing his eyes, he allowed the woman to continue.

As long as this bird realised this was just sex, whatever she fancied doing was fine by him. For the next hour, at least because after that, he'd got things to do.

As the girl whose name he couldn't remember, moved to work him with her mouth, he placed his arms behind his head and tried to relax. But he couldn't.

It wasn't that she was doing anything wrong. She was doing everything just fine - more so in fact. *It was him.*

Despite his reluctance, Zane's mind returned to what he didn't want.

Tensing, his irritation built. How the fuck could he get on with life if he was constantly plagued with thoughts about the person he could never get even with?

Damn whoever had taken the pleasure of retribution out of his hands. And despite Zane's insistence, Marco still hadn't said which one of the firm had rid the world of that two-faced bastard, Flame.

Recently, it had become apparent that there had been a lot of things Marco hadn't said. It also seemed there was plenty more he *had* said too.

And Zane would get to the bottom of that soon.

Still, none of it changed *this…*

Against his will, the glaring image of the man he'd spent the last six years despising projected into his brain - the face crystal clear, every detail excruciatingly vivid.

He screwed his eyes shut, but this only made the hated face

clearer, taunting him over the only thing he wanted, but could no longer have.

Flame's light blue eyes, too pale to be anything other than abnormal, were staring - fucking *laughing* at him. His shock of red hair shone like a beacon; his face holding the same hint of smugness it always had.

Go on, fuck off, Zane thought, his anger mounting.

His lips pursed. To think everyone thought the man an asset to the firm...

Even he had. *At first...*

There was something he'd never quite liked about the bloke, but to say he'd thought him a contender to go against the firm and betray the close-knit crew and throw it back in their faces, then he'd be wrong. No one had thought that.

It was one thing going against the orders everyone was given, but because Flame wasn't a hands-on member and part of the back-end workings, he was the *last* any of them suspected.

But it wasn't *their* faces Flame had thrown everything back in, was it?

It was *his.*

Zane's body trembled. It was barely noticeable, short of the low buzzing in the deepest of his veins, but unless he quit thinking, soon it would become all-consuming.

It was driving him crazy.

He wanted to know the ins and outs of how Flame pulled off the job everyone was warned off. He wanted to know how it went ahead without anyone noticing. He also wanted to know about that fucking evidence. Had Flame planned that all along? And if so, why?

Plus, how had the firm discovered Flame's guilt?

Most importantly, he wanted to know who had caught up with the man and how the fucker had died.

He wanted to know every last fucking detail.

'Am I doing something wrong?'

The voice jolted Zane from his thoughts. His eyes flashed

open to see the blonde girl between his thighs and his teeth clenched. That bastard's image had now disappeared, but it was too late. *Would that wanker invade his life forevermore?*

Swinging his leg over the girl, he pushed himself to the edge of the bed. There was no point doing this. He had to work things out of his system another way.

Zane smiled at the crestfallen barmaid. At least he thought he was smiling because his mouth was doing something similar to what it was supposed to.

Reaching over, he placed his finger under the girl's chin. 'I've got a lot on my mind, sweetheart, that's all.'

Pulling the sheet around her nakedness as if she no longer wished to be exposed, the barmaid's blue eyes studied Zane. 'You were well up for it last night...'

'I've got somewhere I need to be,' Zane said sharply. *He explained himself to no one.*

Yeah, he'd been different last night. The drink he'd consumed stopped his mind from turning over long enough to concentrate on other things, but sober, he thought of nothing *but* that.

His jaw clenched. He refused to be constantly half-pissed in order to stop that ginger-haired twat invading his head.

Standing up, he pulled on his jeans and slipped a white T-shirt over his head, aware the woman was staring at his well-muscled torso. The only bonus about his drawn-out incarceration was it had kept his frame honed to perfection, possibly even more so during his sojourn at Her Majesty's Pleasure.

And that's where he was going now - to the gym he'd seen in that advert last night.

Doing weights and smashing the fuck out of a punch bag would cleanse his mind. He was no good to anyone with his head stuck in a loop.

The girl moved to the edge of the bed. 'I'm working tonight, but after the pub closes we cou...'

'Maybe, but don't expect me,' Zane said bluntly. He didn't

want to hurt her, or for her to think he'd used her for a shag and was binning her off. Except he probably had and probably was.

Either way, no one was becoming a limpet.

Ignoring the hurt in the woman's eyes, he grabbed a towel, a spare T-shirt and a pair of tracksuit bottoms. It was the best he could put together from his meagre resources for a gym kit. He knew the girl was desperate to ask where he was going. Maybe she thought he was one of those tossers who wanted a bit on the side before running back to his wife and family?

She couldn't be further from the truth, but he wouldn't dissuade her. It was less hassle.

'I'd better go,' she said.

Turning his back, Zane smiled. The woman was waiting to be asked to stay. *Again, she'd be wrong.*

He nodded to the unpleasant tea-making facilities. 'Help yourself to a drink before you leave if you wish.' *Wow. I'm all heart...* he thought, stuffing the towel into a carrier bag.

Zane shrugged on his jacket, not bothering to speak again as he left the room. There was nothing to say.

But one thing he did know, was that the woman had better have gone by the time he returned.

Grabbing his crash helmet, Zane thundered down the stairs towards the front door. His hand was on the latch when someone touched his back. Freezing, rather than swinging around to punch whoever had touched him without permission, he reminded himself where he was.

'I couldn't help but notice you bought a guest back with you last night.' The landlady's voice was clipped. The words weren't rude, but her tone was.

Is she questioning me or telling me? Zane wondered. Turning slowly, he glared at her, his hand still on the door handle. The urge to kill her was strong, but he remained where he was.

'The rules are clear.' The landlady's watery green eyes looked Zane up and down, her bony hand flapping in the direction of an A4 piece of paper stuck to the hallway's floral wallpaper:

No guests in rooms after 10 PM

'It was impossible not to hear the noise coming from your room. If you don't adhere to my rules, then I'll have to ask you to leave.'

Zane's lips twitched with amusement. *If only she knew what he'd spent the best part of his life doing.* He controlled the urge to laugh and instead, replied, his voice calm, but his tone left no room for misunderstanding. A little like hers.

'I've paid for a room in this shit hole for three days, Mrs Baker, therefore I will be staying for *exactly* that. During that period, the room is *mine* to do with exactly as I wish.' His mouth curled into a smile. 'Do we understand each other?'

As her expression froze, his hard eyes didn't leave hers. *She understood.*

Nodding politely, Zane turned on his heels and left the B&B. Hopping onto his bike, he fired the throaty engine and headed into the city in the direction of the gym.

• • • •

THE WATER RUNNING over Erin's hair and down her back was soothing. Concentrating on the high-pressured gush helped deflect her racing mind.

Anthony had left for the day. After hearing him stir this morning, she'd pretended to be asleep. Not that he'd touch her. His attentions always followed the same routine and the burning between her thighs served as a reminder of that.

Her fists clenched.

Don't let it bother you, she told herself, uncurling her hands.

She ran her fingers through her hair to remove the last traces of shampoo and any stubborn remainder of Anthony's scent. His very essence impregnated the air. The same air *she* shared.

Turning off the shower, Erin stepped from the tiled

enclosure and grabbed an oversized fluffy towel. The underfloor heating was warm though the thickly tufted bathmat under her feet, yet the coldness within her remained.

Wrapping the towel around her, she fashioned a smaller one into a turban over her wet hair and wandered back through to the bedroom to choose a suitable outfit for the lunchtime drinks with the 'girls'.

What fun that would be...

Erin found her mind wondering what her life would have been like had she not made the decision to take this road. Would it have been better? Less offensive?

Her towelled turban slipped as she shook her head. How could it be less offensive?

But soon she would not have to put up with *any* of it.

She carefully applied her makeup, taking a few minutes to select the most appropriate set of false eyelashes. She pressed them into place, not impressed her hand was shaking. Only very slightly but shaking all the same.

It wasn't because she'd been stupid enough to let Anthony get to her. She'd trained herself too well. She'd trained herself not to feel; not to respond; not to react. That would not happen until the appropriate time.

Irritation bloomed. If she'd trained herself so perfectly, how come things *were* getting to her? Even thinking about what was done to her father at the hands of that firm shouldn't have this effect anymore. Not since she'd devised her plan.

But it did...

Sometimes it would be a song or a sound; a name that sounded similar. Other times, thoughts would sneak in for no reason. Thanks to her immense effort, this had lessened as time went on, but occasionally – like now, they'd catch her unawares.

Her father was far from blameless. By running a firm like his, what happened was always a risk. But for his end to have been undertaken so dirtily – so callously, by a firm who he'd always been on good terms with, was unforgiveable. The lowest of the low.

Slamming her tweezers onto the glass top of the dressing table, Erin didn't care if it cracked. She scrutinised herself in the illuminated mirror - its reflection so clear it accentuated all flaws. But she didn't need to worry, being as she didn't have any.

Not on the surface, anyway.

She frowned at the missing set of lashes on her right eye and stared at the black spidery things waiting to be attached.

Don't frown, it makes you look old, she told herself, wanting to smile, but failing. Thinking of the phrase her mother had used didn't bring amusement - just sorrow. The same as when her dear mother had died six months after her father – from what Erin believed was a broken heart.

Pushing away the stabbing memories, she snatched the tweezers back up. She needed to hurry if she was to make herself into what Anthony required in time to get to the Golf Club this afternoon.

There was little point dwelling on what had been. It wouldn't bring her family back, nor change what her life now revolved around, but keeping the anger fresh did at least fuel her sole purpose.

• • • •

'WHAT DO YOU MEAN, you couldn't get hold of anyone?' Marco roared, the tendons on his neck taut. 'Did you even fucking bother trying?'

'Of course I did!' Bill bristled. 'I called both those screws, but their phones went to voicemail.'

Marco frowned. It was unlike his two officials on the inside not to take calls. That's what he supplied the burner phones for. *If they weren't doing their fucking job...* 'Has there been a riot or something?'

'Not as far as I know,' Bill shrugged. 'I'm sure we'd have heard, if that was the case.'

'Maybe the phones have died?' Sonny suggested,

shrugging his massive shoulders.

Marco climbed from the sunken hot tub, taking his time to slip his bathrobe over his well-muscled nakedness, knowing his physique was a good reminder to his men what a machine he was and how much damage he was capable of inflicting with his bare hands. Bill and Sonny might be hefty fellas, but they weren't ripped and in their prime, like *him*.

He eyed Sonny scornfully. 'Both phones wouldn't have died. If those screws think they can take the piss and not be on call as and when required, they'll be dealt with. Just call Fennel.'

Bill frowned, uncomfortable with the subject no one liked. 'I thought that since... since...'

'I don't pay you to think!' Marco roared. 'If no one else is available, for reasons I'll get to the bottom of, I still want an update. And I want one now.' His cold blue eyes rested on Sonny. 'Decide which of you will call. I don't care who, just get me a fucking update!'

Sonny shifted his weight from foot to foot, wanting to ask what sparked this sudden urge for updates. The usual was twice a month, so why an extra one? His eyes flicked to Bill, who looked to have reached the same conclusion. 'We'll get onto it.

He jerked his head in Bill's direction. The quicker they left the apartment, the better. It was never good when Marco was in one of these moods. He was too unpredictable and neither of them wanted repercussions. Once out of earshot, they could argue which one of them had drawn the short straw to get in contact with that tosser, Fennel.

SEVEN

SWEAT RAN DOWN ZANE'S BACK and trickled between the ridges of his shoulder blades as he pumped the weights on the bench press. His biceps screamed for him to stop, but he couldn't. He needed the pain to bridge the assault on his senses. Systematically flaying himself from one machine to another for two hours, concentrating only on the choice of equipment in this gym, worked.

It was vital to only think of what was relevant. And he'd managed it.

Zane smiled, impressed. The plan to keep his mind centred was succeeding and dare he say it, he'd enjoyed the workout.

Hoisting the barbell onto its metal mount, he closed his eyes and allowed the background music to filter out the noise of the other machines.

His head was clear.

He sat up. He could happily train until he passed out, but he'd done more than enough for one day.

Grabbing his towel from the side, Zane mopped his face and walked over to the water fountain, aware several pairs of eyes were on him.

A wry smile formed, knowing everyone was wondering

where he'd previously trained and who he was.

That was okay. He'd let them wonder. They weren't to know he had his very own gym under the firm's headquarters in Battersea, were they? Neither did they realise a prison gym had kept his fitness in order this last six years. He hoped no one was stupid enough to ask.

Gratefully swigging down the ice-cold water, he slung the paper cup in the bin and glanced around for the showers. He presumed this city gym had better facilities than the dubious looking bathroom down the corridor in the B&B, which shouldn't be too difficult, considering last night the shower was as powerful as a watering can. One thing he couldn't fucking stand was a feeble shower. Correction. One of *many* things he couldn't stand...

Spotting the sign for the showers, he made his way towards it. In a way it was a shame to only be around for a couple of days. If things were different, he might have taken up the doll-like receptionist's offer of a years' membership, rather than three free sessions. Perhaps he'd consider taking the offer of what else he believed she was offering too.

Zane moved into the showers, the thought of steaming hot water and pleasant-smelling body wash a welcome balm.

Bollocks – there were no free showers.

Entering an open changing cubicle, he glanced in the mirror, refusing to let the scar dominating his right cheek irritate him.

He hung his bag on a peg, then whipped his tracksuit bottoms and T-shirt off. He was half-turned away, wrapping a towel around his waist, when he glimpsed a man walking past; brown hair dripping onto his shoulders.

Zane swallowed his smile. That man had clearly spent more time on a sunbed than Donatella Versace, but aside from this, it meant there must now be a free shower.

About to step from the cubicle, he froze, his veins turning to ice. Instinctively, he flattened himself against the partition wall, watching the man remove the towel from around his neck to dry his hair.

Focusing on a tattoo, the blood drained from Zane's head.

No! It couldn't be.

Heart crashing, the sound of his own breathing deafening, Zane focused harder as the man moved to the opposite cubicle.

He'd been present the night that tattoo was done. Branding the man his namesake, a piss-take. The flames on this man's neck were in the same place - *exactly* the same place and *exactly* the same design.

What the fuck?

But the hair? That bloke's hair was wrong. Flame had red hair, this guy's was brown.

But there was something...

The buzz of adrenalin ramped up Zane's arms into the tips of his fingers and the urge to pull this man out of the cubbyhole to scrutinise him was uncontrollable.

Stop. Just stop!

He leant back, barely able to breathe. He didn't dare move in case he lost control and launched himself at this stranger, who he suspected wasn't a stranger at all...

Zane peered closer. The man he'd dreamt of killing for years had distinctive and strangely colourless eyes. Neither grey nor blue, but the palest version of both.

He shuddered, his nails digging into his palms as the man opposite moved in slow motion, his eyes shut as he dried his brown hair.

This is stupid... Zane thought. He rolled his shoulders, desperate to shed the resentment. He'd shed it for a while, yet now it was back with a vengeance and all because of a fucking tattoo that probably hundreds of people had?

Tugging on a clean T-shirt, his gaze still fixed on the man, he watched him fish a small case from a leather wash bag and turn to face the mirror.

The man's eyes opened...

Seeing the reflection, Zane dragged air into his flat lungs.

It *was* him.

Flame.

The man slipped something from the case and if Zane had blinked, he'd have missed it.

Like magic, those soulless eyes were no more. They were now brown. *Like his hair...*

Zane's whole body shook. He had to think about this. He couldn't kill Flame here. He wanted to - God, he wanted to, but he wasn't going to prison for that tosser for the second fucking time.

He pressed his head against the tiled wall, hoping it would ease his burning brain.

Whatever happened, Zane couldn't be spotted. When he took Flame out, which he would, there would be no warning.

That was a *promise.*

As the man made to leave, Zane grabbed his bag and followed at a distance, his blood thundering in his veins.

• • • •

LEAVING AT LEAST three cars between him and his target, Zane carefully tailed the silver Mercedes, not wanting to lose sight of who he believed to be in the driver's seat.

It was a straight route down the A45 to reach Solihull and had only taken about half an hour. He'd presumed this was the destination, until the silver car continued, therefore so had he.

But he hadn't expected *this...*

Watching the target car pull up in the high street of a large, but quaint village, Zane pulled over further down, glad to take his sweaty hands off the handlebar grips.

Cautiously removing his crash helmet, he walked some way behind Flame - or the person he believed to be Flame, past several old black and white buildings.

If the creepy eyes and tatt weren't enough to confirm the man's identity, the swaggering cocksure walk was. The way that prick moved had always irritated Zane and was another tick on the list convincing him that, despite being told otherwise by his own bloody brother, the man he wanted revenge on was alive, well and *there*.

Zane leant against the wall of a building, pretending to stare at his mobile phone, when really keeping a clear eye on where Flame was heading. He had to be certain he was correct.

Come on you bastard, Zane fumed, his senses on full alert.

He felt he may snap. The urge to smash the man to smithereens grew. He could easily bludgeon Flame to death in broad daylight and not care what that brought, but he had to stay focused. He hadn't come this far to return where that bastard had put him.

But what if it wasn't Flame? What if was just someone who *looked* like him?

Zane's grip around his phone tightened. No, it was him. He didn't know how, but it was him without a doubt.

Motionless and alert, Zane watched Flame enter a building opposite.

AW FINANCIAL SERVICES

It made sense for the fucker to be working in financial services. He'd been the firm's accountant, after all.

His jaw tightened. Not that Flame was ever a qualified accountant. They'd all known that, but the man knew his stuff, as well as the loopholes available to move cash around. As it turned out, he knew about those far too well.

Sweat gathered in the nape of Zane's neck as the glass door of AW Financial Services shut. He was too far away to see what, if anything, was going on inside and couldn't peer through the window in case he was recognised. If he'd recognised Flame, despite whatever he'd done to disguise himself, then it worked both ways.

Zane chewed his lip. He needed a library or Internet café. He'd used the computers in nick enough to know how to search for that company. Or maybe find out where the bastard lived?

He seethed with frustration. He didn't want to walk away. What if Flame couldn't be located again? But he had no choice.

His eyes narrowed. There was lots he *could* do now he knew the man still breathed, but not without a cost. Enough had been shelled out on that cunt's behalf already.

Eight

ZANE WAS RUSHING, every part of him on hyperdrive. Every elapsing second meant another wasted moment which could instead be used in butchering the bastard who'd trashed his life.

Taking a deep breath, he forced his fingers to function normally as he keyed information into the computer.

He glanced around the other people in the library, busy tapping away on the small collection of available machines. Every old duffer interested in researching their genealogy or antiquities collections was in here today, but at least that meant no one took any notice of *him*.

His impatience rose as the tired computer continued grinding away, the egg timer in the centre of the screen taunting him. Refraining from swearing out loud in the silent room, he dug his teeth into his bottom lip.

Ah-ha!

Zane scoured the returned results: an article from the local Gazette about a new financial services business to open in town; Anthony Walker's profile from a local business directory; the AW Financial Services website...

Okay, but what was he looking for? Info on that business?

The staff? The person? He needed a goddamn name – an ID. A fucking home address? Something. *Anything.*

Clicking the first link opened an archived newspaper article:

New Financial Services Business to Open

Knowle will shortly benefit from a company to help local investors with their property portfolios, ISAs and investments.

Anthony Walker has chosen to move his business from London, and with many years' experience as a financial adviser for a range of top clients, his expertise will be greatly appreciated.

Mr Walker will commence trading this Saturday and cordially invites people to join him for welcome drinks and a free ten-minute appraisal of their investment portfolios.

Zane scanned the rest of the waffle, searching for a date. If Anthony Walker was Flame, then this company could not have existed before 1996.

There! 21st of February 1997. It was the correct time frame.

Closing the internet page, he moved to the next, his excitement building. Opening the company website, his eyes darted across the screen seeing a photo of the building he'd seen earlier, along with a collection of glowing reviews.

With his pulse ramping up, he clicked 'Meet the Team'.

There he was. A headshot studio portrait of the cunt himself.

Zane squinted, the sunlight from the window behind shining mercilessly onto the screen.

In the photograph, dressed in a tailored suit, was Flame; the collar of his crisp white shirt hiding the tattoo Zane knew was there.

Able to study the face unhindered, Zane mentally replaced the brown hair with burnt orange, and imagined the eyes back to the original soulless shade that lay somewhere underneath.

Without any shadow of a doubt, it was Flame.

The fake tan might hide his alabaster skin and freckles, but the face; the mean curl of his top lip; the aquiline nose – the rest... It was all there.

Zane grinned. *Gotcha!*

So, Flame was Anthony Walker? Maybe he'd *always* been Anthony Walker? Flame was always 'Flame' within the firm, the name borne from the man's ability to be shit hot with fudging the books. That, and the colour of his hair.

Quickly reading the rest of the information, Zane closed the webpage and chewed the end of his pen. *So now what?*

More was needed – like where the man went or a home address, perhaps? But as much as it was preferable, it was too obvious steaming into his house to finish him. It might still be his only choice, but not until Marco had levelled on why the hell he'd lied about this bastard being dead.

Returning to the search page, Zane moved through the remaining items from the search results. Another newspaper article? What the fuck was Flame around here? Some kind of local celebrity?

Businessman's Batchelor Days Are Over

After several years together, Anthony Walker, owner of AW Financial Services, became officially engaged to the beautiful Erin Langley this weekend. Their wedding will follow next summer.

We wish Anthony and Miss Langley many congratulations and best wishes for the future.

Zane frowned. This article was dated 2000 – last year. So,

Flame was either already hitched or would be soon.

A nerve in his neck twitched as his rage bubbled to the point of overflow. This man had got to carry on with his life, whilst *he* hadn't?

Erin Langley? The 'beautiful' Erin Langley?

Yeah, right. Anyone who would marry that cold, weird fuck couldn't be beautiful. Or normal.

Besides, Flame wasn't into women - he wasn't much into *anything*, short of figures. Everyone joked the only time he got a hard on was when Casio released a new model of calculator.

His eyes moved to the small photograph accompanying the article.

There he was again – standing stiffly, a pompous smirk on his face, next to a blonde.

Zane peered closer at the woman on Flame's arm. Well, he'd got one thing wrong... The woman was nowhere near a pig and a *lot* prettier than he'd have imagined, especially for someone Flame had bagged. But with her expensive clothes and soft, fawning look – one usually reserved for demure, upper-class women, it was obvious Flame mingled in what he'd class as 'useful' circles.

A far cry from where the bastard had spent his previous life...

But whoever Erin Langley was, she possessed something to float Flame's boat. No doubt she was rich. Possibly titled? Or could it be that perhaps Flame *genuinely* wanted her?

Either way, the woman was important.

Very important.

A smile curled Zane's lips as he deleted his search history, closed the browser and stood up, the embryo of an idea forming.

Rather than giving Flame the satisfaction of a quick death, he'd systematically destroy him. Everything that mattered would be taken bit by bit. He'd be forced to beg and only *then* would he be finally finished off.

And Erin Langley was now step one of that plan.

With no time to lose, Zane left the library and headed back

to his motorbike.

. . . .

ERIN PRETENDED TO LISTEN to the droning voices of the
surrounding women, not giving a toss what they said or thought.
From the table where they sat, her eyes slid to Anthony the other
side of the Golf Club. The sight of him casually leaning against
the polished wood of the bar made her want to throw up.

She knew what he was doing. He was pretending to be
comfortable and that it was second nature to exchange good-
natured banter about which one of them fluffed up at hole
eighteen, but it wasn't second nature at all. He had his agenda,
which was nothing to do with camaraderie. It was about
fleecing as much money from people as possible.

Erin turned her white wine spritzer around on the glossy
tabletop, wondering how these people would react if they knew
the truth.

What would their opinion of Anthony Walker be if they
knew he had no formal qualifications as a financial advisor?
They wouldn't be so eager to ask his advice and plough their
money into his preferred investment choices if they did.

If they knew, as she did, that he was concealing his real
identity and had been the brains behind the money laundering
of London gangsters, as well as being instrumental in supplying
the Morelli firm with the information where her father's money
was kept, therefore enabling his murder, they'd see him in the
same light she did.

On the other hand, they would be reluctant to give *her* the
time of day too, if they knew her father had also once run a firm
- one no longer in existence, thanks to his death. That wouldn't
help her mission to get this done.

But *she* knew Anthony must have lifted her father's money
after the murderer had stolen it. Why else would he have done
a bunk behind his firm's back?

And she knew this, because on the final day of the trial,
when that new evidence came to light, her legal team informed

her a member of the Morelli firm had turned snark. She'd slipped out of the court room and there, she'd set eyes on the person being handed a few quid by a lawyer. They'd clearly believed themselves to be out of sight.

Well, *she'd* seen them. She'd seen who was behind that new evidence. And that person was *Anthony*.

It was at that point she'd decided on her plan – the plan that she'd always been two steps ahead with.

The money Anthony used to build his new identity, his new life, home, business and what he'd lavished on her with pointless gifts, was *her father's* money and she wanted it back.

Hence why she was here now – so everything could revolve in a circle back into its rightful place.

Once they married, that money would be hers. And then it was time for them all to die.

Erin suddenly realised the women were staring at her. 'Sorry,' she said hastily. 'Did someone say something?' *Like she cared*...

The women clustered around the table exchanged over-concerned glances. 'Kate wondered if you're nervous about the wedding,' a redhead called Belinda simpered. 'We all do. You've seemed on edge lately. Are you okay?'

Erin smiled. 'I'm fine. I'm just side-tracked with wedding preparations. It's a real bother being undecided on the table favours. There are two styles I like and I can't decide between them.' *Really? Was that the best she could come up with?*

'If you show us the examples, we can help decide which would best suit your colour scheme,' Jocelyn enthused.

'That would be great!' Erin shoved gratitude onto her face, happy the bullshit she'd spouted was allaying their scrutiny. 'I want everything to be perfect.'

'It will be, I'm sure,' Jocelyn soothed.

Erin flinched as Jocelyn's hand rested over hers in a gesture of sisterly solidarity, itching to dig her talons into the woman's spindly fingers and snap every single one of them in half. Instead, she swallowed down the urge. If these women felt something was bothering her, it showed she was losing concentration. And that was not good.

She had to get away, if only for a few minutes.

Pulling her hand away from the grasping fingers, Erin stood up. 'I need to call my dressmaker to change the time of my next fitting.' She smiled at the plastic faces around the table. 'So, if you'll excuse me.'

She walked towards the expanse of doors leading to the bar's garden terrace where she could breathe fresh air.

NINE

HAVING HELPED HIMSELF to another large wrap he'd skimmed from the coke supply for his own personal use, Marco emptied a liberal amount on the glass-topped table in the living room and chopped at it with his Platinum MasterCard.

His heart was already pounding with building stress surrounding the nagging feeling prodding inside his veins. And that was even before he'd snorted a much-needed top up of this finest Colombian.

Opening the carved, initialled box he'd had commissioned specially to keep his coke stash in, along with his favourite rolled up fifty-pound note used for snorting this particular pleasurable hobby of his, he fished out the bank note and admired the way tiny particles of cocaine left from the last use glistened like microscopic sequins in the glare of the overhead lights.

It had been less than an hour since Marco had last snorted a line, yet he was already noticing the first twinges of a downer which must be stopped in its tracks.

Expertly hoovering up the fine powder into one nostril, he sniffed loudly and dragged his hand under his nose, not wanting any tell-tale residue lurking. That never failed to look cheap and cheap, he was not.

Inhaling deeply, feeling slightly less strung out as the cocaine rush moved straight to his brain, Marco carefully placed his stash box back in the wooden drawer unit next to his huge sofa.

He leant back against the leather cushions and let his eyes roam over the framed photographs and oversized covers of some of his most recent films that he'd adorned the walls with.

His mouth curled into a smile as he reached for his glass of finest brandy. These photographs and film covers were a mere snapshot of how successful he'd made this new arm of the business. Why no one had seen to do this before, he didn't understand. It made a killing, not to mention the many perks which came alongside…

After only four years of acquiring a film studio for little more than a song, thanks to his irresistible ability to 'charm' people into doing his bidding, Lunar Motion Films was up there alongside the best in the industry.

And very shortly, it would be top of the tree.

Marco's eyes swung to the photograph of Lisa Tequila amongst the others on the wall.

It was perhaps a little premature including her on his wall of fame, considering she wasn't yet a part of Luna Motion Films, but she soon would be. Shortly, not only would the porn industry's most wanted leading lady be making films for *his* company, but she would also be his wife.

The latter reason alone gave him justification in displaying the picture. That, and he loved looking at her.

Feeling his groin tighten, Marco all but salivated with the prospect of finally sinking himself into the woman he'd fantasised about since first seeing her over ten years ago.

Now aged thirty, Lisa might not be what people classed as a spring chicken, compared to some of the bright young things parading around his film set, but she was worth ten of those other chicks, hands down.

It had been his best idea *ever* offering her management -

who happened to be her father, the deal of not only a mega amount of money for the sole control of her film rights and performance, but also, along with the money, he'd thrown in the offer of marriage into one of the most successful London firms this side of the river.

It went without saying that once the deal was sealed, Lisa would have protection and standing for the rest of time.

What father wouldn't want that for his daughter?

Marco smirked. As long as Lisa remained looking the way she did now and didn't fall prey to anything unfortunate, such as saggy tits a few years from now, then it was all good. The minute *that* sort of thing occurred, she could fuck right off back to where she came from. He'd think of something to get himself out of that one if or when the time came.

But for now, he was more than happy with his genius idea.

And so, it appeared, was Lisa's father.

Marco's eyes narrowed. Yeah, her father was pleased with the arrangement. That was on the proviso that his daughter was wed to the legitimate heir and owner of the Morelli firm.

He clenched his jaw, finding himself reaching yet again for his stash box for a rejuvenating line to halt the clawing demons from getting a foothold.

Well, he *was* the heir and owner of the Morelli firm. He was the man with one hundred per cent ownership and control of the business. That would not change, come what may.

Ever.

The only thing to change if he didn't receive an update as to the latest from Winson Green soon, was that the staff who he paid to supply him with relevant information would shortly find themselves waiting outside the job centre in fucking wheelchairs.

• • • •

KICKING UP THE SIDESTAND, Zane revved the throttle and glanced behind before pulling away.

He hadn't had time to properly check out this bike when

buying it yesterday. If that fucker had sold him a dud, the man would regret it because he knew where the bloke lived.

Out on the main road, Zane opened up the throttle for the first time, the wind rushing over him. He'd missed this more than he'd realised. A motorbike was far removed from his Lotus, but his Ducati - one of many motorbikes within his collection back in London, offered a sense of exhilarating freedom that he enjoyed over a fast car any day – something which has always been a source of amusement to his father.

Kicking down a gear, Zane took a roundabout way faster than he should, but it was important to understand a bike's limits and test how well it handled. This Yammy may not be a Ducati, but it held the road well.

He continued up the road searching for a telephone box. He had a number but wouldn't use his new mobile. Not for this.

Spotting a call box, he slacked off the throttle, pulled over and heaved the bike onto its centre stand.

Zane hooked his crash helmet over the handlebars, checking the spare helmet he'd insisted was thrown in as part of the deal was still securely attached to the back.

It was.

Good. He'd need that.

He yanked open the door of the telephone box, exhaling with relief to see an intact phone. Even the unsavoury smell inside didn't detract him – not now he knew what he was going to do.

Picking up the telephone, he fished out the piece of paper containing AW Financial Services' number and lined up his change on the metal shelf.

Stabbing in the digits, he waited for the call to connect.

The high and melodic voice which answered took him off guard.

'Erm, I had an appointment with Anthony Walker this afternoon.' Zane made his voice sound like he thought it should do if he were the sort to make appointments with financial advisers.

Of course, he was stabbing in the dark whether it was correct to ask for 'Anthony' or 'Mr Walker', but it was better than doing what he wanted, which was to stab Flame through the fucking eye and be done with it.

'This afternoon? Can I take your na…'

'Has he forgotten?' Zane interrupted. *He'd failed to think this through. Adlib, quickly.* 'Anthony's always doing this to me!' He laughed, like he was put out, but pretending not to be. 'Has he got any other appointments available today? We can reschedule.'

The woman laughed, like they shared a secret knowledge about Anthony Walker.

Oh sweetheart, you haven't got the first clue, Zane thought bitterly.

'He's not here this afternoon. I can perhaps fit you in on…'

'Off down the wine bar again, is he?' Zane felt more unhinged by the second. 'That's so like him! Forgetting appointments to go for drinks!'

I need to shut up, he thought. Christ, this was ridiculous. He could torture information out of people, kill them without a second thought, scare the living daylights out of the hardest bastards, yet he was drowning like a wet fish over talking to a dippy receptionist? *What the hell was he doing?*

The woman tittered, the high-pitched noise scratching Zane's ear drums.

'Thursday afternoon is golf! He'll be back in tomorrow though. I'm sorry, what did you say your name was again Mr…?'

'Don't worry. I'll call back,' Zane said, desperate to put the phone down.

'But if I could just…'

'Thanks for your help,' he muttered, all nicety falling away.

Slamming the receiver down, he leant against the glass of the telephone box. *There couldn't be many golf courses around here.*

He glanced at his watch. Was there time to see if Flame

could be spotted? If so, then he could be tailed. He may head home afterwards and it was vital to set eyes on this true love of his – Miss Erin Langley.

Zane yanked open the phone box door and stomped towards his bike. *The Golf Club it was then.*

• • • •

'DO YOU DO THIS purely to embarrass me?' Anthony gripped Erin's wrist and twisted it so her hand was forced onto the bar. He made sure his other hand hid his nails digging into her skin.

Erin kept her well-practised smile in place so not to give Anthony the satisfaction of seeing her wince. People were nearby and giving them an indication of how she really felt would go against her when the time came. 'I needed some fresh air, that's all,' she said, throwing a small wave in Kate's direction.

Anthony nodded politely in the direction of the group of women. 'Make more of an effort,' he hissed.

'I'm marrying you, aren't I?' Judging by the sharp increase of Anthony's grip, Erin realised her tone was too harsh. 'Anyway, there's nothing wrong with getting fresh air.'

'I don't want you wandering around on your own.' Anthony raised his hand to brush a lock of hair from Erin's face.

From a spectator's point of view, the gesture looked intimate, but Erin knew otherwise. There was no intimacy in Anthony's repertoire, thank God. Whatever he did was always another form of control.

Her back stiffened as his fingers trailed a line of invisible poison down her cheek, but she stopped herself from shuddering, her heart thumping for all the wrong reasons.

How she would keep things together, she did not know. Two more months until they married and even then it wouldn't be over. Not until the murderer walked free. Could she last that long?

Inhaling sharply, she reminded herself to keep sight of the

end game. She would sorely regret jumping the gun if she didn't. Taking Anthony out at the expense of losing vengeance on the other target would not do.

'We're leaving.' Taking Erin's elbow, Anthony pulled her forward from the stool, the heel of her shoe landing awkwardly. 'Looks like you've had enough anyway.'

His voice was loud enough for people around them to hear. Erin's cheeks burnt. She wasn't drunk. She wasn't even slightly tipsy. Anthony was trying to make her look a fool, using her as the reason they were leaving, when it was *him* who wanted to go.

And she knew why.

Unless they left now, Anthony's ritual would be disturbed. His hot shower, followed by a glass of whisky whilst she got into bed, only for him to follow exactly nine minutes later was always the same.

She felt like telling people about what his rituals involved and how she could set her watch by them, but she wouldn't. Cutting off her nose to spite her face would result in the years it had taken to reach this point being for nothing.

She was counting on the time she'd spent being worth every single drawn-out bloody second.

Dutifully taking her handbag, she gave the brainless women around the table a quick wave and a smile.

'Don't forget to ring me about those favours,' Jocelyn called.

'I won't,' Erin promised as Anthony frogmarched her from the bar.

'Favours?' Anthony hissed. 'What fucking favours? Why are you asking them for favours?'

'Wedding favours, not "favours"!' As they moved through the Golf Club lobby, Erin avoided looking at Anthony. His eyes were deader than usual tonight. He'd clearly lost at golf. Not that she'd ask. She couldn't care less.

'I thought everything was organised for the wedding.' Anthony said suspiciously.

The heels of Anthony's Italian brogues clacked on the marble steps. Erin wanted to nail his feet to the floor so she would no longer have to hear that sound. *Clack. Clack. Clack.*

'It is. It's just women's chat,' she said amicably, the twilight masking her sneer.

Of course, she'd organised everything. Everything was arranged with military precision. The wedding would run exactly to plan - like everything else. It was what kept the blood pumping through her veins.

She glanced around for Anthony's top of the range silver Mercedes. 'Where are you parked?' The sooner she got home and through the nightly ritual, the better.

It meant another day closer.

• • • •

ZANE'S WHOLE BODY TENSED. It was definitely Flame. And because it was Flame, it meant that woman must be *her* - Erin Langley.

From what he could see, she was identical to the photo he'd seen earlier. *And they were leaving...*

This was unfortunate and wasn't how he would have planned it. Up until this morning he hadn't believed there was even the need for a plan. It wasn't something on the cards.

He glanced around for the silver car he'd previously tailed, but there were absolutely *loads* of similar motors. It was impossible to tell which one was Flame's.

Fuck, there were risks here. Anyone could witness what he was about to do, but he had at least checked the CCTV. Two cameras covered the car park, so as long as Flame and his bird didn't go closer to the clubhouse, it was safe.

He shrugged. Whether it was safe or not, he was doing it. It could be the only chance he'd get for a while. Now he knew the fucker wasn't dead, closing his eyes for one night, let alone several, would be impossible.

Zane's hands clenched into fists, his only concern not to let rip at this bastard right here, right now. Yet doing just that was what each beat of his heart screamed for.

Kill him! This is your chance!

It would be easy. Enjoyable.

Quick...

However pleasurable, it would be short-lived. *This* way would be much more gratifying.

He watched the two figures make their way across the car park.

This would require precision timing, but Zane wasn't top of his game for nothing. He may have not participated in his usual areas of expertise for a long while, but some things didn't fade, no matter how much time passed.

The element of surprise was key.

Just about now would do it.

Pulling back on the throttle, his visor open a crack, Zane manoeuvred along the rows of parked cars, his headlight bright in the deepening twilight.

Keep a lid on yourself, he chanted as he turned the corner at the end of the row towards the figures. His pulse ramped up when Flame's face illuminated in the headlight.

This was merely a taste - a smidgen of what was to come.

Flame would hurt. And it started now...

TEN

EVEN THOUGH Erin didn't want to touch Anthony, as a motorbike screeched to a halt in front of them, her hand involuntarily grabbed his arm. Immediately sensing something was far from right, she froze as a huge man jumped from the bike and slammed his fist into Anthony's face.

Her mouth opened to shout, scream, *something*, but in that split second before her brain processed the signal to her voice box, she was gagged. What with, she didn't know.

Flailing, her handbag dropped to the floor as she was turned and pressed against a car and her eyes darted to Anthony lying crumpled on the floor.

No! She wouldn't be taken out like this. there was too much yet to do.

Shit. Her bag! If only she'd bought her knife she could run this fucker through.

As the man grabbed Erin's hands, the weight of his body holding her steady against the cold metal of the car, Erin forced her brain to stay rational. If he was about to attack or rape her, she'd make it difficult.

The gag cut into her face as she attempted to shout, managing only a strange, muffled sound.

'Don't struggle,' a voice growled.

Erin concentrated on the thudding of her heart. The voice was slow, husky, calm - not one she recognised.

'I don't want to hurt you,' the voice continued, 'but I will, if you don't do exactly as I say.'

For some reason Erin wasn't overly frightened. Maybe the sight of Anthony on the floor made the situation of being gagged and pressed against a car by a lunatic, almost pleasant.

I must be stranger than I believed, she thought with a tinge of hysteria.

'Get on the bike.' The man's voice, although still calm, contained a sense of urgency.

He wanted her to get on a motorbike? What the fuck?

With a jolt, Erin realised the man had tied her hands behind her back.

'Hurry,' he snarled, pulling Erin away from the car.

Now Erin began to panic. How could she get on a bike with a skirt and her hands tied behind her back? She'd fall off! Perhaps that was the plan?

For the first time she properly looked at the man but could see nothing behind the black visor of his crash helmet. Her eyes then slid back to the club house lights glowing in the distance. *Surely someone could see what was going on?*

Erin made to move towards Anthony. She wasn't sure why. Maybe to kick him while he was down?

Suddenly her feet were no longer on the ground. Yelping through the gag, her legs wheeled in the air as they span through nothing. Her skirt was yanked around her waist and in the space of two seconds, she was on the bike.

'This will mess your hair up, but tough shit,' the voice said, as a crash helmet was crammed onto Erin' head; thick fingers encased in leather attaching the uncomfortable buckle under her chin.

After securing a thick strap around her waist, the man jumped on the front of the bike, clipping the other end of the strap around his own waist.

The ear-splitting roar as the bike's engine came to life hurt Erin's ears. This helmet was heavy, but even if it wasn't, she couldn't think straight. Her sensibilities were well and truly floored.

A helmet suddenly collided with Erin's as the man looked over his shoulder. 'Lean against me. You won't fall off. Just follow whichever way I move.'

Erin remained silent. She didn't even nod. What was the point? She had no clue what was going on, but whatever was happening, she would find out soon.

Or not, as the case might be.

Her throat constricted. Her father had primed her with what to do in the case of a jump, but nothing he'd ever warned her of was similar to *this* scenario.

As the bike moved forward, the jolt made her jerk to one side, convinced she would fall. A gloved hand grabbed her thigh.

'Don't struggle. This won't take long.'

What wouldn't take long? Her death?

From what she could see through the weird field of vision the helmet offered, Anthony was starting to move from where he lay on the floor, but as the bike continued forward, she could do nothing. Nothing at all.

• • • •

PUTTING HIS FEET UP on the coffee table in the lounge area, Marco paid little attention as the buckle on his shoe scraped a gouge into the etched glass surface. It wasn't like he'd shelled out for the table. In all honesty he didn't much like it. It was just somewhere to put his drinks. Or his feet...

The petite brunette gazed out of the balconied window onto London's skyline. Yes, she wanted a job and yes, she'd love to have a man like Marco on her arm, but she wasn't blind. Neither was she deaf. It was no secret the Morelli firm ran a vicious ship.

All her friends had urged her not to get involved, but

Pauline Albiges had always possessed the urge to better her station. The lure of the glitz and glamour was a heady thought. Headier still, was the prospect of being Marco Morelli's girlfriend...

It had taken months of hanging around the studios before anyone noticed her enough to offer her an audition for one of their films. But when the boss himself asked if she'd like to view the footage privately, she'd grabbed the chance with both hands.

If she played things well, then she could become something special in Marco's life. Imagine the benefits that would bring? She'd never have to worry about anything!

Pauline turned to face Marco. 'Wow! This place is amazing!' she gushed, making sure she wore her most alluring smile. 'I can't believe you own this!'

'Why?' Marco snapped. 'Do I look like I can't afford it?'

'I-I didn't mean it like that,' Pauline said hastily, uncomfortableness brewing at the ferocious glint in Marco's eyes. 'I-I just meant th...'

'Whatever...' Marco flapped his hand uninterestedly. He knew it was him with the hang up about this place, presuming people were having digs. No one ever had. They wouldn't dare...

No one had said a bean when, within days of Zane getting sentenced, he'd put his brother's apartment to good use. For once there had been no need to ask, like he usually had to.

And that was just it. Marco was sick of receiving scraps. Sick of everyone assuming Zane was the one who did this, did that, owned this, decided that... The only fucker, since their father died, who held any clout. *He* never got a look in. But then, Zane was the only one out of the two of them who ever had and therefore, had always been the one to call the shots.

And why? Because that was the way it was - the way their father had decided and the way of the world, when it came to eldest sons...

Not anymore. Zane wasn't here and Marco had promised to

manage the apartment in addition to everything else his brother could no longer do. And no, that might not have given him authority to make the changes he had, but he wasn't ever going to have to explain anything or return the place.

The familiar sense of deep-seated irritation clawed his insides over the advantages of being the eldest son had brought Zane.

This resentment Marco held made him look paranoid and defensive. He didn't have to be either of those things now he'd reached his goal.

Swapping his scowl for a grin, he leant forward and grabbed the brunette by her tight little skirt. Hoisting her onto his lap, his hand delved straight inside her knickers. 'Enough talking, sweetcheeks. Let's have a bit of fun. Act out that scene you made such a good job of at your audition this afternoon.'

Pauline's eyes lit up as Marco released the belt of his trousers. 'Did I look good, Marco? Did I do everything right? Shall we watch it now?' she asked, wincing as Marco's rough fingers scraped across her intimate and delicate skin.

'Yeah, yeah, you looked just the ticket,' Marco said, guiding her hand directly onto his cock. *How would he know? He hadn't seen the film yet. But she looked okay in the flesh and that's what mattered.*

'Have I got the job?' Pauline asked as her head was pushed into Marco's groin.

'Depends how much you impress me,' he grunted, ignoring her silly little giggle, which he promptly silenced by pushing into her mouth. *She thought he was joking? Oh, well...*

Trying not to choke, Pauline was already imagining how envious her friends would be to hear she'd been in this amazing penthouse apartment. She could even be *living* here soon, if she played her cards right. Marco was loaded - anyone could see that. Plus, she'd seen the host of posh cars and motorbikes in the underground garage. She'd be set for life.

Everyone said how pretty she was. Marco must think so too, otherwise he wouldn't want her in his films. He certainly wouldn't invite her back to his personal apartment if he didn't want something more between them.

With added resolve, Pauline put extra effort into the task at hand.

Lying back, enjoying the moment, Marco had almost forgotten the other things on his mind when his pleasure was interrupted by the shrill ringing of his mobile.

Reluctantly pushing Pauline's head away, he snatched his phone off the table. 'Yeah?'

Marco blanched, realising his mistake. He promptly swapped his abrasive tone for a pleasant one. 'Mr Grimes! I've literally just put the phone down from one of those bloody cold callers and I thoug...'

He paused, hearing his soon to be father-in-law's less than impressed tone. 'That can't be right! I...

Pauline remained on her knees warily watching Marco's expression change from irritation to annoyance and then into anger.

'No, I'm not saying you're wrong, just that the information must be incorrect.' Covering the phone's mouthpiece, Marco glared at Pauline. 'Push off! I have to deal with something... No, I'm still here...' His head pounded; his eyes drawn to the rolled up fifty lying on the table from his most recent snort. He'd need another line after this!

He forced himself to sound nonplussed. 'Yeah, don't stress. I'll get onto it straight away and confirm there's been some kind of miscommunication. I can assure you nothing has changed... Yes... Yes, I will.'

Ending the call, Marco stared at his mobile in disbelief. When he found out who had been spouting this shit, then heads would fucking roll.

Ignoring the girl still sitting between his legs, he reached over her and snatched up his full glass of brandy.

How fucking embarrassing. This made him look a right cunt. Bill and Sonny had better have made headway and touched base with the contacts inside that bastard nick. They'd best get a move on finding out who was behind this bullshit and make it clear what would happen if this latest round of grapevine bollocks wasn't immediately rectified.

Whoever these pricks were who thought themselves clever by starting rumours, would be discovered and when he found out who had started spreading this crap, he'd ensure they met their end via an unfortunate accident.

Having to undo this fuckup wasn't a great start to the upcoming arrangement with the delectable and extremely hot Lisa Tequila. If her father thought the conditions of their deal had changed, then he could pull the plug.

Marco wanted to hyperventilate. 'Fuck!' he hissed, the word spewing through his clenched teeth. '*FUCK*!'

'What's happened?' Pauline asked, wide-eyed. She placed her hands on Marco's knees. 'Has someone died? I'm so sorry if th…'

'I thought I told you to go?' Marco roared, his eyes wild. He felt like he would spontaneously combust. Jumping from the sofa, he shoved Pauline backwards and swung for her. 'When I say, leave, it means fucking *leave*!' he screamed, the pitch of his voice hurting his own ears.

Pauline scrambled from the floor, devastated by Marco's abrupt change of attitude. She glanced at him out of the corner of her eye.

'What are you staring at, you nosy bitch?' Marco screeched, slamming his fist into Pauline's face. The sheer force of his punch immediately flattened the girl's nose.

With blood pouring down the front of her top, she stumbled towards Marco, her hands clutching at her smashed face.

'And *still* you won't fuck off? For Christ's sake!' Marco dragged Pauline across the room by her hair, oblivious to the pitiful wailing or the nails gouging into his hands as she attempted to remove the pressure from her burning scalp.

He didn't need this bleating cow asking questions. God knows what she'd heard. He couldn't even remember what *he'd* said. He could have said *anything*. Things went wrong because of stupid women with loose mouths. There was no room for people causing further problems.

Reaching the balcony, he dragged Pauline onto it and pushed her up against the waist-high railings. 'You're leaving now!'

Pauline's eyes bulged, fear choking her, as well as the blood running from the back of her nose into her throat. 'No! What are y...'

'Too many questions. And questions cause accidents,' Marco raged. 'You should have gone when I told you to. Now fuck the hell off!'

Pushing Pauline over the railings, Marco didn't bother watching as her body backflipped over the wrought iron balustrade. The strange thud he heard a few seconds later, giving the only answer he needed.

Growling, he stomped back inside the apartment. No doubt he'd get a visit from the Old Bill, but what could he say? Drunk women inviting themselves around and waiting on balconies whilst he showered were recipes for disaster...

• • • •

ZANE PULLED UP outside the B&B in Ladywood and killed the bike's engine. It had been a long ride with a struggling, tense woman in tow.

Unclipping the thick strap around his waist, he clambered off the motorbike, holding Erin steady as he did so, ignoring the hostile glare through the open visor of his passenger's helmet.

In his initial eagerness to floor Flame, he hadn't noticed much about this woman until the man he despised had crumpled to the ground. It was only then he'd taken a proper look at the female insane enough to be betrothed to that lying, cheating bastard.

And he hadn't expected her to be so astoundingly beautiful. So much so, that for a second, he'd lost the thread of what he was doing.

Gone was the demure look of the woman he'd seen in the

photograph, instead replaced by a sour, hard-looking face. *A stunning wildcat.*

Recovering quickly, he'd wasted no time securing her on the bike, but on the ride over to the B&B with her strapped against him, the feel of her body against his back, her breasts pushing against his spine, her presence had become forefront in his mind.

Now they were at the B&B and for his plan to work and have full effect, he needed to be mindful of what was at stake. No matter what this woman looked like, he shouldn't forget there had to be something fundamentally wrong with her to be with a cunt like Flame. Secondly, he wanted nothing Flame had previously possessed.

Zane just wished his cock realised that.

Shaking his head, he lifted Erin from the bike, like she was a doll. Putting his arms around her waist, he untied her wrists. 'Don't think about making any rash moves. Your fiancé is counting on it.'

As the man pulled her crash helmet off, Erin shook her hair out, revealing eye makeup spidered across her face from the rushing wind and false eyelashes stuck to her cheek.

Zane chuckled as she snatched the eyelashes from her face. *A right diva, this one.*

Erin glared at the crash-helmeted figure looming in front of her. *Nothing could be worse than what she'd experienced with Anthony, could it?*

She was sick of this. What would her life amount to if she let this lunatic scare her? What did he even want? The contents of her handbag? *Her?*

Giving her body to Anthony was bad enough and now this?

But why would a robber or a rapist take her off like this? She didn't have anything. She was a nobody. A nothing.

Anger overtook. She wasn't having a random maniac screw up her plans. She jutted her chin out defiantly. 'What makes you think I won't scream for someone to call the police?'

Before she even acknowledged the answer or lack of one,

she found herself against the wall of the building, a large hand around her throat.

'I wouldn't advise that,' Zane growled, his patience wearing thin. He had no wish to hurt a woman, even one belonging to Flame, but if this spoilt bitch believed threatening him was a good idea, he'd make an exception to that rule.

The back of Erin's head scraped against the Victorian brickwork as she thrashed about, fighting to breathe.

She swallowed dryly, her bravado diluting as her eyes searched for a face behind the visor. This was more than a mere mugging. Was this man a disgruntled investor? Someone Anthony had cost thousands with bad advice? It could be…

But if this nutter presumed Anthony cared about her well-being, then he'd picked the wrong person.

'Now,' Zane continued, his initial anger at this prima donna having passed. 'Are you accompanying me without fuss, or not?'

Erin's mind whirred. She'd played the game long enough with Anthony, so she'd play it again with *this* man. She'd comply with whatever he wanted, as long as it didn't hinder her end plan. No one was stopping that. She gave a slight nod. 'Without,' she muttered.

'Good!' Zane removed his hand from Erin's throat. Taking her elbow, he steered her up the steps of the B&B.

Eleven

USHERED INTO THE ROOM, Erin stared at the damp peeling paint in dismay. How long would she have to stay in this dump?

'You may as well sit down,' Zane mumbled, fiddling with his crash helmet strap. If this woman was as sneaky as Flame, she'd be the first to give a description to the police. But that was on the proviso she walked away and that would not be an option any time soon. *If ever.*

He would hold her for as long as it took. Flame would go to his death believing this woman had been tortured, raped and killed. If he loved her, that would hurt more than anything.

Zane's mind turned over the options. He couldn't keep the woman in this B&B for long. He couldn't take her back to London either because then he wouldn't have access to Flame. Neither could he keep this helmet on indefinitely.

Gingerly lowering herself onto the edge of the bed, Erin watched the well-built man pace up and down, his back to her. Being away from Anthony was a relief, but it didn't change that she didn't know why she was here or who she was with.

Since being pressed up against the wall outside she had remained silent, but the urge to ask questions burned the tip of her tongue. 'What is this about? What do you want from me?'

she snapped, unable to refrain.

'Nosy bitch, aren't you?' Zane muttered from underneath his visor. Most people would be shitting themselves. But it was a good question. What *did* he want from her?

Finally pulling his crash helmet off, he placed it on the cheap chest of drawers and rummaged for two bottles of beer inside a carrier bag.

Biting her tongue, Erin stared at the man's back, her temper rising. What the fuck could be worse than being stuck with Anthony Walker? Yet now she found herself in a B&B with a random stranger, with no word as to why she was here and what was wanted from her.

Every minute she remained here pushed her further away from completing her task. Too much was invested in it. It was the only thing to keep her heart beating this past six years and she was buggered if anyone, including *him*, would infringe on that.

No. Fucking. Way.

As a metal bottle top was spat onto the floor, her brows knitted. This man had the manners of a pig. Most likely, judging by his bottle opening technique, the teeth to boot.

Her eyes scanned the room. If she was going to make a run for it, she had to do so quickly because this thug would turn around any second.

The ghost of a smile formed. This guy thought himself so scary that he didn't need to lock the door because she wouldn't dare run?

How slack to underestimate her.

It would take a lot more than a handful of snarling threats to stop her. She was not afraid of *anyone*.

Without a second left to spare, Erin bolted towards the door. She'd slam her way through if she had to.

• • • •

SENSING SUDDEN MOVEMENT from the corner of his eye, Zane lunged towards Erin, his panther-like speed belying his large frame.

Slamming his hand against the door, he swung Erin around and threw her on the bed, his heavy weight following to push her into the sagging mattress.

'I made it clear not to make rash movements and you seemed intelligent enough to understand that,' Zane growled, his face inches from hers.

Erin fought pointlessly under the weight of the hard body on top of her. 'Get the fuck off me!' she screamed, staring into the eyes boring into hers.

'Don't fret that I might touch you. I've no need to steal such amusements, Erin.' Zane's gaze moved slowly over Erin's unblemished face, down to her mouth. 'That particular pleasure is always freely given from the women in my life.'

Trying to work out how this lunatic knew her name, Erin couldn't stop the sharp intake of breath from escaping as she took in chiselled cheekbones and a jaw covered with dark stubble. At close range, the man's piercing blue eyes were unavoidable and they shot heat into her very soul.

The thick scar running down his right cheekbone was the only thing marring his otherwise perfect features.

She resented herself for even acknowledging his good looks. He was nothing but a thug and one, by the looks of it, one who might force himself on her...

That was not happening, even if it killed her.

'I said, get off!' she hissed.

Zane's sarcastic smile showcased straight white teeth. 'You really do have a complex. As I said, I ain't no rapist, darlin', so don't worry your overly-madeup face about that!'

Erin was about to hit back with a retort, when the man pushed himself off her, exposing his whole face and something stirred in the deep recesses of her mind.

Heart pounding, she studied the face again, her treacherous mind drawn to the man's full lips, before ice flooded her veins.

Feeling faint, she willed her brain to function. It couldn't desert her now. Her anger had clouded her to the obvious, which she could now see in clear and blinding clarity.

It was him - Zane Morelli.

This was the bastard who had murdered her father and the man she was waiting to kill.

Her brain crashed between plunging her talons into his eyeballs, to throttling him, but she knew he was far too quick - even for her.

She had to think and think fast.

How could she not have heard Morelli had been released? How the fuck had she missed it? She'd been waiting and watching to hear of the moment he walked out of those prison gates, yet it had happened without her knowledge?

No. No. No. This ruined everything.

Suddenly reasoning filtered into her speeding mind. This was what it was about. Morelli had killed her father and now he'd got out, he'd come for *her.*

But it didn't make sense. Whilst she was on the back of his motorbike, he could have ridden down a country lane and easily dispatched her. There would have been no witnesses and no come back, with no one any the wiser. If that was his aim, why had he not done it? Why was she still here?

Erin's breath came in ragged pants, sure steam was coming out of her ears.

She could be wrong. Morelli might not have noticed her sitting at the back of the courtroom obscure and unnoticed six years ago. Thanks to the collection of fake, overdone hair and makeup Anthony insisted upon, she looked vastly different to the twenty-two-year-old she had been back then.

She must think logically. Morelli might not recognise her and her overwhelming instinct was that he *didn't.*

If this man hadn't already crushed her rib cage, she would laugh out loud.

It was true! Zane Morelli *didn't* recognise her. He had no clue, which meant this was only about one thing. And that one thing made sense with the comments he'd made.

It was about Anthony.

Morelli must know, like she did, that Anthony had turned snark and had been the one to get him banged up. But one thing was certain - she wasn't letting him take Anthony out. That was hers to have. And hers *alone.*

In the meantime, she'd bide her time. She hadn't got any other choice right now, but she'd do it anyway. Okay, so her plan may have altered, but she could still achieve her aim, just in a different way.

Erin knew she had a decision to make and one to make quickly.

She must hide that she recognised him.

Her mind fused with resolve. What Morelli didn't know and wouldn't until it was too late, was that she would get to him first. And he would have no hint about that until it was upon him.

• • • •

SWIGGING HIS BEER, Zane eyed the bottle. He hated warm beer, but at least it diverted him from the woman sitting on his bed.

Despite his intentions, his eyes slid back to the shapely legs under the silky black material of Erin's skirt; the way the button ripped from her blouse allowed a tantalising hint of cleavage.

Damn it, he thought. *Remember where she'd been.*

All he had to do was move his attention back to the woman's scowling expression - her stunning face twisted with contempt like a sulky child, to put him off.

Except it didn't...

It intrigued him...

Why was Erin Langley not terrified?

On a standard day he put the fear of God into grown men three times her size with one look, yet she was barely fazed – merely angry. Far from the shy, fawning creature she'd made herself out to be for the pictures in the paper.

Interesting...

His eyes narrowed as he reminded himself of the task in

hand. He wanted information and if this chick thought she could play clever, then she'd regret it.

Snatching up Erin's handbag from the floor, Zane tipped the contents onto the rickety table.

'What the hell are you doing?' Erin gasped. 'You've got no right to go through my bag!'

Zane rummaged through the haphazard contents, his fingers closing around a gold case. 'Relax! I have no intention of stealing your makeup.'

Erin scowled as Zane threw her lipstick over to her, annoyed that, try as she might, her eyes remained fixed on his strong hands as his fingers curled around her mobile phone.

This was too weird. Everything Morelli had said so far had proved to be true. He hadn't laid a finger on her, just handed her a beer and sat silently watching her for what seemed like centuries.

He'd asked nothing. Nothing about her, about Anthony. *No one.*

Only the constant pounding in her veins showed the consistent anger for the bastard who had murdered her father. This man's deeds had led her to share her body and life with Anthony Walker. Zane Morelli's underhand decision to break her father's firm had been the first, last and every thought invading her mind since the moment she'd been able to put a name and face to the person responsible for ruining her life.

Keeping this hidden was becoming harder with every millisecond. It crept up her veins and over her skin, the push to release it getting stronger.

But she had to remain vigilant. Unbeknown to Morelli, *she* was in control here, not him. She would not let herself down.

'What happened to your face? I take it someone didn't like you? I guess there's quite a list...' Erin enjoyed her comment triggered a flash of emotion akin to rage, combined with self-consciousness, before the mask dropped back down over Zane's face like a shutter. 'It doesn't do you any favours, does it?' she continued. Getting a barb in on something that was clearly a sore point was gratifying.

'You'll find out yourself, if you wish,' Zane snarled, staring at Erin until she could do nothing but look away. 'The code?'

Erin's head snapped back up. 'What?'

Zane tapped the phone's screen, his eyes drilling into Erin's. 'Your phone's entry code?'

Erin's lips pursed. *She should make him guess. Anything to piss him off.*

Zane sighed and leant forward, his muscles straining the material of his shirt. 'You can make this easy or I can make it difficult.'

'Ditto,' Erin snapped, immediately regretting it. The longer she dragged this out, the longer she would remain trapped. Luring Morelli into a false sense of security was the key. 'Okay, okay, if you're that interested, it's 3622. Not got your own phone?'

Tapping in the digits, his fingers too large for the tiny buttons, Zane smiled. A cold smile - one that didn't reach his eyes. 'I do have a phone, yes, but *you* have the number I want.'

'Anthony's, by any chance?' Erin sniped. 'I presume your plan is to blackmail him? If so, then I doubt you'll get very far.' Her voice became dull and devoid of feeling, for that was the truth.

Zane glared at Erin. She was way off if she believed he wanted money like a cheap thief. Money wasn't anywhere *near* what he wanted. It was of no consequence. He had more than enough of his own. He wanted Flame's pain and eventual death, but Miss Langley could think what she liked. 'If you believe I want money, then feel free.'

Erin flinched. She knew the Morelli's were in no need of money. That firm was rolling in it, but wasn't Zane going to contact Anthony? What was he waiting for?

Zane copied Flame's mobile number into his own phone. So, Erin Langley was pretending the man she was set to marry didn't give a shit? *Yeah, right!* She had something special to win that cold bastard's attention and that was why she was here.

His bargaining chip.

A nerve in his neck twitched. For Flame to be involved with this chick showed that she meant more to him than anything. The man would pay, alright.

Erin watched Zane rise from the chair and pull his T-shirt off. The smattering of hair covering his wide muscular chest made her throat dry. 'What are you doing?'

Zane sluiced cold water on his face from the wash basin in the corner. Turning around, he dried himself with a towel. 'I'm going to bed.' He nodded to where Erin sat. 'As are you. Don't worry. The *last* thing I want to do is touch you, so you're perfectly safe.'

That wasn't entirely true. Flame having already staked his claim on this woman's flesh hadn't diluted the questionable urge to run his hands over that delectable body of hers or from imagining how her lips would feel around his cock. *That* was exactly what he wanted.

He wouldn't be doing that, of course. He *couldn't*. However, he would make that bastard *think* he had.

'Tomorrow, I'll tell you what I need you to do,' he said confidently. Because now he knew exactly what that would be.

TWELVE

MARCO COULD HAVE GOT A TAXI. He could have also called any number of his men to get their arse out of bed to come and pick him up, but the walk would clear his head and grant him the answers he needed.

In reality, all the walk had done was give him sore feet, but he was here now.

Climbing the steps to Bill's maisonette, he knocked on the cheap green door.

After thirty seconds passed with no sign of movement to signify anyone would let him into this crummy dump, Marco banged his fist repeatedly against the door. He wasn't being kept waiting like a twat. If Bill didn't get a bloody move on, he'd kick the fucking thing in.

He knocked again, his jaw clenched. *Bill had ten fucking seconds…*

'Alright, alright, keep your fucking hair on!' Bill yelled, his hangover already making its presence felt. He begrudgingly made his way towards the front door and yanked it open. 'It's not even six o'fucking clock yet, so wh… Oh!'

'Get the kettle on!' Marco barged into the hallway, stopping at the bedroom. Standing in the doorway, he glared at the woman in the bed covering her nakedness with a squashed pillow. 'Time's up love, so sling your hook, there's a good girl.'

Behind Marco, Bill pulled his thick fingers through his tangled hair, resentment brewing. He'd planned on a couple of shags this morning before getting rid of this bird. Now that wouldn't happen. 'Yeah, off you go. Business calls,' he grunted, deciding business must be the reason Marco had turned up on his doorstep at six in the morning.

He hoped so anyway, otherwise if he'd forgotten something, his neck would be on the chopping block.

As Marco continued towards the kitchen at the rear of the maisonette, Bill walked into the bedroom and pulled tracksuit bottoms over his underpants. He glared as the woman scrabbled for her clothes from the floor. 'Get a move on,' he snarled, the prospect of losing a shag preferable to the wrath of Marco Morelli. The less time he kept the man waiting, the better.

Pausing only until the woman had enough clothes on to warrant being decent, Bill shoved her through the front door. He closed it swiftly behind her, leaving the remainder of her clothes to fall from her hands onto the floor outside.

He strode into the kitchen, hiding both his annoyance and concern. 'Sorry about that. What's up?'

Watching the woman from Bill's bed stagger down the road, Marco turned from the window and took a drawn-out swig of his tea. Being as Bill had made him wait whilst getting rid of that tart, then he'd do likewise. It would do the man good to bloody sweat for a while, as he clearly thought this was about him, rather than anything else.

But it didn't change that he needed input on how to play things. Regardless of Bill's lumbering ways, the man was always useful for ideas.

Marco stared suspiciously into his mug of tea, not liking the rancid taste. 'The reason for my early visit is because I've just got out of the cop shop.' Seeing the panic on Bill's face, he winked. 'Nothing to do with me. Just doing my bit for the community by making a statement...'

Bill's stomach found its way from his mouth back into its rightful place. 'What was it about then?'

'Something and nothing. Some bird decided to chuck herself off my balcony last night.' Marco shrugged. 'Can't handle their drink, women.'

'*Your* balcony?' Bill stared at Marco. People didn't just fall off balconies - not usually, anyway. And certainly not from balconies like the one in *that* apartment.

'Yeah, she was pissed and must have toppled off, the stupid bitch. The first I knew of it was when I came out of the shower and heard the commotion below.'

Catching Bill eyeing the scratches on his hand, he swapped his mug into his other hand. 'Anyway, like I said, I had to give a statement. They'd already deduced there was no foul play.' *Amazing what money could buy...*

'Anyway, that's not why I'm here,' he continued, his brow creasing. Even uttering what he knew out loud made him want to smash the place up. 'I got a call last night from Trevor Grimes. And he wasn't best pleased...'

Bill frowned, Marco's narrowed eyes making him want to take a step backwards. 'Everything's still set for the stuff with Lisa, isn't it?'

'You tell me?' Marco roared. 'Grimes has heard from his own contacts on the inside that apparently things have changed regarding Zane's release.'

'What?' Bill cried. 'How? Surely our brief would have said if anyth...'

'Yeah, I know. I told Grimes it was bullshit or a mistake, but it made me sound a right mug,' Marco griped, his eyes flashing dangerously. 'I want to know who the fuck thought it a good idea to bandy that shit about. I want them fucking killed!'

Bill nodded enthusiastically, when really he wasn't looking forward to sifting through who the bloody hell would be stupid enough to start a rumour such as this. He risked a glance at Marco, seeing the fury evident in his eyes. He couldn't say he blamed the man for his reaction. He knew as well as everyone else that the deal with Grimes, as well as many other things, would be off the table if Zane was released from prison.

For a long time they'd done well containing the rumour mill, ensuring it confirmed Zane wouldn't be released for many years - more than long enough not to expect a firm to remain with a standby heir for such a length of time, even if they knew different.

And that was one of many reasons why it was imperative Zane remained banged up. *Or dead.*

'I take it you still haven't heard from those wanker screws or that tosser, Fennel?' Marco barked, making Bill jump.

Bill shook his enormous head. 'No, but it's not for want of trying. I was planning to make another call this morning. If I get no joy, then I'll demand an emergency VO and go to see Fennel myself.'

Marco nodded, wanting to be placated by this, but he wasn't. Not even slightly. If there was even a smidgen of truth to what had been said, he'd go batshit. 'Make sure you do. I'll get on to the brief and find out if he's heard anything.'

He stomped out of the kitchen towards the hall. 'Oh, and Bill? That bird who was in your bed? She was ugly as fuck. Get yourself a shower. You stink of fucking mange.'

• • • •

AS THE MORNING SUN filtered through the thin curtains, Erin pressed herself up against the warm body next to hers, her hand splayed across the hard muscular torso.

Despite her dream state, a burning question filtered into her mind. She'd conditioned herself over the past six years to *never* stray near Anthony, even during sleep. How much had she drunk at the Golf Club last night?

Even being paralytic wouldn't prompt her to touch his tainted flesh or...

Jolting to full consciousness, her hand jerked away. *This wasn't Anthony. It was Morelli. Zane fucking Morelli.*

'You seemed comfortable?' Zane's husky voice growled.

'There's nothing comfortable about sharing a bed with *you*!' Swiftly moving to the edge of the mattress, Erin pulled down the hem of the long T-shirt Zane had given her last night. She'd have kept all of her clothes on, had she not been convinced they would end up infested with bed bugs.

Ignoring the persistent throbbing of his raging arousal, Zane couldn't stop a slight smile from creeping onto his face. This woman really hated him. She'd hate him even more after he'd killed the man she planned to marry.

Should he wind her up further by mentioning that he hadn't taken offence to waking up finding her stroking his cock? Not that she had, but even the light touch of her silky hand on his chest had achieved the same effect and the resulting erection was driving him to distraction.

Flame would resent thinking someone else was using this beautiful creature for their own enjoyment. Even more so when he found out exactly who that someone was…

Zane's face darkened, the thought of Flame having an immediate deflating effect. It was probably a good job. He had to concentrate on the task that would begin in earnest today. Reaching over, he tossed a clean towel in Erin's direction. 'The bathroom's down the end of corridor.'

'No en-suite?' Erin snapped. 'I'm surprised someone like *you* would lower themselves to basic conditions such as this...'

Immediately realising she wasn't supposed to know a thing about Zane Morelli, she paled. She mustn't blow her cover. Deciding that ignoring her mistake was the best option, she avoided looking at him, but knew he was staring at her strangely, she could feel it. *Damn her stupidness.*

Getting up and adjusting the thick tracksuit bottoms he'd forced himself to wear to bed, Zane frowned. Why would Erin Langley presume he had loads of money? He had nothing on him to hint at his wealth - not even his Rolex.

To distract himself from the disquieting question and to quell the urge to stare at the woman opposite in just a T-shirt, he flicked on the antiquated fourteen-inch portable television and twisted the makeshift coat hanger aerial in the hope of getting a picture.

The rolling screen crackled until a half-visible reception was achieved. He pressed the greasy buttons on the front. *Good Morning Britain? No thanks... The news?*

Zane stared at the flickering screen, only half-watching the tail end of a report on Pope John II's historic visit to Syria. He rolled his eyes, wishing Erin would go and take a shower so he no longer had to pretend to ignore her presence.

Just about to give the TV up as a bad job and switch the bloody thing off, Zane's arm stretched towards the on/off button, but froze as footage of an apartment came into view.

His apartment...

The camera panned to a balcony. *His* balcony! Then the view changed to the walkway below, showing the landscaped gardens surrounding the building.

The volume was low, but there was no point looking for a remote control. Leaning forward, he strained to hear the newsreader's words.

> *"... The woman who fell to her death last night had, according to Mr Morelli – who owns the apartment where the accident occurred, believed her to have been drinking heavily. Attending paramedics pronounced the woman dead at the scene, but do not suspect foul play. This lady is yet to be named and..."*

Zane switched the television off, his mind racing. *Mr Morelli? Marco? Marco was in his apartment? What the fuck?*

Chewing his lip, he nodded dismissively as Erin left the room, not noticing the expression on her face.

THIRTEEN

IGNORING THE LEER of the fat, balding man appearing out of an adjoining room as Erin walked down the landing in nothing but a towel, she hastened towards Zane's room, still wondering what could have bothered him so much about that television report.

Because *something* had.

She hadn't caught what the reporter said, but she'd seen Zane's face. He may not have outwardly reacted, but there was a definite change – something akin to confusion and shock.

Erin continued down the corridor from the bathroom, the question why she was choosing to return to the room of her captor, pushing into her mind. Zane had been distracted enough to let her use the bathroom without accompanying her, so he was either stupid; didn't believe she would attempt to escape or that news report had derailed him.

What could those apartments have to do with him? Unless one of them was his?

How remiss of him.

She could just run down the stairs and out into the street, screaming to the nearest passer-by that she was being held against her will. The police would be called and Zane Morelli, the murdering bastard, would be locked up again.

This time they would throw away the key.

So why hadn't she?

Erin glared at the drooling man loitering in the doorway and refused to allow her gaze to be drawn to his grubby underpants.

She couldn't contemplate involving the police. As well as bringing unwanted attention on her when she was on the cusp of achieving everything she'd waited for, why would she place the man she was going to kill out of her grasp?

A grin moved onto her face. Despite the odd way this opportunity presented itself, not only was her target now right under her nose, but as an added bonus, she was away from Anthony. It was the best of both worlds.

And *that* was why she hadn't taken the opportunity to escape.

But she had to know what Zane had planned. Last night he'd said he'd tell her today, but he'd mentioned nothing yet. If his plans involved Anthony, which she suspected they did, they would clash with *hers*, therefore she'd have to remove Zane from the picture first.

If that was required, she had to ensure she wasn't caught.

Hearing someone coming up the creaking wooden stairs, Erin rushed into the bedroom and slammed the door behind her, acutely aware Zane's open scrutiny of her towel-clad body.

Erin snatched up the fresh clothes that had mysteriously appeared on the bed. She eyed the underwear suspiciously. It was a nice set and looked to be in her size.

How?

Did Morelli have a drawer full of spare underwear for his many conquests? A cocksure bastard if ever she'd seen one.

'Is there a problem?'

Zane's voice jolted Erin from her thoughts. She looked at him disparagingly. 'Just wondering why you have a selection of women's underwear to hand? Is snatching women off the streets and bringing them to your room a common pastime?'

She turned away, pretending to look for somewhere private

to dress, but in reality, she'd seen the flicker of rage on Zane's face. She should not forget the man she was stuck in the same room with was a killer. Worse, and to her horror, she felt an almost grudging respect that he'd thought to provide clean clothes for her, even if the circumstances were dubious.

Zane watched Erin curiously. Here was a woman who had been snatched by an utter stranger, who, as far as she knew, could attack her at any given minute, yet she was flippant, snappy and quite frankly, bloody rude.

Despite this attitude usually guaranteeing his fist to drive into someone's face or a knife between the ribs, he was intrigued.

He rubbed his finger over his lower lip. Erin Langley was either a self-obsessed little madam or was hiding something. Either that or just plain mad. He was unsure which it was, but he'd better deduce it quickly. His plans could not be scuppered by a strung-out bitch with a chip on her shoulder.

His eyes lingered as Erin fumbled to fasten her bra with one hand, the other ensuring the towel kept her covered. His mouth twitched into a smile. Spoilt, mad or hiding something – she was too stunning for the likes of Flame.

Pulling himself up from his chair, Zane walked behind Erin, grabbed the strap of her bra and effortlessly hooked it together. Ignoring her shock, he smiled coldly. 'With reference to your snide remarks, the underwear is from a shop in town. I called them first thing this morning to arrange a delivery for you.'

Having the good grace to redden from her previous rudeness, Erin nodded and turned her back once more to override the incessant burn Zane's fingers left on her skin.

She clenched her jaw, determined not to allow anything - not even weird, misplaced sensations to divert her. 'Why exactly do you feel the need to stare at me?' she snapped as the piercing gaze seared into her.

Morelli may have redeemed himself with the story about the underwear, if it was true, but she wasn't deluded. She was under close watch. She'd had enough of that over the years from

Anthony and didn't need another man doing it. And *certainly* not this one.

'I was just thinking how much better you look without that fake shit in your hair and on your face,' Zane remarked without thinking. He meant it, but it was stupid to voice it. Erin Langley was stunning anyway, but without that rubbish and heavy makeup, she was... *perfect*.

He swallowed dryly and prayed for the aching in his groin to subside.

Erin blinked in surprise. It was true that whilst in the bathroom she'd grabbed the long-awaited opportunity to rip off the bloody hair extensions and fake eyelashes she hated so much. She'd shove everything back in place before she returned to Anthony, but for the time being, she was free to be herself, even if that meant being trapped here with a different lunatic.

But no one had ever said she looked nice...

To deflect from her confusion, she snatched up a brush and dragged it through her hair. 'I hope you haven't got lice,' she muttered.

Zane threw the mobile on the bed. 'When you've finished preening yourself, you're to call your boyfriend and say exactly what I tell you.'

That's what you think, Erin thought. She knew what Zane was doing; he turned on the charm via underwear and compliments to lull her into doing his bidding, but it wouldn't work. She'd play his game to a certain extent, but she'd kill him before he got the chance to move on Anthony.

That was hers to have.

'What are you hoping to achieve by this? What has Anthony done to you?' she asked. *Like she didn't know...*

'That's not your concern,' Zane said gruffly. 'Just do what I say.' Meeting Erin's stare, he held it with the same defiance she held his. 'Tell me exactly what *you* stand to gain by marrying this man? His money, by any chance?' *The money he'd gone to prison for...*

Erin felt like screaming at this murdering bastard that it

wasn't Anthony's money, it was her father's - *hers*, but she caught herself just in time. 'Because I love him!' she snapped. 'Why else?'

How those words choked. How poisonous they felt burning a treacherous line as they slipped from her mouth.

'Of course… Love… What else?' Zane smirked.

Erin turned away. If Morelli knew the real reason, he'd get as far away from her as possible, rather than being stupid enough to remain in the same room.

. . . .

HAVING TAKEN EXTRA TIME applying specialist coverage makeup to his blackened eyes, Anthony was confident no one would notice. The area was still swollen, but he could pass that off as hay fever. The most pressing thing was to behave like nothing was out of the ordinary.

And it wasn't as far as anyone else is concerned, both at work and from people at the Golf Club last night. No one had mentioned anything and there had been no talk of him getting clumped by a psycho on a motorbike.

Anthony stared at his reflection in the mirror for the same amount of time as he always did, following the routine of counting from one to thirty-six in increments of three and then back down again. This particular ritual was tantamount to maintaining his well-being and putting him in the frame of mind of being Anthony and Anthony alone. Because that's who he was now.

His botoxed forehead would have creased if it were possible.

No sign of Erin still? She really was a pointless bitch and, from what he suspected, a devious one. Whoever had punched him in the face last night was for a distraction.

A thought *had* fleetingly passed into his mind when the biker had first appeared, but he'd quickly dismissed it. Had it been to do with *his* past, it would have been *him* to have disappeared, not Erin.

The man on the motorbike must be someone she was dallying around with behind his back. Was Erin so stupid to undermine him and risk losing the luxury becoming his wife guaranteed?

Turning the tap on, he ran his fingertips under the cold water and smoothed his eyebrows once, then twice before reinspecting his reflection. Erin would pay for this when she returned. And she had better return soon, because whether he liked it or not, he relied on her to deal with the social side of things, however tiresome she was.

He would not relinquish the steady growth of his business for anything.

Leaving the toilets, Anthony headed through the reception back to his fishbowl office that was sectioned off from the main pool by floor to ceiling glass. It offered 360-degree surveillance of his eager and willing to please workforce.

'Mr Walker...'

Irritated, Anthony turned to the receptionist. He didn't like being interrupted when walking. It broke the pattern of treading only on the black floor tiles. Now he'd have to retrace his steps. 'What is it, Maisie?'

Maisie smiled sweetly, eager to impress. 'You had a call yesterday from a man about an appointment you had arranged.'

'Yesterday?' Anthony frowned. 'I had no appointments booked for yesterday afternoon.'

'That's what I thought, but the way he was joking about things, I think he must be a friend of yours.'

'Joking? About what?' Anthony's interest piqued. Plus, he had no friends - never had and never would. It was the way he liked it.

'Oh, erm, just that you were always forgetting his appointments,' Maisie said awkwardly, realising by the look on Anthony Walker's face that she probably shouldn't have mentioned that part. 'I mean, I explained you were at golf, as usual for a Thursday and he seemed aware of that.'

'Did he now...?' Anthony raised an eyebrow. 'Who was this

person?'

'Erm… he didn't leave his name,' Maisie continued, now flustered. 'He said he'd call back but hasn't so far.' She glanced at the diary. 'Should I...' She stopped, realising Anthony was already halfway across the open plan office heading towards his fishbowl.

Forgetting he was supposed to tread on the black floor tiles, Anthony stormed into his office. *So that woman had told a nameless man he was at the golf course?*

Possibilities brewed. Was this linked to the visitor in the car park - the one that had sped off with his property on the back of that motorbike?

He should have called the police, but how could he have them sniffing around? Apart from questions that were impossible to answer, he wasn't being embarrassed with the speculation about his fiancée that would surely follow.

When his mobile rang, Anthony closed the door. Pulling the phone from his pocket, his eyes narrowed at the incoming caller's name flashing on the screen:

...Erin...

'Finally!' Anthony spat. 'You're determined to wind me up! Get your sorry arse back here right now! Have you any idea how embarrassing this will be, if people ask why you're not with me for drinks tonight.'

FOURTEEN

'IS NO ONE putting effort into this today?' Marco barked, glaring at members of the crew on set and making no effort to mask his foul mood. 'In case it's escaped your notice, we're in the bleeding middle of production, so get your arse into gear or fuck off. I'll replace the lot of you!'

He stomped off the set, casting an extra nasty glare at the naked redhead skittering out of his path. He felt like twisting one of her tits clean off. That would give them something to moan about, rather than acting up just because a bird who'd been to this studio *once*, ended up splattered on the fucking deck.

What did it matter? It wasn't any of them! This lot didn't even know the girl - no one did, short of a couple of 'hellos' and a fuck in front of the cameras! Who the hell cared?

Slamming the door of his office extra loudly for added effect, Marco snatched a new wrap of cocaine from the top drawer and cut a line on his desk. 'Bloody joke, they are! What's the matter with them?' he snarled, expertly hoovering the coke up his nose with a fresh fifty-pound note.

If anyone had anything to worry about, it was *him*, not them. Yet was he the one running around with a boat race like a slapped haddock? No, he bloody wasn't.

But he wanted to. He wanted to fucking scream.

Sniffing loudly to ensure the remnants of cocaine in his nostril reached his brain, Marco hawked and spat a thick ball of phlegm on the floor. He glared at Bill. 'You aren't much better either. You look like you've sat on a fucking hedgehog!'

'Everyone's on edge and a bit nervy, that's all,' Bill muttered. No one had said a thing, but it wasn't difficult to see people were thinking along the same lines as him... *That girl plummeting to her death from Marco's apartment was no accident...*

Everyone knew how Marco got when the fancy took him. And *they* didn't know about what had come to light yesterday that held the power to flip Marco's temper either.

Bill glanced through the one-way viewing window which allowed a front row seat of the filming action.

People were used to waiting to see which one of them would be on the receiving end of one of Marco's legendary outbursts. Even he and Sonny frequently trod on eggshells when Marco was on one. But if Bill's suspicions were correct and Marco *had* launched that girl from the balcony, it didn't bode well.

Bill's bushy eyebrows gathered into one. It wasn't the girl's death that was the problem. He didn't give a rat's arse about the stupid tart, whoever she was. It was those closest to Marco who bothered him. Especially now the man was extra stressed.

'I realise the, erm, accident has caused problems, but we need to keep the girls and crew on set comfortable,' he reasoned. 'Shouting at them could cause issues with, erm, speculation...'

Bill didn't want to keep his gaze locked on Marco as the words left his mouth - he knew what he'd said wouldn't go down well, but Marco hated deference. He also hated *non*-deference. Bill was one of the few who was expected to level with his boss.

'Speculation?' Marco yelled, swiping his glass from the

desk to smash on the floor. 'Fuck speculation! What are you saying? That they'll insinuate what happened to that slut was down to me?'

Jumping from his seat, he paced the office, his movements becoming more erratic as the latest line of cocaine took hold in his brain. 'Is that what *you* think?' he roared, his eyes glittering with mania, the tiny pupils making the cold blue colour even more unnerving.

'I didn't say that, I...'

Marco swiped his shoe through the fragments of broken glass, sending them skittering in all directions. 'Fuck that! And fuck you! You said this morning you were calling the screws again, so did you?'

Leaning both his arms on the desk, he lowered level with Bill's face. 'What. Did. They. Say? I shouldn't have to chase you on this!'

Bill leant back in his chair in a bid to look relaxed, but realistically he wanted to get as far away from Marco as possible, like he always did when the man was on one of his rants. 'Still no joy. I couldn't get anywhere with securing a VO for Fennel either.' *He'd been dreading breaking that bit...* 'Something odd is happening in there,' he added. 'I don't know what, but the shutters have come down and we need to find out why.'

Marco threw his hands up in the air. '*We* do? *We* need to find out why? Don't you mean, *you* do?'

'Well, yes, that's what I meant an...'

'Oh, don't bother!' Marco stomped back around his desk and dropped heavily into his seat. He jerked his head at the drinks cabinet, silently ordering Bill to replace the brandy he'd launched across the floor. 'I tell you what, I'll do it my fucking self!'

Snatching up the phone, Marco stabbed in the digits, whist watching Bill reluctantly move to the cabinet to retrieve a fresh glass. 'I want to see you now!' he barked down the mouthpiece. 'Yeah, now!'

Slamming the phone down, he snatched the brandy off Bill and then dragged his forearm over the desk to mop up the spirit which sloshed over the side of the glass. He necked the drink in one. 'If you can't obtain a VO or find out what the fuck is going on, then I'll get the brief on it. He's coming over now. The nick has to answer to a fucking solicitor, so he'd best do a better job with getting me an update than you have.'

• • • •

JUST HEARING THAT VOICE made Erin's skin crawl. She willed herself to remain calm and ignored Zane staring, waiting for her to follow his instructions.

She didn't want to follow his instructions. Neither did she want to listen to Anthony's berating voice. She hated *both* these men and doing either of their bidding was grating more than ever.

'Are you listening, Erin?' Anthony's voice boomed through the mobile's loudspeaker.

Erin glared at the phone in the middle of the bed. Despite watching her get dragged away on the back of a motorbike, Anthony hadn't even asked if she was okay. Humiliation stung.

'ERIN! Answer the fucking question!' The harsh voice yelled. 'You disappear with a man and have the cheek not to return? You really are a let-down. Do you really think I'll stand for this? Your idea for him to punch me didn't work either.'

Erin blinked. Anthony thought *she'd* set this up? She glared at Zane, seeing him jerk his head, prompting her to speak. All of this was *his* fault. Furthermore, this call was pointless. Anthony didn't give a shit about anything, providing he kept face.

Fuck it. She'd say exactly what Zane had instructed and then the lunatic would see for himself that it was a futile exercise.

'I'm being kept against my will.' She forced herself to sound frightened. 'I don't know where I am... and...'

'Held against your will?' There was a sarcastic chuckle.

'For what reason would anyone take you? Stop bullshitting and get back to the house. I need you at the drinks tonight.'

Erin made realistic sobbing noises. She hadn't kept this shit up for so long without being adept at doing what was required. 'This man... he's... he's...'

'If it's true you're being held against your will, you'd hardly have a phone to use,' Anthony sneered.

The cold laughter which followed made Erin dig her nails deeper into her palms, her knuckles whitening. 'H-he told me to call. He's been threatening to...' She clocked the slight nod from Zane. 'This man is someone you used to know...'

There was a snort of derision. 'Who would I know that would do something like this?'

'I-I don't know... He said you owe him six years and...'

'Six years...?'

Erin smiled to herself. *Had the penny dropped yet?* Of course, she had to pretend she had no idea what this referenced, but *she* knew where Zane had been during the last six years because she'd kept track every single day.

Morelli had the cheek to be put out about Anthony setting him up? They were all part of the decision to rob and murder, therefore deserved exactly what was coming to them.

'Erin, what do you mean, six years?' For the first time in the conversation, Anthony's voice held a hint of wariness. 'What does this man look like?'

Erin saw a nerve twitch in Zane's cheek - the *scarred* cheek... *What does he look like? He looks ready to murder. He looks...* 'Erm, he's got dark hair an...'

Lurching over the bed, Zane snatched the phone and turned off the loudspeaker, his anger simmering further with the proof that Flame was just as obnoxious as always. But the man's attitude had uncovered one thing he hadn't bargained for.

He hadn't once asked how Erin was.

How come this woman was so spiky and trappy towards him, rather than being scared witless, yet she put up with being spoken to like shit from a man who she purported to love? He'd weighed this up incorrectly. He couldn't put his finger on it, but something wasn't right here. Either way he was going in for the kill. It was time to make things *very* clear…

'I have something of yours, cunt. Something you want…' Zane snarled, a smirk twisting his mouth with the confused pause the other end of the line. 'Recognise my voice yet…?'

Erin waited in anticipation. *Did Anthony recognise Zane's voice or not? Surely, he must?*

'You don't speak very nicely to a woman you're marrying…' Zane continued, imagining Flame's twisted, lying face. His eyes narrowed, no longer aware of Erin's presence, his full concentration only on the man the other end of the line. 'Now, let's get down to business. You set me up. I know what you did, so don't even *think* of denying it.'

His pulse thumped through his head, deafening him to everything, short of his own heartbeat pounding mercilessly in his ears. 'You should be dead! And you will be if you don't do as I say. As will *she*… You owe me, you piece of shit. And it starts *now*…'

His temples pounded with the adrenalin coursing through his body. 'She must be special to you, eh? Well, I can't take from you what you're taken from me, but I *can* take her.' Zane's mouth twisted into a savage snarl. 'I'm going to fuck her – fuck her hard. I will remove every trace of you from within her.'

He laughed coldly, vengeance burning. 'She won't want to come when I push her over the edge, but she won't be able to help it.'

Erin shuffled uncomfortably. Zane looked possessed – like he was seeing straight through her, the venom as he spat the words into the phone transfixing her to the story he was spinning. He hadn't laid a finger on her. Nor even *tried*.

She strained to hear Anthony's response.

Suddenly grabbing Erin's face, Zane pulled her head up, his fingers pinching painfully into her jaw catching her unawares so that she let out a yelp.

'Hear that, you cunt?' Zane spat into the phone, his eyes

unseeing, the only person in his mind was Flame. 'I'll ruin her the same was as I'll ruin you, unless you give me a good reason not to. And then once everything is trashed, you piece of shit, I'll kill you...'

The first change to Zane's face was when his twisted snarl morphed into the ghost of a smile. 'So, think carefully what you're going to do now. I'll expect your call back later today.'

Ending the call, he threw the mobile on the bed. Finally aware of his actions, he dropped his grip of Erin's face. 'That will do for now.'

'How *dare* you grab me like that!' Erin cried, fury twisting her face. The complete change in Zane's countenance had taken her off guard and disarmed her. But only momentarily.

How could Morelli even *think* she would sleep with him? Or would he give her no choice after all?

Laughing coldly, Zane dragged his thumb across Erin's cheek. 'Wait, let me dry your non-existent tears...'

Erin slapped away Zane's hand. 'Don't touch me, you bastard! How dare y...'

'Shut up, you stupid cow! I can act just as well as you!'

Flinching, Erin jerked away. She now had her answer as to which way this was going and how she would need to play it. Zane Morelli was an utter lunatic. He would kill Anthony. He would do it before she could if she didn't get moving.

He would also kill *her*. There was no way he would let her walk away now. And that meant only one thing.

She had to take him out first.

FIFTEEN

'JUST CANCEL IT!' Anthony roared, glaring at the woman entering his office. 'I'm not dealing with any appointments today.' His hands clenched underneath his desk. 'Get out!'

As Maisie quickly scuttled away, close to tears, Anthony closed his eyes and began counting. *Three... Six... Nine... Twelve... Fifteen... Eighteen...*

He drew in a long breath.

Zane Morelli?

He'd been assured this would not happen. That was why he'd agreed to it. Yeah, he had the money and a new identity, but what good was that only for Morelli to appear back in his life and take his fiancée?

His skin prickled.

Morelli taking Erin would do him no favours.

His jaw tightened with the thought of that man shoving his filthy cock in his property. Anthony needed Erin in order to keep up appearances and maintain his fast growing, lucrative business. If it got out that she'd slept with another man behind his back, and so close to their wedding too, he'd lose face.

He'd lose *everything*.

Not only would all the important people he dealt with and

planned to deal with, think him an utter joke, but without Erin on hand to cope with the networking, everything would fall apart.

Anthony felt his throat begin to close like it always did when he forgot to count to stabilise his anger. The tremors in his hand began too and he slapped both his palms on the desk; the stinging fuelling his resentment.

Had Erin already been screwed?

Not that he gave a fuck - the woman was a commodity - no more, no less.

The pounding in Anthony's veins increased. If this got out, he couldn't even use the abduction excuse to explain why he should remain with the stupid bitch. If people thought she'd been forced, rather than going off with another man of her own accord, then in many ways, it was *worse*. Her reputation would be sullied. She'd be damaged goods - not fit for purpose.

Certainly not fit for someone like *him*.

Nausea rolled. What if that bastard got her pregnant and left her with an everlasting reminder? If that happened, he'd kick any leftovers from that man out of her. Or kill her.

Possibly both.

If she'd been possessed by Morelli, he'd do that regardless.

Snatching up his phone, Anthony stared at Erin's name in the recent call list. He should call back now and sort this out. It was more than likely bullshit - a tactic to get money. Morelli was a greedy cunt - the whole lot of them were.

Thinking about it logically, he'd worked for that firm long enough to know that Zane wasn't the one out of the two Morelli brothers to force women into bed. *Marco* was the contender for that accolade. *And Marco didn't have Erin...*

And as for Morelli promising to kill him, well, that wouldn't happen. It wouldn't happen because he was going to do something about it.

Slamming the phone down, Anthony tugged open the bottom drawer of his desk and rummaged around for the pocketbook he knew to be in there. He could pinpoint the location of any item he'd put away. Another useful facet of his brilliant mind.

Retrieving the book, he flicked to the page containing the number he'd promised not to use again.

The agreement might have been never to get back in contact, but that was before conditions were broken. The side of the bargain keeping Zane Morelli from ever seeing the light of day was now null and void. The man was close on his heels and had his property, therefore something had to be done.

Anthony stabbed the numbers into his desk phone. If Zane wasn't stopped in his tracks and removed out of his orbit, then he'd do it *himself*. Somehow.

Anthony cut the call and quickly redialled, his botoxed forehead straining, yet failing to form a frown.

`...the number you have dialled is no longer in`
`service...`

He slammed down the receiver and dialled again and again, only to receive the same response.

Not in service? Were they no longer in the same premises? Or had Zane got to them before coming for Erin?

Anthony pulled his fingers through his brown hair, pausing as a single hair fluttered down to land on the pristine page of his leather appointment book.

He'd never get used to this colour, even though it had been many years. When accepting the offer, he'd moved heaven and earth to comply with the instructions. Yet in return, after all this time, a major part of what was promised had now collapsed.

Anthony stared back at his desk phone, abandoning the idea of dialling again.

Morelli had called the shots and outlined what he wanted, but he'd take the gamble of giving it a bit longer before he made the decision on what to do.

He opened his laptop. If he got nowhere with making contact over the next few hours, he'd be left with little choice but to pay Morelli off. Doing that would buy time in the interim until he *could* make contact.

. . . .

ERIN HOPED she was correct by believing Zane faced away from her whilst he loaded his gun. Again, another silly assumption on his part. Having had enough practise over the years being with Anthony, she was good at pretending to be asleep and prided herself on mastering that art.

This wasn't what she'd planned though. How Zane would meet his death the day he was released from prison had been decided in meticulous detail. It was fool proof and guaranteed success, whilst leaving her blameless. Now that was out of the window.

She now had to find a way of killing him, not only immediately, but with no equipment to name of. And worse, doing it somewhere containing God only knew how many others - all of which would probably hear, as well as be able to attest to her presence.

It was a disastrous idea, but she had no other options.

Daring to slightly open one eye and check she'd been correct in her assumptions, Erin consoled her present situation with that her senses were spot on.

Which only underlined the urgency...

Her eyes snapped shut as Zane made to turn around, like his sixth sense was as alert as her own.

Her fingers closed around the penknife she'd found in the bathroom. It had been an utter stroke of luck glimpsing it stuffed down the back of the washstand. How long it had been there was anyone's guess, but the small blade clogged with dust and cobwebs revealed it had been there some time, as well as how seldom the shared bathroom was cleaned.

Someone had lost a penknife and it was now hers...

It was small, but a knife was a knife and at the end of the day, it was all she had. It would have to do.

Erin knew what must happen when Anthony had failed in

doing what Zane had counted on. He'd been sure Anthony would call back, but her fiancé wasn't in the least bothered about her supposed predicament or Zane's threats.

Maybe the full extent that his past had finally caught up with him, hadn't hit Anthony yet? Unlikely, but now there were no signs of him following expectations, Zane would go after him with that gun.

She'd even offered to call Anthony back - *anything* to buy time, but Zane had brushed her suggestion aside. He was hellbent on getting to Anthony, so there was no alternative but to get Zane during the one night that remained.

This night…

Hearing Zane cross the room, followed by the sound of him dragging his boots out from under the dressing table, Erin stiffened, her heart thumping. *He was going out? He was going for Anthony now?*

Her anger mounted, her fingers shaking. This couldn't happen. It would ruin everything. She'd have to kill Zane right this very minute, instead of when he fell asleep.

Holding her breath, she prized the rusty blade from under the cover of the duvet, her fingers gripping it so tightly she felt she might crush it.

Risking another squint through one eye, she focused on Zane's big hands tying the laces of his boots surprisingly carefully.

How should she do this? Wait until he turned his back?

Getting him from behind was the only option. She'd be killed otherwise and she hadn't come this far to allow this bastard to take her out, rather than the other way around.

This was insane, but she owed it to her father. And to *herself…*

With the thought of her father and the atrocious way he'd met his end, any doubts as to the justification of stabbing this man in the back dissolved, and when Zane stood up and headed towards the door, she made her move.

Erin covered the distance from the bed to the door faster

than she believed possible and Zane had no chance to turn before she drove the knife into his back.

Even if it wasn't the perfect place to stab someone or that, from this angle, the small blade was unlikely to do enough damage to kill him, it was enough to disarm him and get more attempts on a place that *would* kill him.

Erin saw Zane twist at the sudden movement, the shock sliding onto his face as he felt the impact. It took a split second after that for her to register that the knife hadn't embedded into his flesh and instead, she was being pushed backwards with raw force, by a hand underneath her jaw.

How could it have not impacted? How? Now she was dead. She'd failed everything - her father; her plans - *everyone*.

Crushing Erin down onto the bed with his body, Zane pulled the useless blade from her hand. He glanced at it scornfully before launching it across the other side of the room. '*That*, is one very good reason not to use shit equipment. It does you no favours,' he hissed, his face thunderous.

He'd clearly got one here that would be more difficult to deal with than he'd thought. She was like a creature possessed. Perhaps it was necessary to remove her from the equation, along with Flame?

Erin fought under Zane's weight; her self-control blown. She could barely believe it had come to this, but now she'd got nothing to lose.

Trying to break from his steel grip to claw his face or gouge his eyes - *anything*, she struggled like a wildcat. 'Get off me you fucking lunatic! Go on, kill me! Go on! Kill me, you scarred-up piece of shit! Do your worst. I don't care!'

Seeing the raw hatred in Erin's eyes, Zane increased his grip to control her flailing hands. 'You're fucking crazy!'

Erin opened her mouth to speak, then promptly shut it. Her rage had almost made her blurt out the truth – that she knew what he'd done and that was why he had to die. But she couldn't. Not yet.

Instead, she spat in Zane's face.

Without relinquishing his tight hold, Zane wiped Erin's saliva away with the sleeve of his T-shirt. His mouth formed a tight smile. 'I see that you're as much of a devious cunt as your boyfriend…'

Sixteen

5 AM it may be, but Zane wasn't tired. His nervous energy and knack of leaving no routes open to chance in any given scenario was honed to perfection, giving him the ability to run through the night any time it was required.

There had been *several* occasions both in and out of prison when this had been necessary and it had served him well. The ability served him well now.

This woman couldn't be trusted. She could have no leeway, nor be left alone. Not even to use the bog.

His eyes narrowed. Because of the stunt this bitch pulled last night, Flame was still breathing, unaware just how much he would suffer and Zane did not appreciate the man's pain had not yet begun.

To detract from ploughing his energy and resentment into the beautiful and psychotic, vicious little spoilt bitch in front of him, Zane forced his mind to return to the news report from this morning - or rather, being as it was now daybreak - *yesterday*.

Since seeing it, the whole thing had festered. Aside from deviating his brain from deciphering this strange woman, the report helped keep his mind from focusing on the stiffness in his thighs and the nagging ache in his lower back, courtesy of the hours he'd sat unmoving in a chair, keeping watch.

That Marco was using his apartment, or at the very least, been there at the time of that woman's death was one thing, but why would his brother not mention he was staying there?

The longer Zane hung around here, rather than returning to London, only prolonged discovering what had *really* gone on in his absence and why Marco hadn't told the truth about Flame. About *lots* of things...

And he had the nagging feeling that whatever he found out, he wouldn't like it...

The main reason Zane was still here, with the additional burden of babysitting a bird who'd tried to kill him, was because Flame was not six feet under, like he'd believed until yesterday.

That his own firm had let the bastard walk free after what he'd done was unfathomable, but the proof had been right in front of him. And if seeing that man in the flesh wasn't enough, then listening to the robotic voice he'd recognise anywhere, was.

His hand rested on the loaded gun in his lap, shifting it slightly before fixing his concentration back to the woman lying on his bed.

In any other circumstance there would be no way a bird looking like this would be lying on a bed in his vicinity whilst he remained in a chair. But then, the experience of a chick trying to murder him wasn't something he'd previously encountered either.

His eyes narrowed at the equally motionless form of Erin Langley, who like him, was able to bypass the concept of sleep.

Waiting for another chance to try and stab him, was she? Well, she wouldn't get it.

But one fact remained the same. Had that knife not snapped, things might have been very different.

Zane rolled his shoulder - the side of Erin's attempt. Only a slight puncture wound was achieved before the blade broke. It hadn't even bled, but it could have been disastrous.

Jesus Christ. Had her plan worked, the bitch would have

succeeded in killing him!

His brow furrowed. He hadn't even seen it coming and that bothered him more than he wanted to acknowledge.

'Exactly how long are you planning to keep me manacled to your bed?'

Erin's voice cut sharply into the silence, but Zane didn't bat an eyelid as the quietness of the room was broken. 'As long as I need. And that looks like it will be for the foreseeable, being as I underestimated how little you can be trusted.' His mouth curled into a sneer. 'Considering you're with that piece of shit, it should have come as no surprise. Attracted by his morals, were you?'

Erin stiffened. 'I'm nothing like Anthony.'

'Then maybe you'd like to embellish as to why you're with him?' Zane crossed his leg over the other, casually reseating the gun in his lap. If this treacherous cow made any move to escape her tethering, he wouldn't hesitate in blowing a hole through her pretty head. It seemed a shame to ruin her looks, but in her case the old proverb, 'beauty is only skin deep', was most apt.

Erin remained silent, aided by biting the edges of her tongue. It helped deflect the agony of her limbs being held at such an uncomfortable angle.

It was fast becoming unbearable, but she wouldn't let Morelli know this. No one *ever* bore witness to her pain, physical or otherwise. And that still applied. Now more than ever.

And no, she wouldn't like to embellish why she was with Anthony Walker. She'd been stupid to ruin her chances of resolving this. Now, her opportunity of killing this murdering bastard had failed, she had lost her only chance.

There was no way Morelli would let her out of his sight now. He would kill her and all of the excruciating, horrendous years she'd put up with Anthony; forcing herself to sleep with him and everything else life with him had entailed, had been for nothing.

Now she was truly being held prisoner by the other bastard

she'd dreamt of removing, everything she'd wished for – what had kept her going, was evaporating.

Rage climbed further as the burn of hopelessness threatened to manifest as tears. *Don't you dare cry*, Erin thought.

Morelli could kill her - he could do what he wanted, but she wouldn't give him the satisfaction of seeing her cry. Neither would she allow him to know a thing about what she'd done or what she'd planned to do every single second of her life since he'd robbed and murdered her father.

Fighting the urge to lay her eyes on the list in her bracelet box, Erin bit deeper into her tongue, the taste of blood strangely calming.

This was only the second day in years that she hadn't feasted her eyes on those names on that list.

It wasn't like she didn't know those names. She'd lived with one of them for six years and was now sitting in the same room with the other. Each name was indelibly ingrained into every fibre of her being. Every curl of each letter of those words she could visualise as clearly as if the list was in front of her. But it not being physically here usurped the driving force she'd maintained in order to cross those names off.

Erin's angry eyes remained on Zane, his piercing glare penetrating into her marrow.

She watched as he reached over to the dressing table and scooped up her phone. Unlocking it, he scrolled through the contents.

'Rude of you to ignore the texts you received yesterday,' Zane muttered, his face illuminated by the screen's glow. 'Hmm, they were really important too...'

Bristling, Erin itched to ask who the texts were from, but remained silent. She wouldn't say a damn word to this piece of shit.

'Your life must be so stressful...' Zane's smirk grew. 'It must be difficult worrying about the colour of wedding favours...'

Erin internally grimaced. *The texts were off Jocelyn?* She'd hoped there had been contact from Anthony, but she shouldn't have been so naïve.

Despite her reluctance to move her eyes from Zane, she turned her head to block him witnessing the defeat she felt most keenly.

Zane continued scrolling through the phone, finding a thread of many texts from Anthony Walker.

He scrolled back to the ones from the other day:

7 May 23:30

Where are u?

7 May 23:23

Erin do NOT ignore me

7 May 23:40

If u don't return my messages u will regret it

Frowning, Zane moved to the next text:

7 May 23:58

U think I don't know ur game whore??!?

All of these texts were sent after he'd ridden off with Flame's fiancée. And there were also these two from yesterday morning before Erin made the call.

8 May 6:20

Out all night???? U taking the piss???

8 May 6:28

Fine. You've made your choice. I hvnt time for
pathetic games. U can be replaced

Scrolling back further along the long list of messages, Zane randomly picked a few from several months ago.

3 February 15:22

Important drinks at 8. Look decent if possible! U
know what 2 do to clinch the deal.

10 March 11:12

Call Simon's wife about tonite. Do something useful
for once and make it realistic.

Zane's brow creased. What the fuck was wrong with the bloke? Well, he knew *lots* was wrong with Flame, but this wasn't normal conversation. This was...

His eyes moved back to Erin. There were things going on behind the scenes with Erin Langley. She might be a wild cat and a mercenary bitch who was involved with Flame, but something didn't add up. He couldn't fathom what that was, short of that Flame - or as she knew him, *Anthony*, didn't behave like anyone about to get wed.

Before he could stop himself, the words came out. 'Why do you let him treat you like this?'

Erin's stomach lurched with the unexpected question and willed the dim light of the room not to expose the raw humiliation burning her cheeks.

Why did she allow it? Because it was the only way to achieve what she needed - the point that was now disappearing into the ether. 'Relationships work in different ways.' She shrugged, her eyes defiant. 'What makes you the expert?'

Zane snorted. 'It doesn't take an expert to work out this shit isn't normal.' He watched Erin unsuccessfully stretching her legs to give her muscles relief. 'But then, normal isn't your kind of thing...'

'Anthony won't pander to your pathetic threats,' Erin snapped, desperate to remove herself from scrutiny. 'Talking of which, what are you going to do now?'

'*Anthony*...' Zane sneered. 'Yeah, Anthony...' How he'd enjoy telling this snotty, crazy bitch that her fiancé didn't even

127

resemble who he *really* was. How he would love explaining that Anthony Walker was 'Flame' - the man who had worked for the firm she believed had killed her beloved father.

Correction. She believed *he'd* killed her beloved father - a bit like, thanks to that wanker's fake evidence, so had the court.

Zane ran his finger across his top lip. 'Tell me, what do you get out of your life, short of a comfortable lifestyle and pointless kudos?' He smirked coldly, his eyes intense as he leant closer, forcing Erin to meet his penetrating stare. 'I also notice the look you wear for him and on photographs isn't *you*. Who are you, Erin Langley? Apart from a fake?'

Every single hair on Erin's neck tingled. Her eyes flashed with venom. 'Yeah, that must be it. That's me, you're right, I'm utterly fake!' Zane Morelli would not get the benefit of knowing who she was until the last drops of his cursed blood spilt from his body. *Then* she'd tell him. *Then* he was welcome to know everything. *Then* he'd realise why he'd lost his life.

Folding his arms across his chest and then thinking better of it, Zane placed one hand back on his gun. This woman really was unhinged. Something was fundamentally broken in her beautiful head. But that was her problem, not his. Once he'd achieved what was required, he'd happily give her back. Not that there would be anyone left waiting... 'Being as neither of us are going to get any sleep, you might as well tell me wh...'

The shrill ring of Erin's mobile cut Zane off in his tracks. Hastily scooping it up from the dresser, he stared at the screen:

...Anthony...

Zane's eyes narrowed. 'It's him... Get ready to talk to your boyfriend again, you crazy bitch.'

• • • •

ANTHONY FELT STRANGELY CALM as the call connected. He strained to make out the background noise - anything to give a hint of where the stupid cow was. That's if she was even still breathing. Knowing the way Morelli worked, nothing was certain.

Although he could hear something on the other end of the line, there were no clues as to location or whether it was Morelli who had picked up. Regardless, he got straight to the point.

'I want proof you've got my fiancée. I want to know where she is.' Anthony's skin rippled with deep-seated irritation. Having to do this was unpalatable enough, let alone making this wanker think he'd dance to his tune. But after trying Marco several more times since yesterday, then spending half the night researching whether the firm's headquarters had moved and drawing a blank on any other plausible person to contact, it left this as the only short-term choice.

The only way of getting hold of Marco, if he was still alive, was to travel to London himself.

Not only was that too risky at the moment, but he didn't have time. People would ask questions if he wasn't at the networking event at the Copthorne tonight. Even more questions would be forthcoming if Erin didn't accompany him. Under normal circumstances the less time he spent with her, the better, but her ability to do what he couldn't overrode personal taste.

Erin had to be back here tonight.

No ifs, no buts.

The twitching in Anthony's hands began in earnest. Counting in increments of three wouldn't suffice in this instance. 'Morelli! Answer the damn question,' he screeched. 'Where is she?'

'She's here... With me...'

A sharp pain shot through Anthony's front teeth as he clenched his jaw. 'Like I said, I want proof.'

'I'm surprised you're up this early,' the voice chuckled, making Anthony's teeth grind harder at the veiled sarcasm.

'Proof, Morelli. Then you'll get your money.' Anthony's nails dug into the skin of his palms. That was what Zane Morelli wanted, wasn't it? *Money*. That was what any of them were interested in. Money was the only thing *everyone* was interested in.

Next, Anthony tried silently counting in nines. Nines, he reserved for emergencies. That or half-numbers. 'I need her back tonight.'

'Need or want?'

Anthony found it difficult to hold his phone as his hands jerked around out of control. 'Send me proof and you'll have your money. That's all there is to say.'

The throaty chuckle from the other end of the line only made his hands twitch and jerk harder. This fucker was laughing at him? If he thought it would piss the man off, he'd let him know the truth. But he wouldn't. Not yet. 'Erin's phone - the phone you're speaking on, is very expensive and it has a camera.'

Anthony preferred to pretend this was a normal conversation and that this man wasn't ballsing up his entire business reputation and social standing. If he didn't get the stupid bitch back, it would look to all and sundry like she'd left him. He would not have that. It was embarrassing. 'Use the phone's camera to take a photograph of her and text it to me. Once I've got that, I'll sort the money for you and then I'll get back in touch.'

Anthony buttoned the call before he lost sight of his aim. The squeaking in his head was loud and his concentration was fading.

He examined his hands, checking each fingernail was the correct length and contained no particles of dirt.

Now he would wait to see if Morelli delivered.

He wouldn't part with a single penny until he was certain his reputation and ability to grow his business would continue unharmed. And to do that, he had to make sure *she* was still intact and usable for that very purpose.

SEVENTEEN

HOPING IT DIDN'T DAMPEN the material, Marco doused himself with Lynx deodorant, giving his shirt and trousers, especially the crotch area, a good spray.

Jesus wept, why the bloody hell had Grimes shown up here at this time in the morning?

Marco ran his fingers through his unbrushed hair, glad he'd asked Bill to come over early. If his right-hand man wasn't here, he wouldn't have got the heads up about the visitors and have been dropped right in it.

He glanced at the digital clock inlaid within the bathroom tiles. Okay, so it was almost midday, but still, this was his personal space - not business premises. How he wished he hadn't given Grimes this address. But being as he was marrying the man's daughter, it might have looked odd if he hadn't...

Sliding her arms around Marco's waist, the brunette eyed herself in the huge bathroom mirror. 'Do you have to rush off?'

Pulling out of the woman's arms, Marco swung around and slammed her against the tiled wall. 'What the fuck are you doing?' he hissed, smoothing the creases in his shirt. 'I told you something's come up and to stay where you were.'

Dragging the woman out of the en-suite bathroom, Marco

slung her on the unmade bed. 'Don't move until I come back. Don't even breathe! Make one sound and I'll cut the tongue clean out of your fucking head. Do you understand?'

Seeing the now terrified woman nodding, Marco snatched his suit jacket off the occasional chair at the foot of the bed and shrugged it on. Darting out of the bedroom and along the long landing, he made his way down the stairs of the split-level apartment.

Christ, if he'd known Trevor Grimes was paying an impromptu visit, there was no way he'd have brought that chick from his latest film back last night. If Grimes got wind that he wasn't waiting patiently for the hand of his daughter, then the whole thing would be called off. And that would be a disaster, both for his firm and for his cock.

Plastering on a confident smile, Marco strode into the open-plan living area, his hand outstretched. 'Trevor! Great to see you! What brings you here unannou...'

Stopping dead, he stared at the woman sitting beside her father. 'Lisa! How lovely to see you.'

Signalling to Bill to make himself scarce with a jerk of his head, Marco moved towards his perfect idea of a female lounging seductively in the leather armchair.

There weren't many, if *any* people in this world who rendered Marco Morelli into a nervous, jittery teenager, but Lisa Tequila did. Or rather, Hazel Grimes, if her real name came into it. But to him, she would always be *Lisa*. And Lisa turned him into a gibbering wreck.

He moved towards her, refraining from pulling his already swelling cock from his trousers and running his hand down it to satiate the overbearing arousal. Clasping one of Lisa's hands, he leant in and kissed her on the cheek, wondering how he was acting so well-behaved around this stunning specimen of womankind, when all he wanted to do – all he'd *dreamt* of doing for so long, was to ram himself between her peachy buttocks and slam into her for hours.

Even that wouldn't be enough and the image of that playing

in his head as his lips brushed her velvet cheek, did nothing to quell his desire.

'Marco,' Hazel Grimes drawled uninterestedly, making sure her cheek was turned as far away as possible from his lips. Shaking her long-taloned fingers from his grip, she looked at him disparagingly. 'My name is "Hazel". I expect you to call me by my real name, unless you are specifically referring to my films. And, I have to ask, do you *always* wear such overpowering scent?'

Marco laughed loudly, hoping it would hide his utter panic, along with the unfamiliar sense of not knowing what to do with himself around this woman. 'Erm okay, Hazel, erm yeah, I was having a bit of a lie-in and wasn't expecting to s...'

Seeing the suspicion on his visitors' faces, he rolled his eyes theatrically. 'I had a late night. Last minute edits on the latest film. Knowing the industry so well yourself, I'm sure you appreciate it's important to get things right.'

He'd ignore the second question. Being as he hadn't had chance to take a shower, the overpowering scent was to hopefully mask the whiff of sex from the sweaty night spent with the brunette. *The brunette that was still here... In his bed...*

Marco's eyes darted to Trevor Grimes and sweat prickled along the back of his neck. *Had they guessed there was another bird here?*

'I hope you're not intending having lots of late nights once you're married to *me*.' Hazel arched one manicured-to-the-point-of-death eyebrow.

'Not unless you're the reason!' *God, he sounded like a prick.* Furthermore, Lisa/Hazel or whatever she wanted to be referred to, spoke to him like dirt. She even *looked* at him with contempt.

Anyone else he'd kill for that, but her... She inspired awe - his very own, real-life beautiful film star... His soon to be wife...

Aware he was behaving like a gawping lunatic was not enough to stop Marco from feasting his eyes over his dream woman. With her thick glossy blonde hair, perfect complexion, long lashes which framed her eyes and a mouth that would make members of 'Impotence R Us' hard, she was stellar.

Probably everything about this woman was fake, but that wasn't the point.

He watched her dainty hands twirl a curl of platinum around a long-nailed finger before letting the hair fall tantalisingly down over the cleavage of her enhanced chest.

God, she was hot.

Marco self-consciously adjusted his jacket to hide the tenting of his trousers.

'Thought we'd drop in to follow up from our conversation yesterday. Have you an update?' Trevor Grimes' voice collided with Marco's train of thought. The only good thing it achieved was deflating his embarrassing arousal.

Shit, yes – That Conversation. 'Erm, well both I and some of my men are at present getting cast-iron confirmation to prove that what I said yesterday is correct.' Marco smiled. 'I'll soon put your mind at rest that my brother will not be released within any acceptable length of time to make our alliance invalid. As far as my standing in this firm is concerned, it's exactly as I've already specified.'

His chest puffed out with self-prowess. 'I am and will remain the sole controller of this firm, as well as Luna Motion Films, so my offer to you and your daughter is one hundred per cent valid.'

Hazel stared coldly. 'I won't enter into a marriage with anyone other than the owner of this firm. Should it prove otherwise, I will not hesitate from pulling out of the deal. I expect to get what I've been assured of, otherwise nothing will happen.'

Marco smiled tightly, a twinge of irritation colouring his obsession. No one questioned his judgement. *Ever.*

But Lisa's intoxicating allure allowed him to override this oversight just this once.

Once they were wed, Lisa Tequila would be the one acting with reverence to *him*. He would make her more famous than ever and she knew it. However, he wouldn't rock the boat by reminding her or her father of that at the moment.

With this treasure as the star, nothing would stand in the way of putting Luna Motion Films at the top of its game. Equally, nothing would remove the gratifying thought of having the same woman he'd watched on screen for many a pleasant hour from being in his bed.

And if that over-priced brief did as good a job as before and delivered what he'd faithfully promised by later today, then everything was just as it should be.

Marco looked between Trevor Grimes and Lisa. She would always be Lisa to him, but if she wanted him to use her real name in private, then he'd somehow have to retrain himself.

His smile was wide, even though he had one ear open for any noise alerting his esteemed guests that he hadn't been on his own in the bedroom.

He was quietly confident that despite his initial misgivings over the stupid rumours doing the rounds and the aggro that silly bitch on the balcony could have dropped on him, had he not been so clever, life was heading in the direction he'd specced out perfectly.

· · · ·

ZANE HAPHAZARDLY PRESSED buttons on Erin's phone, his annoyance growing. How was he supposed to know how a camera on a phone worked?

Rather than waiting all morning - the sole aim of letting Flame stew before sending the 'proof' he so desired, perhaps he should have used the time working out how to use this bloody thing. Before last week, he'd barely even *seen* a mobile and certainly not one with a camera as part of it.

He had no idea that sort of thing existed, which showed just how much life had moved on whilst he had been absent.

The tendons in his neck pulled taut, refusing to admit defeat.

Erin stared at Zane, swallowing the temptation to make a

sarcastic comment. She had more than his lack of technical ability to worry about because Morelli was complying with Anthony's wish of supplying proof that he had her within his clutches, alive and unharmed.

Not that Anthony had asked whether she was unharmed... And she didn't need that rubbed in her face any more than he already had.

The only reason Anthony had called was to keep up the meticulous appearance they had created as a couple. He must have tried other avenues first, otherwise he'd have called back last night as instructed.

But what were those avenues? The one thing he *hadn't* done was involve the police. Erin was glad about that because it would delay everything, but the question was, why hadn't he called them? As far as she was aware, supplying evidence to a court of law was not a crime, so why would he not involve the police?

To her annoyance, her skin became slick with perspiration. She didn't want Morelli reaching the conclusion she was scared of him.

Because the truth was, she wasn't.

She frowned. If she possessed one sane strand inside her, she *would* be scared, but all semblance of normality had deserted her a long time ago. Where her body and soul were concerned, there wasn't much left to lose. But there was *plenty* to lose from what was left of her life.

If Morelli sent Anthony a photograph and then went to meet him, Anthony would die. Which in turn, meant her plans were trashed.

Unless she'd been right all along and all Morelli wanted *was* money? It was feasible he no longer had access to his firm's ill-gotten riches. During his incarceration, her father's stolen money could have been used up. Maybe there was none left?

After all, it wasn't like he'd rushed back to London to pick up where he'd left off, was it?

Erin eyed Zane's rigid posture as he concentrated on the

phone in his hand, like a tiger waiting for unsuspecting prey. A glimmer of hope surfaced. If all he cared about was money, like it now seemed was the case, there was a chance she could still see through her plan.

Her brow creased. But after her attempt on him last night, her chances of her walking away from this once he'd got his payout, was minimal. However, she wouldn't dwell on that.

It wasn't over yet.

Erin's mind waded through a complex web of scenarios that might unfold but were impossible to pinpoint. Everything was speculation. And that was half the problem.

She frowned. Her head felt like imploding as the truth suddenly crashed over her.

That was it! Anthony must have called the police. That's why it had taken so long for him to phone back. A sting must have been arranged to intercept Morelli when he arrived and fine-tuned to make sure she escaped unscathed.

No, no, no! Police involvement or Anthony's death before she was ready could not happen!

Things were now even worse. She had to make an attempt on Morelli's life again before he got to Anthony or before the police swooped.

But how?

Christ, she needed air. She couldn't breathe. There were no answers. None at all. How would she sort this?

She rolled her neck to ease the stiffness, barely able to feel her arms or the bottom of her legs any longer. She had to get him to untie her. 'I need to use the toilet,' she muttered, not holding much hope that her request would be granted, but she had to try something.

'You'll have to wait,' Zane hissed, his back still turned.

'Are you taking this picture then or what?' Erin immediately wished she'd remained silent when Zane swung around, his eyes radiating darkness.

'That's happening now,' he snarled, propping the phone on the dressing table.

He craned his neck to check what the phone camera could see. 'I'll use the timer function,' he said, his eyes glinting, satisfied he now understood how the poxy thing worked. 'We'll pretend we're on a picnic! Won't that be nice…?'

Zane walked around the bed. 'Let's make this look the part.'

Erin yelped as Zane knelt on the bed and promptly tore open her top, buttons pinging around the room.

Her first reaction was to cover herself, but her tethered hands failed to comply. Her second reaction was anger when Zane's fingers hooked into her bra, pulling the cups down to spill her breasts out for all to see.

Fear and loathing surged as the underwiring dug painfully into her flesh. Would Morelli do what he'd threatened? Would he force himself on her?

Coming to the abrupt decision that she wouldn't give herself up to this beast without one hell of a fight, Erin tilted her face up in defiance. To her surprise, she found Zane Morelli looking into her eyes, rather than her exposed chest. His gaze then moved to her mouth and her breath hitched.

'I apologise for doing this,' Zane muttered. 'I'm afraid that authenticity dictates that needs must.'

He jumped from the bed, leaving Erin flummoxed with his behaviour, as well as confusion over her own reaction. *She'd wondered for a split second if he might kiss her…*

She tugged harder against the restraints in a further fruitless attempt to free herself. 'You can't do this,' she hissed.

'It won't take long. Now play the fucking part.' Zane moved towards the mobile on the dresser and pressed the timer button before hurrying back towards her. 'Ten seconds.'

Jumping back on the bed, he pulled Erin forward. Sliding in behind her, he yanked her against him and clamped his hand over her mouth. His other hand pushed between her splayed legs to grab the inside of her thigh. But it did not stray higher. 'By the way, it's good that your nipples are hard, but try not to look like you're enjoying it too much…'

The extent of her vulnerability finally hit Erin. Zane Morelli could do anything he wanted and she could do nothing at all to stop him.

How she resented this man. How she hated him at a level previously unattained.

Or was it that she hated herself more?

She squeezed her eyes shut with utter mortification and fought for air through the constraints of his hand. Aware of the hard masculine body pressed against her back, all she could smell was a mixture of tobacco, body wash and *man* on the hand over her mouth and nose. A heady combination.

Power…

As the camera shutter clicked, Erin cursed her treacherous body for reacting in ways she could not control, as well as the thoughts taking her somewhere she wholeheartedly did not wish to go.

Eighteen

WHEN HIS PHONE BLEEPED, alerting him to the arrival of a text message, Anthony spent several minutes continuing to consider the business proposal he'd been working on for a client he was eager to get on board. The association would prove vastly profitable, but he could stare at the proposal all he wanted - a bit like he'd been doing the entire morning. It wasn't like he'd taken any of it in.

Despite his usual ability to switch off from distractions, the knowledge that every second which ticked past as the morning wore on was Zane Morelli's way of making him sweat, drove him crazy.

As much as he resented admitting it, having always possessed the ability to keep an aloof persona and stable countenance on all matters - important or otherwise, on this instance, he'd failed.

Ever since ending the call to that nutter first thing, he'd been waiting, yet the *whole* morning had elapsed with no word. He'd even degenerated to standing in various areas of the house clutching his phone in case the normally consistent mobile signal had inexplicably dropped.

Which, of course, it hadn't.

Neither had the calls stopped coming through from his stupid, brainless receptionist to rearrange his appointments for today. Another thing Morelli had screwed up.

Anthony looked down at his pristine suit - the trousers freshly pressed, as always. Even when at home he would not be without his suit. It reasserted the professional he was.

His face screwed into a scowl. He despised working from home, but what else was he supposed to do? He'd been forced to cry off from going into the office today. It was the only viable option since cancelling his attendance at that important networking event at the Copthorne last night, thanks to Erin. Explaining both of their absences on falling prey to a stomach bug was one thing, but there was only so long he could pass off his and that bitch's lack of presence as illness.

He glared at his paperwork. He'd probably lost this client now too...

There was another networking event at the end of the week and also golf to deal with. Further questions would be asked if there were more no-shows.

He'd already had that ugly bitch, Jocelyn, calling up asking for Erin and waffling on about some bullshit about the wedding. Apparently, Erin hadn't answered any of her texts.

Well, it was unlikely she would be able to answer texts, being as she was being held by Zane bloody Morelli.

Anthony stared back at his mobile, knowing he'd have to read the new message. If it hadn't come from Erin's phone, like the last eight texts hadn't, he was at risk of smashing the damn thing to smithereens.

Anthony knew Morelli had Erin, but he needed proof she lived. There was no point shelling out money if she was dead.

Dead was no use.

Refusing to allow further distractions, Anthony snatched up his mobile. Taking a deep breath, he opened the text:

MMS message received

Erin

141

He stared at the unopened message. If it was a picture of Erin's corpse, then he was fucked.

Pressing the button, his hands shook, waiting as the image downloaded.

As the photograph filled the screen, Anthony heard the squealing ramp up in his ears and as the image seared into his vision, his nausea grew stronger.

Erin was tethered to the bed with Morelli behind her. He still looked the same as always - dark eyed and psychotic.

The phone jerked in Anthony's twitching hands at the sight of Erin lying like a whore between Morelli's legs, her breasts exposed and her splayed open thighs revealing pink lacy knickers. They weren't anything *he'd* allow her to own. Wearing them for *him*, was she?

Although her arms and legs were tethered, there was no ignoring Morelli's hand had been in those knickers. No doubt, his dick too because he could hang his jacket on Erin's hard, puckered nipples, the wanton slut.

The shaking spread up Anthony's arms, consuming him as he rapidly realised he'd been wrong in his initial assumption.

Morelli *had* fucked her, just like he'd threatened to.

Erin might look wide-eyed and angry, but her body had responded to that psycho's touch - just *look* at it. There was no denying that she'd *wanted* it.

Slamming the phone face down on his desk, Anthony seethed. If Morelli had left a permanent reminder of being inside his property, then he'd kick it the fuck out himself.

Snatching the phone back up, he tapped out a response and pressed send.

Morelli could have his pay off and give back the goods. And this was where he would arrange for the money and the whore to be dropped off.

Within a couple of moments, the sudden shrill ring of his phone jarred in his head.

...Erin...

Answering, Anthony listened and quickly decided his plan of action. 'This is the way it has to be, Morelli.' *There was no way he would do the exchange in person. He wasn't stupid.*

'Drop Erin where I've said and the minute I'm told she's there... No... No... the money will have already been deposited, but once I receive word she's there, you'll be texted the location of the cash. And, Morelli, that will be it. I've paid my dues.'

Anthony ended the call, his heart thumping. Morelli would be there. The man wasn't stupid either. He knew the money would be where it was promised. Morelli knew where he worked and probably even where he lived, so the cash would *have* to be there.

But if Anthony knew Zane Morelli even to the basic degree – which he *did*, the man wouldn't just accept that the money alone, although substantial, would suffice for the years he'd been banged up.

No, he'd be back for more. Or to kill him. Most likely the latter. This had to be rectified.

He smiled. But doing this today would give him time to get in contact with those who *would* sort this out. And that was worth the money he was about to shell out.

• • • •

SEEING LISA TEQUILA THIS MORNING, coupled with a few nicely loaded lines of cocaine, had placed Marco into a frame of mind where he could conquer the world.

He wasn't just imagining it. No, certainly not. He was Marco Morelli. *Anything* was possible and he was the very real, living embodiment of that.

Things kept getting better and better. Small hiccups presenting themselves every so often could scratch the surface of his good fortune. He was The King - the king of his life, his staff, his firm, Luna Motion Films and, well, *everything*.

Soon he would be Lisa Tequila's king and she would be his

queen.

And he couldn't wait.

Just the mere thought of that woman and everything about her triggered the familiar throbbing in his groin. Luckily, he'd scratched that all-encompassing itch shortly after Lisa and her father had left this morning by utilising the brunette he'd left stashed in the bedroom.

And utilise her, he had. It had relieved that particular itch for sure, but now it was back.

His current view wasn't helping the situation...

From his special initialled directors' chair, Marco ran his eyes over the scene in front of him - a pseudo-office set where a buxom redhead was being taken from behind by a man dressed in a corporate suit.

He wouldn't bother doing this particular bird tonight being as she'd so recently been in use. It never paid to be sloppy.

Marco then caught the brunette from earlier staring at him. The minute his eyes met hers, she looked away. Ignoring the wariness and fear behind her lashes, he told himself she was hoping for a repeat performance.

He thought not. Another thing that didn't pay well - making these women think they could be anything more than a passing fancy.

No way. The thought of having a session with the same woman more than once in any given fortnight bored him shitless.

Besides, it wasn't like he'd run out of choices. These bitches fell over themselves queuing up for a piece.

Marco frowned, unsure how he'd play this once he was wed, but his intentions were that nothing should change. Lisa would soon learn to realise that what he said, stood.

Marco Morelli – The King of the World.

Leisurely lighting up a cigarette, Marco leant back in his chair and exhaled a long curl of smoke, pausing to send two perfectly formed smoke rings drifting up to the high ceiling.

See - even his smoke rings were spot on.

He then frowned as the mobile in his jacket pocket started to buzz. He glanced up as a second man moved into frame to take his turn with the redhead and resented the interruption, just as the action was cranking up a notch.

Marco winced as the phone continued to buzz. He could ignore it? But then, it might be the brief calling with an update...

Rising from the chair, he pulled his mobile from his pocket and glanced at the screen:

...Private number...

It must be the brief. *About time!*

Taking a final glance at the action, Marco slipped from the studio into the plushly-carpeted corridor, then ducked into a small side office he knew to be empty. He didn't want anyone overhearing his business - especially on *this* subject.

Answering the call, he got straight to the point. 'How did you get on with th...'

He paused. *This wasn't the brief...*

Listening to the voice on the other end of the line, his eyes narrowed. 'Oh, it's you! Finally returning my man's calls, are you?' *How many times had Bill left messages for this waste of space screw now? How many days had those messages been ignored?* 'Right? So why the fuck are you ringing me, rather than him? I'm busy!'

As the prison officer on the other end continued talking, Marco rolled his eyes. If this joker thought he'd continue getting paid to keep his ear to the ground when th... '*What?*' he roared, his hand clenching the phone a little too tightly. 'Dead...? When?' His mouth twisted into a snarl. 'Who the fuck did it...? Find out! That's what I pay you for, is it not?'

Marco paced around the small confines of someone he couldn't remember the name of's office, his shoe knocking a box balanced on several others, spilling several tapes to the floor.

'No, I mean it... Find out wh... *What?* What did you say?'

Marco's face turned a funny shade of white as what he was sure he must have misheard was repeated. 'When...? Right... Update me as soon as. No fucking excuses!'

Ending the call, he remained shell-shocked for a good thirty seconds.

Marco dragged his fingers through his thick black hair. This couldn't have happened. Fennell had been murdered and the useless bastard screw didn't even know who had killed the man? He didn't give a fuck if the screw had been on off-site training for the past few days. He'd give him training, alright - in front of the fucking express, the pointless cunt.

But that wasn't the worst thing...

Zane was out? *Released?*

His brother had been out of prison for *four* days and he'd only just been made aware?

Marco scrambled from the room in search of Bill, dialling the brief's number as he went.

If Zane had *really* been released, then why the fuck hadn't that bastard brief told him? The appeal had been *months* away, so what had changed?

Furthermore, if Zane *was* out and wasn't back in London, then where the fuck was he?

• • • •

THE HEDGES WHIZZED past worryingly close to both Erin and the bike as Zane took the country roads with wild abandon. She knew where he was heading because she knew this area all too well.

And this route thwarted her plan of finding a suitable opportunity to throw herself from the pillion seat and make a run for it.

This hadn't been an option beforehand, as when leaving Ladywood, it was only a short distance before they'd joined the motorway. Doing it there would have guaranteed suicide.

Opening the throttle, Zane had swung out into the fast lane, overtaking trains of thundering lorries. With her hair whipping through her open visor, all Erin could do was close her eyes and concentrate on her whitening knuckles clinging to the metal bar behind the pillion seat.

A small part of her wished she'd clung to Zane, rather than the metal, but the thought of touching him and being closer than she already was, overtook the terror of being on the back of this death trap.

Now, on these country roads, even if she jumped without sustaining catastrophic injuries, there was nowhere to run. Not out here.

She blinked her watering eyes to clear her vision. She longed to pull her visor down but couldn't bring herself to release one finger of her vice-like grip behind, let alone a whole hand.

Her heart thundered as they sped past the turning for a road leading to another, which led onto the very road she lived.

Her home - or rather, *Anthony's*.

She had no idea how Zane would play this. He'd refused to give her any inkling about what would happen.

Surprisingly, her hands weren't tied this time, but the prospect of being returned to Anthony was as horrific as remaining with her father's murderer.

Humiliation stung. It didn't help that she didn't know where Zane had arranged to do the swap over - where she would be passed on for a chunk of money.

This wasn't much different to before, except *that* time she'd made the decision herself, so if there was one opening - *anything* enabling her to make a run for it, then she'd take it.

But there had been nothing. Not one chance. Neither had there been another chance to kill Zane Morelli. Instead, she was en route to witness Anthony die and her dreams go down the pan when Morelli was arrested and sent back to jail, further stripping her of hope.

Her brain burnt with fast escalating panic.

Shunting forward into Zane's back, Erin realised they'd come to a halt. She glanced around. They were in Knowle?

Anthony's office was only around the corner. Morelli would never get away with this!

Zane heaved the bike onto its centre stand and cocked his leg over the bike, leaving Erin staring through her visor incredulously. 'What are you doing? Can't you see he's setting you up?' she hissed. 'The police will be somewhere here waiting for you.'

She watched Zane laugh, his teeth bright in the sunlight. 'Do you want to go back to prison? Is that it?' *This wasn't funny.*

Zane's smile dissolved as he pulled Erin from the bike. 'Neither of those things will happen, trust me.'

As if she'd trust him... Erin tried to snatch her arm out of Zane's grip, but his hold was too tight.

'Don't make a scene,' he spat. 'We don't want to draw attention.' He pulled his crash helmet off and took a pair of aviator shades from his inside pocket. 'Remove your helmet and walk with me.'

Erin wanted to refuse, but Zane placed his arm around her shoulders and pulled her against him. She had no choice but to walk alongside him, knowing that to passers-by, they looked like a couple.

She fought against screaming to anyone who would listen that this man had kept her prisoner; humiliated her; would most probably rape her.

If she did that, she'd thwart her chance of vengeance. For now, at least, she had to go along with his plans. There was still a chance none of this would materialise, so she couldn't afford to stop now. Not whilst there was a sliver of hope.

Her brain ticked over feverishly. Surely he wouldn't hand her over in public? If they were heading somewhere secluded, there may be a chance to get them both. Using what, she didn't know, but the chance might be there all the same. 'You have to at least tell me what you're planning.'

'I don't have to tell you anything, short of to follow my instructions,' Zane smirked.

'What makes you so sure this isn't a set up?' she asked, smiling at a woman heading towards them on the pavement. 'Has it not crossed your mind that someone might recognise me? I do live around here, you know?'

Zane laughed once again. 'You've clearly forgotten you look different since that shit is out of your hair and off your face.'

Erin paled. She'd forgotten about that.

'The police *won't* be here to save you either. I know that much.' Stopping suddenly, Zane looked down at Erin. 'You really don't get it, do you? You haven't worked it out?'

'Worked it out?' Erin spat. 'What's there to work out, apart from that you're blackmailing Anthony and...'

'I don't want his money,' Zane whispered, his breath hot against Erin's ear.

Erin's throat constricted with the feel of Zane's lips against her ear lobe, hating herself even more. 'I don't believe you,' she countered. 'You're full of shit, Morelli. Like I said, you just want money. You lot are all the same.'

Zane knew his eyes betrayed his fury over Erin's words when she immediately silenced. How he'd love to slap the taste out of her spoilt mouth. He didn't know how, but she knew *something* about this. How did she know he'd been in nick and what did she mean by, 'you lot are all the same'?

Was this bitch part of the original set up? Had she known it was happening? Had she helped Flame or had he filled her in at a later date with what he'd achieved?

He studied Erin's face carefully. It triggered a memory, but he couldn't place what or where from. For now though, Erin Langley, what she knew and what she was, would have to wait. 'I'll let him know you're in place.'

'What?' Erin cried as Zane walked her up the road. 'Where am I going now?'

Zane shrugged. If this stupid cow was part of more than what he'd originally believed, or refused to see the wood for the trees, then he wouldn't waste his breath explaining a thing.

'Nowhere. You're going nowhere…'

NINETEEN

SITTING IN HIS MERCEDES, Anthony stared at his watch. *Still no word.*

He eyed the bag on his passenger seat. That wouldn't go anywhere until he'd received word Erin was exactly where he'd instructed her to be.

His mouth cracked into a sneer. Even Morelli wouldn't be stupid enough to take him out in full view of his business premises. Yes, it was awkward being back over this way, considering he was supposed to have the trots, but he'd passed it off as one of those twenty-four-hour bug things.

Besides, no one would dare question him.

But Erin couldn't go inside his office. She must stand in full view *outside*. He'd made that clear. Nothing could happen to her in broad daylight and she'd be fine waiting there until he'd placed the money. It was only a couple of minutes away.

As his mobile beeped with a text, Anthony snatched it from the passenger seat:

```
In general location
```

Anthony grinned. If Erin got a move on, they might even

make drinks with Simon and his wife later. It would help make up for last night's absence. Only after he'd rectified the mess with his clients, would he deal with Erin and what she'd allowed Morelli to do.

But first things first...

He tapped in his reply:

```
    Erin to wait opposite my office. Outside Delish
                          Deli.
      Once I have word of her arrival I'll text the
                  location of the money.
```

Anthony chewed his lip as he waited for confirmation. He didn't have to wait long:

```
                      2 minutes
```

He dialled his office switchboard. 'Maisie? It's Anthony. Yeah, I'm feeling a lot better now. Yes... Look, could you do me a favour? Can you look out of the window and see if Erin's waiting opposite? She insisted on getting some fresh air, but I don't want her walking home the way she's feeling, so I'm coming to pick her up. Yes, okay... thanks.'

Hearing the phone being laid on the desk and a shuffling sound as Maisie moved to the window, he waited. Setting his phone to loudspeaker, he keyed in a text ready.

He heard Maisie pick back up the phone. 'Hello? She's not? Okay, well I'll stay on the line until she's there. It saves parking up or ringing again. She's making her way there now.'

She'd better be, anyway.

'What? She's just turned up? Okay, I'm literally a couple of minutes away. Oh, and Maisie, don't invite her into the office just in case she's infectious.' *And now she'd been with Morelli, he suspected she'd have a plenitude of diseases.*

Sending the pre-written text, Anthony ended the call, not wanting to answer any more of Maisie's stupid questions.

Getting out of the Mercedes, he glanced over his shoulder and moved to the chosen area. Quickly depositing the bag, he dashed back to his car and started the engine.

Screw you, Morelli. Just take the money and give me time to contact the people who will stop you.

He screeched off down the road. Now all he had to do was get Erin back to the house and make it clear she had a shed load of making up to do in order to put right the clients she'd probably already lost him.

Anthony turned the corner of the road, his eyes searching the street. He'd said outside the Delish Deli, hadn't he? Maisie said Erin was there, but where?

Jesus!

Anthony squinted through the bright sunlight at the dishevelled woman outside the delicatessen. What had Erin done to her hair and face? And those clothes! Was she trying to embarrass him?

That Maisie should actually recognise Erin looking like *this* showed she needed to put in a lot more effort, even on a standard day.

Gritting his teeth, Anthony scoured the road for somewhere to park - the only available space on the road in front of his office.

Furious, he pressed the handbrake button and went to scramble out of the car when the door was kicked shut in a blur of black.

Momentarily disorientated, he grappled for the door handle, his eyes searching for the culprit. *If his car was dented...*

And then he saw it.

Morelli on that fucking motorbike. And…

Shit no!

Lurching from the Mercedes, Anthony stumbled across the road as Erin clambered on the back of Morelli's bike. Within seconds the motorbike disappeared amidst a screech of tyres.

Had Anthony immediately got back into his car and given chase, there was a slight chance he could have caught up with them, or at the very least, clocked the reg plate. But the ten seconds wasted rendered frozen in his tracks put paid to that.

He glanced around and to his horror, saw Maisie watching from the window. He swallowed down his exploding rage of being turned over and instead thought of an excuse to explain why his fiancée had disappeared with a leather-jacketed lunatic on a motorbike.

Now he was back to square one.

Fuck.

. . . .

UNABLE TO HELP IT, Erin was laughing so hard she struggled to keep grip of the metal bar.

As dire as this situation was, Anthony's expression had been pure quality. Him darting across the road towards her, narrowly missing an old dear trundling along in a green Vauxhall and then the slow-motion mixture of horror sliding across his face as she'd clambered onto the bike... He'd been unable to do one single thing about it. *Priceless.*

So, Zane was correct. There were no police. If they *had* been there ready to swoop, they'd been far too slow.

Reality inched back into Erin's mind and her laughter fell away. Enjoyable that may have been, but it didn't change the outcome. She was still trapped with Zane Morelli and no further towards her goal.

She suddenly realised the bike was pulling over. Her eyes darted around. *Why had Zane stopped?*

Of course, he'd come to pick up the money.

Shit. The police could be waiting here instead. She'd been naïve to think otherwise.

As Zane clambered off the bike, Erin grabbed his arm and shouted through the visor in the hope of making herself heard. 'Forget the bloody money! We need to get out of here!'

Shaking Erin's grip away, Zane held a finger up, nodding for her to stay put and walked towards a bench.

Erin floundered, her eyes darting from right to left. Zane's back was turned. She could make a run for it. But where would she go? Back to Anthony and miss her chance to finish this?

No.

She watched Zane speaking to two people sitting on a bench. Were they part of this as well? Other members of his firm summoned from London?

Perhaps the plan was to take her there next? How could she do anything if that happened? But those people on the bench looked like tramps... They couldn't be part of his firm, surely?

As Zane walked back towards her, she squinted through the bright sun, her frown deepening. 'What's going o...'

Her question was drowned out as Zane started the bike and they roared off up the road.

Erin's pulse thumped in her ears, the noise overtaking even that of the bike's large engine. Her heart thundered. She had no idea what Zane had said to those people, but she had a horrible feeling about it. Now they were heading out of Knowle, but not to the motorway or the A45. They were on another country lane.

Fuck. Where they'd stopped before hadn't been for the money. They were heading there now. Anthony would have had time to get there too. There was no way that son of a bitch would allow his money to be collected without exchange of the goods. *Her.*

The police would be there too.

Fuck, fuck, fuck.

Erin's head felt like it would explode within her helmet. Her temples throbbed, her mouth dry. She had to stop this. *Had* to.

Braving taking one hand off the metal bar, she pounded on Zane's leather-jacketed back. 'Stop!' she screamed. 'You've got to stop!'

Her thumping and vocal protest went unheeded. Zane's only response was to flick the bike just enough to make Erin feel like she would fall off. In panic, she clung to his back, both hands now off the metal bar.

The hedges whipped by dangerously close to her face as Zane lent the bike to take the bends at top speed. Her fingers clutched onto his jacket, her palms slick against the leather.

He'd kill them both.

Jaw clenched, too paralysed with fear to even swallow, Erin forced her eyes open. *I have to stop this. Have to stop this...*

Throwing caution to the wind and without stopping to consider the implications of what she was doing, Erin pushed forward, her hand reaching for Zane's right forearm. Grabbing on, she pulled his arm sharply back towards her.

It all happened very quickly after that. The bike flicked: the front wheel shot to one side, the back end of the machine jerked.

Tarmac rushed closer and the grind of metal was the last thing Erin heard as the bike went one way and she went the other.

TWENTY

MARCO TURNED up yet another corridor, kicking open each door he passed. None of the rooms contained Bill. It felt like *hours* he'd been looking and the bloke had vanished into thin fucking air?

It wasn't good enough.

Continuing, he glared at a young man heading his way with a sheaf of paper in his hand.

'Mr Morelli? Could I ask y...'

The crack as Marco delivered a headbutt ricocheted along the shiny walls. A low growl rumbled from the back of his throat as he glared at the staff member on his knees, both hands over his nose to stop blood from splattering the paperwork waiting for signature.

Marco purposefully placed his foot on a sheet of the paperwork now scattered over the floor. 'Pick this shit up,' he muttered, before continuing on his way. That would give whoever that dickhead was something to do, other than speak to him. He didn't have time for *anything*, short of finding Bill Wainwright.

Turning the corner into the next corridor, Marco's stress levels ramped up to level six. *Still no sign of anyone.*

He needed another line and he needed it now. *Where the fuck was everybody?*

Raising his right leg, Marco slammed his foot against the door of the next room. No door was ever locked to him, but it was easier than unclenching his fists to turn the handle.

Fully expecting the room to be empty like the others, Marco did a double take as he walked past the doorway. With a grimace, he stormed into the room and yanked a woman, naked from the waist down, across the room by her hair.

Along with the woman's shrieks of pain and panic at this unexpected interruption, he kicked her discarded clothes across the floor towards the door. 'Think you can waste work time? You can't! You're fired!'

Slamming the door in the face of the now sobbing woman, Marco turned to glare at Bill.

Bill scrambled to pull his trousers up from around his ankles. 'Come on, that's a bit harsh, isn't it? It wasn't her fau...'

'Fennel's been killed. Someone got to him in the sick bay...'

'*Killed?*' Bill's mouth dropped open, his hope of getting Marco to reverse his hasty decision on firing that bird falling to the wayside. 'Fennel's dead? Shit! Do you kn...'

'It's worse than that... Zane is out...'

Bill froze, his brain barely ticking over at this information. 'He's been released? But... but how? When? How will we arr...'

'He got out four fucking days ago.' Marco's eyes narrowed. 'That screw that you left messages for finally returned the call. I want to know why we, or more importantly, *I*, wasn't informed by that bastard brief either. Furthermore, being as Zane hasn't shown up here, I want to know where the fuck he is. And lastly, I need your opinion on what the hell to do about this. What we planned, if his release was on the cards, has now gone to shit.'

Bill remained poised like a cardboard cut-out, rendered speechless. He had no idea what to say. What even *could* he say? 'What does the brief think? Maybe it's something different an...'

Marco paced the room looking like he may erupt. 'He hasn't called back either. I've left messages, but I'll phone again now.'

He glared at Bill. 'And Bill, don't let me catch you screwing on my time again, otherwise I'll have you killed.'

• • • •

'YOU STUPID BITCH!' Zane roared, undoing the buckle of Erin's chin strap. He lifted the helmet slowly from her head, his eyes alight with murderous rage. 'You trying to get us both killed?'

Erin blinked, the sky above her changing from a blurred mess into crystal clarity. Zane's face was inches from hers, blood dripping from a cut on his cheek. 'W-What happened?'

She tried to clear her mind from the torrent of swirling confusion and automatically went to raise her hand to touch the gash on his already scarred face.

Wait! She couldn't move her hands or arms. Smoke and the smell of hot metal crowded her nostrils. *Shit! The bike!* She'd pulled his arm to stop him! They'd crashed! They'd crashed and now she couldn't move...

Zane's fury only escalated further at the panic flooding Erin's face, the blood dripping onto her cheek tracking slowly towards her lips. Trapped underneath his body in the ditch, he guessed she hadn't got her head around where she was and what state she was in. He was too angry to care. Let her worry. She deserved it.

He'd broken nothing and it was likely neither had she, considering it was *him* who'd taken the majority of the impact and his bike was still lying heavily across the back of his legs.

With immense effort, he pushed the bike to one side.

As the weight rendering her immobile eased, relief flooded Erin. She freed her arms. 'Oh Christ! I thought th...'

'Yeah, I know what you thought,' Zane snarled.

'A-Are you alright?' Erin stammered. 'I'm sorry... I...

You've cut your face an…'

'Sorry?' Zane yelled. 'You're fucking *sorry*?' Pushing Erin into the wet grass by her shoulders, his face closed in. 'I should kill you for this, you crazy cow! We could both be dead after that stunt!'

Memory rushed abruptly back to the fore. Why the hell had she apologised? She'd asked if he was alright too! What the hell was she thinking?

She'd failed yet again. He might have another gash on his face, but he wasn't dead. Far from it.

And neither was she…

Further relief mixed with torment poured over her, harder than before. 'Yes, we could *both* be dead, but unfortunately, we're not. Especially you…' She struggled to roll her body out from under his. *He was too close. Too overpowering. His mouth…*

Zane trembled with the conflicting urge to smash his fist into this spoilt woman's face and kiss her at the same time. The black smudges of dust and blood on her cheeks, coupled with the strands of grass stuck in her tangled blonde hair set his veins on fire with both hate and lust.

Questioning how he could feel attraction for this mad chick who had tried to kill him for the second time was not on his mind when his mouth crashed down onto to hers. All that he knew - that he *felt* at this second in time, was that he had to claim those beautiful lips he'd wanted to taste since the moment he'd seen her.

The air disappeared from Erin's lungs, the primal need to reinstate that she was still alive tricking her into responding to the powerful mouth on hers. Molten heat exploded within her as she returned the kiss, the urgent possession of her mouth blowing a hole in the base of her being.

Then it disappeared. Stopped.

Breathless, Erin opened her eyes to find Zane pushing himself off her, his penetrating eyes glaring with unconcealed anger.

With an abrupt shake of his head, he jumped to his feet and brushed the dirt from the elbows of his leather jacket. Grunting, he pulled his bike out of the ditch. 'As long as there isn't a petrol leak and the handlebars aren't twisted, this should be okay to ride,' he muttered, leaving Erin drowning in confusion.

What the fuck had just happened?

Zane Morelli, that bastard, had just kissed her with raw passion and she'd *let* him? She'd given her mouth to him freely. *What the fuck?*

Now he was acting like it hadn't happened? Like none of this was happening and that he hadn't just slammed her soul out of her body and left her lying in a ditch - the ditch he'd also been in. *Because of her.*

Erin pushed herself on to her elbows, her whole body aching mercilessly.

She didn't trust herself to speak. Not until she'd justified how she could have allowed the man she despised to kiss her. Or how she would override the guilt that she'd actually *wanted* the man who had murdered her own father to put his mouth on hers.

• • • •

MARCO VICIOUSLY PULLED the back of his hand underneath his nose, snorting loudly to shift the stubborn powder clinging to the inside of his nostrils.

He needed another drink. Another line. *Lots.*

For fuck's sake, this day had turned beyond the pale. The whole thing was a fucking joke.

His brain careered from one dead end to another as he weighed up his options. A bag of shite, the whole lot of it. He'd kill someone for this. He'd kill *everyone* for this.

Bill watched Marco pace up and down, his movements becoming more erratic as the cocaine took hold. *This was bad.*

'I'm telling you this has gone *way* past the point of no return,' Marco barked, breaking the loaded silence apparent since he'd stormed into Bill's office.

Looking at his boss's face, Bill quickly reached the conclusion that it was preferable to say nothing and wait for the man to speak, rather than ask questions. Marco hated being questioned - even more so when he was in one of his moods. And by hell, he was in a *blinder* of a mood. Which, dare he say, had worsened considerably even *since* the bombshell was dropped about Zane.

None of it boded well.

Marco glared at Bill, daring him to ask what happened purely to warrant an excuse to let rip. Unable to wait any longer, he continued regardless. 'You won't believe this,' he started, his pinpoint pupils centred on his right-hand man. 'I finally got through to that arsehole brief. You know, the one I paid a fortune to?'

'Yeah, of course I know of him.' Bill had been present when Marco hired the man to act for his brother, or rather, for *himself*. 'Why did he bring the appeal forward?'

'Well, that's just it. He didn't. He's been putting off telling me.' Marco's eyes were wild with rage. 'He got through to the prison to request a meet with Fennel, like I asked. Clearly at that point we weren't the only ones unaware of what had happened, but it turned out that he did this *yesterday*!'

'Right...' Bill fidgeted, not liking the way this was going. 'So, if he knew this yesterday, then why didn't he ring you to tell you th…'

'I'm getting to that! He said the prison refused to go into much detail because he was "no longer in Mr Morelli's employment".'

'You sacked the brief?'

'I didn't, you fool!' Marco slammed his fist on the desk, the pen pot jumping across the surface. 'Not me. *Him*! Zane fired the brief. He fired him by leaving instructions with the prison office. And get this – it turns out that some other fuck of a brief brought the appeal date forward. It was done under wraps. He got the evidence overturned and voila – Zane was released!'

Bill blinked. 'Zane used a different lawyer? Without telling us? Without saying anything?'

Marco nodded, the frantic movement jarring his neck. 'Yep! That brief's been paid thousands for his part in this and for what? To bugger us up? To make my life bastard difficult? He knew this *hours* ago, but the fucker only levelled with me after I threatened his wife and children.'

He'd make that wanker pay fourfold for not informing him immediately of his sacking, the fucking useless bastard. 'The brief will die. As will whoever this new one is, when I find out,' Marco snarled. 'But first, I need to work out how to deal with my brother!' *Especially now he was out.* And out, without telling *them*!

Zane had planned this. And if he'd planned it, it meant he must know something. Why else would he do this behind everyone's backs?

It was just a question of when Zane would be back and what they would do when that happened.

To cut to the chase, that *couldn't* happen.

Marco rubbed his hand over his chin. 'We should have dealt with this and done what was needed long before now,' he muttered. 'We knew what we'd planned to do, should this happen, so why didn't we just do it while we could? We could have avoided all this, yet now we've got to do things out in the open. In the meantime, I've asked Sonny to look at Zane's accounts and check for withdrawals.'

'Maybe Zane won't come back?' Bill suggested, knowing his words were lame. Where else would he go and, furthermore, why? As far as Zane Morelli was concerned, he had a waiting apartment and a firm to run. Or did he? Could he have found out what had *really* happened?

'My brother will be back,' Marco hissed. But that he'd been out for four days and not yet arrived, was strange. Not easy on the nerves either. 'We *have* to locate him.'

He paced around faster, the circling making him dizzy and driving the incessant thumping of blood pounding in his brain. He felt his temples expand, the veins throbbing. Rubbing his fingers on the sides of his head, he continued wearing out the floor. *Think, think.*

Bill nodded pointlessly. If they knew where Zane was, it would be simple. Not that he'd bother stating the obvious - he'd only get grief.

He watched Marco nearing the drinks cabinet, praying the man didn't start on the spirits. If he did, it would be even more difficult controlling the outbursts.

Jesus Christ. What a shit mess. They'd planned it so well too. Marco's original idea was good. Keeping tabs on Zane in nick had been achieved. Their two screws on the inside and, when that couldn't happen, Fennel, kept them abreast of this. They'd placed tons of opportunities in Zane's path to help add to his stretch, but even when that failed, it wasn't too much of a problem. They'd had seven months clear before the appeal, allowing plenty of time to fix it so that an unfortunate and fatal accident befell the incarcerated heir before then. So what the fuck had gone wrong?

Marco had made it clear that if his brother didn't do the decent thing by getting more time inside, then he had to die. Yet he was out. *And not dead.*

Seeing Marco reach for the rum, Bill decided now was an opportune moment as any to deflect him. 'Is it possible the information's wrong? Maybe that screw has got mixed up and Zane's not out at all?'

Marco paused, his hand almost on the bottle. 'They wouldn't have got it wrong! Neither would the brief have been sacked. The prison wouldn't say th...'

'There's been a withdrawal!'

As Sonny burst into the office, Marco and Bill swung around. 'I did what you said and put a trace on Zane's accounts. He withdrew a large amount of money four days ago.'

'Fuck!' Marco snatched up the rum. 'There's the proof there! He's definitely out! Where was it withdrawn?' *They'd set up a hit this very minute.*

Sonny placed a print-out of the transaction on the desk. 'It was from a branch two miles from the nick and it happened thirty minutes after his release. No other transactions have occurred since.'

The three men stared at each other in silence, apart from Marco who released a guttural growl from deep within his throat.

They all knew what this meant. If the one and only withdrawal had taken place minutes after Zane was released and it was done two miles from the prison, then he could be *anywhere* by now.

And the other thing this showed, which in some ways bothered Marco more than anything else scooting around his brain, was that if this knowledge got out before he'd had chance to sort it, then the deal with Lisa Tequila and her father would also be in the dust.

TWENTY ONE

KEEPING HIS EYES firmly on Erin, Zane delved his fingers back into his bag of chips. At first, the taste of salt and vinegar after so long without, was delicious, but now the soggy greasiness was losing its appeal. As was his failure in exhibiting self-control. Kissing Erin like that yesterday was slack. *Very slack.*

He might have come to his senses soon enough and stopped what he'd been compelled to do, but that the compulsion had succeeding in overtaking logic in the first place was unforgivable.

He may be holding the fiancée of that bastard hostage; using her to torture every ounce of payback Flame so deserved, but its effectiveness would lessen if his inexplicable attraction to Erin Langley was allowed to dilute the plan.

It also didn't help sitting in a chair all night, alert and awake.

It would serve him well to remember that whatever this woman said or however much she, for unknown reasons, intrigued him, the magnet she possessed which pulled him headlong into a crushing attraction, only gave her new openings to kill him.

That stunt on the bike was the second attempt. There was no room for a third.

Zane wiped his greasy fingers down his jeans, then tossed the remains of his chips in the bin in the corner of the room.

There was no doubt Erin would try something else. She was a risk, so it was vital to remain aware. And being aware didn't include the animalistic urge to possess the woman who hated him so, to take precedence.

Following suit, Erin got up and placed her chips in the bin. She wouldn't throw them in, like Zane. If she missed, it would only give him more reason to think her a joke.

He hadn't said a word since yesterday, apart from informing her not long ago that they were fetching food. The night was long - filled with thoughts she didn't want and recriminations she deserved.

She'd tried not to fall asleep, but at some point, exhaustion must have overtaken, as when she'd next opened her eyes, it was light and Zane was still sitting in the chair opposite.

Erin wished he'd stop staring. His eyes left searing hot trails and she resented that the memory of his mouth on hers haunted her, reminding her just how much she had allowed herself to be deviated away from her aim.

Shameful.

The added humiliation of it being *him* who had pulled away, rather than her, was the final insult. It should have been *her* to make that judgement. It should have been *her* recoiling in horror.

Should, being the operative word...

She should have immediately taken umbrage at his touch. It should have sickened her.

But it hadn't.

And *that* sickened her the most.

What was wrong with her to have allowed that to happen? Did her father mean so little to let the man who murdered him take liberties?

No, he didn't. Her father meant *everything*. It was why she was here. But that did not stop the incessant thoughts from plaguing her as to what might have happened last night, had Zane not pulled away.

Erin shook her head in self-disgust. It was irrelevant because it would not happen again.

She cleared her throat. 'Being as you're still acting like a sulky child and refusing to speak, I can't work out whether you're angry about your bike's smashed indicator or whether it's over being too late to risk picking up your money by the time we got back on the road yesterday.'

She defiantly met Zane's eyes. She would show him that her brief snippet of losing reason yesterday would not be repeated.

'I had no intention of picking up the money.'

Erin stared at the sneer on Zane's mouth. *He really thought he was something else, didn't he? Pathetic.* 'Oh, right... I know you've got plenty of your own money, but that's never enough for people like you.' Her eyes danced with malice. 'It must really piss you off to miss out on a few quid!'

Zane prickled. 'What do you mean by that?' *This was the second time she'd alluded to him having money.*

Erin's stomach sank realising she'd let slip and quickly deflected. 'Nah, I get it now - the reason you instructed me to jump on your bike outside Anthony's office, rather than sticking to the deal and giving me back, was a ploy to pull more money out of him.'

'Hmm...' Zane made out he was in deep thought. 'Maybe... But on the other hand, it's odd you didn't seem too put out about not returning to your lovely fiancé. I wonder why...?'

And he did wonder why. Something did not add up with Erin Langley.

Erin couldn't stop the colour from draining from her cheeks fast enough for Zane not to notice. 'Think what you like,' she snapped.

Zane *was* thinking. *Very hard.* No, he didn't know what was going on behind the scenes with this woman and didn't particularly want to, but she was both a threat and a necessity. He had to do something to make this work in his favour and wanted her involvement in this finished, sooner rather than later.

It was only a matter of time before she found a way to take another attempt on his life, but it wasn't like he could let her go. Not only would he lose his bargaining chip, but she'd make sure the police were all over him. But if he *didn't* get her off his hands, there was a very real danger that he would fuck her for real. And that bothered him more than anything.

There was also the other issue over how long he could keep his control over Flame in check. Three times now he could have grabbed the opportunity and launched himself at the man. He doubted whether he'd be so constrained a fourth time.

The next time he came face to face with Flame, the man would die. He had to ramp up his plan. *Fast.*

Zane frowned. To do this properly he had to get Erin Langley to work with him, rather than against him.

Erin could see Zane's mind furiously ticking over. No doubt dreaming up more bullshit or sarcasm to throw her off guard.

Well, it didn't fool her. She knew exactly what his game was. Like most men, it was to exert control. As Morelli was choosing not to use violence on her, like he would normally do to people, he was pulling on the *opposite* side of his repertoire.

Much as she hated to admit it, the sexual draw Zane commandeered - this power he possessed, which had no doubt provided him with plenty of success with the opposite sex in the past, would not work on *her*. Yes, she'd felt the unmistakable pull several times and yes, she may have stupidly succumbed for a very brief period yesterday, but she was one woman he would fail to control in that way.

Thought he could blind her with a kiss and blatant lies, did he?

Her lips flattened into a thin line. 'Okay then, if you had no intention of wanting that money, like you expect me to believe, then why did you agree to the deal? Why go to the trouble of making arrangements?'

She cocked an eyebrow, daring him to blag his way out of this one. She'd heard too much bullshit in her life. She'd seen too much manipulation to fall for this crap and experienced more than enough herself, not to be able to play people at their own game. 'Come on, if you expect me to believe that was your intention, then explain *why*?'

Zane held Erin's stare for a few moments in silence, weighing up whether to do things *this* way, or not. Making his decision, he leant forward, his arms resting on his thighs. 'As I said, I had no intention of collecting the money. You were correct - I don't need it.'

Ignoring Erin's snort of derision, he continued. 'When I received the text about where the money was being left, do you remember I stopped to talk to people on a bench?'

Erin frowned. 'Those tramps? Are they *your* people?'

'*My* people?' Zane laughed. 'Whoever they were, I don't know, but I figured they needed cash more than your boyfriend needed it back, so I told them where, if they were quick, they could find a lump sum.'

Erin laughed and then stopped, realising Zane was serious. 'But why?'

Zane's eyes narrowed. 'It's simple. I'm playing with that bastard boyfriend of yours. I'm reeling him in. I've got what he wants and I'll finish him over it.'

Erin's mouth dropped open. *She hadn't expected that.* She knew Morelli didn't need money, but for him to actually admit this? Before she could say anything else, he spoke again.

'Look, I don't know who you are, Erin Langley, or what your game is, but I know for sure that you fucking have one. I reckon you hate that boyfriend of yours as much as I do, so this is your opportunity to either work with me so that we both get what we want or you can work against me, where you will lose.'

Standing up, he grabbed his crash helmet. 'Think on your answer for as long as it takes for us to get to my bike. We're moving on today.'

. . . .

BILL AND SONNY trailed Marco from the underground swimming pool which formed one of the many benefits of living in an exclusive apartment. They glanced at each other as they followed the trail of chlorinated water dripping from their boss's wet torso onto the shiny marble floor of the building's reception.

They waited in silence as Marco jabbed the button to call the lift, knowing the concierge was busy eyeing the mess on the floor, realising there would be an equal amount in the lift that he would also need to get cleared up.

Nothing would be mentioned about this, of course, because *no one* would dare question anything the Morellis saw fit to do.

This was also the reason why they were waiting for Marco to decide when to tell them what conclusion he'd reached. Or worse, whether he assumed one of *them* had the hallowed answers.

It was bad enough witnessing Marco getting shitfaced last night at the impromptu party he'd insisted on throwing. The only guests, apart from himself and a shed load of brandy, champagne and cocaine, and of course themselves, were three girls from the studio - all of whom he'd got heavy-handed and sadistic with, his sexual expectations and actions verging on perverted and illegal.

That culminated in another hefty payout being brokered during the small hours to ensure nothing came from the once pretty mouths of those women in future. Of course, the payout didn't include the extortionate fee of the doctor, kept on the books for instances such as this, and summoned to patch the women up.

That was Marco all over. Rather than deal with pressing issues, his way of initially coping with problems was to ignore them, replacing them with other pursuits to take his mind off thinking about them.

Although unsaid, both Bill and Sonny knew Marco would have to give orders soon, otherwise they would all be in the shitter.

Following inside the apartment, Bill closed the door and waited until Marco flopped into a leather armchair, still in his sopping wet swimming trunks before he risked voicing anything.

As it turned out, Marco didn't wait to be questioned. Cutting a new line of coke on the glass tabletop, he looked between both Bill and Sonny in turn.

'I'm sending a man up to the area my brother was last seen on a fact-finding mission.' Without drawing breath, he snorted the entire line of coke in one go. 'One of you can accompany that man. Choose between yourselves who that will be.'

Bill looked at Sonny and then back at Marco, guessing he was the one lumbered with stating the obvious. 'But Zane could be anywhere by now.'

Marco's eyebrow twitched with the beginnings of annoyance, but reined himself in, proud he was able to keep a lid on things. He'd got it all worked out now but didn't expect these two to have the same ability as someone like *him*. 'Why do you think Zane hasn't yet returned here?' He fixed each man with a long stare. 'Sonny? Why do you think this is the case?'

Sonny cracked his hefty knuckles. 'Erm, perhaps he found out what you've done... as in, that you've changed how the firm works?' He shot a quick glance at Marco, hoping he'd said nothing that could be perceived as accusatory or antagonistic. To his relief, Marco nodded.

'And what about you, Bill?'

'He's angry because he wanted to deal with the target himself?'

Marco nodded again. 'I'd say that's the closest. I know Zane and how he harbours grudges. I also believe he topped Fennel.'

'But we apologised for the mistake about what happened to Zane's face!' Sonny exclaimed. 'He'd accepted it.'

'Zane accepts *nothing*, so never presume that. I also think Bill's right about him being pissed off that retaliation over his jailing was taken away from him.' Marco's eyes narrowed. 'I think he's digging around to make sure it's been done.'

'What?' Sonny gasped. 'But why, if you said th...'

'Because I know my brother!' Marco snarled. And it was exactly that, which made his clandestine release so worrying. 'I want you to make contact. You know who with...'

As Bill's bottom lip dropped in shock, the cigarette balancing in his mouth fell into his lap. 'But we swore that we'd be...'

'I know what was said,' Marco spat. 'But we need to make contact with the prick and see if he's seen or heard anything out of the ordinary.'

'We don't know where he's gone, apart from somewhere up north,' Bill cried, his mind going into overdrive as he scrabbled to retrieve his dropped fag.

'Then I suggest Sonny uses his technical powers to fucking find out. The wanker hasn't disappeared off the face of the earth, therefore he's locatable, right? So fucking locate him!

TWENTY TWO

ANTHONY WANTED TO type the words, 'fuck you', in reply to the snotty e-mail he'd received from Simon Clarknett. His fingers hovered over the laptop keyboard, itching to stab in the relevant keys.

A loop of *Unchained Melody* played on repeat in his head and he slapped his right ear several times, not stopping until the burn of his reddening skin drowned out the irritating tune.

Placing his twitching fingers back on the keyboard, he began typing:

```
To: simon.clarknett@gildedhotels.com
From: anthony.walker@awfinancialservices.co.uk
Subject: Availability


Dear Simon,


Thanks for your email. Unfortunately, a short
illness this week prevented myself and my fiancée's
presence at several functions we were both eager to
attend.
I can assure you that our recent absences do not
```

```
affect the provisions arranged in relation to your
investments. Everything I have advised on is still
valid and on track, should you wish to proceed with
my suggestions.
Like we previously arranged, I look forward to
receiving you as my guest at the golf club on
Thursday.


Until then, kind regards


Anthony Walker
```

Hitting send, Anthony sat back, his headache growing. That would do for now. He'd think up something else to embellish his and Erin's disappearance when he saw Simon during golf on Thursday. Because regardless of the man's doubts, he'd be there.

And so would Erin.

Once more Anthony stared at his mobile sitting silently next to his laptop.

Nothing. No response to his voicemails or any texts he'd sent since yesterday. Not a bloody thing.

It wasn't like Morelli. The man wouldn't be happy with what he'd achieved so far. Oh no, there would be more. It was just case of *when...*

But Anthony couldn't afford to wait. He needed to move on this. Erin had to return. She should *already* be here. And she would have been, if Morelli hadn't welched on what had been fucking agreed.

Busy screwing her again, was he?

Anthony wanted to frown. He wanted to frown so badly it was times like this he wished he hadn't had so many Botox injections. Showing his utter displeasure would help to remove a small percentage of his gut-churning, teeth-grinding rage.

But he couldn't.

And neither could he do anything about the rest of it.

He picked up the cup of tea Maisie had dutifully placed on his desk some time ago and then put it back. *Even that was cold.*

For fuck's sake. Word would soon spread like leprosy - or rather 'speculation' over his unusual absences from his previously well-attended networking functions would.

It was no secret that he was no longer ill – not that he'd ever been. If people began suspecting Erin was the one behind his ability to flourish in public, he'd become a laughing stock.

He'd be even more of an object of ridicule if it got out the leather-jacketed biker who had left with his fiancée wasn't her brother, like he'd told his nosy fucking receptionist.

Anthony picked at his manicured nails. Maisie hadn't said she didn't believe his explanation about crossed wires and that Erin had thought her *brother* was coming to pick her up, rather than *him*. But she hadn't said she *did* believe it either…

She wouldn't though, would she? Maisie would hardly question his explanation.

But she could be discussing it… She could have already told the other staff during their gossipy breaks, lunchtimes or after work drinks that he never got invited to. She could have emailed all her friends – people who lived in this town or anywhere around here, laughing at him.

And if that stupid cunt, Jocelyn, rang one more time…

Anthony snatched up his mobile to quickly compose another text message, identical to the last ten he'd already sent:

```
call me
```

However, there was one major issue that he'd so far failed to adequately address.

Nothing explained why Erin had *chosen* to get back on Morelli's bike. She'd been waiting outside the Delish Deli as arranged, so why the hell had she got on the back of the damn bike again the second that bastard roared up the street?

Anthony's lips curled into a snarl. Unless she was part of it… If Erin was part of whatever Morelli was doing, then…

No, that was ridiculous. Morelli must have threatened her further.

Anthony's teeth made a horrible grating sound as he clenched his jaw.

He shunted his chair back and one of the castors stuck, forcing the chair to skid across the floor with a dull scraping sound, which only worsened the tightly coiled fuse inside his head.

If he didn't receive a call from Morelli within the next hour, he'd drive to London himself. If that was the only way to find the people needed to sort this, then so be it. He'd go today.

Anthony got as far as tugging his suit jacket from the peg on the gold coat stand in the corner of his office, when the shrill ring of his mobile rendered him frozen.

Finally!

Lurching for the phone, he booted a ceramic pot holding a Japanese fern which promptly tipped soil and gravel across the highly polished floor. 'Fuck!' he hissed, snatching the mobile off the desk.

'What the fuck do you mean by...' The voice that interrupted caught Anthony off guard and he fell silent.

As he listened, he scraped his fingers through his dyed hair. He then stomped across to the floor to ceiling glass partition, tugging the cord which closed the slats of the Venetian blinds, blocking the faces in the open plan office from sight.

'I've been trying to get in contact with you... Yes, I know you did... Unusual? You could say that... Yeah, he has... And he's got my fucking fiancé too, so what are you going to do about it?'

• • • •

JUDGING BY THE landlady's face when Zane informed her he wouldn't be further extending his stay at her B&B, Erin reached the conclusion that the sour-faced woman was not unhappy about it.

The woman's green eyes dripped with distrust as well as

dislike, but another emotion was also present as she snatched up the keys deposited on her makeshift reception desk.

Fear.

Erin then noticed the 'no visitors' sign and inwardly cringed, aware it must be presumed she was a two-bit whore Zane had picked up on his travels.

This aside, Erin couldn't say she'd be sad to leave this crummy place. Not that she knew where they were heading...

And she was still stuck with *him*.

Her eyes bored into Zane's back as he grabbed the small holdall containing his possessions and with a final scowl at the miserable landlady, jerked his head in the direction of the door.

Erin reluctantly made her way down the steps to where the bike stood, surprisingly untouched.

She eyed three young men in hoodies surreptitiously watching from their perch on a wall a few yards away. Not exactly a desirable neighbourhood and one she would not miss.

She pulled the rucksack containing the few items Zane had provided her with onto her back and watched him stand in front of his bike, his arms folded.

Yes, she'd made her decision.

With a lazy smile, like he cared little either way, Zane jumped astride the bike and shoved his arms through the rucksack straps to shrug it into place on his back. 'What's it to be, then? The easy way or the hard way?'

'I'll do what you want,' Erin muttered, putting her crash helmet on. 'But only on the proviso that you tell me what the plan is.'

Zane laughed as he started his bike. 'Providing you tell me why you dislike the man you're marrying!'

Ignoring his comment, Erin took her place on the pillion seat. Zane Morelli could demand whatever he liked, but there were some things she would not share - *that* being one of them.

Aside from having little choice, she'd work with him to bring Anthony in. It could work in her favour.

As they sped up the road and out of Ladywood, her lips

curled into a smile.

She'd make out to this lying, murdering bastard that she'd dance to his tune, but only because this was the best - actually, the *only* way to bring her goals to fruition.

And yes, the plans to reach her end game had been altered yet again, but this was her final chance. As long as she didn't mess up and if Zane believed she wanted the same as him, the time would come when both Zane *and* Anthony were in the same place.

Then and only then, would her finale unfold.

Twenty Three

ERIN STARED AT the estate agent shop front in confusion. 'We're going in here?' she shrieked, hating that Zane's arm around her shoulder forced her closer to him. His underlying male heat was stronger than she could comfortably withstand without sending her mind down a spiral of unanswerable questions.

This was madness! They'd moved from a grotty B&B in Ladywood, only to stand outside an estate agent in Solihull? It was closer to Anthony - closer to where she didn't want to be, but equally closer to where she *must* be. She had to remain wherever Morelli was, until the opportunity arose.

Hearing what Zane had planned made things even worse. Pretend to be a couple? Rent a house and live there together?

Mortifying.

Erin felt sick. Considering she found it almost impossible, both physically and emotionally, to comprehend her unacceptable attraction towards the last person on earth she should experience anything but hate for, this was a nightmare. Being in a house – just the two of them, more alone than in that awful B&B, wasn't something she thought she could bear. But his hurried explanation made sense, even it if was less than palatable.

It was true that different premises other than the B&B were required if Zane was to succeed in holding Anthony. And therefore, needed for *her* to take revenge on them both too. But *here*?

'What are you thinking?' she hissed, trepidation avalanching once again. 'This is crazy!'

'Never mind what I'm thinking,' Zane said, his hand on the handle of the heavy glass door. 'Just do what I said. Like I told you, we're a couple looking for the perfect place to live, so play the part. Follow my lead and don't attract attention.'

'But...'

'You're supposed to love me, remember? So act like it!' Flashing a smile which completely changed his entire face, Zane kissed Erin's cheek. The dangerous psycho with cold blue eyes morphed into the gorgeous, chiselled featured dark-haired Italian-looking man that he was. This overall look was one which even that scar and a fresh cut wouldn't deter most women from doing an appreciative double take.

Feigning resignation whilst masking the immediate pull she felt, Erin plastered on an equally bright smile and grabbed Zane's hand to enter the estate agents. She could act better than most and if that got her where she needed to be, then it was worth not over-analysing why his large rough fingers entwined with hers shot electric all the way up her arm.

Pulling Erin towards the nearest sales desk, Zane kept his showstopping smile in place for the benefit of the attractive brunette who eyed them curiously.

She's interested, Erin thought bitterly. If this woman only knew what Zane Morelli had done, then she wouldn't be drooling at him, like her knickers were already off. Realising her hand had involuntarily clenched to dig her nails into Zane's palm, she quickly relaxed it.

'Can I help you?' the woman purred.

'We're looking for a place that's available immediately.' Zane looked at the wall to his right with printouts of available rental properties on display. 'It needs to be fully furnished and somewhere out of the city.' He glanced down at Erin, his eyes still miraculously clear of all wrongdoing. 'We'd like somewhere in a rural location that's quiet, as well as private...'

Erin returned the smile, hoping it was as convincing as his. *Follow his lead, he'd said.* 'Yes, somewhere rural...'

The brunette's eyes flashed with a hint of irritation that Erin should dare break her conversation with this extremely handsome stranger. She pushed herself from her chair, drawing the movement out so that her manicured nails remained on show on the desk's surface, like she needed them to lever her from her seat.

Sashaying past, she brushed against Zane to pluck a printout from a see-through slot on the wall. 'We have *this* one.' Ignoring Erin, she handed the sheet to Zane. 'It's in Knowle, which isn't far from here. It has more of a countryside setting an...'

'I don't fancy Knowle.' Zane pretended to consider the options. 'Where would you suggest, babe?'

Erin almost choked realised he was talking to her. *Babe?* She cleared her throat, remembering her supposed part. 'Oh, erm... Let's think... Dorridge? How about Dorridge? Have you anything there?'

The brunette frowned. 'You want to be *that* far away from the city?'

Erin's irritation spiked. The woman had just looked her up and down! It may not be obvious from a male's point of view, but *she'd* seen it.

Meeting the brunette's inquisitive stare, she purposely leant into Zane, her hand splayed against his chest. 'Yes, we *do*. We want to be away from everyone, don't we, hon.' Calling Zane anything other than a murdering bastard was difficult, but then so was refraining from punching this woman in the face.

'My boyfriend's a musician.' Erin pretended to laugh. 'He always tells me I shouldn't say that to "random" people, but being as you're questioning us, I will. He needs peace and quiet in order to work on his new album.'

The brunette fawned at Zane. 'I should have guessed with the leather and stuff. Rock, is it?'

'So, have you anything in Dorridge that's available now and fully furnished?' Zane said somewhat uncomfortably. *Christ, Erin didn't need to make him out to be a bloody rock God. Don't attract attention, he'd said.*

Erin enjoyed the wisp of embarrassment flitting over Zane's face. *Two could play at the game of uncomfortable-beyond-words positions to be in.*

'We do have one, but unfortunately it's not available for another few weeks. The landlord is away at the moment and...'

'Is there anyone that I can speak to about "changing" that?' Zane asked, spotting a man in a pin-striped suit sitting in a separate office at the rear of the shop.

The brunette shuffled awkwardly. 'Well, I...'

'That's the main man in there, isn't it?' Zane flashed another smile.

'Wait! You ca...'

'Have a look at the other stuff on the wall whilst I'm gone, babe, in case there's anything else you prefer while I talk to the gaffer and see what he can do to sort this out for us,' Zane called over his shoulder as he walked past the woman towards the office.

Turning away, Erin pretended to peruse the properties adorning the walls, trying not to laugh at the expression on the brunette's face over being totally and blatantly sidestepped.

A glimmer of hope for this situation returned. A furnished house would contain knives, as well as other things that could be used as weapons. As it stood, she had nothing and no means of obtaining any. But *this* way...

If she kept her wits about her and her acting up to par, then she could do this. *She could actually do it!*

She'd work hard to gain Zane's trust – convince him she was willing to work with him. He already had suspicions that her and Anthony's relationship wasn't what it should be, so if she thought about this and made out she was 'confiding' in Zane about what things were really like with her fiancé, then it would explain why she was looking for a get-out clause.

Zane didn't need to know the *true* reasons for any of it.

And when Zane had Anthony and believed he'd gained her trust, then she would strike.

• • • •

'FUCK OFF! I'M BUSY!' Marco screamed at the woman tapping the office door at Luna Motion Films.

His pounding head swivelled back to Bill who was, as usual, crammed into the opposite chair and then over to Sonny, frantically tapping away into a laptop over in the corner. The raging hangover from last night had got its claws embedded since he hadn't had chance to put his normal tactic of starting on the spirits before it gained traction.

He hadn't had chance because he'd been dealing with *this*. It was something he couldn't quite get his head around. And something that if Sonny didn't come up with anything useful, like *now*, then he might blow a fuse.

He drummed his fingers on the desk to stop them from forming a fist. 'Why the fuck was no one aware the bastard relocated to the Midlands?' His eyes narrowed. 'Or were you, but decided not to tell me because you deemed it unimportant?'

Marco jumped from his chair, the sudden movement sending a ricochet of pain through his skull. Wincing, he allowed the pain to subside before continuing. 'Perhaps you thought it not relevant mentioning this "small" detail when my fucking brother was transferred from the nick in Manchester to one in Birmingham?'

Bill inwardly sighed. Marco's paranoia was worsening on a daily basis. He really needed to cut back on the gear. It was untenable dealing with him when he was like this. 'None of us were aware of it. We knew Flame went up north, but as to where, we never found out. The instructions were that no contact or connection remained.'

'You mean, *my* instruction? Is that what you're implying?' Marco raged.

'It was your instruction, yes,' Bill said. He waited for the expected impact of Marco's fist to the side of his face for daring to speak of anything that might put him in a less than favourable light, but nothing came.

Instead, Marco dropped heavily back into his chair, for once too exhausted to give Bill a clump for speaking the truth. He *had* given that instruction. He remembered now. He'd wanted all connections with Flame broken because there was no point in retaining any – it would only link the firm to the person who had dropped his brother in the shit. Why would they do that? That would have been the question asked by other members of the firm - especially those who were predominantly Zane's men - the first to go, once *he'd* taken control.

Besides, Flame was not a contender to cause trouble. He was a bean counting prick - no more, no less. He'd gone and wouldn't return, so there had been zilch point in keeping tabs.

Now it seemed that wasn't quite the case.

Marco snatched up his packet of cigarettes and lit one. 'Where exactly is this prick now? What's he doing with himself?'

Bill nodded at Sonny. 'That's what he's finding out.'

'You mean you didn't fucking ask when you spoke to him?' Marco spluttered. Sometimes he wondered how anything got done around here surrounded by shit-for-brains.

Bill cleared his throat. 'I was more concerned in hearing what happened when Zane got in contact with him…'

Marco's eyes widened, his jaw setting in a ferocious snarl. 'So, Zane *has* been in contact. For God's sake. Did you not think to tell me this immediately?' His big fist slammed onto the desk.

Bill heaved his huge frame from the chair. *He'd had enough of this shit.* 'I did tell you and when I did, you smashed the fucking cabinet!' His big head jerked towards pieces of broken wood littering the far corner of the room. 'For Christ's sake,

Marco. You don't listen!'

'I'll be the judge of what I'm fucking listening to or not!' Marco bellowed, knowing somewhere in his addled mind that Bill was right. He was forgetting things and that was not good. *Was he going mad?* 'Tell me what else was said,' he added quickly.

Bill reluctantly sat back down, still bristling. 'Flame said that if we don't sort this, he'll make sure the truth gets out.'

Marco laughed. 'What? He won't do that. Flame's a cunt and has too much to lose.'

'You could say that...' Sonny swung around on the chair, his laptop in hand. 'From what I can see here, his financial firm is extremely successful. He's doing well for himself.'

Marco grinned. 'See. He's got too much to lose. I expected him to get himself set up with something like this with the payout he received.'

Walking over, Sonny placed the laptop on Marco's desk, tilting it so that both Bill and Marco could see the screen.

'That him?' Marco cried. 'What the hell has he done to his bloody hair?' Peering closer, he chuckled. 'Looks like he forked out for a makeover. I'd never have recognised the bastard.'

'That was probably the general idea, but it didn't work - not if Zane found him,' Bill muttered.

Sonny scrolled down the screen. 'And this must be the fiancée that Zane's taken hostage.'

Marco stared at a picture of the man he could barely recognise standing next to a blonde. 'She's hot! How the fuck did Flame manage that?' He was about to laugh again when his face fell. 'Wait! Did you say Zane has taken this woman?'

'Yes, I told you that before as well,' Bill sighed.

'Yes, yes, I know,' Marco lied, covering his worryingly sketchy memory. 'But why has he taken her?'

'Blackmail, of course and Flame wants us to sort it.'

'What, so he don't have to fork out any more of his fucking money?' Marco sneered. His eyes scanned the rest of the text on the screen. 'Knowle? Where the hell is that?'

'Somewhere up by Solihull,' Sonny said. 'He's been there for a few years and is due to marry that bird in a few months.'

'Well, well, well...' Marco clapped his hands together. 'So now we know Zane must be somewhere around there. Let's get up there and do what's needed.'

Bill frowned. 'Zane will have gone elsewhere by now. The woman was snatched a few days ago.'

'Nah.' Marco pulled his shirt sleeves down, feeling more settled now he knew where his brother was lurking. 'He'll still be somewhere near. We just need to find out exactly *where*.'

'There's been no more withdrawals since the original one,' Sonny added. 'I've been watching the accounts closely.'

Marco stood up. 'Nevertheless, let's get sorted.'

· · · ·

MARK SILL glanced up at the uninvited interruption. Unless he specifically requested it, Jane knew damn well that customers were not permitted into his private office under *any* circumstances.

His mouth opened to tell the leather-jacketed layabout that it was unlikely *Sill & Co* would have anything to suit his requirements, when his annoyance gave way to fear at the barrel of a gun pointing in his general direction. 'What th...'

'Apologies for barging in like this, Mr...' Zane glanced at the wooden block emblazoned with a name and initials of qualifications on the man's desk. '...Mr *Sill*. I'm trusting you'll be able to help me.'

He kicked the office door shut behind him without taking his eyes or his gun off the shell-shocked man. 'Where I come from, I don't normally need to ask for things because my firm's reputation precedes me, but I realise that up here you may not be quite as au fait with how things work, so I'll explain a little more about what I need.'

Using his gun, he waved away the man's hand from resting near the telephone. 'To start with, don't get any silly ideas whilst I'm here, after I've left or *ever*.' Zane's eyes narrowed menacingly. 'Unless you and your family wish to die, you'll keep quiet. I have plenty of men who will be watching you for the foreseeable, so it's in everybody's interest to be sensible.'

Casually sitting in the chair opposite, he crossed one leg over his knee and held the gun in his lap, making sure it was still aimed at the chest of Mr Sill. On the off chance the brunette or anyone else thought to interrupt, they wouldn't see it and therefore would be no further people to threaten.

Remaining silent for a moment to let his words sink in, he weighed up the man in front of him, up. A classic loser who thought himself a high-flyer. *Easy*.

Mark Sill wanted to say something - *anything*, but his abject fear kept his tongue from moving to form coherent words. He also wanted to put his fingers in his collar and release some of the heat flooding his body. His crisp white shirt was already clinging to his sweat-soaked back.

'Now,' Zane continued, satisfied the man understood his position. 'You're clearly the boss of this place, so this will be a piece of piss for you to organise. I need a house and I need it now.' Leaning forward, he slapped the printout of the Dorridge house on the man's desk. 'This one, actually.'

Flinching, Mark Sill stared at the property particulars, the words swimming haphazardly through his thick glasses.

'This is furnished, right? And empty, yet your woman out front reckons it's not available for several weeks because the dickhead who owns it is away.' Zane absentmindedly examined his fingernails on the hand holding the gun. 'I thought to myself, that's silly. I doubt whether somebody such as *you* – an estate agent, wouldn't be in possession of the keys of *all* the properties you market. There's no way someone like *you* would struggle, in this particular situation, in making this property immediately available, if you saw fit, yes?'

Mark Sill's eyes darted over the details in front of him once more, at the same time remaining well aware of the gun. 'Well, I... erm... I...'

'Good - that's all I wanted to know,' Zane grinned. 'See? If you deliver, then you don't get killed. Not difficult, is it?'

Mark Sill flinched for the second time when Zane thrust his hand into the inside pocket of his leather jacket, terrified any movement would cause the gun to go off.

Zane chucked an envelope on the desk. 'The place is marked up for six hundred a month. I only want it for two weeks. Maybe three at a push, so you've made a right nice profit.' He nodded to the envelope. 'Five grand will cover any inconvenience and all before the landlord even gets back from his hols!' His eyes twinkled. 'Now, do you have the keys here or do you need help to fetch them?'

'N-No, I... I have them here.' With his eyes still fixed on the gun in Zane's hand, Mark Sill fumbled with the bottom drawer of his desk and pulled out a large metal box. His trembling fingers rooted through the many pairs of keys held within, sweat now dripping from his forehead.

Finally locating the correct keys, he pushed them across the desk.

'Cheers,' Zane smiled. 'I'll get them back to you once we're done there.' Standing up, his smile dropped. 'Now, remember to keep quiet and there will be no repercussions.'

Leaving the pale-faced man nodding furiously, Zane shoved the gun back into his inside pocket and reinstated his smile as he opened the door.

Holding the keys up, he jangled them, trying not to laugh at Erin's face as she turned, her expression making it clear she could see the terror on Mr Sill's face behind him. 'All done, babe. Let's go.'

TWENTY FOUR

ERIN WALKED AROUND the old two-bedroomed detached cottage, inspecting the small rooms. It was tiny, but quaint and contained all the furniture and equipment needed to live comfortably. She especially liked the original inglenook fireplace complete with garlands of dried hops hanging around the brickwork, as well as the brass ornaments. It was the sort of place she'd like to live in in real life.

But this wasn't real life. *Far from it.*

She peered out of the leadlight windows into the rear garden. Surrounded by fields it was a beautiful space and held an important feature - a detached brick outbuilding, possibly used as a workshop. It was perfect for Zane to keep Anthony and the right kind of place where she could murder them both.

She glanced up as Zane walked into the lounge. Taking his gun from his pocket, he laid it on the oak sideboard, then slung his leather jacket on the back of the chair, like he'd been living here for years.

'I don't know how you swung this with that estate agent,' Erin said. 'Although I can probably guess…' She raised an eyebrow, her gaze moving pointedly to the gun. 'I kind of noticed the expression on that man's face.'

'Yeah, well. It's not important. That we have no neighbours was what I was looking for. And we haven't. You did good suggesting here.'

Erin clocked the word 'we' in Zane's comment. They might have been a 'we' for that brunette's benefit, but now, behind closed doors, they didn't need to retain that act. Nevertheless, the reference caused a small, yet distinct flutter in the pit of her stomach.

Shaking away the disconcerting feeling, Erin concentrated on what she must do - win Zane's trust and lull him into a false sense of security. 'It's a bit close to Knowle,' she admitted. One of the main roads out from Dorridge led straight into the centre of Knowle. *And that was where Anthony was.*

'Not necessarily.' Zane flopped down onto the sofa and much to Erin's irritation, put his big boots up on the coffee table. 'I've studied the map and we're out of the village in the other direction. This place is out in the sticks closer to Hockley Heath than Knowle, yet still close enough. It's perfect.'

Deep in thought, Erin pushed Zane's feet off the coffee table. Even though there was no one around to keep up the necessary act, he hadn't returned to the brooding scowling persona that she'd come to recognise. The handsome man she'd witnessed in the estate agents - the one who made her further question her sanity, was still in residence.

It was like something had flipped in his head. It was unnerving. She preferred it when he resembled exactly what he was - a murdering bastard. That way it was easy not to forget.

But make no mistake, he was Zane Morelli - the violent, psychopathic criminal who had killed her father and ruined her life. And she would do well to remember that.

'I suppose we'd better go and get some food and bits and pieces,' she said hastily before she allowed the steadily rising hatred to build. 'If I remember rightly, there's a couple of food shops on the High Street in the village. We can't live on thin air.'

'You're right.' Zane jumped to his feet to grab the bike

keys. 'Let's go.'

· · · ·

'THERE'S NO QUESTION about it,' Trevor Grimes' owl-like eyes centred on Marco's hands. 'That's what I've been told. Being as it's been over twenty-four hours since you promised proof of your standing and you've failed to deliver it, I have little choice but to reach the conclusion that what my trusted source has informed me of, is true.'

Marco bit his tongue to stop the expletives he itched to roar at this condescending jumped-up prig of a nobody. He knew Grimes could see his hands were shaking. The muppet no doubt believed that he – *Marco Morelli* - was fazed by this inflated act of power.

The trembling of his fingers was sod all to do with that. *Imagine it? Marco Morelli being scared of a prick like Trevor fucking Grimes? An utter joke.*

He had the shakes because he was due another line of cocaine and his downer had set in at the rate of knots.

The only reason this slimy toad was even permitted to set foot on his premises, let alone use a second of his time, was because the greasy wanker had somehow shoehorned his way into being the crème de la crème of the adult film industry. That, and Marco wanted to bone his daughter whilst making a mint from her film rights.

If it wasn't for those things, this spindly turd would be gargling with what remained of his cock after it had been removed and shoved down his fucking gullet.

However, those two things *did* matter, hence why the man was still intact and why Marco was putting up with him. But there was a limit. And Grimes was sailing close to it.

Marco fixed his reptilian stare on the gaunt features of Trevor. Today, he couldn't even be arsed to smile at the man. 'I'm not sure who this 'source' of whom you refer is, but like I said, I'm afraid their findings are incorrect.' He pulled open a drawer of his desk and retrieved a black leather Filofax. It wasn't something he ever used, but it looked important, which was the main thing.

He took his time flicking through the pages. This gave his trembling fingers something to do, other than fucking shake and also because he'd rendered Grimes temporarily speechless and he was enjoying the egotistical bastard scraping around his brain for something to say.

He wouldn't give him too long though.

'I should also add that it wasn't that I "failed" to update you or that I had something to hide...' Marco slowly moved his eyes from the blank pages of the Filofax to Trevor Grimes. 'It was because when I attempted to call you last night after receiving confirmation from my solicitor, you didn't answer your phone!' He raised one eyebrow, daring the man to deny it. 'I'm a busy man, so funnily enough, I didn't have time to spend the evening pressing redial!'

And Marco hoped that for once his memory correctly recalled what Lisa had said the other day about attending an award dinner last night...

Marco smiled. The lack of response signified he was right. 'I hope that's now put your mind at rest over any "confusion"?'

Trevor Grimes fidgeted uncomfortably. His sources *were* good and he had no reason to believe they had failed him. But there was always a small chance... He might hold the upper hand with what he had to barter with, but he couldn't match Morelli when it came to violence. Plus, his daughter made it clear that she would not accept the mere words of Marco Morelli. She wanted *proof.*

If Hazel wasn't happy, then she would make sure *he* wasn't either. Without her, he had nothing on the table. Plus, he wasn't about to walk straight into a trap without any benefit.

Marco watched Grimes curiously and didn't hide the narrowing of his eyes. He knew it unnerved people. *Why was Grimes still here?* Wasn't the bullshit he'd told him what he'd wanted to know? Still, he didn't want to completely antagonise the situation.

Trevor looked at Marco. 'You need to let me know what's going on quickly, otherwise things can't happen.'

'Look.' Marco smiled thinly. 'I realise that you don't yet know me well enough to merely accept what I say. It's strange really, considering most people find that more than good enough...' *If they wanted to live, that was...* 'But being as we'll soon be family, how about you speak directly to my brief?'

He scribbled a number on a piece of Luna Motion Films headed notepaper and pushed it across the desk. 'Here's his number. He'll clarify everything I've said - Zane will *not* be released from prison and that I am and will remain the sole owner of the Morelli firm.' He stood up, signifying the conversation was over.

Pacified, Trevor Grimes stuffed the paper in his pocket and made his way to the door.

Marco waited until the footsteps faded before snatching up the phone.

'Yeah... it's me... Listen, expect a call from a prick called Grimes. Tell him what I said... Yeah, he has... and yeah, I know... Just fucking do it, okay?'

Slamming the phone down, he pulled his coke stash from the top drawer. *Fucking idiot.* At least this was one thing that moron brief could do to make up for being such a pointless loser before he got dispatched.

Grimes would get what he needed to hear and that would buy more time to do what was required. After that, there really would be no worries.

Marco snorted a fat line of coke and inhaled, satisfied the irritating trembling would now die down.

He glanced at his wristwatch. Yep, by this time tomorrow, none of this would be an issue.

• • • •

ZANE HAD PLANNED on only picking up something to eat and a few supplies for around the house - the necessities Erin insisted on: washing up liquid, toilet rolls etcetera. All the stuff that was usually wherever he stayed without thinking about it.

But he'd changed his mind.

Maybe getting one step closer to revenge on Flame was what did it? Knowing that wanker was a few miles away sweating like a stuck pig because all the texts and voicemails he'd sent since his fiancée has disappeared for the second time had been purposefully ignored, was satisfying. The dickhead realising he'd given away a chunk of money for nothing would also be driving the man to distraction.

It would be gnawing away under the brown hair dye of that bastard's head as he wondered exactly what was happening to the woman he deemed so important. Because of the enforced silence, the turd would imagine all sorts. It was a soothing balm to Zane's psyche.

Or was it because this strange woman who both infuriated and intrigued him, had finally seen the light and was working with him, rather than against him? Had Erin Langley now realised it was in her best interests to play things *his* way?

He wasn't sure, but neither was he stupid. Erin may be toeing the line, which made things less frantic, not to mention less dangerous, but the unknown reasons for her sudden change of direction only strengthened his urge to discover what was *really* going on behind the scenes. What was so not right with her life with Flame to make her agree to work with him?

But try as he might, Zane couldn't help but let the experience of being out of a grungy living environment, along with a short break from worrying about what was going on with his firm, make him uncharacteristically relaxed.

Perhaps it was a combination of *all* of those things that, when seeing the genuine joy on Erin's face as she looked around the little cottage, had been the final thing resulting in him doing something completely out of character.

And going to the pub was what he felt like doing. *The food shopping could wait.*

Plus, he was enjoying this pint. It was the first decent one he'd supped since getting out of nick. It was lovely, even if he was confined to just having the one being as he was the one with the wheels.

'I wouldn't have put you down as a steak and chips girl,' he remarked as Erin sliced off a piece of the perfectly cooked sirloin on her plate.

'You've no idea how long I've yearned for a steak like this,' she said, shielding her full mouth as she spoke. 'It beats smoked salmon and olives any day!'

Dabbing her mouth with a napkin, Erin drained her third glass of wine and looked around the pub. A cosy and quaint 16th century inn - all dark wood, large fireplaces and low ceilings. A universe away from the soulless, sterile wine bars and fancy restaurants she'd been forced to frequent for the last six years.

But she wouldn't think about *Anthony* or anything to do with him just now. She'd grasp this unexpected slice of freedom and experience life as a 'normal' person for once - as much as it could be with the present company...

Soon her life would be even more removed from normality, so providing she didn't focus too carefully, she could pretend that life was good for a couple of hours.

She would need to bottle the feeling when it became all too apparent that life wasn't good and never could be.

Zane studied Erin as she ate. He'd been wrong about her. She was nothing like Flame. The complete opposite, in fact. Neither was she the demure and upper-class persona depicted in those photographs. She was a wildcat, make no mistake, but with the addition of loving simple things.

She confused the hell out of him.

Erin felt self-conscious knowing Zane was staring at her. And much to her horror, it was making her shy. *Nervous, even...* 'Why are you looking at me like that?'

'Like what?' A lazy smile tugged at the corner of Zane's mouth.

'Like you're studying me.' With rising dread, Erin realised her cheeks were burning.

'If you must know, I was thinking how beautiful you are when you don't scowl.' Zane's eyes twinkled with rarely seen mischief. 'Do you realise you've only scowled four times today. It makes such a difference. It must be the country air.'

Erin laughed, mainly to hide her embarrassment. *Zane Morelli thought her beautiful?* Why did this make her stomach flip with anticipation? 'The country air must be having the same effect on you because you haven't been snarly all day!'

'Snarly? What sort of a word is that?'

Zane laughed – a throaty laugh and one that rumbled through Erin's body making all her hairs stand on end. She'd never heard this man laugh – not *genuinely*. Not until now.

It suddenly hit her that this conversation was verging on the edge of flirting! What was she thinking? She groped for her glass to deflect from how exposed she felt.

Averting her eyes from the man, who she admitted held a powerful pull at levels she didn't quite understand or *want* to understand, Erin concentrated back on the delicious dinner in front of her, her mouth now worryingly dry.

Zane continued watching Erin. She fascinated him. It was a surreal experience. How could someone who had been sleeping with Flame, trigger anything but revulsion?

He hastily shook the wisp of thoughts of that man from his mind. For now, at least. However strange and unexpected it was, he was actually *enjoying* Erin Langley's company. And no matter which way he tried, there was no telling his cock that it shouldn't go there.

Adjusting himself slightly, he smiled. 'So, tell me - did you grow up around here? What do your family do?'

Erin's fork paused halfway to her mouth, the make-believe world she'd cleverly manufactured to last a couple of hours shattering around her. Who the person sitting opposite her at this cosy table in this quaint little pub really was, hit her between the eyes - like seeing the big picture with a fresh outlook.

Horror descended once again. *He had the cheek to ask*

about her family? The one he'd ruined? The ones he'd killed?
Her throat constricted as she reached for her glass of wine.

Keep it together, she told herself, mentally reinstating what
this was all for. 'I didn't come from around here. There's not
much else to say, really. My life isn't very interesting.' Draining
her glass, she reached for the bottle. 'My parents are dead.' *Like
you didn't know...*

Zane faltered. 'Oh, I'm sorry to hear that.'

'Yeah, course you are,' Erin muttered under her breath.

Frowning, Zane took a pull of his pint. *There it was again.*
That flash of something that was now hidden back under the
mask. That was clearly a bad subject to raise, but then, hardly
surprising, if her parents were both dead.

Erin's brain span. She'd overreacted and she shouldn't
have. *Stop it. Do not react.* She stared at the now empty bottle
of wine.

Zane got to his feet. 'Fancy another?'

Erin smiled tightly. 'Yeah, why not.'

She watched Zane make his way to the bar. She'd been
stupid thinking she could go for a meal with a man who had
held her hostage for the past week and murdered her father. It
was insane. How long could she keep this up for?

All sentiments of playing the game unravelled as the pent-
up frustration and stress of the past few days, along with the rest
of her life, began reacting with the alcohol.

TWENTY FIVE

ANTHONY WAS fast drowning from his inability to hold a conversation without the low-down Erin tweaked from these people's wives. This alone made him angrier with her disobedience and absence.

He resented his lifelong struggle with social skills. It made many aspects of doing business such as this, difficult, and he hated it even more that he required Erin for it.

Tonight was making him look like a bloody dolt in front of the people he needed to impress.

His fingers curled around his mobile phone, wanting to crush the plastic casing and watch the components within scatter to the floor.

It was a second-by-second battle to stop from refreshing his text messages, only to find nothing new, or dialling his voicemail to get the same automated message: *'no new messages...'*

But doing this distracted him from what he already found unbearable. He'd never had the first clue how to engage in the mindless, yet expected prattle of general conversation that came naturally for everyone else. But after too many emails questioning his unusual absence from the events he and Erin usually vigorously and unfailingly attended, he had little choice but to go to at least one of these latest gatherings alone.

So, why had he not heard anything back from Zane?

And why had he not received further confirmation and instructions from Marco? He'd made it clear what would happen if no one sorted this out. He wasn't waiting around forever, just to let his world come crashing down around him.

He needed Erin back and Morelli out of his goddamned life *now.*

'I was beginning to think you'd jumped ship with my information and bond portfolio!' Jeffery, Jocelyn's husband, slapped Anthony on the back.

Anthony stared at the man in front of him - far too close in his personal space. Resisting the urge to step back or bark at him to move away, he instead weighed up whether the man was joking or whether it was indeed a veiled insinuation.

There was a smile on Jeffery's face, but it might not be real. How could he tell? If Jeffery's ugly dog of a wife had been rattling on about being unable to get hold of Erin, then all sorts of things could have been speculated. 'Why would I run off with your bond portfolio? I'm investing it for you, aren't I?' Anthony countered. *Or was Jeffery saying he'd changed his mind and was moving to another adviser?*

Sweat trickled along the collar of his light blue shirt as the tic just below his right eye went into overdrive.

Jeffery frowned. 'Hey, I was only joking! I meant because you didn't go to the Copthorne the other night and Jocelyn said th…'

'What else have people said?' Anthony barked, seeing Jeffery's face dropped in surprise. *Stop it. You're making it worse*, he told himself. It was no use. He could feel the twitching starting. He was going into freefall. *Blast Erin and her stupid, stupid games. If she'd sided with Morelli, then…*

'Who's Morelli?'

Anthony's head swung to Jeffery, realising he'd been staring up at the ceiling, instead of looking at the man. 'What?'

'You said something about siding with Morelli? Who's that?' Jeffery pressed. 'Are you okay, Anthony?'

Feeling heat barrelling along his neck, Anthony wanted to scream. *Shit. He'd said that about Morelli out loud?*

He tried his best to block out the cacophony of clanging and high-pitched squealing that only he alone could hear. *And no, he wasn't okay.* 'Sorry, sorry. I'm very tired and still not one hundred percent after being ill.'

He looked around feverishly. He had to get out of here. Everyone was looking at him. *Shit. Shit!*

Seeing the concerned, yet suspicious look on Jeffery's face, Anthony's pulse drummed harder. He tried to pull a smile into place but couldn't make it slide into the correct position. He knew it must look like a frozen grimace. He should say something witty - something funny to neutralise his mistake, but he couldn't think of anything.

Suddenly, his mobile buzzed and Anthony held it up like it was covered with nuclear waste. 'Excuse me. I'd best see who that is. It might be Erin. I didn't want to leave her tonight, as she's still not at all well.'

After this, when he finally got his hands on her, the bitch wouldn't ever be well again.

Racing from the room, Anthony turned into the corridor, his sweaty fingers fighting to enter the screen lock.

He pressed the button to display the text message:

U want your missus back then come and get her

Anthony's pulse thundered in his temples. *Zane...*

Where was backup? Should he reply or call the number Marco's man had contacted him on?

• • • •

ERIN SLAMMED THE corkscrew down on the wooden countertop and leaned against the kitchen unit for support.

Zane raised his eyebrows. Returning from the bar in the pub

with a fresh bottle of wine, he'd been greeted by Erin with a face sourer than hell itself, requesting they returned to the house. She'd even had her jacket on ready.

He didn't proclaim to understand what had changed so dramatically, but he was damned if he'd got the time or energy to put up with histrionics. *This* was why he hadn't got saddled into anything serious with a woman. They were too unpredictable.

Especially this one...

If Erin no longer wanted to make this unfortunate set-up less uncomfortable, then he wouldn't make the effort either. Not that he'd particularly had gone out of his way to do that. Strangely, he'd found the unfamiliar feelings since the estate agents required little prompting. However, with the return of her hostile attitude, that had now dissolved.

Oh well, back to business. Better now than later.

He nodded to the bottle of wine in Erin's hand. 'I'd save that until after you've made the call.'

Erin's hand paused on the corkscrew she'd picked up for the second time, noticing the moody and aggressive look was back behind Zane's eyes. *That was fine with her.*

Her resentment swelled. If she wanted another drink, then she'd bloody well have one. That bottle of wine in the pub was nowhere near enough to quell the avalanche of crushing emotions swamping her. 'What call?'

Zane pulled Erin's mobile from his pocket and tapped in the entry code. 'The call to your boyfriend... It's time to action the bullshit messages he's being leaving since yesterday.'

Ice flooded Erin's veins. *He wanted her to call Anthony now?*

Witnessing the waves of anger and panic crashing over Erin's face, Zane shrugged dismissively. 'I've purposely ignored him, so he'll be spitting chips by now. I know what he's like, so it's time to up the ante.'

Turning her back, Erin stabbed the corkscrew into the bottle of white wine, her fingers shaking as she wrenched the metal handle. The base of the bottle skidded along the work surface and she steadied it before it fell from the surface to smash on the quarry-tiled floor.

This was all a joke to Zane, wasn't it? Revenge because he'd been the one to go to prison.

Both Anthony *and* Zane were guilty of their part in what they'd done, yet their argument was all because one had taken advantage of the other. *Pathetic!*

Pulling the cork from the bottle with a pop, Erin yanked it from the spiral thread. She swung around, glowering at Zane's expression. 'Why would you know so much about what Anthony's like? Exactly how do you know him so well, being as you've never told me?'

Let's see what he makes of that, she thought, the alcohol and anger diluting her rationality. *Let's see what lies he spews this time...*

With heat flushing over her chest, she stumbled forward. 'You've always been vague about why you hate Anthony so, apart from the, "he's done something to me", rubbish, so why don't you tell me exactly what that is?' *Because she knew. Oh yes, she knew.* 'I'm sick of you acting like the wronged fucking party!'

Zane eyed Erin warily, the corkscrew in her hand the centre of his concentration. A nerve twitched in his neck as irritation bubbled. 'I could say the same about you... Why would *you* be so eager to help me bring in the man you profess to love?'

His face cracked into a sneer. 'Despite giving you the benefit of the doubt and that you've tried to attack me twice, you're the one having a hissy fit!' Eyes blazing, he stepped forward. 'Didn't he give you enough spends for a new dress? Is that it? Is that enough to push you over the edge? Fuck's sake! Whoever you are, Erin Langley, *you're* the one acting hard done by. You don't know the first thing about that! You're more unstable than a...'

'*I'm* acting hard done by?' Erin saw red. She'd had enough of this bullshit.

This man had the audacity to say she didn't know what it was like to suffer? What the hell did he know about the things she'd endured to take revenge on others' decisions? The decisions *his* chain of events had forced her to take?

Tears of rage brewed in her eyes and she burnt them away with the power of thought alone. There was no way this lying monster would witness her cry.

'Fuck you!' she screamed, blind to everything, including what she'd set her mind to do. She lunged towards Zane with the corkscrew. *She was ending this here.*

Zane blocked the oncoming corkscrew aimed at his neck. Gripping Erin's forearm, he held her at bay which required a lot more force than he'd expected. Manhandling her against the stone kitchen wall, he pushed her against it using his body. 'What the fuck is the matter with you?'

His hand tightened on Erin's arm to make her relinquish the grip of the pointed spiral she was determined to dig into his jugular. 'Sort yourself the fuck out!' he hissed. 'I haven't got time for hormonal ramblings. Make the fucking call, otherwise I'll...'

'Otherwise you'll *what*? Get off me, you fucking lunatic!' With wild eyes, Erin pushed with all her might against Zane's rock-solid body and resisted the pain his fingers inflicted on the muscles of her arm.

She wouldn't drop the corkscrew. *Wouldn't.* She'd kill him now. Anthony would have to wait. In fact, he could just fuck off. She didn't care about money anymore, nor marrying him to ensure her back remained clean. It was pointless. She'd happily go to jail. She just wanted this to stop. She was done. 'You want Anthony that much, *you* phone him!'

Knowing his body held Erin in check, Zane grabbed her under the jaw, his cold eyes penetrating. 'I *do* want him that much. I fucking hate him and I'll have him!' *But not as much as he wanted her - this crazy chick.*

Ignoring the pain in her jaw, Erin wrenched her hand from Zane's grip and stabbed the corkscrew into his muscular thigh.

'You won't have him. Anthony's *mine*. As are you! Have you any idea how long I've hated you?'

As Zane stepped back, pain twisting his face, Erin swung the corkscrew again, this time, the newly-opened space between them allowing a clear aim at his neck.

Deflecting the dangerous point as it closed in, it was worth taking the jab to his hand in order to twist the tool from her fingers.

With blood trickling from his thigh and now his hand, he slammed her back up against the wall, the corkscrew now in his possession. His eyes glittered with rage. 'Fucked that up, didn't you?' he spat, the urge to kill this woman as powerful as the need to rip the clothes from her body and possess her right here, right now.

Erin refused to drop her gaze from those piercing cold eyes. If she allowed her line of sight to move to his mouth...

Heat pooled with the memory of his lips on hers.

No! She should have pulled a knife from the block when she had the chance, but it was too late now. If she couldn't take Anthony or Zane's life, then she was better off dead. 'Go on then, kill me!' she screamed, her voice splintered with pain. 'Kill me, like you killed my father, you scarred-up piece of shit! Do you worst. I don't care!'

With one last ditch attempt, her fingers clawing towards his eyes, she lunged for Zane's face. He wasn't going to stare into her soul any longer.

Seeing the base hatred, Zane quickly regained control and restrained Erin's flailing hands as he processed her words. *Killed her father?*

The corkscrew clattered to the floor. *He didn't know what the fuck was going on here, but this wasn't working.* 'You're fucking crazy! I haven't killed your father! I've never killed a woman before either, but this time it looks like I'll have no choice...'

'Still denying everything, you son of a bitch?' Erin roared. She'd blown her cover now. She could say what she liked. It mattered not. *It was over. She'd lost.* 'The whole lot of your shitty firm killed my father by what you all did - including Anthony. However, don't forget it was only *you* who slit his throat!'

Unflinching, Zane pulled Erin away from the wall and dragged her arms behind her as he frogmarched her from the kitchen. The action of her being turned away from him helped to conceal his shock.

Erin Langley was David Masters' daughter?
Holy shit!

TWENTY SIX

BILL PUFFED HIS WAY up the many flights of stairs to Marco's penthouse apartment. It would have to be today the lifts broke, wouldn't it?

Yeah, yeah, the electricians were working on it, so the concierge said, but that was no help to his bloody legs! Not when he'd received a garbled message from Marco half an hour ago asking him to come over immediately.

Or something like that...

The man sounded so mashed it was difficult to work out the exact words from the slurred-together jumble in the voicemail.

Bill grabbed hold of a gleaming banister to aid hauling his hefty frame up the next flight of stairs. He looked up into the rest of the never-ending stairwell with trepidation. *Christ, his legs would be buggered after this.*

The last thing he needed was for his boss to be still two sheets to the wind after whatever mess he'd got his head in last night.

For once, Bill had cried off attending the latest after show party Marco insisted on, after filming wrapped up for V*irgin Night*. It was more important to return that phone call. Marco would think so too, once he knew what it was about, considering he'd been adamant in getting things lined up for his problem of a brother.

As always, Marco liked delegating everything to the rest of them - namely *him*, whilst he concentrated on getting lashed and coked up. Yet he'd be the first to kick off if things weren't arranged when his brain finally remembered what they were supposed to be doing.

Not to mention the urgency of it all.

Sometimes, no - *half* of the time, Marco switched off his brain about taking in how serious things were. And he was certainly doing that at the moment about the Zane situation and what the implications would be if they didn't follow through with what they'd planned from the start.

Living in a drug and drink-induced escape was all very well, but it was *his* head on the chopping block if Zane returned to London, as well as Marco's. And that, Bill didn't want.

When it suited him, Marco might dream up bullshit and dampen the urgency down within his own mind, but *he* couldn't.

Now he'd got the news they'd been waiting for, Bill needed the nod from Marco. He'd sort the rest. He just hoped the bloke was capable of a serious conversation.

Finally reaching the top floor, Bill trudged along to the front door of the only apartment on this entire level. He pressed the gold doorbell, hearing the brash tune of *Dixie* ring out from within. Marco had thought it funny swapping out the original door chime for this one, but it was hideous. *Did he think he was in the Dukes of Hazzard?*

And that was Marco all over. Everything was either rage-inducing or hilarious. Sometimes the same thing swapped from one end of the scale to the other within minutes.

Getting no response from the naff doorbell, Bill frowned and keyed in the code within the wall recess to release a sliding panel. Entering a further code into a small strongbox within, he twisted the dial and released a little door to retrieve the spare key.

This was an idea he'd suggested to Marco in the event it was required. And it was required *now* because there wasn't time to mess about.

Opening the door, Bill let himself in. 'Marco!' he called, stomping along the hallway. *Where the bloody hell was he?* 'You here? You asked me t...'

'Up here!' Marco leant unsteadily over the galleried landing of the split-level landing above.

Bill looked up, his face creasing with irritation as Marco staggered back towards the bedroom. By the looks of it, the man was still off his head. *This was not good.*

His eyes scanned the destruction of the living area as he made his way to the stairs. Beer cans and bottles were littered everywhere. There were even fag ends stubbed out on the floor. Marco needed to get a grip. He'd lost control on his drug intake and that was no good to anyone.

Taking the stairs to the bedrooms above, Bill gritted his teeth. More bloody steps... *He'd need callipers at this rate.*

'I got word last night and I'm waiting for a message this morning to confirm the address,' Bill shouted. He rounded the half-twist at the top of the stairs and headed towards the main bedroom, guessing that was where Marco was, no doubt nursing his head. 'Providing I receive it, we'll need to head north today. A meet's been arranged for... Holy shit!'

Stopping stock still in the doorway of the immense main bedroom, Bill gaped at the surreal scene, bile fast rising up his throat. Dragging his eyes from the grotesque sight, he stared at Marco. 'What the fu...'

'She needs a doctor.' Marco jerked his head dismissively at the woman spreadeagled on the bed, the bloody mess between her legs making it impossible to tell what was what.

Despite his normal stoicism for brutal violence and gore, Bill retched, unable to rationally understand what his eyes were seeing. *What the fuck had this lunatic done? It looked like the woman had a chainsaw put to her privates. Oh Christ...*

Gagging again, Bill staggered to the French windows, his

big fingers fumbling with the patio doors leading to the balcony.

Promptly remembering the 'accident' that other woman had met with, he rapidly changed his mind and instead turned to Marco casually cutting a fresh line of coke on the dressing table. 'What the fuck have you done?'

'*Me*?' Marco raised an eyebrow. 'It's what she wanted.' He flapped his hand in the direction of the horribly injured woman - the very same woman who'd starred in his most recent film. 'We were brainstorming for new movie plots. It was her idea.'

A low laugh escaped his mouth. 'I think she's got the fear that Lisa will take the star roles once we're married. She was trying to outdo ideas.' He bent to snort the line. 'You'd be amazed how many of these birds fall over themselves at the moment to suggest plots they reckon only they can handle!'

Bill's mouth flapped open and then shut as he forced his eyes back to the woman. 'But... but she's... Christ! What did y...' Stopping, his eyes fell on what he guessed had inflicted the horrific and undoubtedly permanent injuries on the woman's genitals. At the sight of the discarded screwdriver and a claw hammer covered in blood and bits of flesh, his hand flew to his mouth. 'Fuck!'

'Hardcore, eh? Still, it worked a treat!' Marco grinned. 'I'm just gutted we didn't film it. Ripping open a tart's cunt will make a killing on the film rentals. But you'd better give that quack a call to sort this one out.'

'What?' Bill squeaked, unable to drag his eyes from the mutilated woman. 'Is she even alive? Christ, Marco! How do you think this looks? Jesus!'

'Ah, fuck's sake!' Marco pulled himself to his feet and staggered over to the bed. He poked the woman's pale face, getting a weak moan in return. 'See? She's fine!'

Folding his arms, he stared at Bill. 'What's the matter? You some kind of fucknuts? All she needs is a once over with one of them gyny... gyno... The doctors that deal with women's bits will sort this out. Fuck me, it's hardly a big deal! No worse than having a kid!'

Bill shook his head in despair. He'd had three kids with his ex-missus and her nether regions never once looked like *that*. Surely someone would flag this up as not right.

'Go on!' Marco roared. 'What are you waiting for? I can't find the quack's fucking number, that's why I called you. Just sort it out and quit flapping, like an old mare!'

Reluctantly locating the number, Bill slammed his mobile down on the dressing table and used Marco's landline to make the call. He was fucked if he was calling this in from his own phone!

Jesus Christ. Marco was sick in the head! This would take some explaining, not to mention the mother of all fucking payouts.

• • • •

HAVING WOKEN in the same uncomfortable position she'd eventually gone to sleep in last night, Erin was sure her shoulder was ripped from its socket.

Now Zane had untied her from where she'd been manacled to the bed yet again, she rubbed her hands up and down her arms to regain feeling and detract from the pain. Every muscle felt like they'd been stripped out, stretched and shoved back in different places.

Manacled to the bed - held prisoner once more... Just in a different building. But it was hardly surprising, considering what she'd done last night.

Erin shivered with cold, helplessness and defeat. She'd done this to herself. Why, oh why had she lost sight of things? Why had she blurted out what she'd promised herself she wouldn't?

Her eyes darted to the bedroom door as it opened, quickly looking away as Zane ventured in, wearing nothing but a towel around his hips.

Her throat constricted as she concentrated on something other than his muscular torso as he strode across the room to fetch a pair of jeans from his holdall.

Aside from her own heartbeat, the silence was deafening.

Erin dared to peek out from under her lowered lashes and watched Zane with his back to her, drop the towel to pull on his jeans.

And *that* was the problem.

Enjoying the evening last night; enjoying his company - *that man's* company; the way the conversation had turned flirty from both sides...

That's what had sparked the crazy, over-defensive reaction to bring her entire plans crashing down around her ears. That she'd seen him as something other than *Zane Morelli* had knocked her for six.

It was only the question about her family which had been the trigger to force the harsh truth back into her stupid brain.

The suffocating guilt of allowing herself to slip and see him as a *man*, rather than the psycho who had ruined her life had, coupled with the alcohol, tripped her down the path of reacting in a way to ruin everything.

Busy fighting the unanswerable argument in her head, it had been Zane's demand to call Anthony again which pushed her over the edge of the precipice she'd been teetering on.

Erin closed her eyes in despair, needing to blank Zane from the room as the electricity and magnetic pull of his presence closed the walls in and crushed her from all angles.

Why had she lost sight of what she was doing? He'd never trust her now. *Never.*

And that wasn't just because she'd attempted to attack him again, but because he now knew who she was.

She could have achieved everything she'd aimed for. Now all she'd succeeded in doing was making the grief, misery and every single hated second of her life with Anthony Walker an utter waste.

And for what?

Now she'd lost. Lost it *all*.

In fact, she was amazed that she was still breathing. Zane said he'd have to kill her and yet she was still here... *Why?*

Unless his plan was now to kill both her and Anthony at the same time?

Erin screwed her eyes shut harder and for the first time, real panic swirled. She couldn't die alongside Anthony. Dying was one thing, but dying next to *him...*

No! She wouldn't!

'Come on.'

Zane's gruff voice made Erin jerk her head up so sharply she banged it on the wall. Her eyes flicked open to see him standing over her with his jacket on, his face set like stone.

Was this where he killed her? Perhaps he'd do her the decency of making it separate? Maybe she wouldn't be dispatched alongside the other most hated person in her life?

Despite the hopelessness, Erin felt a fresh surge of resentment. Why the hell was she glibly accepting Zane had the right to kill her just because she knew what he'd done and who he was?

It was reasonable to want vengeance for what he'd taken from her, but his barefaced cheek of denying his actions and treating her like she'd betrayed *him* was unbelievable!

He really thought that by saying he hadn't killed her father somehow made it all right? Like she'd believe it?

Christ! Why was she acting bloody grateful for the bonus of dying alone, rather than with Anthony?

She wasn't grateful at all.

This injection of renewed fury was just what Erin needed to free her from the debilitating sense of defeat.

Glaring at Zane, she wrapped her arms around herself defensively. 'I can tell you right now that if you're planning on killing me, it won't happen without a fight!'

'You never give up, do you?' Zane dragged Erin from the bed. 'I *should* kill you, yes, but like I said last night, I've never killed a woman and don't intend to start now, even if that said woman keeps trying to kill *me!*'

'What exactly do you expect?' Erin hissed, skittering across the wooden floor, fighting to keep her footing as she was pulled by her wrist.

Grabbing her by the shoulders, Zane slammed Erin up against the door. 'I expect you to help me and help yourself at the same time, that's what! You need to see the wood for the trees, love. Why the fuck do you think I want to kill your boyfriend, eh?' His eyes darkened with anger. 'He set me up! *He's* the one you want in relation to killing your father and robbing his money, not me!'

Erin froze, cold seeping into her even though Zane's fingers pressing into her shoulders radiated hot embers over her skin. *Anthony was a sad, self-obsessed freak, interested only in numbers and business kudos. He might be a control freak, but a killer, he was not.* 'Don't be ridiculous! It wasn't him!'

'Really?' Dropping his grasp of Erin's shoulders, Zane took her wrist once more and pulled her towards the stairs. 'Are you so sure? Work it out. If you know so much about everything, doesn't it cross your mind that's what he *wanted* it to look like? Why the fuck do you think I ended up in nick? Because of fake evidence! *His* fake evidence.'

'*Fake* evidence!' Erin snorted. 'I don't know about that… But yeah, I knew he'd given over evidence, being as I watched him hand everything over to your lawyer that got you *rightly* locked up!'

Zane stopped, his foot hovering over the top step. 'You were in court?' *That's where the initial jolt of recognition stemmed from?*

'Of course I was there, although I looked a bit different six years ago! Why wouldn't I want to witness my father's killer get put behind bars? You're fucking disgusting, Morelli! Your firm was on good terms with my fathers, yet y…'

'Wait! You saw that cunt hand evidence to *my* brief?' Zane knew Flame had set him up, but handing phony evidence to his own brief? 'You're sure it was my brief and not the Crown's?'

'I watched you all long enough to know who was who, so yeah, it was *yours*. And from what I saw, Anthony got a nice payout for it too,' Erin scoffed.

Zane's eyes narrowed. 'You're lying.'

'Whatever.' Erin shrugged. Zane Morelli could think what he liked. She knew what she'd seen and didn't give a shit whether he believed it or not. 'Do me a favour - stop denying everything. It makes you look like a cock!'

Snarling, Zane continued down the stairs, his hand still firmly around Erin's wrist. She could be playing him - yet another manipulative trick in her arsenal to fuck him over, the sly bitch.

She must be on in on this with Flame, she *had* to be. But whether she was or not, one thing he would ensure came out of this before it ended, was that she would learn and *believe* her arsehole of a boyfriend was the one who killed her father.

However greedy and manipulative this stunning woman was, by the way she'd reacted last night, her father had been very important to her. Whatever she had going with Flame and whatever cash she hoped to reap from it, he was pretty certain she'd be unable to gloss over the fact that the man she was due to marry was the one who had dragged the knife across her father's throat.

But this also underlined more questions of his own...

Marco had paid thousands for the services of that brief, plus additional bonuses giving the man incentive to push for a lesser sentence.

However, Zane had personally never liked the guy. Each time he'd pushed for the appeal date to be brought forward, the brief had dragged his feet, always giving some kind of excuse. That's why he'd eventually fired the tosser and brought in the services of another.

And yes, he'd kept this from Marco because his brother would have had a fit, saying he'd already spent thousands so why pay another?

But was there another reason?

TWENTY SEVEN

PICKING UP HIS MOBILE, Anthony tapped in the address he'd received last night via text. Pressing send, he raised his gaze to his receptionist standing in the doorway of his fishbowl office.

If Anthony's stony face could be translated into inflicting physical harm, then Maisie would be seeking immediate medical attention.

As it was, the look in his eyes made her contemplate, not for the first time, whether she'd be better off seeking alternative employment. Her boss's behaviour and general attitude towards her was affecting her sleep. Consistently treading on eggshells wasn't doing anything for her nerves and the uncomfortableness it provoked caused her to forget things; to slip up and make mistakes.

Today, she'd even put the internal mail in the incorrect pigeonholes, earning her a collection of snotty remarks and even a rather nasty e-mail from Shawn in Accounts.

Anthony Walker's demeanour had never been what she'd class as 'great', but this past week it had been *unbearable*. She couldn't do anything right and it had worsened since she'd seen his fiancée disappear with the man Anthony said was her brother.

There had already been much speculation in the break room over Anthony's more-than-usual standoffish behaviour, including his noted absences from events he normally attended without fail. Of course, Maisie hadn't mentioned anything about seeing a dishevelled-looking Erin Langley and that man. It was none of her business. She didn't need further reasons to be glared at, but now she was so on edge she couldn't do her job properly and that was not good.

She hovered in the doorway, loathe to relay this message, but equally loathe not to. If Anthony found out she'd failed to inform him of *anything*, let alone something relating to one of his impending business acquisitions, there would be hell to pay.

'Is there something else?' Anthony barked at the timid woman; aware her loitering presence was gathering inquisitive stares from the main office. 'I've already told you that due to unforeseen circumstances I need to cancel my afternoon appointments.'

Something else Morelli had caused. But despite Marco and his men now being en route from London and the planned meeting tonight, Anthony knew, even with his sterling ability, there was no way he could offer full concentration to anything but what lay ahead.

Aggravating wasn't the word. But after tonight he could get on with things the way he had previously been doing and the way he should have *always* been able to do. This situation should *never* have arisen.

Anthony stared at his mobile, like it was wired to the mains. He hadn't expected a reply to the text. He'd been told last night that if he hadn't sent the address by 10 a.m., then he'd receive a text containing just a question mark. If he didn't receive this, he should take it that the message was received, understood and the arrangements were in place.

He glanced at his watch. 10.06 and no question mark text. *It was on...*

In reality, Anthony should be unnerved that the psycho was

now in possession of an address only a few miles from here, but that Morelli had texted him that address - actually *texted* it to him with an actual time to come and take Erin back into his possession, was insanity.

It just proved the imbecile didn't have a clue. Morelli must have lost most of his semblance during his sojourn at Her Majesty's Pleasure.

But Anthony was glad that tonight was going ahead, otherwise today's meetings had been called off for nothing.

Raising his eyes back to the woman fidgeting in his doorway now wringing her hands, Anthony's mouth formed a thin line. 'Did you hear what I said? I've already told you I needed my appointments for this afternoon cancelled.'

'I-I realise that Mr Walker, sir. I've started rearranging them. Unfortunately, I can't get hold of the 3 o'clock at the moment, but I'll keep trying. The other – the 5 o'clock was less than happy you should requi…'

'Are you trying to wind me up?' Anthony slammed his gold pen down on the desk. 'What exactly do you wish to achieve by making out everyone has such a problem with my rearrangements? I don't expect to have to explain myself to you or anyone!'

'I know, sir! I didn't mean... I...' Maisie's voice trailed off, tears welling in her big blue eyes.

Taking a deep breath, Anthony knitted his fingers. He'd recently read that doing this invoked a sense of calm. That he needed because he couldn't let Morelli's latest stunt backfire further on his business.

He forced his mouth into something resembling a cold smile. 'Then may I ask why you're still standing there?' He gestured at the paperwork on his desk. 'There are things I need to tie up before I leave, so if I could just get on with it?'

'I... erm...' Maisie did a strange mini dance on the spot, contemplating whether it was more sensible to leave this next part until Anthony returned tomorrow, but then thought better of it. 'It's just I thought you'd want to know that Mr Clarknett called... Simon Clarknett from the Gilded Hotel Group?'

'Yes, yes, I know who he is!'

'Well, he's, erm... he's cancelled golf on Thursday. 'He's also decided to... erm... to use another firm to...'

'*What*?' The squealing immediately started within Anthony's head.

'Erm... Mr Clarknett is dispensing with... erm... I suggested he spoke to you about this, but he refused and...' The words tumbled from Maisie's mouth before she could stop herself. Her fingers trembled harder underneath the sheaf of paper she clutched as she searched Anthony's face for signs he was about to blame her for his latest lost customer.

Anthony wanted to punch Maisie in the face but knew that wasn't socially acceptable. Especially now every pair of eyes from the main office were burning into him.

So, Clarknett, the supercilious bastard, had binned off his firm? How he wished he'd stuck with his first email and told the guy to fuck off.

Something *else* Zane Morelli was responsible for.

Instead of exploding, Anthony nodded calmly in Maisie's direction. *Morelli would pay tonight*. It didn't bring back his deal with the Gilded Hotels Group, but there would be plenty more where that came from once Erin was back in situ. 'Okay, thanks for letting me know.'

Maisie hovered in the doorway as Anthony returned to his paperwork, unsure whether she'd just hallucinated his lack of reaction. She quickly decided her best option was to propel herself back in the direction of her reception desk, rather than allow him to change his mind.

Anthony only raised his eyes after he was sure Maisie had gone and none of the other ghouls he employed were still staring at him like an exhibit.

Half an hour to wrap things up here and then he'd go home, have a shower and get his mind ready for the arrival of the people who would put his life back to normal again.

· · · ·

ZANE'S BLOOD thundered in his ears as he pulled Erin's protesting figure up the pretty garden path towards the outbuilding. Her squawking and wailing were driving him to distraction. He fought to keep his thoughts in line as his brain swirled with the information he'd learnt.

Oh, he knew Flame had been the one behind those fake testimonies as last-ditch evidence. He knew because the firm had gone to great lengths to discover which of their members had sold out the Morelli heir. But what had his own lawyer got to do with it?

This sparked thoughts off at tangents down roads he was reluctant to go. They pointed in directions he was reticent to even *think* of, let alone act on.

But as much as he didn't like the implications, *could* it be a possibility that his own brief had been working against him throughout? If this were true, how had this been missed by Marco and the rest of the firm? They'd had more to do with the man than he ever had.

Zane would never forget that night he'd been locked up.

Every single member of the firm present when the police smashed their way into the Morelli headquarters, including his dear father, had watched, horrified. Word on the grapevine usually alerted them to any up and coming trouble, yet it had been silent, making them helpless to foresee it.

None of what happened was expected. *No one* had guessed anyone would go against Giuseppe Morelli's clear instructions that David Masters was to be left alone.

They'd heard from Giuseppe's own mouth there would be no retaliation against the man he'd been on good terms with for forty years. As far as Giuseppe was concerned, the bad-mouthing of the Morellis that Masters was accused of was an out of control rumour. He hadn't believed it to be true and was adamant there should be no reprisals.

Admittedly, both Zane and Marco had been unhappy with their father's decision. In their opinion, there was no smoke without fire and believed Masters should be pulled up over it.

Marco especially. He always chomped at the bit to avenge *anyone* sullying the Morelli's good name.

But Giuseppe's word was sacred. Everyone adhered to it. Apart from *him* - or at least that was what the firm believed. The bullshit Flame manufactured - the list of witness statements attesting he'd been heard on numerous occasions boasting he would kill Masters for insulting his family, along with the damning selection of character witnesses stating his fiery and uncontrollable temper had seen to his downfall. That the eldest Morelli son was known to be a hot-headed lunatic, possessing the strength, power and, in this instance, *incentive*, to feel an honour murder was well-founded had been his undoing.

Zane's jaw clenched as the unwanted flashback of hearing this evidence presented whilst he had one foot out of the dock, about to walk away a free man, filtered into his brain. Circumstantial, it may have been, but it was enough to sway the court's decision to send him down for a long stretch.

Flame had manufactured the whole thing to conceal that *he'd* been the one who had gone against the firm, killed Masters and robbed the money. He'd spotted the opportunity and bloody taken it.

The quietest were always the least suspected and the most convincing...

Well, Flame had certainly succeeded in convincing the rest of the firm of Zane's guilt too – until doing a runner exposed him for what he was.

But by then it was too late.

Zane's fingers traced the ragged scar on his right cheek that remained testimony to what Flame had managed to get his own family and firm to believe.

That Giuseppe had died shortly after believing Zane to be a traitor was the worst insult of all. Yet no one had thought to look in Flame's direction until he'd disappeared?

But none of this explained why Marco had lied about taking revenge, rather than telling the truth - that Flame, the bastard who had shafted and betrayed both his brother and firm, was still out there...

And now, if what Erin had said was to be believed, his brief was part of it...?

None of it made sense. None of it at all. But the end would begin tonight. Once Flame had replied to his text last night, like Zane knew he would, it sealed the bastard's fate.

Now the man was in receipt of this address, he would be arriving here of his own volition in a matter of hours...

Zane looked around once more. There wasn't much left to sort in this outhouse ready for the arrival. Once he knew Flame was coming, Zane had set out most of what was needed, but he wanted to be here, ready and waiting with plenty of time to spare.

Flame knew this meeting would eventually happen. Stalling it only delayed the inevitable. He might have thought he'd escaped - and got away with it. Or perhaps, since there had been no retaliation from anyone after so long, believed things had moved on?

Zane's brows knitted. *He* hadn't moved on. He hadn't forgotten either. *He never would.*

Although it seemed odd, it sort of explained why Marco had lied. It all stemmed from his brother being too ashamed to admit he'd let things slide.

He shook away the underlying nagging doubt and forming guilt over the premise of even considering there could be any other reason. Zane knew more than anyone how erratic Marco's decisions could be.

At least, *used* to be. It was a long time since Zane had seen anyone under normal circumstances. Anyway, it was the most logical explanation, but it still didn't stop him from worrying what he might find once he returned to London. Marco was always more interested in women, excess and mindless violence than running a firm. Had his brother let everything run into the ground?

What happened if he got back to find Marco had ballsed everything up? Maybe there wasn't even a firm to speak of anymore... Would that explain why his brother was in his apartment? Perhaps he had nowhere else to go...?

The prospect of their father's hard work having gone down the drain made Zane's blood run cold but shook the sense of foreboding away. This was speculation. He'd tie himself up in knots thinking like this.

Whatever had happened or hadn't happened was because of the bastard due to arrive shortly and knowing what was to befall him was some comfort.

Throwing open the heavy wooden door of the brick outbuilding, Zane dragged Erin inside and flicked on the light, her constant harping scratching the inside of his already fractured brain.

He felt like smashing the place to fucking pieces. 'Will you shut the fuck up?' he roared, his eyes alight.

Confident there were no tools or anything this crazy bitch might stick in him, he dropped his grip of Erin's arm and watched her eye him warily. 'Praying a grand piano will miraculously fall out of the air onto my head?' Zane didn't even find his own sarcasm pleasurable any longer.

He was sick of this. Sick of not knowing what was going on. Sick of *her*. Sick of feeling things about Erin Langley that he didn't want. *She was an enemy.* An enemy playing with his fucking head. No one did that and got away with it.

'Being as we've got a couple of hours to spare, we'll take another picture to send to your boyfriend,' he snapped. *She could have a taste of what games could do.*

Erin paled. 'No! You're not humiliating me like that again. I won't let y...'

'Why? Because you can't stand that I know your boyfriend doesn't give a crap and that I made a mistake by picking *you* as a bargaining chip? I should have nicked something he *really* gives a toss about - like his calculator!' Zane sneered. 'Doesn't it pain you shagging the man who killed your father? You must be bloody desperate to whore yourself out to that fucker!'

Seeing the flash of deep-seated pain on Erin's face, Zane

regretted his words. Erin wasn't a whore. She was far from it, but he wanted her to suffer for being the only person in living memory who got under his skin in this way.

'You know nothing about me, Morelli.' Erin's attempt to sound harsh failed, the tinge of hurt exposing her pain.

'After last night, I know more than I did!' Zane sighed. Whatever this woman had done and whether she was party to Flame's plan or not, or whether she made him feel like he couldn't trust himself, he gained no pleasure from scraping the barrel to score points.

Erin felt a sudden compulsion to cry. She was becoming a nervous wreck - lurching between anger and despair, as well as mind-bending confusion over how this beautifully-damaged man set her nerves on fire in ways that could not be justified.

'Why did you change your surname?' Zane asked suddenly. 'Why not your whole name?'

The energy needed to jump to a defence, poured out from Erin like a water through a sieve. Now Morelli knew who she really was, remembering a web of lies for one concocted story after another was futile. 'I had to distance myself from my father's firm. Not that there was anything left of it after what *you* did, but the surname connected me, so it had to go.' Her defiant eyes met Zane's. 'I wanted to be ready.'

Zane smirked as the truth behind Erin's odd relationship with Flame suddenly became clear. *She hadn't been working with that bastard.* 'You've planned this all along, haven't you? Does *Anthony*, as you call him, know who you really are? That as well as me, you're planning on killing him too? You might as well tell me because it will come out in the end.'

'Anyone who is or *was* part of the Morelli firm deserves to die,' Erin hissed. 'You, more than most.'

'If you got things correct, things would be a lot easier!' *Christ, this woman was even more attractive when she faced him off.*

Zane dragged a cabinet away from the wall into the centre of the room, the metal base screeching against the concrete floor.

'Help me finish setting this place up. This is where he will be kept. Now I know that wanker is on your kill list, you've gone up slightly in my estimation. If you stop being such an idiot, I'll change my mind about putting you through another one of those photographs!'

And she hadn't just gone up 'slightly' in his estimation... Knowing that Erin had no intention of being with that tosser in the first place only made him want her more.

Scowling, Erin grabbed the opposite end of the cabinet. Zane Morelli may have worked it out, but if he thought he was off her list and that she'd happily step aside to allow *him* to take Anthony's life, then he had bricks in his head.

TWENTY EIGHT

'NOT NOW!' Marco blocked Bill from entering the open-plan lounge. 'I'm kind of busy.'

The twinkle in Marco's eyes, his hastily done up trousers and untucked shirt, spelt out quite clearly to Bill *exactly* what Marco was busy with. But this couldn't wait. He hadn't expected his boss to ask after the welfare of the woman who had been removed from his bed earlier, but he did need to talk to him about the other big thing in their lives.

The one in the shape of Zane Morelli. 'Look, I need to talk to you ab…'

'Mate,' Marco hissed, pushing himself closer to Bill's large head. 'Lisa's here, yeah?' He jerked his head towards the lounge. 'We're discussing our wedding arrangements, so be a good fella and fuck off, would ya? Give a guy space to plan his nuptials, eh?'

Bill gritted his teeth. 'Don't you remember what I said this morning about Zane? I received the message I was waiting on and now I've got the address. We need to get on the road this very minute!'

Marco looked at Bill blankly, irritation combining with confusion. *Message? Had Bill mentioned a message?*

'Do you not remember?' Bill cried in disbelief. 'Christ, Marco! I came round this morning only to find that bird and now you're sayi...'

'Shh!' Marcus dug his fingernails into Bill's wrist. 'Did you not hear? I said Lisa's here and...'

'Who's this then?'

Bill feigned a smile at the tall, slender and exceptionally voluptuous figure of Lisa Tequila gliding out of the open plan lounge into the hallway.

'Ah! Here she is!' Marco grabbed Hazel around the waist and pulled her possessively against him. 'This is Bill, my right-hand man and Bill, this is Hazel, my gorgeous wife-to-be.'

'Hazel?' Bill blinked. *It was Lisa Tequila.* Anyone who watched their kind of films knew what this stunner looked like.

'Hazel is Lisa's real name,' Marco explained, clocking Bill's confusion. His voice was amicable, but his death stare aimed at Bill spoke the direct opposite. 'Bill's just popped round with some info, but I've already told him we're too busy to discuss trifling matters.'

Bill wanted to nut Marco. Did the guy not take anything on board? 'Yeah, I was just saying I now have the exact address where we can find what we're looking for...' He spoke through clenched teeth, aware Lisa or Hazel - whoever the hell she really was, was scrutinising him. 'You remember, Marco? The address and details in relation to, you know... erm...'

Suddenly, the coke fuzz dissolved in Marco's brain. *Shit. Zane...* He gave Hazel's buttock a squeeze. 'Pop yourself back on the sofa, doll,' he winked. 'I'll just quickly sort this out.'

Hazel's highly arched brows pulled into a perfectly formed frown. 'Now I'm your official fiancée, shouldn't I be kept informed of anything that could affect *me*?'

'Of course,' Marco smiled, concealing the adrenaline now thundering through his veins for altogether different reasons. 'And you *will* be, don't worry about that, but this is nothing to do with anything concerning *us*. It's just about some crap with an overdue invoice.'

Except it was very much to do with her. Or it *would* be, if word got out that Zane was on the loose.

His memory returning, he shot Bill a warning glance. He'd instructed some of his men to go up north to dig on his brother's whereabouts, but no one had gone. Not yet.

Quickly. Think! What had Bill said this morning? Fuck! He couldn't bloody remember. He'd been too hyped over that chick and the hammer.

Was Bill saying that he'd got Zane's *current* location?

Steering Hazel back into the lounge, Marco pulled the door closed, knowing she'd more than likely still be earwigging. 'Are you telling me you know where my brother is?'

Bill nodded. 'Yes, and a meet has been arranged for seven tonight. We need to get on the road now!'

A wide smile split Marco's previously stressed face. 'Then get the van.' Lowering his voice, he nodded towards the lounge. 'I'll find a way to get rid of her. I'll say I'm off to buy a ring or something and then...'

'A *ring*?'

Marco flapped his hand. 'Don't worry about it. Get the required tools and the usual clobber from the lock up and we'll leave shortly.' He rubbed his hands together, a hot knot of excitement balling in his stomach.

This was it! By tonight he would put an end to speculation or risk to his empire. And his marriage. He'd wipe his brother off the map and leave no stones unturned that might come back to haunt him at inopportune moments.

His eyes gleamed. *It was all good. It was all just...*

Standing directly below the doorbell speaker, the tinny sound of *Dixie* caught Marco off guard. He covered his ears as the scratching melody ricocheted around his brain. 'Jesus!' he muttered. 'Is that Sonny? Is he accompanying us?'

'I haven't yet mentioned anyth...'

Marco pushed past Bill and yanked the door open. 'Good timing! We're just about to...Oh!'

'Marco Morelli? We're arresting you under suspicion of

causing grievous bodily harm.' One of the four burly policemen grunted whilst the other officers bundled into the hallway and between them, secured Marco in handcuffs before he'd even had the chance to react. 'You do not have to say anything, but it may harm your defence if you do not mention when questioned, something which you later rely on in court. Anything you do say may be given in evidence.'

Bill's eyes darted from Marco to the policemen. *What the actual fuck?*

'And that also includes you, sir.' Light work was made of securing Bill in handcuffs, the operation made easier by his shell-shocked state. 'Bill Wainwright? You are also under arrest.'

'What the fuck is this?' Marco roared as an officer read Bill his rights, his temporary spell of suspended animation broken. He pulled savagely against the restraints to no avail. 'I demand you release us both this very minute!' *He had to reach that address. He had to deal with his brother before it was too late.*

Hazel barged from the lounge into the hallway. 'What's going on?'

'Don't worry, babe. Everything's fine,' Marco smiled, dampening down his snarl. 'There's been a mistake. It will be sorted out at the station really quickly.'

And it had fucking better be. If this wasn't wrapped up and sorted, along with a grovelling apology from the Old Bill within half a fucking hour, there would be hell to pay.

• • • •

AFTER HER INITIAL MELTDOWN about being dragged into the outhouse, hearing more lies and coming to terms with royally ballsing up her own plan, Erin had calmed down enough to think.

If she worked with Zane - like *really* worked with him, then the fear of him butchering Anthony while she was stuck, unable to step in and do it herself, was no longer suffocating. If she played this ultra-carefully, she could jump in at the last moment and stop that accolade being swept from under her nose.

At least she was still here. Now Zane knew the truth about everything there could be no more losing control.

She would do everything required until the very last minute. All she had to do was steel herself for Anthony's arrival and go from there. But as Zane was planning on bringing and holding Anthony in this outhouse, he could drag the torture out for weeks...

And he was insistent she be present at all times...

Nausea brewed deep within Erin's belly. The prospect of setting eyes on Anthony again at close quarters made her skin crawl. Zane may have worked out she planned to kill Anthony - fine, but the added humiliation of him witnessing for the second occasion - this time in glorious technicolour, how little she meant to her 'fiancé' was additionally insulting.

In fact, it choked her to the point where she could barely breathe.

Not that it bothered her in the slightest what Anthony and Zane Morelli thought. *Did it?*

No.

It was what *she* thought and how she felt about being deemed so thoroughly and utterly pointless that bothered her and her father would turn in his grave if he knew she was being treated this way.

She stared blankly at the wall as if the bare bricks could answer her questions or give her ideas.

Zane trying to convince her that her father's murder was by Anthony's hand, unsettled her. It brought things kept at arms' length back into her mind and made her jittery. And jittery, she didn't need. But she couldn't stop from fixating on how much more horrified her father would have been to discover his firm had folded within weeks of his murder; that his beloved wife had died from a broken heart six months after that, and then his only child had disappeared, removing all traces of his name and association with the firm he'd once been so proud of.

Feeling her breath catch in her throat, Erin controlled it

from escalating into hyperventilation. Doing what she'd done was the only way to achieve revenge. The murders she would soon commit would be for payback, not honour.

Honour, she'd lost trace of many moons ago.

But if her father knew she harboured powerful and unexplainable feelings about the monster who had taken his life, then...

She watched Zane lining up tools on the workbench, no doubt to torture Anthony with. How long would she have to endure being enclosed in here with the two of them before she could strike?

And what else was Zane planning to do?

Spotting a makeshift camp bed rigged up over the other side of the outhouse, her heart crashed loudly in her chest. Were parts of Zane's torture plans to follow through with his original threats? Was he aiming to use what he'd previously threatened to do *in front* of Anthony?

The burn emanating from deep within her at this thought was way more disturbing because it wasn't the burn of dread or horror. *It was the burn of anticipation...*

Panic pooled. But Zane Morelli touching her wouldn't achieve what he wanted. It wouldn't hurt Anthony. Not at all.

All it would achieve was proving she was responsive to Zane's touch. Her traitorous body had already made known that it would let her down. How could she live with herself?

No, no, no. Not her father's murderer.

Erin's chest tightened. Admitting a relentless attraction that she didn't need or want was bad enough, but for Anthony and Zane *himself* to witness it...

Erin's toes would have curled up with crushing shame within her boots were they not so tight.

'Now it's just a question of waiting,' Zane remarked, like this situation was the most normal thing in the world. 'He should be here within half an hour.'

Erin almost gagged. 'Anthony's coming here now? You never said it would be today! I...'

'How long did you think I would sit on this for?' Zane muttered, his nerves jangling with anticipation of starting the repayment he'd awaited so very long.

'And you've given him *this* address?' Erin squawked, her eyes widening. 'Oh my God! He'll bring the police! He'll...'

Seeing the unusual bolt of panic in Erin's face, Zane reached to touch her shoulder in a gesture of comfort, before stopping himself. Why would he comfort someone who had and still most probably was, hellbent on killing him?

The answer was, he wouldn't. Neither did he know why he'd been drawn to do so in the first place, unless it was the rare flash of vulnerability in this woman which fired the need to protect her.

Zane shook his head in bewilderment. He needed to protect *himself* from *her*, not the other way around!

'Like I said before, he won't involve the police. He's got too much to lose. But...' His eyes narrowed as they met Erin's, '...the one thing he *will* be doing before he goes to hell, is telling you the truth about what he did to your father!'

Erin heard Zane's words but couldn't move her eyes from the camp bed shining in a threat to her sanity. It wasn't possible for Anthony to have been behind the murder. Torturing a false confession from him wouldn't make it true either.

Even if she was starting to half-hope that it could.

TWENTY NINE

WATCHING THE CLOCK on his Mercedes dashboard didn't make the time pass quicker. Neither did it slow it up. Time moved in the exact way it should, but Anthony felt like he'd been sat here for ten years.

In actuality, it had been *two* hours. Over an hour and a half longer than the time he'd requested they show up by.

He shoved his fingers into the high collar of his turtleneck black top to alleviate the building sensation of being slowly strangled by invisible hands. Turtleneck tops and black jeans weren't his usual attire and a lot of time and effort had been put into sourcing something he found both apt and functional within his wardrobe.

Something else Erin would normally advise on, but in her absence, he'd made the call himself. Wearing less usual attire helped separate that this was not his usual mode of business. It partitioned the impending events of tonight by separating Anthony Walker - the successful director of AW Financial Services, from *Flame* - the person he'd once been known as.

When a black Jaguar pulled into Solihull train station's car park and moved along the row of parked motors, Anthony stiffened. *Was this them?*

Despite his solemn promise to remain calm, his pulse notched up as the Jag backed into a space opposite.

Should he get out of the car and approach, or wait until they got out?

He glanced at the mobile positioned in the centre of his passenger seat.

Nothing.

What should he do?

Anthony held his breath as the Jaguar doors opened, his stomach plummeting into his shoes as a blond man, woman and two teenagers exited the car.

That wasn't them!

Snatching up his phone, his eyes darted back to the dashboard clock.

19:38.

They should have been here by six o'clock. That's what had been agreed, so where the bloody hell were they?

Scrolling through his list of texts, Anthony checked the final one he'd sent:

```
Solihull station
B91 1LE
```

That was correct. He knew he wouldn't have got it wrong. There was no way they could miss this place. The station was signposted throughout the city. All they had to do was exit the M42, go up the A41 and they'd pretty much be here - in this very car park.

It wasn't difficult, so where were they?

He had arranged to meet them here before going to Zane's address and there was no way he was giving out *his* home address. He'd gone to great pains so that where he lived wasn't publicly available. For plenty of reasons, none of his personal details were available to be bandied around for public perusal. His previous life being one of them...

Next, Anthony checked his call log. No missed calls... No

unread texts… Full signal…

What the hell was going on? Were they not coming? Had they let him down?

Anthony's blood thundered in his veins. Scrolling to the required number on his contact list, he pressed 'call'.

Yeah, he knew he wasn't supposed to, but he needed to know if they were showing up.

Now they'd be late for the time he'd agreed with Zane and he'd wanted to discuss exactly what would happen before going anywhere near where Morelli waited. Anthony prided himself in meticulously planning things and this was no exception. Now it had gone tits up.

Removing the phone from his ear as the ringing clicked to voicemail, Anthony ended the call, his eyes darting back to the dashboard clock.

19:52

Seething with rage, he attempted to call again and again. And again.

They weren't coming. The bastards had left him to it.

Anthony frowned so hard his brows slightly moved, even through the Botox overload.

He couldn't go on his own. Morelli would be waiting to kill him, no doubt also seething from his no show.

Anthony dragged his fingers through his hair, strands flopping onto his unlined forehead, not caring if the action ruined his usually pristine style.

Morelli would be gunning for him after this and now he'd failed to show, would most likely rock up at his offices. But that wouldn't happen until tomorrow because there was no point going to an office at this time in the evening. No, Morelli would be waiting for him in the morning, which gave *tonight* to work out what to do.

Anthony's mouth twitched with the hint of a smile.

There was no chance in hell he was leaving the city. *No way.*

Those bastards had made a big mistake by leaving him in

the lurch. Zane Morelli could come for him all he liked, but he wasn't being taken down. Not unless he took every single one of those tossers with him.

• • • •

'THE SNIVELLING fucking chicken-shit worm,' Zane snarled, upending the workbench with minimum effort.

As the carefully lined up tools clattered to the floor, his eyes danced with unbridled rage. All evening he'd waited, priming himself into a point of no return; the visions of things he would do to the man who had trashed his life gaining pace, until they revolved around his head at breakneck speed.

At first, he'd put the lack of anyone approaching up the driveway and the silence of cars down the lane to the cottage as an issue with finding the exact location, but this reasoning wore thin after an hour. Now after four and a half hours, it was obvious Flame wasn't coming.

His goosebumped skin burned. He'd been so sure, so completely *convinced* Flame would show that he hadn't factored what to do if that didn't happen.

It had never been an option.

But he'd been wrong. The cunt had played him. Flame had played him *big time* and that alone meant something was being planned. Possibly even, despite Zane's initial thoughts, something involving the police. Maybe Erin was right when she'd said the police would be involved?

All Zane knew was that he'd got it fucking wrong and that it affected *everything*.

In frustration, he booted an old can of paint across the floor, the can spinning off to hit Erin on the side of the leg.

Shrieking in pain and shock, Erin clutched her thigh. 'What the hell was that?'

Zane rushed over. 'Shit! I'm sorry. I didn't mean for that to hit you.' He watched Erin rubbing her thigh and dropped to his haunches to gently raise the hem of her skirt, seeing the reddening patch on her pale skin.

Erin wanted to scream for him to quit peering up her skirt, but was rendered powerless as his fingers gently traced the painful spot left by the edge of the paint tin. Heat flooded her at the feel of his rough fingers.

'It'll bruise, but it's not cut.'

Zane's husky voice sent further shivers through Erin and she pushed his hand away before he sensed her trembling. Snatching her skirt from his other hand, she looked away from the blue eyes piercing into hers. 'You need to calm the fuck down,' she sniffed, stepping out of reach of his hands. 'Anthony's not coming, so you'll just have to live with it.'

Zane pulled himself back up to his full height. Flame's no show was driving him crazy and kicking a paint tin at a woman was the final bloody straw. But it wasn't just that - it was the *implications*. 'How can I calm down? If you think this is all about getting my own back, then you're wrong! Regardless of your assumptions, this affects *you* too. How will you kill either of us if he's gone AWOL? Thought of that, have you?'

He raised an eyebrow. None of this was amusing, but the absurdity of the situation was too ironic. 'Will you console yourself with just killing me? If so, you'll be gutted when you finally believe the truth.' Zane's eyes fixed on Erin. 'Because you *will* discover the truth. With or without me...'

Erin's retort stuck in her throat. *Could there be any truth in this? No. It was preposterous.*

But Zane was right about one thing. She wouldn't be content with just him. She had to remove *both* their names from her list, not just one.

Zane perched on the edge of the remaining workbench. 'The other big factor is that we can't stay here.'

Erin's eyes widened. 'Why not? This is only the second day we've been at the cottage.'

Zane pushed himself to his feet. 'Your lovely boyfriend has this address now and he's planning something. Whether you're right and it involves the police or whether it's something else, I don't know, but whatever it is, I'm not sitting here like a target.

And neither are you!' Grabbing Erin's arm, he pulled her towards the outhouse door.

'Where are we going?'

'To shove some stuff in a rucksack and get the fuck away from here. And we're doing it now!'

Erin limped up the pathway towards the house, her thigh muscle protesting. She glanced at the old brickwork of the cottage she actually really liked. 'But where will we go? It's almost midnight.'

Using his shoulder to open the stable door to the cottage, Zane didn't bother turning around. 'I don't know, but I'll think of something. Either way, we're back to square fucking one.'

Erin squinted against the lights of the cosy kitchen in comparison to the dark of the night outside. *Square one? Maybe, maybe not.*

She'd just had an idea. Call it insane, but it was the only thing that she could think of to sort this out, without having to go back to square one.

Going backwards was not an option up for consideration.

THIRTY

'JUST BE CAREFUL where you put your feet. There's a shit load of potholes along here,' Zane said, his breath forming wisps of white vapour in the unusually cold May night. 'We don't need you getting a broken ankle!'

He felt bad to see Erin limping. She wasn't putting it on, he knew that much. The edge of that paint tin had caught her a right clump in the centre of her thigh and her leg would be as black as Newgate's knocker by the morning.

And it wasn't far off morning.

He stole a glance at the blue-black of the clear night sky, the illumination of the full moon and the clusters of bright constellations scattered in the darkness. Only the countryside, away from the subtle amber glow of streetlamps from towns or cities showcased a night sky like this. Here, out in the sticks, it was as black as the ace of spades.

At least it was dry. Pushing a heavy motorbike along an uneven track in the dark, whilst keeping his footing, as well as keeping an eye out for a limping woman was hard enough, without rain causing the uneven surface of the track to be even more treacherous.

He glanced at Erin wincing as she plodded along beside

him, her face set determinedly.

Zane knew she might be setting him up, but his instinct was telling him that she wasn't. His gut was sure Erin was on the level with her idea. And that was a Godsend because on leaving the cottage, he hadn't got the first clue where to head, except away from where they were sitting ducks.

Erin's suggestion wasn't expected, but it was perfect. *More* than perfect.

Zane wiped the thin layer of sweat from his brow with the back of his leather-jacketed sleeve. 'How much further is this shed you say you have?'

Pausing, Erin scanned the landmarks she could make out in the darkness. 'It's just around this corner. Literally a few yards away.'

Zane nodded, inwardly thankful. Cutting the engine a mile or so ago was logical so not to attract attention, but his arms were beginning to hate him.

'The shed door creaks if you open it too quickly,' Erin added, upping her pace as the silhouette of a large wooden building within the boundaries of her property came into view. 'You need the knack. There it is.'

Zane stared gratefully at the shed looming in the not too far distance. 'How do we get into the house without being noticed? Do you have security lights? Cameras?'

'Yes – both, but I know where they're located and what route will trip them. I'll make sure we get through undetected, trust me.'

Zane stopped, leaving Erin to deal with the shed door. *Trust her? Hardly.* But he had no choice *but* to. It wasn't like he had any better options.

Holding the phone she'd retrieved from Zane between her teeth, Erin flicked on the torch function and turned the numbers on the combination lock, then slipped the padlock off the door.

With a phone now in her possession, she could call the police; text Anthony to warn him; get herself some help. She could do *any* of those things, but she wouldn't. Doing *this* was what *she* wanted, even if it was being achieved in a backward fashion.

Pulling the handle up to raise one of the doors an inch off the ground, she tugged it open soundlessly, then stuck her head inside to make sure nothing had changed. The chances were unlikely. Anthony never ventured into this shed *or* the garden. He certainly wouldn't store anything of *his* in here. The man was as adept at DIY as he was with social niceties.

Besides, this shed was on the edge of the property's large perimeter. The other shed standing at the back of their main garden, was the one housing the lawn mower and other equipment the gardener used, so this larger shed wasn't utilised for anything. Anthony had mentioned several times about knocking the shed down and perhaps building an annex for guests in the space instead. After all, the area had its own separate driveway from the main house.

Erin was glad he'd never got around to doing anything further than talking about the concept, otherwise somewhere to stash Zane's bike would be impossible. Yet this was the perfect place.

The shed was also somewhere that could be used, like the outhouse at the cottage, but Zane had other ideas. His plan of holding and dealing with Anthony within the house itself offered Erin the advantage of knowing everything about the place that he didn't. It would be easier to achieve her own ends, when the opportunity presented itself.

And it would. Because it had to.

She had everything worked out how she would explain it all afterwards too.

Offering Zane Morelli access to her and Anthony's home had, at first glance, seemed ludicrous, but by the time they'd arrived here, she'd realised it offered options she'd previously not had. This was by far the best solution and one she hadn't thought available.

'There's plenty of room here for your bike,' she called, her voice a loud whisper in the silence of the night.

Zane heaved his massive bike onto the centre stand. He shoved the keys in his pocket and turned to face Erin. 'Okay, so now you'd better lead the way.'

• • • •

CREEPING ALONG between the Laurel hedge and the double height fence Anthony insisted on erecting around the property's boundary, Erin felt strangely exhilarated with what lay ahead.

Taking Zane's hand, she guided the way in a zig-zag trail as they neared the rear of the imposing property to ensure they didn't trip the cameras or the plentiful array of security lights dotted throughout the grounds. His rough hand in hers didn't unnerve her - it felt oddly powerful; comfortable; *exciting...*

She quickly shook away the unlikely chemistry this man engendered and instead concentrated on the end result.

Holding her hand up to indicate to stop, Erin paused, her breathing heavier than it should be. 'I need to work out where the cameras are pointing.'

Turning to make sure Zane had heard, she flinched as a twig from an overhanging tree caught in her hair and scratched her face.

'Wait!' Zane moved closer, his hand delicately untangling the thin, gnarly twig. 'It's okay. It's out now.' He rubbed his thumb over the light scratch on Erin's face. 'It hasn't marked you. Not permanently, anyway.'

With the moonlight dancing in Erin's eyes, Zane could almost taste her excitement. She was as up for killing Flame as he was. Combined with her beauty, it was a heady combination. The woman was indeed a wildcat. And a stunning one.

His groin ached with longing. The urge to kiss her again and bin off this whole idea off for half an hour to take her right here and now in the damp undergrowth was tempting. *So* tempting. His lips neared hers, the invisible pull strong.

Erin's breath hitched as Zane's raw magnetism drew her closer, her eyes moving from the jagged scar on his face to the full lips homing in on hers. How she wanted this man.

There. She'd said it. She wanted him badly. *So* badly. 'Zane... I...'

The crack of a twig broke the moment. Zane's head shot up to scan the garden through the dense foliage of the Laurel. 'It's only a fox,' he whispered.

'We had a family of them last year,' Erin smiled, remembering the tiny cubs playing in the uncut wild part of the garden she'd insisted remain, grateful the wild animals' timely return had prevented her from straying from her mission. But things were getting difficult.

Keep sight of your aim, she reminded herself as she focused back on the house. 'All the lights are off, as you'd expect at three in the morning. Anthony will be in that room there, third from the left.'

Pulling himself back to the job in hand, Zane looked at the massive house now clearly in view. The place was huge, expensive and perfectly maintained. *Flame had all of this, whilst he'd rotted in jail?*

His eyes narrowed. 'What if he isn't in that room? Or even in the house?'

Erin snorted. 'He will be. He'll have had his single whisky, a shower and he'll be in bed, turned towards the window with a blue velvet cushion placed on the floor to the left of his bedside table.'

Zane raised an eyebrow even though Erin wasn't facing him. She *couldn't* look at him because she also felt the pull. She wanted him as much as he wanted her.

Still, they had things to do. Sometimes, differences were too large to bypass and resolve. *This* being one of them. 'That a normal night for him, is it?'

'Pretty much. Not much, if anything, deflects Anthony's routine. It's pathetic! You can set your clock by it.' Erin heard the acid in her voice. She wouldn't add the only thing missing from Anthony's routine this last week, was sleeping with her in a cold and callous fashion until he believed he'd hurt her enough to gain control and therefore release. Zane Morelli didn't need to know *those* details.

Zane hadn't missed Erin's meaning. He could take a wild guess at what else this 'routine' included and the thought made him tremble with rage. 'After what happened tonight, he might not be there,' he whispered, his lips far too close to her ear. He could smell her hair, her skin. *Her.*

'He's there, alright,' Erin spat. 'See that curtain? If you look closely there's a bit folded up against the window sill. He does that before putting the light off. If he doesn't, then he can't sleep.'

Saying this out loud sounded even more bizarre than actually seeing it and the prospect of being so near to that hateful man lying in the room behind those curtains, made her blood turn to sludge.

Zane snorted derisively. 'Tonight's the last night he'll do any routine,' he hissed through clenched teeth. His urge to kill the man stronger than ever. 'Come on. We have work to do.'

Erin nodded and clenched her fist tighter around the keys which opened the back door to the house where she'd been a prisoner of her own making for so many years.

What was about to happen couldn't come fast enough. It was just unfortunate that by ending the life of the man who had turned her to stone, she would also be removing *this* man she hated more than anyone, yet who made her feel alive.

· · · ·

BILL WALKED OUT of the police station, purposely rubbing the chafed marks on his wrists from the over-tight handcuffs. He gave the desk Sergeant a withering glare as he passed and then pulled the handle of the glass door so hard, it was a surprise he didn't yank it from its hinges.

Four in the fucking morning?

He wouldn't waste time waiting to catch a word with the brief about where things stood with Marco. The guy knew what he was doing - that's what he was paid for. His boss would soon be off the hook, there were no worries there.

Besides, there was no case to answer.

Bill's heavy-set eyebrows knitted together. The word of a stupid nurse at the hospital counted for fuck all. And it hadn't, hence why he was free to go.

The charges didn't have a leg to stand on. They wouldn't stick to Marco either. But the bitch who felt it her 'duty' to report that tart's 'suspicious injuries' to the authorities wouldn't have *any* legs to stand on soon. That was something that would be put into place very soon, along with making their overpriced private quack pay for his ridiculous notion of taking the woman to a General Hospital in the first place.

A General Hospital? What the fuck was he thinking? Why take the bird there, just because he'd hit a brick wall on how to patch up the silly cow? There were always alternatives, yet the stupid, *stupid* bastard had done that?

The silly fucker would receive no more funding from them. Not that he'd need it where he was going after this.

Marco had been way out of order with that girl, but sticking this sort of shit on him was not helpful. Especially not tonight, of all nights.

Now they'd missed the window. By now, they should have been up north getting everything sorted.

Bill kept his casual demeanour in place until he'd cleared the police station's stone steps and reached the pavement. Only then did he yank his mobile phone from his pocket, his eyes feverishly scanning the screen:

```
7 missed calls
```

Fuck. Like he'd expected. If this balls-up had lost them the chance of taking Zane out of the equation, then he'd go tits.

Throwing his outwardly calm stance to one side, Bill broke into a clumsy run, his boots hitting the pavement with echoing thuds as he lumbered towards the main road where there would be black cabs.

He'd get back, pick up his car and then get on the road to

Solihull tout suite. He'd deal with this himself. He couldn't wait around until Marco got out of clink. Those bastards would drag out the paperwork for as long as possible, purely to piss everyone off.

Nope. He'd sort this and sort it alone.

Bill's lungs screamed in protest as his huge frame careered around the corner to the waiting taxis.

If there was even a small chance that he'd be in time to stop the chain of events that would inevitably impinge on *him*, as well as Marco, then he couldn't waste a moment longer.

THIRTY ONE

ANTHONY SMILED KNOWINGLY as Simon Clarknett rolled his boule in a perfectly calculated line towards the group of gold-topped skittles, each sitting on a coloured square.

His eyes danced with smugness as one, then two, three, four and five of the skittles fell, leaving the rest to tumble like dominos for no reason, apart from it was the only way it could happen.

And that was because it was how he'd arranged it. Things were set to run in a specific order - executed with precision because of his skill and planning.

Anthony smile grew wider at the fawning gratitude on Simon's face as the coloured squares underneath the fallen skittles exploded into sparkling gold glitter, which fluttered down around the group of admiring onlookers, everyone congratulating him on the success of the newly acquired investments for his hotel chain.

'And it's all thanks to Anthony Walker - the best in the business!' Simon boomed, pulling his beaming wife towards him - the wife that looked a lot like Jocelyn...

Wait! Simon Clarknett wasn't married to Jocelyn. Why was he standing with her wh...

Anthony jolted from his sleep, the flash of light behind his eyelids through the thick silk of his sleep mask pulling him rudely from his dream.

Was it morning? The sun must be bright to penetrate this mask. Hadn't he shut the curtains properly? If hadn't, then it would ruin everything!

Pulling the mask off his face, Anthony forced open his eyelids and squinted into the bright light.

What the fuck?

'Good morning! Probably not for you, though,' Zane snarled, his torch inches from Anthony's eyes.

Anthony turned his head from the blinding light that left green neon squares on his screaming retinas. He may be temporarily blinded, but there was no mistaking who owned that voice.

Scrabbling to pull himself out of bed, Anthony found himself pinned back down.

'I notice you don't wear your contacts in bed?' Zane growled. 'Yeah, your eyes are their true soulless shade of creepy nothingness!' Grabbing Anthony's hair, he yanked his head to one side, a low laugh escaping his lips. 'You never got around to having your name lasered off your neck either? Tut tut.'

Standing in the shadows, Erin watched with a mixture of revulsion and fascination. Anthony looked every inch the toad he was. He was no match for Zane Morelli, that was for sure.

It was only Zane's assurance, as they'd stealthily made their way in through the house, that he had no intention of killing Anthony tonight, that she allowed herself to stand by and watch Anthony get a taste of his own medicine.

And she had to say, she was enjoying it so far.

But what was this about his name being on his neck? She'd never noticed anything like that, but then Anthony never took his top off in bed, like the weirdo he was.

'Okay, Flame, you cunt, what's your excuse for not showing up tonight? Why have I had to come for *you*?' Zane twisted Anthony's head forward at an uncomfortable angle.

Erin frowned. *Flame? Is that what the Morelli's called him?*

Anthony tried to get a grip of something around him. *Anything.* He wasn't being taken out by this lunatic. Not ever. 'Who told you where I lived? Her? Did Erin tell you this?'

'Did you not want your lovely fiancée back after all?' Zane spat, dragging Anthony out of the bed to land with a thump on the floor. 'There's a surprise!'

'You're a piece of shit, Morelli! You think you could threaten me with that tart? What have you done this time? Fucked her, then killed her? Where is she? You should be fucking dead by now, y...'

Erin saw Zane's face twist with fury as his fist slammed into the side of Anthony's jaw. The crack as it connected, along with his head snapping back and forth unfolded in a strange slow motion, delicious spectacle.

Anthony crumpled to the floor, out cold. The exhilaration of witnessing him hit the deck quickly morphed into concern. 'I thought you weren't going to lose your temper?' Erin hissed. 'How will we find out what's going on, now he's spark out?'

Zane refrained from pummelling Anthony's skull in case his brain spilled over the fluffy sheepskin rug. 'I haven't lost my temper. You'll know when I do...'

Bending down, he grabbed Anthony's ankles and dragged him across the polished floorboards. 'To be honest, I didn't appreciate him referring to you as a tart. Now, tell me where you have here that's suitable to keep someone trussed up. I don't want to mess up your posh furniture now, do I?'

· · · ·

MARCO SLAMMED THE TAXI DOOR and stormed up the path to his apartment. Or should he say, Zane's...

No. *His.* It was his fucking apartment now, not his brother's.

Reaching the shiny entrance of the complex's security

reception, Marco punched in the numbers he knew by heart to release the door, then glanced around, convinced he was being followed.

There was no one about. It wasn't like there would be at this time in the bloody morning.

Grimacing, he ran his hand over the stubble which had pushed through his jawline during the night. His head pounded, the need for a line of pure and energy-inducing Columbian greater than usual.

As he stomped towards the lift, he stared at the gold clock above the concierge's desk.

5 a.m.

All night he'd been stuck in the cop shop being grilled on a stupid charge that didn't even bloody exist. *Grievous bodily harm, my arse*, he thought savagely.

If they thought *that* was GBH, they hadn't seen what he could *really* do.

That woman had been up for everything, for Christ's sake. She'd said so herself. She couldn't change her mind just because it suited her.

And where the bloody hell was Bill? He'd expected his right-hand man to be waiting when those po-faced detectives said he was free to go.

Of course he'd been free to bloody go! He wasn't the brother who got shoved in the fucking slammer! *That* was reserved for Zane and Zane alone. And the slammer was the very place where his brother should still be, yet for some hideous twist of fate, was not.

He had to get hold of Bill and get up north. Zane would be there still, he *had* to be.

'Ah, Mr Morelli!'

Marco paused, his finger on the 'call lift' button. If this fuckturd was about to tell him the lift still wasn't fixed, he'd punch his stupid fucking face!

Spinning around, Marco stared at the skinny man in an oversized security uniform, complete with gold epaulettes. *Like the addition of those made any bloody difference.* 'Yes?'

The man was acting like everything was normal, when the entire security staff of this building had to already be aware that he and his right-hand man had been publicly escorted through this very reception yesterday afternoon cuffed, to a selection of London's boys in blue.

Bloody embarrassing it was. He had a good mind to sue the Metropolitan Police for harassment and damage to his good name.

The young man scrabbled underneath his gold countertop for his notebook. 'A message from Mr Wainwright for you, sir.'

'Right? And?' Marco glared harder, knowing his piercing stare only made the guy more nervous. Well, if he didn't have the clout to back up the pretence that the whole building wasn't aware of his public arrest, then he deserved to have nightmares, the stupid little prick.

Much to the concierge's relief, he located his notebook and with fumbling fingers, thumbed to the page where he'd scrawled the message. 'Here we are. Mr Wainwright said that he's gone to deal with a client up north. He said it made sense to go straight away being as you were "busy".'

Marco's eyes narrowed. 'You trying to be fucking funny?'

'F-Funny?' The concierge's eyes darted around nervously. 'No, sir. That's what Mr Wainwright said.' He held up the scribbled message. 'I-I just wrote down the words. I haven't...'

'When was this?' Marco barked. So, Bill had gone to kill Zane alone? Kill him or *fetch* him? His lips pursed. It would be better if Bill got his hands dirty, rather than *him*. 'Well?'

'Erm, about forty minutes ago, sir. He stopped to leave the message then went off in his car.'

Marco turned back to the lift. He quite fancied punching the concierge in the face for the fun of it, sure he was having a dig with that remark about being busy. Either that or Bill was.

Marco shook his head to shift the gradual speeding up of his paranoia roundabout. It didn't work. Shaking his head didn't help his fast-building headache either.

The lift door opened and Marco stepped inside with relief. If it hadn't been working, he'd have had no choice but to throw that scrawny little scrote down the fucking shaft to fix the bastard thing himself.

He'd go to the apartment, have a line and a whisky to sort his head out. Then he'd have a shower and put in a call to Bill to find out what the score was.

• • • •

THE INITIAL ELATION of seeing Anthony get floored had worn off and the heaviness of the situation pressed against Erin's head and rib cage, making her temples pound and her breathing laboured.

The longer she remained in this house with its familiar surroundings - every room, every ornament, each piece of *everything*, the longer things chipped away at her.

The week she'd been out of this claustrophobic fortress had diverted from exactly how horrific it really was here. Now it rushed back.

Although the alternative of being held a prisoner of sorts by the man she'd despised more than anyone else - including Anthony, had been horrendous too, it had become less offensive as time wore on. And the reason her time trapped with Zane Morelli had become less offensive was for reasons she still struggled to comprehend.

Erin's gaze moved to Zane who remained fixated on Anthony, tightly bound to a chair and still out cold. His steely gaze was zoned on the man in front of him, the hatred and bitterness rising from his muscular shoulders in waves. It was like she was invisible – only the space containing Zane Morelli and Anthony Walker a reality.

Erin shuddered. Being back within these four walls seared her brain with a stark reminder of the hundreds of days, no - over two thousand days - six long years that she'd remained stoically in place, determinedly following through everything required in order to achieve her ultimate aim. *Revenge.*

And now that revenge was on the cusp, she felt strangely devoid. Maybe it was being here that drained her normally high energy for the task in hand, but whatever the reason, it was running out of her like a leaking tap.

It took a great amount of effort to look at Anthony. The way his head lolled to one side; the trail of dried blood tracking from his mouth down over the white polo shirt he wore in bed filled her with utter revulsion.

Whatever happened now, Anthony would not walk away. The raw hate radiating from Zane pulsed like a beacon, underlining that option a non-starter.

Even if there was a miracle enabling Anthony to escape Zane's wrath, there was one thing that could not happen. She wouldn't marry the despicable creature, no matter how much it had figured in her original plan.

'Why do you call him Flame?' Erin blurted, suddenly desperate to break the surreal atmosphere. Every second she was excluded from the soundless war between these two men twisted her insides.

'Wanker or fucking bastard usually suffices just as well as any name,' Zane muttered, not moving his eyes from Anthony.

'Just answer the question,' Erin snapped.

Zane's eyes slid to Erin's. 'Work it out! Amongst other things, he's a ginger with bright red hair.' His head jerked back to Anthony. 'Oh, you didn't realise he dyed it? I forgot you don't have a clue that he looks *nothing* like you know him in real life. Or that he wears contacts...' His mouth curled as he nodded pointedly to Anthony's groin. 'I'd have thought you might have worked out about the hair...'

Erin shook the blatant reference out of her head. Anthony shaved every single part of his body hair off - *'More hygienic'*, he'd said. But Zane was wrong. She *did* know the real reasons. 'Don't forget I saw him at your trial, so I'm fully aware he changed his appearance to hide from you lot.'

'But is *he*?' Zane's eyes narrowed.

'Why would I want him to know who I am? I already told

you. I've planned this a long time.' Erin's resentment gained momentum. 'He's a narcissistic freak and screwed in the head!'

'And you were prepared to marry the prick, purely to bide time waiting to kill *me*?' Zane's gaze trailed over Erin's face down to her feet. *She really was something else.*

'That, and to ensure I got my financial security back, yes. He may not have the kind of money *you* stole, but he got enough of a payout for that evidence and to disappear. Plus, as a widow, I'd have profited from the shitty business I've helped him run these past six years.'

'You had it all worked out then?' Zane was about to point out that it was a pity she'd set her sights on the wrong man and repeat that she'd been sleeping with the *real* murderer, but when Anthony stirred in his chair, he jumped to his feet. 'Back to the land of the living?' he snarled, grabbing Anthony's swollen jaw. 'Now's your chance to tell me what you did and how you managed it.'

Realising he was tightly bound, a flash of confusion passed over Anthony's face, quickly replaced by a tinge of gloating sarcasm. Being tied up didn't faze him. He'd been constrained his whole life by limitations and routines. But he excelled at his job - the *real* part of it anyway, and nothing Zane Morelli did would take that away. Not even killing him.

Even the throbbing pain in Anthony's jaw didn't dissuade him from his newly found aim. If Zane succeeded in killing him, it wouldn't happen until the man was left feeling like an utter piece of shit for evermore. He would be left with haunting doubts.

Morelli would question *everything* by the time this was finished. And those doubts he would never be able to shake off.

THIRTY TWO

SWEATING LIKE A PIG, Bill stabbed the 'end call' button on the mobile in its holder.

Still no answer from Marco. Or Flame.

He glanced at the cheap clock sitting on the Transit's plastic dash.

Five times he'd called Marco since getting on the road and nothing. He'd called Flame the same amount of times too.

The police must have released Marco by now. Bill had been driving for two hours and it was now 5:45 a.m. The dawn was underway and if he was to singlehandedly bundle Zane Morelli into the back of this van without attracting attention, it couldn't be in full daylight. Now he was cutting things fine.

His memory of Zane didn't fill him with oodles of confidence for pulling this off seamlessly. If his recollection served him well, the man was a veritable machine - both physically and mentally. Certainly not someone he'd go out of his way to cross.

But desperate times brought desperate measures. If this wasn't sorted, Bill was dead meat. They *all* were.

If they lost track of where Zane was now they'd finally pinpointed an exact location, they'd be back to not knowing when the attack would happen and from which angle.

Tearing up the country lanes towards the destination, Bill frowned harder as hedges whizzed past.

Not knowing when an attack would happen worked two ways. And that was what he was counting on *here*.

If Flame had failed to show up, there were only certain options Zane could take: stay put on the off-chance Flame would finally appear, or if Flame *had* been stupid enough to attend the meet alone, Zane would be busy working on the man right now. Flame wouldn't yet be dead yet because the Morelli's liked taking their time.

Usually...

As long as Bill arrived, caught the situation off guard and sorted this before Flame spouted things best left unsaid, then the element of surprise was the only way he stood a chance of pulling it off.

'Shit!' Bill slammed on the brakes, the back wheels skidding on the mud-strewn road. Shoving the gear stick into reverse, he backed up and peered through the approaching dawn at a rickety plaque at the edge of a narrow driveway. *Was this it?*

Bill squinted through his steamed-up window at the faded letters of the wooden sign. *'Hope Cottage'*.

Yep! This was the place.

Pulling across the driveway's entrance to block the exit of any leaving vehicle, Bill cut the engine and killed the side lights. Retrieving his gun from under the seat, he double checked it was loaded correctly, then flicked the safety catch off.

He clambered from the van and a few yards up a mud track serving as the drive, rounded the corner to see a small cottage in darkness. Anyone inside was either asleep, in rooms around the back or the place was empty.

Bill clumped along, scowling at the dust clinging to the hem of his black trousers. Another trip to the dry cleaners in the foreseeable future... However, depending on how this unfolded, he might need to burn the lot...

Busy looking for scuffs to his nice leather shoes, Bill almost missed the track in the mud - a singular tyre tread heading toward the cottage. One that, if his tracking skills still served him well, looked recent. And one that, due to the width and position, could belong only to a motorbike.

This corroborated with what Flame said about his bird's abduction.

Morelli was here with the girl and most probably with Flame. Or *had* been...

Bill's hand tightened around the butt of his Glock as he approached the front door of the cottage. He took a quick glance over his shoulder. He could do without early-rise posties or milkmen appearing. He didn't want more bodies to deal with than necessary.

But that was the next problem...

Did he go in here with the aim of dispatching Zane or bring him back to London for Marco to do the deed?

He'd purposely bypassed that question on the way up here by concentrating on a quiz on Radio 2, but he should have perhaps considered it.

His jaw clenched. Marco should be dealing with this and make the call how it would be played, not *him*. But Marco wasn't here, so what choice was there?

Bill sighed. His ex-missus expected him to cough up for their eldest's university tuition fees and he'd promised to deliver. How could he do that if he was in nick, or worse, dead.

No, he had to act. Zane was out, the net was closing in and therefore, couldn't leave the outcome to pure chance.

Flattening himself as much as possible against the cottage's crumbling brickwork, Bill peered through the ill-fitting curtains of the ground floor, finding it silent and without a sign of anyone.

Paying attention to where he placed his feet, he moved around the side of the house as lightly as his immense bulk allowed, fighting his way through the overgrown remains of a herb garden. The back of the cottage was equally without life.

He scanned the garden. That big outhouse was an option, but he'd check the house properly first.

Pausing, Bill listened again, his hand on the stable door of the cottage. Everything was quiet, short of the melodic dawn chorus of the abundant bird life.

Holding his Glock in front of him, Bill tried the handle. Finding it open, he entered the room, quickly deducing the kitchen was empty. But there were two glasses near the sink - one still with something in it. There had been at least two people here.

Moving into the lounge, he stopped at the base of the stairs and tuned his ears for sounds from above. It was too silent, but that didn't mean anything. Zane could have watched him come up the driveway and be waiting at the top of the stairs.

Bill's heart thumped loudly as he scanned his surroundings. There was little here, apart from furniture. No items to show people were living here, like spare shoes or coats. It was like a holiday let with all the necessary items, but no personal belongings.

But *someone* had definitely been here.

Aside from the glasses in the kitchen, fires didn't leave mess in the grate if they hadn't been recently lit. The fresh pile of wood in the wicker basket was damp too, suggesting it had been collected within the last day.

And then there was *that*...

Bill's attention centred on a single muddy footprint at the base of the stairs. It was large - at a guess, a size eleven and looked very much to be that of a biker boot.

Bill tentatively took the steps, cringing with every creak of the wooden staircase. If there *was* someone here, now they knew *he* was too...

Swinging his gun around the corner into the only bedroom, he covered the area and booted open the door to the bathroom.

Clear.

Making his way into the empty bedroom, he paused by the

unmade bed, straight away spotting the wide open drawers of a dark wooden chest. Sticking his hand in, he felt around and fished out the only remaining item - a pair of pink lacy knickers.

The woman had been here then... How lovely... Zane shacking up with Flame's bird in the interim...

Shrugging, Bill stuffed the knickers into his pocket, then noticed a belt tied to the bed's metal headboard.

It was Morelli's belt. He'd have recognised it anywhere. The metal insignia on the buckle had been specially commissioned in Italy and both the Morelli sons had received one containing their initials.

Into bondage now, was he?

Whatever...

The address Flame supplied was correct. Morelli had *definitely* been here but had since done a flit. The question was, when and where to?

Furthermore, was Flame with him?

Pulling his mobile from his pocket, he scrolled to Flame's number. He'd check the outbuilding next, but he was pretty sure the place was deserted.

If he couldn't get through to Flame or Marco, he'd contact Sonny to do some digging pronto for Flame's business and home addresses. Sonny would have to find them and find them quickly because they were the next two places he would try.

• • • •

AT FIRST, the noise was part of his dream. Marco shifted onto his side and sighed contentedly.

There it was again.

He buried deeper into his pillow, hating it when dreams went on a loop. It was becoming so irritating he'd have to wake up and he was getting to the good bit!

Just as he'd settled back into his dream, it happened again.

Then it hit him.

It was his phone! Bloody hell! Who was calling in the middle of the fucking night!

Wait! He sat bolt upright. It wasn't night at all. *Shit. Fuck. Shit!*

Marco's eyes sprang open to receive confirmation it was indeed morning by the sunlight streaming through the open curtains. The memories of the long drawn-out night of no sleep crashed into his head.

He'd gone for a shower, had a few whiskies and had been about to do a couple of lines, when he thought he'd lie down - only for a minute or so to rest his eyes...

Jesus H Christ!

Jumping off the bed, the shrill ringing torturing his frazzled nerve endings, Marco darted around for his phone. *Where the fuck was it?*

Haphazardly throwing his discarded clothes off the end of the bed, he located his mobile under a crumpled shirt.

```
16 missed calls
```

Shit!

Marco fumbled his way into the call log:

```
Bill - 6 missed calls
Sonny - 3 missed calls
Trevor - 1 missed call
Voicemail - 6 missed calls
```

Sweating, Marco dialled his voicemail. There was only one message and it was pointless – thirty seconds of crackling and shuffling, like the phone was in someone's pocket.

He scrolled to Bill's number. Bill was going up north. Had Bill taken Zane or killed him? *Which was it?*

The phone continued ringing out.

'Fuck!' Marco barked, pacing up and down. When had Bill last called?

An hour ago...

What if Zane had killed Bill? If his brother had got in first, it was feasible.

With clammy hands, he selected Sonny's number, noticing he'd last called fifteen minutes ago...

'Come on, come on!' Marco muttered, jamming the phone in his neck, whilst he juggled to top up his whisky. 'Sonny?' he gasped as the call connected. 'No... no, I didn't hear it ringing. What's going o... When? Right... okay... Where is he now?'

His brows folded as he made sense of what he was hearing. 'If Zane's not there, then where is he...? What do you mean, you don't know...? You are? When?'

Marco stared out of the window down to the road below. Was his car here? He hoped so because he needed it. 'What did you say? You've got it?'

'So, you've sourced Flame's home address *and* work address? You've given them to Bill? Which one has he gone to first?' Marco tipped the full glass of whisky into his mouth. 'Okay... Look, I'll get on the road and head up there now... Of *course* there's point! Just confirm which address Bill's gone to when he calls you back and let me know.'

Ending the call, Marco stared at his mobile for a few moments, then frantically put back on last night's clothes. These would have to do. There wasn't time to dig out new ones.

He paused, his eyes tracking back to the remaining half bottle of whisky and then to the drawer where his coke stash tempted him. *Did Sonny have a point?* Should he be going anywhere until he knew what was happening?

In two hours from now, which was at least how long it would take to get to Solihull, Bill would either be already dead, have done the job or be halfway back down the motorway with Zane in tow. Maybe he *should* wait and see what the situation was?

Marco drummed his fingers on the dressing table. Besides, he could do with another couple of drinks before dealing with anything else.

Making his mind up, a sly smile crept over his face.

Yeah, he'd hang fire until he knew where the land lay. It

was the most sensible solution.

He reached for the whisky. In the meantime, he'd just have a...

The dulcet tone of *Dixie* interrupted him from replenishing his top-up. 'I don't believe this,' he muttered.

Slamming his glass down, he made his way to the front door. *If this was the police again, then he'd definitely file a complaint and sue them for everything.*

He yanked open the door. 'What do y... Oh!'

'Hi babe!' Hazel waltzed into the apartment, her father following behind.

Trevor gave Marco a cursory nod. 'Just wanted to check everything's been sorted out with the police?'

Marco leant against the wall wondering how he could have been so stupid not to check who was at the door before opening it. He really must change the authority he'd given reception about letting certain people up to the apartment without prior arrangement. This wasn't the first time an ad hoc visit from these two had been inconvenient.

'What exactly happened yesterday, Marco?' Trevor asked. 'My daughter informed me of your arrest, which is worrying. Is there anything we should be concerned about?'

'Nah.' Marco flapped his hand. 'It was a mistake.'

'I expected you to call the minute you got out,' Hazel pouted. Now her father had the confirmation Marco was definitely the recipient of the Morelli profits, it was in her best interest to be nice to the man and therefore stake her claim on his fortune. She wound her arms around Marco's waist. 'You knew I'd be worried.'

Despite having the lovely Lisa Tequila's arms wrapped around his middle, all Marco could think of was what he could use as an excuse.

Moving out of her grip, he faked a smile. *This pair weren't going to leave it, were they?* 'I didn't call you because I haven't been back long. The arrest was a clerical error, which quite frankly isn't good enough, so I've been speaking to my brief to bring a case against the police.'

'I couldn't agree more,' Hazel purred. 'We don't want this sort of thing happening, especially after we're married.' Her eyes danced with excitement. 'That's the other reason we're here.'

She nodded at Marco's crumpled clothes. 'Get yourself smartened up. We've got an appointment with the vicar in an hour.'

Marco almost choked. 'The *what*?'

'The vicar...' Hazel batted her false eyelashes. 'About our marriage?'

'Wh...? But...'

'Babe,' Hazel gushed. 'We agreed to get hitched quickly and...'

'It's in everybody's interests to get this done straight away, Marco,' Trevor interrupted, his nasally voice slimier than molasses. 'We both know our businesses stand to profit from this joining, so there's no sense prolonging it.'

Hazel slipped her arms back around Marco's waist. 'Isn't it exciting? We've arranged it with our family vicar to get special permission so that we can get married quickly! Can you believe it? But we must go and see him straight away.'

'Hence why we need to leave now to get to the appointment,' Trevor added. 'If you'd answered your phone, you'd have had more warning.'

Hazel's mouth formed a sulky moue. 'You're not busy, are you?'

'No, no, it's fine,' Marco blathered. *Goddamn it.* Although the prospect of being married to this bird had at first seemed a top idea, he was rapidly going off the idea. 'But... but I haven't got your ring yet.'

Hazel laughed, the trill peal as false as her breasts. 'We don't need a ring for the meeting, silly. But we'll go shopping straight after and get it, how about that?'

'Great...' Marco muttered through clenched teeth. 'Just give me two minutes to freshen up.'

Striding into the bathroom, he shut the door. Leaning back against it, he closed his eyes and pulled his mobile from his pocket. He'd have to call Sonny and tell him there was a change of plans now.

As much as he needed to get his hands on Zane, the chances were that his brother was already brown bread or on the way back to London, so it made more sense to get the ball rolling with this marriage. He'd deal with whatever Bill came back with later.

• • • •

'YOU THINK you're so clever, don't you?' Anthony spat, his resentment outweighing rationality. All that mattered was getting out of this chair and stopping the squealing in his head.

He hadn't even got any shoes on and having bare feet was a pet hate. The worst part was that he was in the garage. The bloody garage! The floor was concrete, for Christ's sake! All manner of germs would be present on the floor in here. Viruses and bacteria would invade his blood stream. He could even *hear* them making their way through the soles of his feet.

He couldn't bear this, he really couldn't.

'Did you really think *she* was a good bartering chip?' Anthony spied Erin's figure sharing the space and breathing the same air. Her witnessing him trussed to this chair like a stuck pig only fuelled his rising anger and erratic thoughts of invading germs. 'Was this your idea?' he screamed, his strange pale eyes homing in on Erin. 'Been enjoying this psycho's company, you whore?'

Erin stiffened, Anthony's fish-like eyes all the more dead. This was the first time she'd seen his real eyes and they were horrible. Just *horrible*.

Unable to prevent it, her fingers shook. Just the sound of his voice brought back memories of all the times she'd endured his disgusting thrusting and grunting on top of her.

Anthony's whole being glittered with malice. 'I saw the photo.' He nodded to Erin belly. 'Is his seed growing inside you yet? Wouldn't that be an achievement.' He laughed coldly. 'I care very little if all the times you've opened your legs for him have paid off, you useless bitch, but if he's left a lasting reminder, it will be rectified. I can't have anything else embarrass me, Erin. You've already lost me clients!'

Zane first watched the unfolding events with interest, but this rapidly changed to base fury. The words now spewing from Anthony's nasty mouth made the adrenalin thunder through his veins in a surge of protectiveness. This man was so deluded that all he was worried about was losing clients?

He hadn't laid a hand on Erin Langley. Hadn't touched her, short of that one kiss. But by God, he'd wanted to.

Erin suddenly lurched forward and slapped Anthony's face. 'You're disgusting!' she screamed. She wouldn't take this anymore. She wouldn't listen to any more shit. Enough was enough.

She snatched a wrench from the neatly stacked tool cabinet. Yet another expensive and unused item Anthony insisted buying to go through the motions of what men should possess.

Zane darted forward, his fingers closing around Erin's wrist. 'Leave it!' he hissed. 'It can't happen like this.'

'Why not? You're not doing it, Zane,' Erin screamed, her resolve blown. *It had gone too far. Gone on too long. It was done.* 'I'm having him now. I...'

'First name terms too?' Anthony mocked, a low chuckle spurting from his bloodied mouth. 'How cosy. For God's sake, Erin. Did you have to stoop so low as to sleep with *him*, of all people? How much did he pay you?'

Erin pulled against Zane's steely grip to reach Anthony, but the increase on her wrist's pressure points made the wrench drop from her hand to clatter to the concrete floor below. 'No! I have to d...'

Spinning around, Zane booted Anthony squarely in the chest, sending him flying onto his back still attached to the chair. Jumping astride him, he knelt on a bound hand, gaining a controlled squeak of pain in return. 'Shut the fuck up with your spate of insults and concentrate on talking instead, you cunt.'

Seizing her chance, Erin lurched towards Anthony once again. 'You think I don't know who you worked for? You think I don't know who you are?'

Seeing the flash of confusion on Anthony's face, Zane held his arm out to keep Erin at bay. 'Yes, she's David Masters' girl. You know, the man you killed? The one you robbed and the one you set me up for?' His eyes narrowed to slits. 'See this?' His finger jabbed at his own face. 'See the scar? Along with getting me banged up, that's what your fucking lies caused!'

Anthony's mouth opened and then shut again, his eyes darting to Erin. *Erin was David Masters' daughter?*

'Sinking in yet, fuckface? Yeah, she hooked up with you, with the aim of killing you! Did you really think you'd get away with what you've done and that it wouldn't catch up with you? Well, now it has…'

Grinding his kneecap down on Anthony's hand, Zane enjoyed the mild fear now present in his pale eyes. He pulled a flick knife from his pocket. 'Let's see what you look like with a slashed face! Don't panic that it will put your customers off because shortly you won't need any.'

The flash of silver was so quick, Erin barely saw the blade connect with Anthony's flesh. She'd thought it a threat until a thin red line across his cheekbone widened and blood cascaded down his face.

Bile rose at the hint of white bone visible through the deep cut.

A flick knife was what had been dragged across her father's throat. Was it like that one? Could that be the very same knife Zane used on her father?

She leant against the tool cabinet, her breath coming in shallow gasps. Her eyes flicked between Anthony and Zane, one thing sticking in her mind: Anthony hadn't countered what Zane accused him of. He hadn't denied the accusation of being the actual murderer…

'The big question is, do I kill you in your posh fucking

house or do I take you back to London to face the music?' Zane laughed hollowly. *He would kill Flame here, no shadow of a doubt.*

It wasn't feasible to drag this out for weeks, like he'd intended. Even another day was too long.

THIRTY THREE

BILL SCREECHED AROUND the corner, hoping this time he'd taken the right turning. Twice now he'd drawn a blank. An address was an address, right? It shouldn't be this bloody difficult to locate the bastard place!

But he had to keep things steady. Screeching tyres and sounding like a getaway driver around a neighbourhood such as this wouldn't go down well. These sorts of people were the type to call the Old Bill if as much as a leaf fluttered onto their manicured grass.

His eyes narrowed at the large houses along the leafy road. The huge properties were all set back from the road behind statuesque gold or black iron railings and pillared columns topped with lions and such like.

Oh yeah, very nice...

This lot certainly believed their shit didn't stink. However, he knew Flame, and in this instance, it *did*. Everything Flame did stunk of shit, which is why he'd been so eager to take their offer up in the first place, the greedy cunt.

And Marco still hadn't called back...

Bill's teeth clenched. Marco had better take on board that he'd gone above and beyond today. He didn't have to do *any* of this. He could have sat on his arse, waiting for instructions, like the gopher Marco treated him as half the time. But there was too much personally riding on this to leave anything to chance.

At least Sonny had come through. Having a technical whizz on their side, *his* especially, was a bloody godsend at times like this. He wasn't sure how Sonny had got hold of Flame's addresses so quickly after previously drawing a blank, but was glad that he had.

Between them, they'd sort this out and put it to bed once and for all. Marco getting off his head and causing himself additional problems wasn't good for *anyone*, so somebody had to pull it together.

But where was this bloody place?

Applying the brakes, Bill slowed the Transit down and scanned the name plaques of the palatial homes. *If it wasn't one of these, then...*

A-ha!

Cutting the engine, Bill retrieved his Glock once again from under the driver's seat and shoved it in the purposely-built pocket of his jacket.

Jumping from the van, it looked to any passers-by that he was a delivery driver. But he'd have to be careful. *Both careful and quick...*

Knowing Flame, the bastard had a state-of-the-art security system in place. And that had to be dealt with.

Glancing around, Bill was relieved to see the road clear of anyone. He casually strolled over to the intercom at the gates and leant against the post, his back shielding what he was about to do.

He hoped it worked without tripping the system.

Pulling a thin screwdriver from his pocket, he slipped it between the sides of the intercom and prised away a piece of casing. Praying the wires were seated on the near side of the unit, he pushed the tiny head of the driver until he felt resistance.

Bill smiled. *Pretty nimble for someone with colossal hands.*

Twisting the screwdriver, he tensed as the wire disconnected.

No alarm sound yet. So far, so good.

Making a few more adjustments, Bill held his breath until the gate mechanism sprang into action. Exhaling with relief as the gates cranked open, he lumbered back to the van.

Wasting no further time, he manoeuvred the Transit up the long gravel drive towards the property.

What followed had to be methodical *and* fast.

• • • •

PANTING WITH EXERTION, Zane sneered at Flame, happy with his handiwork so far.

A further rain of heavy punches had knocked the prick for six, but inflicting this additional damage had not removed his need to finish this.

His self-control had floundered. It was too late to sit back and drag this out. He was doing it now. He'd waited long enough.

Besides, there was no option or need to take the bastard back to London. Killing Flame was his to do and his alone. Unfortunately for Erin, she would not get what she wanted on this score, but she'd have the next best thing - watching this cunt slowly bleed out.

Zane's eyes glinted. But there was one thing left to do before striking his final blow - the truth from this lowlife coward.

It wasn't to remove himself from Erin's absurd hit list, but he knew now more than ever how this piece of crap had treated her. God knows what else she'd been put her through from Flame's freaky madness.

Erin deserved to know the truth. She deserved to know who had really murdered her father and she also deserved to watch that person's life seep out over the fucking floor.

Erin remained frozen against the tool cabinet, hypnotised with Zane's savagery as well as his words. Her desperate urge to end Anthony's life was now in freefall.

'So, what's it to be, wanker? Are you telling her the truth or not?' Zane snarled, then stared in amazement as Anthony's split face broke into a smile.

'How can I tell her something that isn't true, Morelli?' Anthony mumbled through his ruined mouth. 'Take me back to London if you wish, but you're wasting your time... Your brother and the firm know where I am. They always have...'

Anthony's laughter rolled around the otherwise empty space of the double garage, yet all Zane heard was a strange whistling in the back of his mind.

And he saw red. A deep, glowing fiery hot red.

Grabbing Anthony by the hair, he smashed his fist into his slashed cheekbone, the damaged flesh splitting wide open. The bone shattered on impact, leaving no doubt it was broken when it jutted from the deep gouge in his face.

'You fucking lying prick! You'll tell her the truth and you'll tell her now!' Zane screamed, wrapping his hands around his nemesis' neck.

Erin's body remained paralysed as she watched the scene unfold. Zane was killing Anthony in front of her. She hadn't even said her piece!

Hearing a strangulated gurgling from Anthony, Erin knew she had to make this stop. She had to say what she needed to say. She had to hurt him and this was also her chance - the chance she'd been waiting for. The chance to kill them *both*.

Looking at Zane and then Anthony, her heart pounded in her ears. Covered in blood, broken bones and with half his face a crushed pulp, Anthony's eyes still retained that awful dead fish appearance. Despite his dire situation and the state he was in, he defiantly stared as Zane continued to strangle him. It was almost like he enjoyed it.

Anthony wouldn't notice what she did now. And Zane - Zane was back in the zone - fixated only on finishing the man. It was unlikely he'd even see her strike until it was too late.

This is it, Erin, her mind screamed as her sights locked on the discarded flick knife to the right of Zane's foot.

Possessed by the driving urge to complete what had kept her going for years, she inched forward as Zane continued screaming at Anthony, his sneer serving like a red rag to a bull.

'Tell her what you did! Fucking tell her!' Zane roared, his breath ragged.

'I'm. Telling. That. Slut. Nothing,' Anthony wheezed, his eyes dancing with malice, the only sign of life behind the pale irises. 'She thinks *you* killed her father... So I'll let her...'

When Anthony's gaze swivelled to rest on Erin with her hands curled around the flick knife, she froze. *He'd noticed her.*

Anthony's eyes narrowed. 'You're a slut! A means to an end. A whore and a loser. A *nobody*. And you...' His eyes moved to Zane '...Are an equal loser. Who do you think arranged this whole thing? My appearance? *All* of it?' His eyes slowly tracked back to Erin.

Zane laughed. '*Her*? You expect me to believe that *Erin* forced you to kill her own father, helped you frame me and then sorted your change of identity?'

'*What*?' Erin shrieked, dropping the knife to the floor with a clatter.

Zane looked from the knife to Erin before turning his concentration back to Anthony. '*You* killed Masters, Flame. No point lying now. You're dead.'

'As are you, Morelli,' Anthony laughed, the sound coming out as a weird gurgle from the back of his throat. 'You're wrong. *I* know it and so does *she*. You want the truth, then work it the fuck out!'

Erin stood bewildered, her mind churning. What was this bullshit? Anthony hadn't killed her father like Zane believed, but making out that *she* was part of it?

She wasn't part of it, of course she wasn't part of it! But Anthony said to 'let her believe' that Zane had... So if it wasn't Zane... and it wasn't Anthony... then...?

'Stop the fuck lying!' Zane reared up and grabbed a hammer which he brought down upon the back of Anthony's bound hand.

The splintering of bones shattered the eerie silence and Erin heard Anthony's scream. *Or was it her who had screamed?*

She picked the knife back up from the floor. She had to finish them both.

Didn't she?

Wasn't this what she wanted?

Anthony yes, but Zane...?

'Time's up,' Zane spat, raising the hammer above Anthony's head. 'May you burn in hell.'

Zane didn't hear the door open, neither did he hear Erin's shout of warning before his world went black.

THIRTY FOUR

MARCO'S ERECTION grew as Hazel pressed closer, her hand tightly holding his against his thigh. She was doing a superb job of acting her half of the loved-up couple they needed to appear as.

Not that either of them were. He knew their marriage was a business deal - especially from *her* side. As for him, well, he didn't love her. Of *course* he didn't love her. What he felt was big time lust! That, and he'd make a killing from having her on the books at Luna Motion Films.

Those things were why he was sitting here.

He didn't do churches and neither did he do vicars, but if that's what it took, then fine.

Sitting in the vicarage drawing room, Marco tried to keep the sneer off his face as he stared at Hazel's vicar. *Family vicar, my arse*, he thought.

Trevor must have secured this ultra-quick marriage via a hefty donation to the church fund for the repairs to the steeple or funding a poxy mother and baby group in the dilapidated church hall. This bloke here wouldn't arrange this without any benefit to *him*.

Marco's take on the vicar's dubious attitude was

exemplified by his thinking it acceptable to wear small and weirdly over-tight dark-red canvas shorts as a normal form of clothing. It showed he wasn't a person with many morals.

It was also doubtful the man was blind to what this member of his parish did for a job. Or that her own father profited from his daughter spreading her legs. That didn't fit well with the great book itself, did it?

Marco had already deduced the vicar was aware, or had been conveniently *made* aware of what the Morellis' standing was this side of the river and therefore knew better than to put a spanner in the works. After all, it would be a dreadful shame should retaliation be required on this man and his family. Or his church...

Yeah, it was easier all round to swing what was needed with the powers that be, to fast track the paperwork and gain special permission for this marriage.

And the sooner that happened, the better.

Marco resisted the urge to look at his phone to see if there was an update from Sonny. He trusted Bill was wrapping things up and doing it well. There was no reason to think otherwise. But there was *every* reason to get this deal between Grimes and Luna Motion Films set in stone. Not forgetting the extra bonus of getting to stick his dick in the lovely Lisa Tequila. *Sorry, Hazel.*

Pulling his suit jacket down to hide the bulge in his trousers, Marco smiled at the balding, bespectacled, shorts-wearing vicar and thought about asking whether he was planning on wearing that shit when he married them. Perhaps he might consider chucking in a pair of sandals with socks to add to the overall grotesqueness of the look, but he decided against asking. These people had no sense of humour. *Not that he was joking...*

'So, is everything in order, vicar?' Marco's voice boomed around the room, the large wall-mounted cross and framed picture of Jesus beginning to grate on his wick. 'Of course, it goes without saying that my company also wishes to make a donation to whichever cause you feel most pressing.'

The vicar ran his tongue over his thin lips and clasped his fingers together in barely concealed satisfaction. 'That's most kind, Mr Morelli.' He crossed his blue-veined spindly legs over one another. 'And yes, I prepared the paperwork and took your request to the Archbishop of Canterbury, who agreed to waive the twenty-eight day notice period.' He smiled ingratiatingly. 'My church is lucky have a particularly longstanding relationship with the Bishop.'

What do you want, a medal? Marco thought, but instead smiled warmly. 'That's most fortunate.' *Shut the fuck and get on with it, you prick.*

'It's nice to see a couple so genuinely in love,' the vicar simpered.

Marco knew he'd rolled his eyes. He hadn't meant to, it just happened and hoped old Vic here hadn't noticed.

'Can you confirm the date then, Vicar?' Trevor asked, as impatient as Marco to get this done. From his side it was security. He didn't want Morelli changing his mind, especially now he'd done more digging on the company finances and had a better idea of what Morelli was worth. He wanted to ensure his daughter, and therefore *he* got his cut.

Smiling, the vicar turned the stamped paperwork around on his desk so his guests could see it. 'Saturday, at 2 o'clock.'

Hazel squealed right down Marco's ear. 'Oh, that's fantastic, isn't it babe? Thank you, vicar!'

'Yeah, wonderful...' Convinced his ear drum was bleeding, Marco bypassed the ringing in his ears, making a mental note to punch Hazel in the face at some point for that one. *But this weekend? Pretty swift, but fine by him.*

'Okay, well if that's sorted, then we'll leave you in peace, vicar.' Standing up, Marco did the gentlemanly thing and held his hand out to Hazel.

'Let's go shopping now, babe,' Hazel exclaimed excitedly, clutching Marco's hand. 'We can get the ring and my dress. I know *exactly* what I want.'

Great, Marco thought, silently wondering how much that

would set him back. Still, it was worth it. He must speculate to accumulate. Everything he'd gambled with so far had paid off.

As would this.

. . . .

BILL BLOCKED OUT the woman's screeching and concentrated on ensuring Zane Morelli's hands were firmly tied behind his back. On the off chance the man regained consciousness, it was vital he had no room to strike.

He should probably bind the ankles too, but he needed to move fast, being as he'd yet to deduce whether any sensors had been tripped. A silent alarm could presently be summoning a bunch of coppers in this direction from the nearest nick.

Bill turned to the man in the chair, unrecognisable aside from the eyes he knew belonged the accountant he'd once known. He'd never forgotten that weird fuck's eyes, even if the rest of him was a fucking mess and the ginger hair had long since changed colour. 'You got an alarm linked to the cops here, Flame?' he barked. 'You'd best be fucking honest about it, otherwise I'll fuck you up even more.'

Receiving a slight, but distinct shake of the head from the battered creature, Bill traced the outline of his Glock inside his pocket for good measure. He was about to deal with the woman, when a flurry of movement made him turn just in the nick of time to stop the blade driving into him.

Blocking Erin with his huge arm, it didn't take much effort to send her flying the other side of the room to land in a crumpled heap on the floor.

Stomping over, he kicked the dropped knife out of her reach. 'That was a fucking stupid manoeuvre, wasn't it?' he mumbled, primarily to himself, now glad that he hadn't utilised his spare rope to further constrain Zane.

He quickly bound Erin's hands and chuckled to himself as she glared at him with open malice. 'You're a feisty one,' he remarked, silently wondering how Flame had pulled such a fiery, hot chick.

Maybe he'd have a bit of her himself when they got back to the smoke, but for now his only aim was to get this lot out of here and back on the road.

Who should he start with?

Bill stared at Zane, still out cold. *Him.* He'd secure Morelli in the van and then come back for the other two.

Being as this tart was engaged to Flame, she wasn't likely to be much of a problem, even if she had just attempted to stick him, the stupid cow. She'd calm down soon enough when her weird fuck of a boyfriend was untied and didn't look quite so much like Freddy Krueger.

Wiping his hands down his trousers, Bill hefted up Zane's dead weight. 'Weighs a bleeding ton, the bastard!' he griped, his back already giving him jip.

'Where are you taking him?'

Surprised at the unexpected question, Bill saw Erin studying him intently. 'The same place you're going...'

'What? But...'

'Shut your missus up, Flame,' Bill growled. 'She ain't helping matters. And neither of you fucking move. I'll be back shortly.'

THIRTY FIVE

ERIN WATCHED Zane get dragged from the garage, his boots scuffing a groove across the dusty concrete floor.

As the door slammed, she heard the distinct turning of the key in the lock.

Her mouth was dry and her lungs burnt. *Would Zane be killed when he could do nothing to defend himself?*

Erin shuddered. She'd seen that man enter, but his presence had only registered over Zane's yelling and Anthony's pitiful howling for a split second before the metal curtain rod had thwacked across the back of Zane's skull.

She tried to warn him. Or at least she *thought* she had. Whether her yell had been just before or after the rod connected, she couldn't be sure. Neither could she be certain the sound had left her mouth or whether it remained locked inside her mind. Or even whether Zane had heard it?

What was certain though, was the warning, if she'd managed one, had been too late.

Biting her bottom lip, Erin stared at her bound hands and tested to see if she could release them. The movement only succeeding in tightening the knots. *Shit.*

She scanned the garage, spotting the knife lying against the wall in the far corner. If only she'd succeeded sticking it in that man... The man that Anthony - or as he was known, *Flame*, knew well...

He must be connected to Zane's firm...

But if that was the case, why would he attack Zane? The man hadn't much time for Anthony either...

Something very wrong was going on here and for the first time in all of the days, months and years since her father had been murdered, did Erin begin to think that maybe she'd been wrong about who had actually carried out the act.

Was Zane speaking the truth when he'd said it was Anthony?

Fear churned. Had she slept next to the person who had killed her father all of this time, whilst ploughing the majority of her hatred into the wrong person?

But even after the horrific beatings Zane had unleashed, Anthony hadn't admitted it. Nor had he denied Zane's part in anything.

Nothing added up and whichever way she looked at it, she was not in a good position.

Panic raged. That man said she was going to the same place as Zane? Would they all be killed? Or just her and Zane?

But why would Zane's own firm want to kill him?

Unless...

'I bet you wish you'd stayed where you were now, you stupid bitch!' Anthony suddenly said.

Due to his smashed face, Anthony's voice sounding nothing like the voice Erin had always despised, sliced through the silence. She hated it even more now. Did she wish she'd stayed with him and not chosen to get back on Zane's bike?

Never.

But her reasons for getting back on that bike were a thousand miles from where they had been that day last week.

Erin's brain hurtled through the conflicting events of the last few days; the last few hours especially difficult to contemplate.

Was Zane already dead?

She couldn't stop her heart from thrashing within her chest at the prospect of Zane no longer being there. Would she be left with Anthony... *Flame*, or would she die?

Bile rose into her mouth, the acidic taste making her gag. She wouldn't sit here waiting to be dumped next to Zane in a shallow grave whilst Anthony and that man went on their merry way.

It was now clear that Anthony knew who had really killed her father. But it wasn't him and neither was it Zane, so was it the big man who had carted Zane off? Him or someone to do with him?

She had to get out of here, away from Anthony - away from that man. If she could locate Zane, she might be able to release him.

He was the only one who could stop this now.

Rolling onto her side, Erin got to her knees, wincing as the concrete pushed against her bruised kneecaps. *If she could just reach the knife...*

Her progress and embryonic plan were thwarted hearing the key turn once again in the lock.

• • • •

'DON'T TRY ANYTHING STUPID,' Bill hissed, swinging the van around the large turning circle on Anthony and Erin's drive. The gravel crunched as they drove towards the gate. 'I've only untied you so not to alert nosy fuckers who might see you when we stop at traffic lights.'

But Bill didn't believe he'd have problems with any of these silly cunts. Now her boyfriend was untied, the tart was subdued. Zane was still out cold in the back of the Transit and wasn't going anywhere, short of racking up a few more bruises as he rolled between the bulk heads.

Sparking up a cigarette, Bill grinned. *All in all, not a bad job. Three brought in alive - just about...*

Marco could do the deed to Zane. Fuck knows what would

happen to Flame. He'd probably need to go too, being as he'd be the only one remaining alive who knew the ins and outs of the original deal.

As for this silly cow... Bill's eyes slid from the road to steal a glance at Erin numbly staring from the van's window.

Yeah, she knew her place. A swift punch to her pretty little face when he'd returned from chucking Zane in the van, made sure of that.

She didn't look quite as fetching now one of her eyes was black and almost swollen shut, but it served to remind the slut that he wouldn't put up with screaming ab-dabs and silliness. The message had clearly hit home, along with his fist, because now she was complying with his instructions like a docile lamb.

Bless.

Bill shook his large head. The strange idiosyncrasies of women never ceased to amaze him. That was probably why he was no longer married. It was too much fucking hassle.

He had no idea what Marco would do with this bird once they reached home turf, either. Personally, once her eye had sorted itself, Bill reckoned it wouldn't hurt putting her to use in some of the films. She was a tasty looking wench and they could always get rid of her afterwards, if she proved more trouble than she was worth.

Slipping his mobile back in the dashboard holder, he quickly called Sonny. He wasn't wasting time trying Marco again. 'Sonny? Yeah, it's Bill... Yep! All done! I've got all three and we're en route back... No, I haven't been able to get through, so can you let him know? Okay... Laters!'

Ending the call, a sly grin formed on Bill's face. 'Don't fret, chick. We'll get lover boy's face patched up when we reach London. He'll look as good as new.'

Erin made a point of sniffling, like she might burst into tears. She didn't have a clue what she was planning or if there was anything she could do. Right now there wasn't, but if she acted obedient, then an opportunity might present itself.

And if it did, she would be ready.

Pressed next to Anthony in the proximity of the van's cab, her skin crawled at being so close that part of her touched him.

Gritting her teeth, she stared out of the window with the one eye she could see through, her mind trawling through the possible scenarios as to what state Zane was in.

He could be lying in the back with a fractured skull. He could be dead... Either way, she was sure he must be horribly injured.

Her nausea increased as she scanned the cab and her mind for ways of stopping the van and preventing this man from taking her to God knows where with Anthony – and Zane.

Why hadn't she believed what Zane said when she'd first questioned the discrepancies? She *knew* things didn't add up, yet she'd pushed the discrepancies away. She'd used them as an excuse to divert from her self-hatred about the intense attraction for the man she'd believed had killed her father. This alone had blinded her heeding any truth in his words.

The attraction was still strong - now more than ever. Yet it was too late to do anything about it. *If only she could go back and change things...*

Erin turned to peer through the transparent partition between the cab and the rear of the van, seeing nothing but darkness. There was no sign of movement from within.

Desolation slammed through her as the extent of her hopeless situation gained pace. She'd be better off throwing herself from the moving van and taking her chances by running through a hedge into a field, praying she could outrun the inevitable chase.

Now all was lost, dying from an escape attempt was preferable.

And then she saw it.

Erin's eyes widened at Zane's face a couple of feet away from the partition. Her pulse raced as he gestured to the driver and motioned for her to do something.

How had Zane freed his hands? It didn't matter – he'd done it, but how could she distract the man driving?

'Face forward!' Bill growled, his hand flying off the wheel. Throwing his arm across Anthony's chest, he grabbed the front of Erin's top. 'Don't make sudden movements, otherwise I'll tie you back up.'

Immediately spinning back around, Erin scrabbled for what to do. *Quickly, think.* 'I-I wasn't turning around,' she lied, her hand rushing to her mouth. 'It's just that I think I'm going to be sick... No, I *am* going to be sick! Oh God... I...'

'Christ! Stop the fucking van!' Anthony jumped about in his seat, crushing himself against Bill. 'I can't stand vomit. I can't bear the smell. I...'

'Quickly!' Erin pleaded, making a very good job of an authentic gag reflex, pleased Anthony still had his strong phobia of vomit. 'Oh God... I...'

'Jesus Christ!' Bill muttered as Anthony all but crawled onto him in his desperation to move away from Erin. Glancing in his wing mirror, he swerved to the side of the road. 'If anyone comes round the corner they'll slam straight into us, so get a move on!'

He squashed Anthony back into the bench seat and clamped his hand over Erin's seat belt connector. 'You're not getting out! I ain't stupid! Open the fucking door and throw up. Make it quick.'

Erin so wanted to turn and look through the partition again, but she couldn't. All she could hope for was that Zane had a plan.

Scrambling for the door, knowing she could do nothing apart from exactly what the man said, she leant out and pulled everything from her acting ability, hoping her stomach muscles would play the game.

'Ugh!' Anthony cried at the loud retching. 'I can't stand thi...'

'Hurry the fuck up!' Bill yelled, acutely aware that every minute the van wasn't moving was a danger as well as an impediment. His eyes flicked between the wing mirrors and Erin, missing the split-second warning he had before the partition smashed in from behind.

. . . .

EVEN BEING DOWN thirty-eight grand in the space of an hour and a half, thanks to Hazel's choice of ring and wedding dress, wasn't enough to dent Marco's good mood.

He strongly suspected this was the tip of the iceberg, compared to the final amount his wife-to-be's tastes in what she deemed 'vital' for their wedding would rack up to. But it didn't matter. Whatever the cost of Saturday afternoon ended up, didn't compare with what he stood to gain in royalties and payments once Lisa Tequila was on his cast list. Or should he say, when Lisa Tequila was the *only* relevant person on his cast list?

With her topping the bill, the rest fell into obscurity.

Lounging back in his director's chair, Marco lazily flicked his cigarette ash onto the floor, rather than lean forward to use the crystal ashtray on the table next to him.

He shrugged. Someone would sweep it up. They could do it with their tongue, for all he cared. He paid these people, so they could damn well work for their money.

But things were okay. During the expensive shopping episode, he hadn't failed to notice the admiring glances from people in the jewellers and on the streets. He was pretty certain a hefty percentage of them recognised the woman on his arm from the films they watched behind closed doors. The films that *he* would soon own the rights for.

These people could dream all they liked. Hazel or Lisa, as they saw her, was now *his*. Or she would be at 2 o'clock in three days from now.

Marco looked back at the scene in front of him. The redhead with the massive tits had the main role in this film. It was the third in this particular series and most probably the last, once next week arrived. Oh well, if she had a problem with her downgrade to an extra, she could work at Tescos.

From that point on, he'd concentrate solely on what his wife was doing, because that's what she would he - his *wife*. With her looks and popularity, she'd be the one bringing the spoils to the table.

The percentage agreed for Trevor's cut from this would be a *pinch* of the takings. Furthermore, Trevor had failed to negotiate a cut for accompanying merchandise or endorsements, the stupid bastard.

Marco grinned. *Not his problem.* It would have been rude to point out the skinny twat's shortfall in negotiating ability.

In the meantime, this lot would suffice well enough. They'd serve as an additional income stream using the less adept film crews.

It was all good.

Now he'd left Sonny to get on with getting everything ready and in place for when the van returned with the awaited cargo, there was nothing to impede his success. Neither was there sod all left to do, apart from sit back, relax and wait until he got word that it was time.

Marco frowned. Short of getting himself suitably wired to deal with his brother...

But even *that* wasn't a hardship.

He topped up his whisky and sighed contentedly. A few more lines of coke once this next set of takes had finished and he'd be good to go. It wouldn't be long now.

Marco exhaled a long thin stream of smoke towards the ceiling. He knew he could count on Bill. He'd always been able to. And Sonny receiving word that all three were in Bill's possession, alive and on the road back, was the news he'd wanted.

Okay, so at first, he'd thought it would be easier for Bill to deal with Zane, but when push came to shove, it should be *him* to pull the final curtain on his brother. It should be *him* showing Zane he no longer held the reins and that he, Marco, wasn't in his shadow any longer and hadn't been for quite some time.

Besides, he wanted to see the realisation seeping into Zane's brain that the changes in the firm during his absence proved there was no room in it for *him*. Marco didn't need or want his brother's involvement. Furthermore, Zane hadn't the *option* to be part of anything.

Marco wanted to witness Zane's anger and resentment, knowing all the things he'd taken pains to setup, maintain and keep, were old hat, obsolete and long gone.

After all this time, Zane could meet back up with their father. It couldn't be more apt. Considering there had been minimal room for *him* where their father was concerned, now they'd have eternity to spend in each other's company...

Company of which Marco finally didn't feel aggrieved to be excluded from.

Zane was always the favourite, the heir, the only one worth anything...

He smiled inwardly. *Funny how things changed...*

As for that dickhead, Flame, and that tart he was supposed to be marrying, well they would be easily dispatched. It made sense to do them all here, rather than elsewhere in the country, where they didn't have the same network of associates to help remove the traces.

THIRTY SIX

THE HEAVY PUNCH to the back of Bill's neck was enough to knock him off kilter long enough to release his hold of the seat belt, giving Erin chance to jump from the van.

As Anthony started squawking and trying to release his seat belt with his one good hand, not looking where she was going, Erin leapt onto the tarmac of the country lane. She raced around the back of the van, her fingers fumbling to open the back doors from the outside. *If these were locked, they were finished.*

Tugging the black plastic handle, whilst Zane pushed from inside, the door flew open, almost knocking her over.

'Keep yourself clear of what I'm doing next,' Zane hissed, his eyes meeting hers for a split second as Bill clambered out of the driver's side.

Zane jumped from the van; aware time wasn't on his side. His head pounded, but his skull was still intact. It wouldn't be if he didn't get this right though. *Nobody's* would be.

Bill Wainwright would have a gun on him or in the cab and it would be ready to fire.

Hoping Erin stayed out of the way as instructed, Zane darted around the side of the Transit, slamming straight into Bill as he did so.

Throwing a punch, Zane failed to connect with Bill's face and instead grappled with the man. He was right. A gun was in Bill's hand and he had to get it off him.

He only had one go at this and he couldn't afford to misjudge anything else.

Positioning his leg behind Bill's, Zane drove his weight against the man's barrel chest, meeting equal resistance. He then put his power into pointing the barrel of the gun in the other direction.

Racing around the van's rear, Erin stared in horror at the two men struggling to gain control, the barrel of the gun wedged underneath Zane's chin.

Zane was roaring, the other man was roaring. It was a battle of brute strength for the prize of only one life.

If that gun went off, Zane would die.

Erin's heart clattered so fast the separate beats became a continuous thrum.

Then the men toppled over - Bill crashing to the floor with Zane on top of him.

Moving his foot from underneath Bill's massive bulk, Zane didn't feel pain, he was just grateful his plan to overbalance the man had succeeded. *But this was far from over.*

Bringing his knee up, he jammed it into Bill's neck. Pushing forward and down with as much pressure as possible, his hand remained firmly gripped on Bill's, only his fingers stopping the trigger from being pulled.

Sweat poured down Zane's back as he twisted harder, his fingers searching for pressure points on Bill's hand and fingers. This was taking too long. He'd run out of energy soon with the amount of power needed. *Come on, come on!*

'Fuck you, Wainwright!' he snarled, willing for a much-needed burst of power. He then gained traction. Only a few millimetres of the gun's grip, but it was something. Aware the gun's barrel pressed directly into his windpipe meant there wasn't long to rectify this, he upped the downward pressure of his knee on Bill's neck.

Another millimetre or two...

Zane's fingers dug harder, his arm upping the twist. His third and fourth fingers were now in full contact. *This was it. He'd got this.*

With a final twist, hoping the sudden movement wouldn't trigger the gun, Zane jolted backwards as Bill was forced to relinquish control. Knowing there wasn't a moment to spare before Bill was back on him, he raised the gun and pulled the trigger.

Erin remained motionless with both horror and relief as the bullet ripped through Bill Wainwright's face and head, gore and flesh splattering over her. There was a dull silence in the second his body remained upright before it crashed to the ground.

'Is he dead?' she blathered, amazed she possessed the ability to render understandable words. Her eyes moved to the pieces of pink bloody flesh peppering Zane's face.

'He'd dead,' Zane muttered, his head then swinging around as the engine of the Transit fired into life and with screeching tyres, backed towards them.

• • • •

WHEN ANTHONY HEARD the gun, he knew he had to make a decision. He'd known that even before it went off that one of those fuckers would die. Whether it was Morelli or the overgrown orangutan, Wainwright, was irrelevant. That's why he'd grabbed his chance and moved into the driver's seat.

He wasn't being dragged back to London by whoever remained alive. Nor would he be dispatched. And he wouldn't be. Not now he had this opportunity.

It wasn't *him* who had backtracked on the agreement. He'd done everything agreed. He'd built a new life for himself - a good and profitable one and he wasn't leaving that behind.

He was getting out of this and he was taking Erin with him. She owed him plenty. Even more so now and he intended to call in every last bit of it.

Careering backwards through the dust the tyres flicked up,

in the reflection of his left wing mirror, Anthony saw Erin standing motionless, her mouth hanging open like a gormless bitch.

Reaching level, he watched the implications of what was happening dawning on Erin. Her eyes widened and she opened her mouth to scream, but he knew as well as she did that she'd left things too late.

Not feeling the sea of pain which was now his face, or the smashed remains of one of his hands, Anthony jerked to a stop and leant over to fling the passenger door open, following with his body which enabled him to gain a secure hold of Erin's arm.

'Get in,' he snarled. 'Get in the fucking van.'

'Get off!' Erin yelled, suddenly coming to life. There was no way! Nothing would make her go *anywhere* with Anthony ever again.

As Anthony gained a better grip of her top, Erin found herself pulled closer to the van. *If he got hold of her arm, he would manhandle her in there.*

She tried to slam the door on his arm, but all that achieved was her being dragged closer.

No, no, no!

'Get the fuck in!' Anthony snarled, his bared teeth in his ravaged face showcasing him for the monster he was.

'Zane!' Erin yelled, her voice filled with panic as Anthony pulled the top half of her body into the cab. Her heels dug into the floor, but it was no use - they scuffed and scraped in vain along the surface of the tarmac.

Running up the side of the van, Zane aimed his gun through the driver's window. The back of Flame's head was in his sights. He could shoot him dead this very second. But if breaking the glass slightly changed the trajectory of the bullet, or if Flame moved one centimetre either way, the shot could pass him by and hit Erin.

Fuck. It was too much of a risk. There was too much to lose. He'd lose her...

Zane tugged the locked driver's door and when Flame

glanced around and spotted him, he knew he had seconds before Erin was entirely dragged inside the van. Flame would be gone and so would Erin, leaving him with a dead body and no means of giving chase.

As Erin's hands flailed around to connect with Anthony's face and eyes, Zane fired a shot, aiming purposefully high enough to miss them both.

When the driver's side window blew out, covering him with splinters of shattered glass, Anthony knew he had to move. Ducking down, he kept his grip on Erin and shuffled back to the driver's seat.

Zane raced around the passenger side as the gears crunched and the revs of the accelerator rose. As the van sped forward, he grabbed Erin's feet sticking from the open door and pulled her out, leaving her to tumble onto the tarmac.

Raising his gun, Zane squinted through the dust cloud and fired once, twice, three times at the fleeing Transit. If he couldn't shoot Anthony face to face, he'd blow the tyres out and *then* shoot him.

Giving chase on foot, he slowed to a stop as the air cleared and he realised the van and Flame had gone.

Fuck.

Remembering Erin was lying in a heap on the floor, he raced back down the road and scooped her into his arms, his anger blooming with the swollen mess of her left eye.

But she wasn't in that van; she wasn't dead and for that alone he was grateful. He pulled her against his chest. 'Are you alright?'

Overwhelming relief cascaded through Erin as she sagged into Zane, her fingers clutching his sides. Against her will, the tears that never genuinely flowed, started.

Anthony had gone, but she hadn't and Zane wasn't dead. This beautiful, yet savage man who she'd wrongly blamed had saved her again. 'I'm okay. Are you? Your head?'

Zane's frustration was palpable. 'My head's fine, but I didn't stop him... I tried to blow the tyres... I...'

'You did all you could. But what do we do now?' Erin whimpered. 'We've got no transport. No nothing and we're miles from anywhere.' *And Anthony had got away...*

'Don't worry about that. I'll think of something.'

Erin swallowed dryly, realising she believed him. She looked up into Zane's piercing blue eyes and before she could talk herself out of it, pressed her lips to his with the overwhelming need to do what she'd wanted again for so long. This time, it was free from guilt.

THIRTY SEVEN

ZANE CONTINUED WALKING, even though his feet were killing. It was only a few miles from where they'd left Bill's body lying on the road in full view, but they'd had to move from that area as quickly as possible.

Dock leaves picked from the verge had helped scrape the majority of Bill Wainwright's gunk off them and with a bit of luck, they'd make it back to the cottage without anybody stopping them.

It was tempting to cut through the fields, meaning less chance of getting noticed, but if they *were* spotted, hiking through a random field was harder to explain. At least this way, they resembled *normal* people, rather than people who had just shot someone dead. At least from *his* side, anyway...

He frowned. Then there was the question of how to retrieve his bike which was still at Flame's house. That, he could not risk collecting in case Flame had returned there or more people had been summoned... Or the police?

He had to weigh up this nightmare and the implications, not forgetting what he now knew. But he couldn't do any of that now. He must concentrate only on getting both himself and Erin out of immediate danger.

Zane was sure Erin's head must be swarming too and that awkward kiss back there hadn't helped.

Had he not wanted it?

It may have been unexpected, but hell, yeah, he'd wanted it.

He'd had no option but to pull away. Every minute remaining at the scene of a blood bath, next to a corpse and holding a murder weapon, was a risk.

And a fucking big one.

If it was up to him, he'd have happily returned her kiss forever more, but it wasn't just the major problem with the vicinity - his head was mashed too.

Shoving his hands deeper into his pockets, Zane pressed on, his eyes fixed on the corner at the end of the road, around which led to Hope Cottage. Once they were back there and showered, he could think straight.

Hopefully.

Maybe it was possible to make sense of what was relentlessly banging inside his brain; the things he'd suspected but didn't want to acknowledge.

Maybe not.

Either way, there was no getting away from it now.

Marco was behind killing David Masters. It was him, or someone else under his orders. The proof was in Bill's phone.

Zane's jaw tightened. All this time he'd believed Flame to have pulled the robbery and murdered Masters. Sure, the bastard framed him, but he'd done that under instructions. *Instructions from Zane's firm. From Marco...*

Marco was responsible for *everything*.

Zane's anger was too fierce to think properly. He couldn't think about *anything*, including the woman he'd been drawn to since day one.

He needed to be back behind closed doors and shower this shit off before he could take stock.

Erin walked beside Zane, desperately trying to keep pace with him, her mind swirling with an avalanche of unanswered questions.

She knew she'd wrongly accused him and attempted to kill him on more than one occasion... But they had a connection - she *knew* they did. Yet, after the initial hungry return of her kiss just now, he'd frozen and blanked her, again...

But they shared something - a *big* something.

Betrayal.

Irrevocably drawn to each other, due to the shared need for revenge, as well as undeniable chemistry, there was nothing now to stop them. No guilt. But there *was* the residue from what today had uncovered and who was responsible for ruining both their lives. *That* would be the most difficult to deal with of all.

After the short kiss, Zane had held her eyes with his piercing blues that spoke a thousand unsaid words. Then someone or something had switched the light off and he'd flipped to another channel.

Turning away, he'd shoved the gun in his pocket, walked over to where that man's body lay and proceeded to go through the man's pockets. Retrieving a phone, he'd walked off, jerking his head for her to follow.

That had been it.

The words Erin wanted to say, the conversations she needed to have, remained stuck in her throat during this never-ending walk. The words and questions were trapped in a place she was unable to dislodge them from.

She trudged on, the tip of her tongue burning with the need to discuss things, but instead they carried on in silence. Zane paced ahead, his full concentration on the phone taken from the man she now knew to be Bill Wainwright. *The man Zane had just shot dead.*

She'd watched Zane's face as he'd scrolled through the call log and texts. She hadn't seen what they said and neither had she asked, but from his expression alone, they held the proof of the conclusion she too had arrived at.

Zane's brother had killed her father and framed Zane, making out it was Anthony.

She felt sick. Anthony must have taken a hell of a payout to be the fall guy. Now his distinct refusal to go near London and his change of appearance made sense.

Marco had done it or was the one giving orders to whoever sliced that knife across her father's throat.

And that person wasn't Zane...

But how would Zane handle it? Where did he go from here? Where did she go from here? Where did *either* of them go from here?

Was there even a 'they'?

And where had Anthony's disappeared to?

There were too many questions which she didn't have answers to. But she needed them. She needed answers more than anything.

Rounding the corner to the cottage, she touched Zane's jacket sleeve. 'Zane, we need to talk. We n...'

'Not now.' Zane stomped towards the house, searching his pocket for the keys.

'But we need to discuss what we now know must be the truth about wh...'

'I said, not now!' Zane spat.

He swung around, his eyes wild with a deep emotion Erin had not before seen on him. *Pain.*

'I can't talk about this right now.' Zane jammed the key in the lock and shouldered open the door.

Walking inside, Erin looked around the cosy interior. Everything was exactly as they'd left it. But *someone* had been inside since they'd left. The hatred and anger bristling in waves from Zane, showed he sensed it too.

'You shower first,' Zane muttered, reaching for the bottle of whisky.

· · · ·

LISTENING TO THE SHOWER RUNNING, Zane stood at the window, not wanting to sit down for anything that had splashed from the body of Bill Wainwright to transfer onto one thing he had to live with.

Not that he could live here now.

He looked blankly down onto the driveway. It was a beautiful sunny day, but all Zane felt were cold needles running up and down his veins. Sharp slivers of pain that no amount of hot water could cleanse.

And along with this numbing cold, was the contradiction of searing hot anger flowing the opposite way.

His own brother had done this to him? His little brother that he'd spent his life looking out for and protecting and honouring what his father expected of them both?

Slugging down the rest of his whisky, Zane raked his fingers through his hair.

Now he'd killed Marco's right-hand man, but where were the rest of his firm? Where were *his* men who had always been loyal to both him and his father beforehand? Were any of them still there and if so, why hadn't they done something about this?

Bill had always been Marco's man, but Zane was surprised at Sonny. Sonny hadn't leant towards one of the Morelli brothers more than the other, but it seemed he'd been wrong on that too. The texts Sonny had sent to Bill with the addresses showed his involvement. He'd also seen the texts from Flame.

His jaw clenched.

And where had Flame gone? Back to his house? To the police? To London?

Hearing the water from the bathroom turn up a notch, Zane glanced in the direction of where he knew Erin would be standing, naked and beautiful.

His heart skipped a beat. And Erin? She'd been destroyed as much, if not more, during the course of this long situation. The things she'd endured to govern her plan of revenge...

It now made sense why she'd got herself involved with Flame and all the things that brought with it.

Zane shuddered with the image of that bastard's hands on her; treating her like shit; abusing and hurting her. And she'd done it all under the proviso of getting revenge on *him* as well as Flame?

But both he and Erin were wrong. All those years wasted planning the downfall of the perpetrator, when the real culprit was someone else.

Slamming down his empty glass, Zane moved towards the bathroom. Too much had been lost and he wasn't about to lose *this* - the singular chink of light in an otherwise dark existence.

• • • •

ERIN LEANT her forehead against the glass shower cubical, allowing water to cascade over her in a hot torrent. She should turn the shower off and leave some hot water for Zane, but she couldn't bring herself to move.

She needed the burn on her skin to infuse her with the will to continue. Water wouldn't remove the stain of what was invisibly dyeing her skin, or her mind, but it was all she had.

Everything was for nothing.

For the second time today - two times more than it had happened in six years, real tears cascaded down her cheeks to mix with the water pouring overhead. The salty tears stung the swollen flesh of her damaged left eye, but she didn't care.

Without even realising, she slithered down the wall to crouch on the shower floor, her chest heaving with racking sobs.

She didn't think she'd ever stop. Didn't *want* to stop. She had to purge the poison building up in her body during her campaign over these past few years. The campaign that had turned out to be fruitless.

She'd achieved nothing. She'd...

As strong arms lifted Erin up from behind, she felt too weak to protest. She knew who the arms belonged to and although she couldn't bear a third rebuff from the man who had slaughtered her own concept of herself, she was too numb to offer resistance and protect herself from further insult.

She wasn't normally unable to put up a fight or challenge a threat, but after today and the past week, she was reduced to pulp. She doubted whether she'd ever rebuild her shattered mind.

Erin found herself facing the man she'd felt so horribly guilty over being drawn to - the guilt she need never have felt. Even being naked and exposed no longer held any meaning.

She stared at the hard, defined muscles of Zane's torso, mindlessly separating the tattoos underneath the smattering of dark hair over his chest and the swirling ink over his arms. What were the pictures of? Did they hold significance? Did it matter?

No.

Zane tilted Erin's head up and gently traced the blackened flesh around her eye, glad he'd killed the man who had done this. If he hadn't already killed Bill Wainwright, then he'd be making it his business to do that now.

The water flowing over his head and face to mingle with the water cascading over Erin lithe body, made Zane's breath hitch with longing.

This time he would not pull away.

He ran his thumb over Erin's bottom lip, her eyes now meeting with his before his mouth crashed onto hers.

Immediately yielding to Zane's lips, Erin snapped from her stupor, a burst of new life breaking forth as intense longing raged through her, like wildfire.

Picking Erin up, Zane pressed her against the cubical wall and wrapped her legs around his hips. He paused, his eyes searching hers.

Erin responded by searching for his mouth once more, her hands grasping his buttocks, letting Zane know in silent understanding that she wanted this, *needed* this as much as he did.

All thoughts of anything else were thrown from her mind as he entered her, giving the unspoken promise, that for a while, short of the intense sensations raging through her, she would be free from everything.

Thirty Eight

WAKING UP EARLY compared to his usual standards, Marco blinked the sleep from his eyes and surveyed the room in an effort to crank his brain into recalling what the state of play was.

Although the cocaine and alcohol hangover pounding in his head was clear, he recalled *exactly* why it was amazing he should have succumbed to sleep.

But then maybe he'd passed out rather than 'slept'. He rolled his shoulders in a bid to release the crick in his neck from sleeping in the leather armchair and brushed a pile of cigarette ash from his lap to the floor.

He snatched his mobile off the table. The battery was almost dead and there still had been no calls from Bill.

All night Marco had snorted cocaine and drank whisky to keep himself in a state of utter frenzy for the minute Sonny gave the nod the van was at the warehouse ready to unload.

That should have happened hours ago. *Hours*. But there had been nothing...

And no matter how many times he'd called Sonny, shouting at him to find out what the fuck what was going on, there were no forthcoming answers. This hadn't stopped him from screaming and roaring and as a consequence, his throat was raw.

But if Bill wasn't picking up his phone to Sonny, there was nothing to relay.

Bill hadn't even answered to *him* and Marco had called how many times?

He flicked to his mobile call log:

Bill (32)

And there was the answer – thirty-two times.

Once the arrival time had been and gone, he'd called Bill every twenty minutes or so, getting angrier and angrier.

Marco knew he must have passed out in the end, otherwise he'd have smashed the bloody phone to bits.

His teeth grated with frustration and the effects of a heavy coke downer.

He'd get hold of Flame if it was possible, but for security reasons, Bill was the only one with that toe-rag's number. And without Bill - surprise surprise, no one could get hold of the tosser.

Marco hefted himself to his feet, wishing he hadn't, when his temples pounded in protest.

Perhaps he should call Sonny again? He'd been instructed to put his skills to work to unearth Flame's mobile number from the techno ether and he'd had hours to do that now, so...

Marco snatched up his phone the second it rang. 'Bill?' His face dropped. 'Oh, hello Hazel. What? Caught me out at what? No... of course I'm happy to hear from you...'

He closed his eyes in desperation, willing Hazel to get off the line. 'What? Today? No, no I can't... I've got loads on... No, I haven't forgotten...'

How could he forget he was getting hitched in three days? And with no confirmation that Zane wasn't on the loose, finalising the marriage was more important than ever.

Realising Hazel was still talking, Marco concentrated, then frowned. 'Honeymoon? Yeah, yeah sure. Whatever you want. It might be a bit difficult at the moment though... Perhaps in a month's time instead? No, it isn't more important than... Okay, book whatever you want and send me the bill.'

Whatever she booked he'd find a way to cancel it. He couldn't go anywhere until this was sorted, but he wouldn't tell her that just yet.

He glanced at his watch. 'Look, I must get on... What? No, I haven't had time to organise a stag party. You have a good time tonight though with the girls at your hen thing.'

Ending the call, Marco chucked the mobile on the chair like it was a hot coal. *Bloody woman.* Stag party? What the fuck for? Every night was a stag party - or it *used* to be, until this shit kicked off.

It wasn't like they had hosts of people coming to the wedding anyway. There wasn't time to invite many, and that was fine by him. The quicker it was kept under wraps and the deal secured, the better. He didn't give a toss if no one was there to see it, as long as he got what he needed, got a shag from Lisa Tequila and sorted this mess out before anyone found out about it.

Namely Hazel and her father...

As the doorbell's irritating tune of *Dixie* rang out, Marco's heart lurched. The only people with passage through the reception to his apartment without consent now were Hazel, Bill and Sonny. And it certainly wasn't Hazel, unless she'd just phoned him from downstairs!

Please let it be Bill, Marco prayed as he stumbled to the door.

'I haven't got Flame's mobile number.' Sonny walked into the apartment, his laptop under his arm. 'The bitch at his office wouldn't give it out, despite the bullshit I fed her, but I'm still working on it.' He plonked his laptop on the coffee table and cranked it into life. 'You need to take a look at this...'

As Sonny brought up an internet page, Marco's annoyance heightened. It was easier to get shit from a rocking horse, than personal details these days. It used to be so fucking easy.

'Look!' Sonny nodded at the screen.

'What is it?' Marco peered at the small text, resenting that soon he'd have to throw the towel in and get glasses. That would look good, wouldn't it? *He'd look a right fucking idiot.*

'The Midlands news website.' Sonny tapped the screen. 'I'm not saying this is... you know... but...'

Frowning, Marco squinted harder, finding closing one eye made things clearer.

Shock Shooting in Quiet Village

A dog walker has been left traumatised after coming across the dead body of a man with gunshot wounds on Tuesday afternoon, 12 May.

Donna Morfett walks her dog, Benji, at least three times a day along the quiet country lane from her house to the village centre a mile away. It was here that she came across the dreadful scene. Donna, who was still visibly shaken, said: "In all my years of living in Knowle, I've never experienced anything like it. This isn't Birmingham, so you don't expect this. It's awful. Just awful!"

The middle-aged white male, with dark hair and a larger than average, stocky build was around six foot three inches tall and had no form of identification on him.

No vehicle was noticed around the area at the time investigators believe the attack happened, but there were fresh tyre tracks at the side of the lane, possibly belonging to a van.

Residents in the affluent village of Knowle are understandably upset and worried by this horrific event. Anyone with information or who thinks they witnessed anything unusual, please call the police on...

'The addresses I gave Bill were in Knowle,' Sonny said

quietly, like speaking louder would make the concept more offensive.

Marco chewed his lip. That website didn't say the dead man was Bill, but it didn't say it wasn't either. *Gunshots, a van and the right area... It all linked up.*

And being as there was still no sign of Bill, Zane, that woman or Flame, it stood a good chance the man shot dead, *was* Bill.

If it was, then where the fuck was the van and the rest of them?

Marco's eyes narrowed.

Zane...

Zane had done this and fucked off, keeping Flame and that tart hostage. *Shit.*

THIRTY NINE

ANTHONY STARED into the bathroom mirror, flinching at the reflection. There was no way he could go to work like this. *None*.

His hands shook in the never-ceasing rhythm stress always brought, his fingertips twitching and jerking in an untimely fashion. It was now even more painful due to the broken bones in his bandaged hand. His ability to type emails and correspondence would also be hindered for however many weeks this took to mend.

He glanced at the painkillers the hospital insisted he take with him when he discharged himself and then snatched up a leaflet the nurse had given him.

His eyes narrowed at the bold type at the top of the leaflet:

Spotting Depression And Mental Illness - How To Get The Help You Need...

Were they taking the piss? Depression? Mental illness? Did they think that by interspersing this rubbish with a pattern of blue squares and circles deflected from the insinuation something was wrong with his brain?

There was nothing wrong with that!

However, Anthony had paid little attention to the doctor's comments. Why would he? He'd only been interested in how long it would take to bolt his cheekbone back together and stitch his fucking face back up.

The only bonus of not being short of money was going private. He'd been dealt with *immediately* at the Bupa hospital. That was the difference if you paid for stuff. No hanging around for weeks on end with incontinent, wailing bastards in a dormitory smelling of piss. Neither was there grounds to keep him overnight if he didn't agree to it. And he hadn't, even though they had 'strongly advised' it.

They couldn't call the police without his express permission either and he'd made it quite clear who was paying for their services. *Him*. If he said he'd been attacked by a gang of hooded men and had no wish to press charges, then that's all there was to it.

He didn't give a toss if they believed him or not.

Scrunching up the leaflet, he chucked it in the bathroom bin. He'd keep the plastic surgery booklet they'd given him though.

Anthony inspected his misshapen, swollen face once again, his anger increasing as he touched the tight tender skin pulling over the puckered stitches. He looked like a patchwork blanket!

How long would he have to remain out of sight? It wasn't like this mess would heal overnight and there was only so much his conceal-all make up could cover. It certainly wouldn't hide these stitches and the lines of scabs once they formed.

The overall state of his face after what Zane had done wasn't something that would rectify itself. So, yes, surgery was something to consider, but he'd go to his usual clinic for that.

He snorted loudly through his nose in derision. Even doing *that* hurt.

At least Zane fucking Morelli had something to think about now. But what the man would do with the snippets he'd been given was anyone's guess.

Now that slag had disappeared again, Anthony suspected it would be for good, but there had been no choice but to drive off, whilst he still had the chance.

How exactly would he explain Erin's permanent absence?

Hearing his mobile ringing, Anthony left the bathroom and moved into the bedroom, eyeing the mess left from Zane's stunt. For it to have happened in his own personal fortress was even worse. Morelli had overstepped the mark ten-fold.

Picking up the phone, he glanced at the screen. *It was the office...*

Taking a deep breath, he answered. 'Anthony Walker speaking.' His throat constricted hearing Maisie from reception. Without giving her chance to say much, he got in first. 'I was just about to call you. I won't be in today. I had an... erm... a car accident last night. No... I'm okay, but my face is a bit of a mess...' *That was an understatement.* 'No, I'll be fine... What? When...? No, you did the right thing. Data protection and all that... Let me know if it happens again or... or if you get any strange... erm... visitors.'

Anthony swallowed the urge to tell the woman and her probing questions to piss off. 'No, I'm not expecting anyone... I'm more worried about you,' he lied. 'I presume you heard about that incident yesterday? Dreadful, yes... and until they find the lunatic responsible, I want all staff to remain on guard. As owner of the firm, I take responsibility for everyone's well-being.'

And if he hadn't had a gun aimed in his direction yesterday, he'd have hung around to run those fuckers over – including Erin.

Hanging up, Anthony placed his mobile down and looked around the room.

Whilst Zane was most likely still in the vicinity, waiting to finish what he'd started before Bill rudely interrupted, the chances of a repeat visit was high, so the next thing to do was to get the doors and windows reinforced.

Anthony also had his suspicions about who had called his

office asking for his mobile number. It *had* to be Marco or one of his associates, but now that dippy receptionist had ensured he couldn't get in contact with the very people who could get him out of this bloody mess.

What remained now was what the hell he did from here with the limited options he had.

One of those things had to be getting rid of the white Transit complete with bullet holes, which was presently sitting in his double garage.

• • • •

AFTER ANOTHER INTENSELY enjoyable session of being brought to previously unknown heights, Erin flopped back onto the bed, satiated. The intense love making which had commenced in the shower and continued most of the night, as well as several times this morning, had been all-encompassing.

She aimlessly twisted strands of Zane's hair around her fingers whilst he trailed light kisses over her breasts.

Popping himself up on an elbow, Zane grinned - a rare expression of relaxation on his handsome face. It was a far cry from the hard look he reserved for normal use, but Erin understood. The base and all-consuming attraction which had haunted her since the start, now being free from guilt removed a huge weight. Being able to act on what she so desperately wanted, without the lurking sense of betraying both her father and herself, was not only liberating, but deflected from the outstanding issues she knew both she and Zane still faced.

She suspected Zane felt along the same lines too. He was a complicated, deep man with many buried issues and a lot of problems on his shoulders.

Of course, nothing had been said, but even if Zane's feelings weren't as intense as what she felt for him, there was no doubt they had more than a basic connection.

It was strange. Strange, but nice and the first time she could say she was understood by someone, with or without words.

But there *had* to be words: Not about how or why they'd

ended up in bed, frantically exploring each other's bodies like the end of the world was nigh, but what might be nigh if they didn't make a move on what to do next. Not discussing it only prolonged the inevitable.

Shifting to lay her head on Zane's chest, Erin listened to the steady, yet distinct beat of his heart.

'Tell me about your father.'

Erin froze at Zane's unexpected question as it rumbled against her temple, but talking about this now was as good a time as ever. As well as the precarious situation they were in, she too had things she wanted to ask - things she *needed* to ask.

'My father was a good man and I loved him.' Erin's eyes misted over. 'He'd do anything for me and my mother, hence why she couldn't bear to go on after he died...'

Zane bristled at the raw pain in Erin's voice. 'I didn't kill your father, Erin. Nor did I rob him.'

Erin nodded. 'It almost finished me when... when he was murdered, but I do now believe it wasn't you who was responsible.' *That* was something she never thought she'd hear herself say, especially to the man she'd held at the top of her despatch list all of this time.

Zane stroked Erin's soft hair, unable to believe how much she affected him. He wanted to shield her from all the shit in this world, along with the people who caused it. 'My father was always on good terms with yours. He was adamant there should be no reprisals.'

Erin tilted her face to Zane's, blown away every time by the contrast of his striking blue eyes with his olive skin and jet-black hair.

'Admittedly, both myself and Marco weren't happy with our father's decision. Our father believed Masters hadn't badmouthed the firm and that it was rumours put around by people looking for trouble.' He shrugged. 'We thought there could be no smoke without fire and that Masters should be pulled up.'

Erin tensed. 'So, you *did* think it right my father should be killed?'

Zane shook his head. 'No. Not that. Admittedly, I was a fiery young man. I still am, just not quite as young.' His mouth twitched with a slight smile. 'I felt some kind of reprisal was warranted for reputation's sake, yes, but not *that...*'

'And Marco...' Erin's voice was barely more than a whisper. 'What did he think?'

'The same.' Zane's brows furrowed. 'At least that's what he said in as many words... What I believed he thought...'

And there it was... The elephant in the room.

'But now...?'

Zane remained silent for a moment, knowing the second he uttered it, despite thinking the very same thing for some time and none more so since yesterday, vocalising it made it that little bit more real.

And that was the difficult part. Because it was difficult *and* true meant there was only one way to deal with the situation. Something he'd never dreamt he'd face. But now he had to and he knew it.

He spoke slowly, his eyes clouding with both resentment and disappointment. 'I don't "think" it was Marco. It *was* him.' He ran his hand over his stubbly chin. 'Marco planned it and paid Flame off to take the flak. He planned it all.' His eyes darkened further. 'They wanted me to believe Flame was behind it. Marco even told me the firm dispatched Flame when they discovered he was the traitor. And Wainwright - the guy who turned up yesterday, he was sent to take me out.'

Erin swallowed. 'I thought he'd killed you when he whacked you.'

'So did he, I expect.' Zane shrugged, like it meant little. 'But I expect his aim was to take me back to London for Marco to have that prize.

'I-I don't understand...'

'My own brother even sanctioned *this*.' Zane stabbed at the jagged scar on his face. 'He said I'd gone against our father's orders and claimed my "injury" was instructed before it was realised Flame was the culprit.'

'But now we know he wasn't the culprit...'

'Oh, but he was. Flame knew what had been done and, being a greedy cunt, took the money and disappeared.' Zane shook his head. 'Then I fucked things up by getting released. I see now that I was never supposed to get out.' He shrugged his large shoulders again. 'I had my suspicions, which was why I changed briefs. Even my original brief was in on it!'

Erin blew through her teeth. 'So now what?'

Zane's eyes narrowed. 'Now I'm going to finish them all and get my firm back. That's if there's one left of any use!'

Flipping himself over Erin, he pressed his lips onto hers. 'I'll get your father's money back for you, okay? I'll get back what was yours and reclaim my firm.'

Erin shook her head. 'I don't want the money. I thought I did, but it was never really about that. I wanted the *murderer*. I thought that by getting my family's money back by marrying Anthony, killing him and then killing *you*, I'd achieve all of those things... As it turns out, I wouldn't have achieved anything.'

Zane smiled. 'But you will now. I'll make sure this time you see justice, as indeed, so will I.'

WIPING THE COKE RESIDUE from under his nose, Marco loitered outside the studio's main dressing room. As this lot shagged in front of a camera for the world to see, he hadn't seen the point forking out to maintain separate dressing rooms for women and men. It wasn't worth the upkeep, so they'd got one to share between them. The deluxe smaller one opposite was only *ever* reserved for the star of the show.

After next week, there would be only one name attached to that hallowed door. But not yet there wasn't and hearing this shit wasn't helping.

Pressing himself against the wall, Marco fine-tuned his hearing to pick up the voices inside, the cocaine heightening his senses.

In many ways he wished he hadn't.

His dark brows knitted as he homed in on the voices, several of which he knew exactly who owned them.

'Well, I don't like it!' a woman said. 'It's all too much of a coincidence. The sort of things that keep happening, don't tend to just "happen". It's *got* to be him.'

'I agree. Plus, he's been arrested twice now,' someone added, a conspiring note clear in their voice. 'First it was over chucking Pauline off his balcony and th...'

'But they said Pauline *fell* off!'

'Oh, come on! You don't believe that any more than the rest of us,' a man sneered. 'It's him alright! Morelli's a fucking loon. That girl was only here one day, yet he made a beeline for her. The next thing – bang! Dead!'

Pressed against the wall, Marco's fists clenched. That voice belonged to a tall blonde surfer dude who, due to the size of his cock, thought himself Don Juan. He'd have no fucking cock at all after this.

'And what about Cherie?' The timid sounding woman was barely audible, but Marco could still make out the words and their poisonous insinuations.

'My sister's a nurse and she told me the extent of Cherie's injuries. She'll never have children now.'

'Disgusting.'

'Fucking wrong, it is.'

As the voices kept coming, Marco's blood boiled to a dangerous temperature the other side of the door. Despite this, he continued eavesdropping on his two-faced staff.

Bastards, the whole lot of them. Every single one of those fuckers would wish they'd kept their opinions to themselves.

'I reckon he's paying the police off,' a man suggested.

'I don't care what or how he's doing it, but he freaks me out!' a woman gasped.

Marco scowled. That was the red-headed bird. She needed a punch in the face. This lot were done. *All* of them.

'You do know when Lisa Tequila turns up, we'll all be out of a job. The stupid bitch must be insane to marry that monster.'

'That's if she's not dead herself by next week...'

Marco was about to barrel through the door and smash every single one of these people to smithereens, when he heard Bill's name mentioned.

'It was definitely about him. That geezer said something about it on the phone. I bet Wainwright's dead too. On top of that, it sounds like the brother's out of nick too. You must have heard about him. He's the one with sense and a brain.'

Marco stiffened, his inner fury solidifying the blood in his veins. *Even now Zane was the hero.*

As much as he wanted to smash these ungrateful bastards' faces in and ensure they never worked again, short of the 'before' pictures for plastic surgery clinics, he had to hold fire. If someone had overheard Sonny on the phone, then that was a disaster in itself. But what would be even *more* of a disaster, was if the news about Zane got out in general circulation or back to Hazel and Trevor Grimes.

If it did, then this lot needn't worry about their jobs being usurped by his wife because there wouldn't be a fucking wife!

His jaw clenched harder. Make no mistake, these tossers would pay for their loose tongues and the ill-conceived notion they had the right to an opinion. No one had the right to a fucking opinion. *No one.*

But he couldn't do anything about it. Not yet.

No, he had to sit on his fucking hands and not move a muscle, until he was married. Seventy-two hours now to keep a lid on things. He could manage that, couldn't he?

The buzz of cocaine-infused adrenaline steamed through Marco's body in a consistent rhythm, urging him to unleash the beast on these trappy bastards bitching in the room that *he* paid for; doing the job *his* company paid them to do...

How he wished Bill was here to calm him down.

It finally hit Marco that without Bill, he struggled to deal with things. Without his right-hand man's level headedness and propensity to think of good ideas, he was at risk of bringing the whole show down.

Marco's knuckles whitened further. He could do nothing until he'd married, dealt with Zane and located Flame. It would only be then that he'd make these fuckers wish they'd never been born.

Every. Single. One. Of. Them.

Whatever had happened to the tarts they pretended to be so concerned about was chickenfeed, compared to what would befall *them*.

But it was time to put his newfound control to the test. *Less than seventy-two hours to play this shit, Marco, then you're good to go*, he reminded himself.

Okay, so he may be unable to react in the way he felt most appropriate, but that didn't mean he had to remain mute.

He could still do *this*...

Kicking open the door, Marco stood in the doorway, his arms folded across his wide chest. With an evil glint in his eyes, he surveyed the immediately silenced dressing room. He slowly and intently scanned each person, his eyes burning purposefully longer into the blonde surfer man. *He'd be the first to cop it.*

Marco could sense everyone's brains feverishly churning as they endeavoured not to make eye contact. *Not quite so trappy now, were they?*

A slow smile spread over his face. 'I hope you're not spending all day in here ladies and gents. Unless I'm mistaken, you have films to make. There are several hours of the working day left before you can justify lounging around gossiping.'

He paused for a moment to let the impact of his words sink in. 'Don't forget speculating can be dangerous. It costs lives, you know...?'

Satisfied he'd made the point without violence, Marco turned on his heels and walked back up the corridor, his Italian brogues clicking on the tile floor.

He'd done well. He'd kept his temper, but he needed to let off his rage and frustration somewhere.

Marco yanked open the door to the foyer of Luna Motion Films. Going to the club where Hazel was having her hen night and getting a shag would do for start. It wouldn't stop his temples from thumping with the buzz of trapped violence, but it would ease the pressure a little.

And he didn't give a flying fig if the groom rocking up to the hen night wasn't the done thing. He was Marco Morelli and could do what the hell he damn well wanted.

• • • •

'ABOUT TIME!' Anthony muttered as he moved to press the answer button on the intercom. He winced at the brash tone coming through the speaker; the tinny pitch amplified by the crackling. 'Yes, come through and drive up to the house. Wait outside the detached garage and I'll be down in a moment.'

Dropping the connection, Anthony moved to the window, watching the ornate gates crank open. He then frowned at the battered pickup truck making its way up his pristine driveway.

Fancy having to resort to this. And the idiot was late...

Anthony hated tardiness. It irritated him almost as much as calling on the services of an outfit so far beneath him.

A bloody scrap man? What was the world coming to?

By the sounds and looks of who had arrived, it was a gypsy, rather than a reputable firm. He might have bloody known.

Anthony moved away from the window, his stomach sinking at the signage on the beat-up old truck: *'Percy's Scrap.'*

Classy... Still, he wanted rid of that fucking Transit, didn't he? Only this guy had availability to come round and sort it so fast. Unfortunately, Anthony wasn't in the position where he could afford to wait for a more palatable firm.

No doubt Mrs Hildegard from number fifteen would be making notes to bring up during the next neighbourhood watch meeting. He just hoped the firm coming tomorrow to reinforce his doors and windows didn't have the nature of their business emblazoned on the side of their van, otherwise that would give the nosy old bitch more to whine about.

Hurrying down the stairs, he made his way outside, checking his pocket for the forty-fifth time to make sure his phone was still there. He didn't want to miss any calls. That was on the off chance that anyone bothered to ring.

He couldn't get into contact with Bill any longer, thanks to Morelli, but surely by now someone else from the firm knew what had happened?

At least he hoped so because he couldn't wait around here indefinitely for Zane to come and finish him off.

Or maybe the man was stupid enough to think this ended

here?

All he knew was that he had to find out what was going on.

Pulling open the front door, Anthony loped down the stone steps to the gravel driveway and stared at the man eyeing him curiously over by his knackered old wagon.

His eyes trailed over the squat man's grubby vest and the paunch of his belly hanging over the belt of the equally dirty jeans and didn't attempt to conceal the distaste plastered across his face.

Wait! This skanky individual was eyeing him! What the...?

It took a moment for Anthony to remember that with his bandaged hand and criss-cross stitching across his face, he didn't resemble anything wonderful either.

Resentment and defensiveness collided.

'What happened to you?' A deep frown formed on the dark-haired man's pockmarked face.

'You've come to collect the van, yes?' Anthony conveniently ignored the man's question and barged past towards the double garage. 'It's in here.'

He was damned if he was explaining himself to the likes of this imbecile. The scrounging twat was here to pick up a vehicle, not to grill him about his bloody life and he'd best remember that.

Anthony's irritation rose as he struggled to open the double doors with one hand, resenting it further when the man lumbered across and made light work of the task. *He'd have to disinfect the door now this creature had touched it.*

The squat man walked into the garage and scratched his head. 'What's this?'

Anthony stared at the man in disbelief. 'What do you mean, "what's this"? It's a Transit van, like I told you on the phone. What did you expect?' *Was this bloke retarded?*

'Yeah mate, I can see it's a Transit. I meant *this...*' The man gestured to the bullet holes in the rear doors. 'You a bank robber or summat? I ain't getting involved in dodgy weird shit!'

Anthony scowled, wincing as the movement pulled the

stitches in his face. 'Do I look like a bank robber?'

The man looked around the garage, his eyes scanning over the upturned chair, rope and unmistakable stains of dried blood on the concrete floor. 'Something ain't right here.'

Anthony's lips set in a thin line. 'I've booked you to take a van away. Analysing things isn't part of your remit.' He folded his arms. 'What I do is none of your business! You're crushing the van and weighing the bloody thing in, aren't you, so don't ask questions!'

What was it with this scum? How dare this slob come round casting aspersions and questioning him. None of this was relevant. Christ, he wasn't even asking for payment and scrap metal fetched a decent price.

The man backed out of the garage, shaking his head. 'Nah mate, I ain't doing this. Some kind of shit has gone down here and with that van too. I don't want no part of it.'

'What?' Anthony screeched. This tramp of a scrap metal person was refusing to take the vehicle? Saying that *he* was dodgy? *Unbelievable...* 'You have the bloody cheek to tell me you're not taking it? I've booked you to take it away and... Come back here immediately!' Raging, he followed as the man moved towards his wagon.

'Keep the fuck away from me!' The man scrambled into his lorry cab. 'I should call the police on you, you nutter!'

Anthony banged the lorry door with his good hand, then reached for the handle. 'Get back here and sort this out right away!' he screamed, his voice drowned out as the engine fired and the wagon span off down the driveway covering him in bits of gravel and dust.

· · · ·

ERIN STARED AT the vibrating mobile phone which had once belonged to Bill Wainwright. She turned to Zane. 'Aren't you going to answer it?'

Zane smirked. 'Soon. But not yet. Do you know how many times he's called now?'

Erin sighed. 'No and neither do I know who's calling because you haven't said.' That phone had been ringing constantly, yet Zane remained tight-lipped about who it was. 'It's clearly someone from your firm, so just tell me. We're supposed to be in this together now, aren't we?'

Being as Erin had done just about everything *else* with this man over the last twenty-four hours, he should level with her on this. Although they'd discussed many things today, she was still unsure what the plan of action was. Being as remaining in this cottage wasn't an option, she needed to know. 'Zane!' she pressed. 'Talk to me!'

Zane picked up the now silent mobile, then placed it back down. 'It's Marco. He keeps ringing and leaving messages for Bill.'

Erin's mouth dropped open. 'Marco? Your brother? He doesn't know what's happened?'

'Oh, he does,' Zane smirked. 'Well, kind of. Last night he didn't, but the messages this morning are different. It seems the "incident" was reported on a website, but no, he doesn't know for *sure* that Bill is no more. But from what he said, he's thinking that way.'

Erin couldn't stop from focusing on Zane's big hands, knowing what they could do - both good and bad. She ached for them to be on her again and although it was tempting to fall back into bed with this man who made her feel alive, there would be time for the enjoyable side of things later.

Hopefully...

The prospect that whatever they did could go very wrong shimmered brightly. *There were so many obstacles. So many unknown factors. So many dangers...* 'What's the plan then?'

'I'll answer next time he calls,' Zane said.

'Are you sure?' Erin frowned. 'As it stands, Marco doesn't know where you are. Where *we* are and...'

'But that's the point. He probably does. He'll have been in contact with Flame by now, so they must all know this address.'

Erin felt sick. 'You mean they could already be in the area?'

'They might be outside now, for all I know, so we've got to move fast.' Standing up, Zane leant down to kiss the back of Erin's neck. 'I won't let anyone touch you, I swear.'

And that was a promise. These people had already done enough to this woman and he would not allow anything else to happen because of what he'd inadvertently brought upon her.

He moved to the other side of the room away from temptation. 'The question is who we aim for first. Flame or Marco? I'm thinking Marco, but I need to know where he is before I can do that and finding out will be difficult.'

Now more than ever, he realised he had enemies on the inside, but he wanted his firm back. And that, he would achieve.

Erin bit her lip. Her list had now changed and the name replacing Zane, was Marco's. But one remained the same. *Anthony's.*

'And,' Zane continued, 'we need to recover my bike from your house.'

'No way!' Erin gasped. 'You want to go back there? Surely that will be walking into trouble. What if...'

'We can't leave it! It's an obvious calling card and like I said, I won't be going back to nick, courtesy of that prick. Courtesy of *anyone*!' Ignoring Bill's phone, he snatched up Erin's. 'I'm calling Flame. I'll find out where he is and where the fuck Marco is.'

'He won't tell you that!' Erin snorted.

'You might be surprised...'

Erin sat back as Zane pressed the call button, unsure if she would be surprised. Zane had already surprised her so much, she believed there was little he could do to render her speechless.

FORTY ONE

PACING UP AND DOWN in his lounge, Anthony didn't think to check the caller ID when he snatched up his ringing phone. He should have done because then he wouldn't have presumed it was that bloody idiot scrap man having changed his tune, or Maisie from the office.

It was his own fault. If his brain wasn't so crowded about whether that skank would involve the police over the van or the simmering anger with being threatened about it in the first place, then he might have thought more clearly.

Luckily, his sense of self-importance dismissed the police's involvement as being unviable. Why would they question someone with a job such as his? Or who lived in a property like *this*?

They wouldn't. It was absurd and he couldn't fathom why he'd entertained the notion in the first place.

Overtired, that's what he was. It was messing with his head.

'Yes?' he barked into the receiver.

Anthony froze. Just hearing Zane Morelli's voice made the stitched gashes in his face hurt more than usual and the throbbing in his plated cheekbone increase.

This bastard had the audacity to call? If he thought he'd

get any more money or another chance to smash up what he hadn't already ruined of his face, then he'd need to think again.

The only thing Anthony wanted was Zane Morelli removed from the planet, so he could get on with the life he'd worked damn hard for over the last six years.

There was nothing Morelli could possibly have as leverage anymore. Erin was out of the picture - she'd made that clear. He'd think of a suitable explanation for her absence and find a way to get round the parts of the business he found difficult without her.

The last few days had already shown he could manage it.

Just.

Not without casualties, admittedly, but he'd learn and improve with time. He wasn't giving up what he'd achieved, so there was no option but to treat this unexpected call with the contempt it deserved.

'I'm not sure what you want, Morelli,' Anthony sneered, his confidence gaining pace. 'Do you wish to know whether you succeeded in making me look as fucked up as you? Well, you failed - I have an excellent surgeon!' He chuckled. 'Or are you calling to apologise for something that you now know I didn't do?'

Even Zane Morelli wasn't so deluded not to have worked out who the *real* person responsible for getting him put behind bars and for David Masters' murder was by now.

Anthony was still chuckling to himself when the words from the other end of the line gradually seeped into the logical side of his brain. '*What*?' he spluttered, his unbandaged hand twitching, making his grip of the phone unstable. 'You can't do that!'

Combined rage and panic bubbled as Anthony fruitlessly tried to control his speeding brain by implementing the counting mechanism he used in times of stress.

It wasn't working...

Especially now the voice down the line was laughing.

'If you do that, then I'll... I'll...' Anthony stopped, realising

Morelli would do *exactly* what he said. Plus, he had vague memories of the photo he was being threatened with. If that got shown to his staff or clients... If they saw that photograph of him bound and trussed to a chair, bleeding...

He couldn't let Morelli take Erin to his office to back up the story either. If she relayed to even a *fraction* of his clients about his former position at the Morelli firm, his involvement in the trial, and that he had no financial qualifications whatsoever, then...

If his staff and clients didn't believe Morelli, they'd believe *her*.

Damn and blast the bitch.

Even if Morelli didn't really possess footage of him admitting his involvement in the murder trial and fixing evidence, there was still enough to finish him. Many of his clients would sue. They'd sue him for pretending to be something he wasn't and for investing their money under false pretences.

Sweat cascaded down Anthony's back.

What he'd presumed to be correct, wasn't. There *was* something Zane Morelli had as leverage after all.

And this was it.

As much as he resented it, the words sticking like shards of glass in his throat, Anthony found himself asking, 'What is it you want?'

Listening to the response, he was taken aback.

Was that it?

That, he was happy to give, but the other part of the request was a different matter.

• • • •

IN THE TIGHT BLUE dress which fitted like a glove, clinging to her surgically enhanced body like it was spray painted on, Hazel perched on the leather-topped bar stool, thoroughly enjoying the attention.

She crossed her left leg slowly over her right, allowing the dress to ride up enough to reveal a flash of matching blue lacy knickers. Letting one sky high stiletto dangle suggestively from her perfectly positioned foot, she placed the cocktail stick into her mouth and took her time closing her plumped-up pout to suck the glacé cherry, knowing the man who had furnished her with champagne and cocktails for the past half an hour could barely believe his luck.

Yeah, he knew who she was. Most of the men in this upmarket club knew Lisa Tequila was gracing them with her presence tonight. And boy, was she revelling in it.

This is what she was born to do: be every man's dream and every woman's inspiration. She knew she was the epitome of what *all* women wanted to look like, so it was only fair to remind everyone of that.

Coquettishly raising her false eyelashes at the man edging closer with every drink he supplied, Hazel inwardly smiled at her immense power.

The girlfriends who she'd invited to her hen night were pretty hot in their own right, apart from a couple she kept around to act as a contrast and accelerate her beauty. Still, no one had a patch on her.

It may have taken several years of time, money and effort to look so damn good, but every day proved worth it. Nights like this, where every set of eyes were on her, was just one example of the adulation she both expected and craved.

Running her bright pink false nails along the length of the man's sleeve, Hazel swallowed the cherry with gusto, rewarding him with a flash of her dentist-perfect white smile. 'You're not leaving a girl without a drink are you, Tony?' she purred.

Deciding to bypass that his name was Pete, rather than Tony, Pete smiled, aware of his mates watching a few metres away in abject envy. 'Same again, babe?'

Hazel giggled in that special way she reserved for flirting with fawning fans and ran her tongue along her bottom lip. That would get this guy going even more. He was already like a dog on heat. 'Oh, I shouldn't really... but being as you asked so nicely, I'll let you persuade me.' She laid her hand on his chest. 'You're not trying to get me drunk, are you?'

Her eyes flicked to her group of friends, noticing one in particular gesturing. 'Get me another champagne cocktail then, but if you'll excuse me for just a moment.'

Sliding from the stool, giving the man a good look at her long legs, Hazel sashayed towards her friends.

Reaching the group, she frowned they pulled her across the illuminated floor towards the ladies cloakroom. 'What is it? That bloke's buying me another drink and I...'

Cut off from her protests, Hazel found herself inside the cloakroom, the door shutting to muffle the loud beat of the club's music.

'You shouldn't drape yourself over that man,' Sandy said, frowning.

Hazel's eyes narrowed as she stared at the brunette. An attractive woman who worked at her father's studio, they'd been acquaintances for some time. Sandy wasn't what Hazel would class as a 'friend' - she didn't count *anyone* worthy of that accolade, neither did she need anyone inveigling themselves into her life to that extent. But Sandy was one of those women who knew the drill, understood the game and wasn't an embarrassment to be seen in public with. Sandy wasn't on par with *her* of course, but acceptable, nonetheless.

However, nothing gave Sandy or any of these women the right to tell her what she should or shouldn't be doing.

Hazel's eyes flicked over the group clustered around her in the corner of the brightly lit cloakroom. 'It's my bloody hen night, so I'll do what I like,' she snapped. 'And I'm not "draping" myself over anyone. The guy's supplying me with drinks! Just because men aren't lining up to buy you lot any, doesn't mean *I* have to turn them down!'

She flicked her hair over her shoulder and stood firm. If this lot didn't want to enjoy themselves, that was their problem. They could go home if they wished. She couldn't care less.

'You must have heard the rumours going around,' Sandy continued, knowing all the other girls agreed with her. 'Are you sure you should be doing this?'

'Doing what?' Hazel barked. 'Accepting a fucking drink or two from a man? What's the big deal?'

Sandy glanced at Billie, a petite blonde with the largest bust ever, then turned back to Hazel. 'I meant... *we* meant, marrying Marco Morelli...'

Hazel's bright pink mouth dropped open. 'Are you serious? Why the fuck not? Do you not realise what th...'

'You must have doubts, Hazel?' Billie said quietly. 'You know I work for his film studio and the rumours going around there at the moment... Well...' She glanced around nervously as if someone might be eavesdropping. 'What happened to Pauline Albiges and Cherie and...'

'Oh, for God's sake!' Hazel scoffed. 'Marco had nothing to do with any of that.' She rolled her eyes. 'If you don't like it at Luna Motion Films, then leave!'

'But he's a crazy, Hazel. A violent nutter,' Sandy added. 'Everyone knows that, even if they don't say it. You don't know how he'll treat you. Plus, I've heard his brother's out of prison now too. Do you know what you're getting yourself into?'

Hazel bristled. Her father had already cleared that rumour up about the elder brother. 'Marco's not crazy and I'll be perfectly fine. He's besotted with me and it's not true about his brother either, so you should be careful what you say.'

Sandy grabbed Hazel's arm. 'We're worried about you.'

Hazel snatched her arm from Sandy's grip. 'I'm marrying Marco. There's no reason not to.' *But several reasons to do so...* Turning on her heels, she pulled open the door, blasting the cloakroom with music. 'You're all just jealous. If you don't like it, then piss off.'

Hazel strutted back across the room, quietly seething. *Who the bloody hell did they think they were?* Just because they could never be as successful as her and didn't have the ability to bag eligible men offering delicious rewards, wasn't her problem.

Yes of course, she knew of Marco's reputation, but what did that have to do with her? She'd get a vast payout and a mega-boost to her career from their union. Her looks and the marriage would put her even more in demand than she already was. She was untouchable and those women best get used to the fact that they couldn't compete. *Ever.*

Replacing her frown for a stellar smile, Hazel returned to the bar where the man and her fresh champagne cocktail eagerly awaited.

• • • •

SLAPPING THE BOUNCER on the back in a gesture of camaraderie, Marco strutted into the Bel Air nightclub, pleased to receive admiring glances from women dressed to the nines, along with wary looks from their accompanying menfolk.

Yeah, everyone knew who he was: Kingpin around these parts. Best they didn't forget that, either.

It had been a long time coming, but he could now safely say he was firmly in place and nobody could scupper that. Even his unlocatable brother was no longer unduly concerning him, neither was the tittle tattle he'd heard in the dressing rooms.

Sonny was on the case for Flame's contact number and there was no doubt he'd achieve it. He probably already had. And as for that lot at Luna films - their days were numbered. He didn't need them. Not once Lisa Tequila topped the bill.

Grinning, Marco continued into the club's main room, the thumping music adding to the pleasant buzzing in his head.

Allowing all of this nonsense over Zane and the brainless gossip to get to him seemed implausible. It was funny what a couple of grams of coke did to shake needless trains of thought away.

'Good evening, Mr Morelli.'

The voice came from a group of people Marco had never seen before. Not that he could recall, anyway. But it proved his point. Everybody knew him, which reaffirmed he had attained his rightful standing.

A. Very. Important. Person.

Marco nodded at the man and purposely refrained from smiling. Stopping to converse with randoms or smiling did nothing for his rep. Although it was difficult not to sometimes grin at his rising social status, especially whilst his veins thrummed with cocaine-induced confidence, the standard surly expression garnering him the most respect should be maintained.

Now he was back to his usual state of mind and had reached the decision not to let the meaningless dross of late get to him, Marco put his effort into locating Hazel, certain this was the club she'd mentioned.

After all, that was why he was here.

He'd take her somewhere offering a degree of privacy, have a much-needed quickie to release some pressure and then leave her to get on with her night.

He wouldn't hang around. Adulation from the grovelling tarts who followed Hazel around was not what he wanted. He needed reminding exactly where he was in his life and once that was done and he'd reasserted his authority, he'd return to the apartment to wait in peace for Sonny's update, which he expected before the night was out.

Reaching one of the many bars, Marco shouted up a whisky on the rocks, not expecting to wait more than four seconds before his request was granted.

Keeping an eye on the second hand of his Rolex, he nodded in confirmation that his personal service levels had been fulfilled in adequate time. He picked up the glass and scrutinised it for any imperfections. None.

Good.

Marco turned his back on the bar, not expecting to be asked for payment and scanned the club for Hazel. It was doubtful he'd recognise any of her cronies. Most women looked the same. They acted the same too.

But Hazel was different. Hazel was something else. Hazel

was perfection. Hazel was...

What the fuck?

His eyes narrowed, seeing someone who looked very much like Hazel, sitting at a bar the opposite side of the club.

Now, he knew his eyes weren't so great these days, but he was fairly sure it was her...

He squinted harder, his jaw clenching as the woman ran her outstretched leg up the thigh of a man who, if he got any closer, would be inside her dress. Anger mixed with the high percentage of cocaine thundering along Marco's bloodstream.

It *was* Hazel. The woman who was on her hen night in preparation for marrying *him*. The woman who was allowing a dweeb to paw her?

Marco's face set in a sinister grimace. He tipped his whisky into his mouth before slamming the empty glass back onto the bar and then strode through the busy club.

This wasn't Hazel's doing. That man thought he could take liberties, reckoning making a play for Marco Morelli's woman gave him cred?

A low growl erupted from Marco's throat. He'd show the cunt what credentials were. *Right. Fucking. Now.*

Juddering with rage, he barged through the group of women standing near Hazel, half-recognising some as people she socialised with.

Not anymore, she wouldn't be. Not after this.

This was lesson one. If Hazel allowed boneheads to treat her like a common slut, then she needed to rethink what was expected as part of their arrangement.

His obsession for Hazel aside, Marco was adamant his rules were followed by anyone connected with him. None more so than his wife.

Ignoring the yelp as he knocked a woman flying, Marco planted a kiss on Hazel's cheek. 'Evening, babe,' he smiled, turning his back to the man he'd just seen place his hands on the woman he was due to marry.

Pete frowned at the big man blocking his view, his

annoyance escalating. He hadn't forked out loads of dosh on posh drinks for this bird only for someone else to elbow their way in. He was that put out, he didn't notice the frantic gestures from his mates. 'Excuse me, mate. What do you th…'

'What?' Eyes gleaming with malice, Marco swung from Hazel to face the man who had touched his property. Pulling a knife from his pocket, he set it with a deft flick of his wrist and slashed a line across the man's good-looking features before anyone got chance to blink.

'Aaargh!' Pete's hands flew to his face as blood spurted down his white shirt.

'Keep away from my bird, you cunt!' Marco hissed. 'You're lucky that I'm only giving you a warning, but if I ever see you again or anywhere near me or my missus, I'll cut you to fucking ribbons. Do you understand?'

Pete was about to stand his ground when two of his mates hastily dragged him off in the opposite direction. Despite the satisfying buzz of victory ringing in Marco's ears, he clearly heard, *'Fucking leave it, Pete! That's Marco Morelli!'*

Yeah, Marco thought. *I am Marco Morelli.*

Closing his flick knife, he glanced at the people closest to him, all pretending they had seen nothing, then leaned towards Hazel. 'Don't give men like that the time of day, eh love,' Marco said, bringing his mouth down on hers. 'Come with me for a while and then I'll let you get on with your hen night.'

Hazel had already clocked the bulge in Marco's trousers and could barely hide her enthusiasm as she slipped from the stool. She beamed widely at her group of friends, ignoring their looks of horror.

They really didn't have a clue! Couldn't they see how much kudos Marco Morelli brought to her already exemplary reputation? Didn't they understand that soon, by proxy alone, she would be as powerful as him? *And she couldn't wait.*

FORTY TWO

SHOVING TWO LARGE suitcases in the car, Anthony glanced back at the house that he'd ploughed so much money into over the last six years.

Refusing to allow himself to fixate on how unjustified it was having to leave and walk away from the business that was coming into its own, he got into his Mercedes and fired the engine.

He grabbed the steering wheel, forgetting several bones in his hand were broken. Overriding the pain, he swapped to his other hand, reminding himself to only steer with one hand from now on.

Keeping that in the forefront of his mind all the way to London would be a feat in itself. His brain was already struggling to concentrate on things he normally took for granted as it churned through the hate and resentment of leaving, as well as the unknown variables of what might happen. Keeping centred all the way to London would be hard going, but there really was no alternative.

'It's only temporary,' Anthony muttered over the dulcet strains of Radio 2. And it *would* be temporary - a short term solution until everything was sorted.

Quickly making headway towards the M42, Anthony gave silent thanks that he'd had the foresight to buy an automatic car. It hadn't been a conscious choice - there were few manual Mercedes any longer and certainly none of the top of the range models, like this.

It had been a good choice.

Pulling onto the motorway, Anthony relaxed as he set the cruise control. With the decent power steering, little effort was required for the foreseeable future, which freed his brain up to think.

He took the opportunity to glance at his mobile in the dashboard holder. *No calls yet.*

He fully expected that dumb-arsed bitch, Maisie, to forget that he was not to be contacted for the next couple of weeks. Knowing her, she'd ring anyway. Or one of his clients that he'd been stupid enough to hand his personal number to, would call to enquire about progress.

No one need worry. He'd set everything up so no ongoing investments would be affected. Everything would pan out just as promised. Besides, he intended to be back sooner rather than later and providing Morelli remained unaware he'd disappeared, like he'd promised not to, all would be good.

Even if it wasn't, it would be too late because the wheels would be in motion to what was needed long before anyone was aware he'd gone.

Yeah, what he'd said to Zane on the phone last night was true. *Partly.*

Anthony *didn't* know where Marco was. He'd also been telling the truth when he'd promised not to involve the police. Those two things were easy. *For now...*

But those conditions were on the proviso that Morelli kept to *his* side of the bargain and didn't involve his business in this. One thing Anthony was sure of, was that Morelli kept to his word, which worked in someone's favour or not, depending on the subject...

The two other promises Anthony had made, he had no plans

of the man finding out that he'd broken them.

A smile formed on his messed-up face, making him wince as the half-healed gashes pulled against the tight stitches.

No, he wouldn't remain at his home out of sight and out of contact with anyone until further notice. Neither would he honour not getting in contact with Marco.

Because that's exactly where he was heading now.

Being as no one from the firm had been in touch since that shit with Bill had kicked off, the only option was to go to London himself.

And yes, his work was shocked to hear he was taking a surprise break - a 'sabbatical', was the way he'd put it when he'd called this morning. No doubt the clients he'd emailed saying he'd be unavailable for a couple of weeks due to 'personal reasons' would also wonder what was going on, but tough luck. This needed sorting out.

Zane Morelli had to go and being as this stemmed from Marco in the first place, he would be the one rectifying it.

The fundamental flaw was, no longer being sure where Marco was, Anthony didn't know where to head. But he'd find out. *Somehow.*

He had to seek refuge under Marco's safety net until the lunatic had done what he promised and got rid of his fucking brother. It was the least he was owed after this. Then he'd return to Knowle and pick up where he left off. His clients wouldn't lose faith. He was far too important for that. Besides, they relied on his expertise.

As for Erin, well - good riddance. He'd use her as the excuse why he'd taken time out. He'd think of a viable reason to lay the blame on her, so she was seen in a bad light, rather than him.

It was a huge relief to be honest. Erin would not be missed.

Anthony smiled. Now he no longer felt it impossible to meet the basic level of social interaction skills, life without Erin wasn't quite so unachievable.

Zane Morelli was welcome to her. They'd enjoy sharing the

same shallow grave Marco put them in.

Suddenly startled by the unexpected ringing of his mobile, Anthony looked up.

...Private Number...

He frowned, hoping it wasn't Maisie. He risked taking his hand from the wheel to answer the call. 'Hello?'

Listening carefully and deciding to live with the pain it brought, his smile widened. 'I'd say you are correct in your observations, and yes, I'm on the way now, so I suggest you tell me where to come. No... it *is* a good idea because I have information you will want.'

. . . .

NOW ZANE KNEW Marco was not presently with Flame, they'd been able to pick up the bike from his house. But things were still far from clear. And riding straight from there into the centre of Knowle had pushed Erin way out of her comfort zone.

'If he says he doesn't have a way of getting in contact with Marco or anyone, why do I need to go in there?' Erin asked, her nerves returning just by being near Anthony's office, the thought of bumping into him more than she could bear. 'They'll ask questions.'

'Because I don't believe what he said!' Zane kept a tight hold of Erin's arm. Although he couldn't clasp her close whilst in the vicinity of Flame's office, he insisted on physical contact with the woman whose very presence set him alight. 'I believe that Marco's not here, but I don't believe no one from the firm has been in contact.'

'And you want me to go in there and tell them his dirty secret? Show them that photo?' Erin stared at the façade of AW Financial Services.

'We'll save that for now. I just want to prove myself right or not,' Zane said. 'It will determine the next course of action. If Flame's there, then he told the truth for once in his life. But if he's not, then he's gone back on what he promised, which is what I'm expecting.' He fixed his gaze determinedly on Erin. 'Now, please go in there and do the rest of what we discussed.'

Nerves fluttering, Erin pulled open the glass entrance door and stepped into the pristine foyer of Anthony's office, half expecting him to jump out from behind the reception desk.

Her eyes darted around the empty space. *You can do this*, she told herself. *It's the only way.*

'Miss Langley?'

The sudden voice made Erin start. Swinging around, she saw Maisie entering through an adjoining door. *Now, remember how to play this...*

Anthony's receptionist laid a mug of tea on her desk, smiling guiltily. 'I grabbed myself a drink whilst it was quiet. I hope you haven't been waiting long?'

'No, I've just this second arrived.' Erin hoped her smile looked genuine. She refrained from looking in the direction of Anthony's personal office. 'Being as I had to come into the village, I thought I'd pop in and see Anthony. Is he around?'

By Maisie's expression, Erin knew instantly that she'd opened a can of worms.

Maisie wrung her hands nervously. 'Y-you mean you don't know...?'

Erin opened her mouth to speak, then shut it again. Whatever had gone on, whatever she'd missed, something had fundamentally changed, *But what?*

Laughing uncomfortably, Erin dismissed her error with a flap of her hand. 'I've forgotten, haven't I? He must be out at meetings. My head's been all over the place since... I... erm... since I've been unwell and I...'

'You mean you haven't heard about the car accident and his sabbatical?' Maisie blurted, her eyes full of suspicion. 'You didn't know? He's...'

'Car accident?' Erin gasped, thinking on her feet. *Of course! He'd say something like that to explain the state of his face, the spineless twat. But a sabbatical? That could only mean one thing...*

'Is... is everything alright?' Maisie moved from behind her desk. 'I know it's none of my business, but you and Mr Walker... If you weren't aware that he...'

'I should have said!' Erin smiled a lot brighter than she believed she could muster as her brain searched for plausible reasons for not knowing about her husband-to-be's unlikely decision.

Anthony never took time off work, let alone for a sabbatical! The speculation over the *real* reason behind his out of character movements would be rife. She had to play this down. 'I've been staying at my brother's to convalesce. The illness knocked me for six and I didn't want to impede Anthony's work. You know what he's like...'

Was Maisie buying this?

Holding her ground, Erin met eyes with the timid-looking woman. 'And, of course, everything's fine between us.' She rummaged in her handbag for her phone. 'He tried to call me a few times over the past couple of days, but my phone's broken and my brother doesn't believe in mobiles, hence why I thought I'd better come and touch base.' She pretended to look distressed. 'I can't believe I missed a call about the accident. I feel dreadful!'

'Is your brother the man on the motorbike that Mr Walker mentioned?' Maisie probed.

'Yes, that's him. I've been staying there, like I said.' *You're making it worse. She doesn't believe you...* 'Erm, when did Anthony leave?'

'I haven't seen him, but he called this morning. I-I must admit I was very surprised that he'd...'

'He wouldn't want anyone seeing him if his face isn't like it usually is. He's a stickler for looking perfect,' Erin laughed, masking the sneer in her voice. It was then that she belatedly realised no details had been given as to Anthony's injuries. She had to leave. She'd got what she come for, so that was enough. 'I'll head back to the house,' she continued, turning towards the door. 'I might be able to catch him before he leaves.'

'I don't know where he's going either, I'm afraid,' Maisie blathered. 'He didn't say much - just that he didn't want to be contacted.'

Erin nodded. 'Don't worry. I know exactly where he's going. Thanks Maisie.'

Erin hastily left the reception before Maisie could pry further. Walking across the road, she grabbed her crash helmet from Zane's hand, knowing without looking that she was being watched from the office window. 'They're suspicious as fuck!' she muttered as she swung her leg over the pillion seat. 'Apparently, Anthony's gone away for a while. He left this morning.'

Zane fired the bike's engine, giving Erin's thigh a quick squeeze. 'Then now we know where he's gone, the lying bastard.'

Revving the throttle, the bike pulled away and Erin clutched onto Zane's waist, knowing London would have to be the next stop.

FORTY THREE

SONNY WAS UNCOMFORTABLE. *Very* uncomfortable. He'd already got wind via some of Marco's enforcers that the boss had publicly striped some geezer in a club last night.

Word travelled fast in certain circles.

Due to the identity of the perpetrator, the bouncers in the Bel Air had willingly let it slide. What they hadn't let slide was from stopping their traps opening and letting the news spread.

Sonny's brow creased with a frown. Marco wouldn't be concerned - the opposite in fact. He would be happy with news of his exploits which hammered home his kudos being wilfully bandied around. Sonny expected it was exactly why he'd done it. For that reason and because Marco was always so coked up, the man believed himself invincible.

Invincible in his own mind, maybe, but in real life and in their world, things were rarely that straight forward. Certainly not straight forward, when there was a hunter on the prowl - one with a score to settle, which they were *all* implicated in. And one that was at large, and more to the point, on the warpath.

Sonny dragged the back of his hand across his brow and made his way through the lobby of the apartment complex. He nodded at the nervous-looking concierge stationed at the reception desk, knowing he would not be questioned why he was heading for the lift that went only to the penthouse floor. No one ever got questioned - not anyone in Marco's inner circle anyhow.

Sonny had never been questioned and definitely wouldn't now his role had shifted from being the firm's technical whizz to Marco's new right-hand man. But this new role bothered him, given the current situation and Marco's state of mind.

He hadn't expected to step into Bill's shoes. It wasn't something he'd wanted, nor thought would ever be an option. But now Bill was no more, this transition had occurred automatically, with no discussion.

If someone's job was about to change, most people would be approached to discuss the change. It was unlikely that would have even crossed Marco's mind and if it had done, the concept was ignored.

It also showed, even though no one knew for certain, everyone presumed Bill dead.

Sonny leant against the metal wall of the lift as it ascended to the top floor.

Both he and Marco knew Bill was dead, but no one could risk viewing the body to be sure. Not without things being uncovered. It bothered Sonny immensely that Bill's body lay unclaimed on a mortuary slab somewhere in the Midlands and they were unable to give the man a decent send off.

Bill may be divorced from his missus, but he'd always made sure she and their kids were well looked after. Now, as far as his ex-wife knew, Bill had disappeared. She'd have no idea he was brown bread and probably never would.

None of that sat well, but there was little point in speaking to Marco about it. He'd just shrug because he didn't give a toss. Everyone was expendable in Marco's world, especially when he was in one of his frenzied moods. And he'd been in one of those moods for some time.

Exiting the lift, Sonny strode towards the door of the penthouse and banged on it.

Regardless of how big the gaping hole Bill's departure had left and how much he'd miss leaning on him when dealing with Marco, it didn't change that they had to act on what was going on right now.

That's why Sonny had come here – to tell Marco the latest about Flame. And he doubted whether it would go down well.

• • • •

MARCO STARED AT SONNY with a hint of annoyance etched across his unshaven face. He'd been happy having a nice chill out session this morning, relishing the phone calls and texts from people who'd heard how he'd successfully staked his claim last night.

Even Hazel had been so impressed, that for once she'd stayed over. They'd had such a good night of shagging, his cock was still sore.

All in all, a top night.

But this had pissed on his chips. Correction - *Sonny* had pissed on his chips, as well as that dickhead, Flame.

Running the back of his arm under his nose, Marco sniffed up chunks of coke-infused phlegm - an unfortunate reminder from last night's blow out.

Crossing his ankles, he wondered how long his patience would last. He leant back in his leather chair, watching Sonny flick through his laptop. He'd smash the thing over his fucking head, if he didn't get his arse into gear. 'When's he due, then?' he snarled. 'If, like you said, you hacked into Flame's email, plus spoke to the twat himself and know he's coming to London, when is he arriving? It's not a difficult question!'

Sonny looked up from the screen, his bulldog face creased with stress. 'He's on his way now, but I don't know exactly when he'll arrive.'

Marco sat forward. 'Why the fuck did you tell him to come to London? Where have you told him go?' That arse-licking baboon, Flame, had no inkling they were no longer in their old premises. Nor did he know about Luna Motion Films and

Marco wanted it to stay that way. 'The wanker's in touch with Zane and I don't want *him* getting an easy road of our whereabouts!'

'I didn't tell Flame to come anywhere!' Sonny protested, his own irritation growing. 'I told him I'd call him back in an hour to let him know where to go, but it's almost been that now, so where shall I send him?'

'Back to where he fucking came would be a good start!' Marco muttered.

Sonny raised an eyebrow. 'You might not be as eager to keep him away when you hear what he's got to say…'

'Which is?'

'That Zane knows the truth about who killed David Masters. As well as who set him up…'

Marco shot out of the seat, like his arse was perched on hot coals. 'You fucking what? After all this time, that two-faced slimy bastard opened his gob? After all the money we paid him? I'll kill him stone fucking dead!' *Then once he'd killed him, he'd dig him up and kill him again.*

Sonny watched Marco's face getting redder and redder, the vein in his temple a hideous bulging contrast of purple in the surrounding puce-coloured skin. 'Flame denies saying anything. He reckons Zane worked it out himself.'

Marco's head swung around like an owl. 'Yeah, right! Nothing to do with my brother torturing him, having already killed Bill and having his missus, then? For fuck's sake! I want all the money back I paid Flame. With interest!'

Sonny knew Marco would blow further after what he would say next but continued regardless. 'He says he's counting on you to take Zane out because *you* broke your side of the arrangement.'

'*What?*' Marco screeched. 'What fucking arrangement am I supposed to have broken, the cheeky twat?' He'd kill Zane, yeah, but not because that wanker demanded it. It would be done because Zane was not steaming back into his life to ruin everything he'd built. *That* would be why his brother had to die

– not for anyone else.

'Zane was never supposed to get out of nick or come after Flame,' Sonny pointed out. Despite Flame being a Grade A wanker, the crack was that both of those things had already happened. And that wasn't part of the deal.

Marco snatched up a bottle of whisky. Chucking the top on the floor, he necked straight from the bottle. If Flame was en route to London, it didn't take rocket science to deduce Zane wouldn't be far behind. There was still two days before the wedding and Zane's presence, nor any of this, could come out before then, otherwise everything would go to shit.

He flopped back into his seat. 'Call Flame and put him in one of the Barker Street flats. He is to go nowhere. Nowhere at all. Arrange an enforcer to guard him.

Placing Flame at Barker Street was a great idea. Zane was always too up himself with 'important' things to waste time registering that *he* owned that stinking hovel of dossholes. It was perfect. Marco sparked up a cigarette and slowly blew the smoke out towards the ceiling. 'I'll deal with him myself tomorrow.'

Sonny nodded slowly. 'Right, okay, but what about Zane?'

Marco shrugged dismissively. 'He'll be here at some point soon. He'll put his ears to the ground and it won't take him long to find out where I am from someone. I want several guards stationed in the apartment lobby ready to incept him. He's bound to come here first.'

He pointed his finger at Sonny. 'It's a case of watching and waiting. And being as I'm busy with the wedding and a honeymoon, you'll have to deal with it.'

Sonny leaned forward. 'You're going on honeymoon? Now? With all this going on? You can't ju…'

Mario cut Sonny's protestations off by grabbing him around the scruff of his shirt. 'Don't fucking tell me what I can and can't do! Who do you think you are?' How could he delay the honeymoon without Hazel getting suspicious? Things were already on thin ice with this going on in the background.

Everything else which had happened, like that stupid Pauline bitch, had almost put a spanner in the works. His marriage and getting Lisa Tequila on the books would not be hindered by anyone.

Marco silently fumed. Things weren't supposed to have escalated to this degree. It should have been simple. Even with the trouble, Bill would have sorted this crap out by now.

He dropped his hold of Sonny's shirt, ignoring the hint of contempt on the man's face. 'Now Bill is no longer with us, you're my right-hand man, so deal with Zane when he turns up. Do what you have to do.'

Sonny's expression of contempt morphed into horror. 'Me? You want *me* to... to do *that*?'

Marco raked his thick fingers through his hair. 'I'm not asking you to *kill* him. I'll do that when I return from honeymoon. Just keep him out of the way and watch him 24/7 so he can do nothing. Do the same with that bird of Flame's he's got in tow as well.'

'But... I...' Sonny's voice trailed off, realising protests were fruitless. This was bad. These days his expertise centred on computers and hacking - locating people and finding stuff. He was out of touch with anything else, as well as reticent. But keeping Zane Morelli constrained? *Zane*?

Reading Sonny's mind, Marco sighed with displeasure, his patience fraying. 'For Christ's sake! What's the matter with you? You worked with me and Bill on the extortion side of the business long enough. You're built like a brick shit house, so what's the problem? Been sat in front of a fucking screen for so long, you now think a bit of strong arm is below you?'

'No!' Sonny cried. 'It's just th...'

'It's just *nothing*. Stop talking shit. Now we're a man down, it's all hands on deck, so shut the fuck up and do what I say. I don't want to lose another man, do I?'

Sonny received the threat loud and clear. His skin prickled. Marco couldn't have been more obvious with his intentions, should he mess this up. Nodding, he rose from his seat and pulled his phone from his pocket. 'I'll call Flame and sort out guards.'

Now things were worse than ever. Keeping Marco on track was something he and Bill had dealt with together. Now he was on his own, he missed Bill more now than ever. Bill was the brains behind Marco's ideas, yet now everything was solely down to him.

And dealing with the wrath of a vengeful Zane Morelli wasn't something Sonny was looking forward to in the slightest.

FORTY FOUR

BEING DELAYED on the M1 wasn't what Erin expected to happen, but when Zane was forced to pull over, they'd had to wait hours before a breakdown service could attend to the problem with the bike's carburettor, so they had little choice but to sit tight.

The enforced wait had seriously hindered things and now it was quite late. Waiting and wasting time hadn't played well with Zane's state of mind and she'd watched him pace up and down the hard shoulder, muttering about Flame having a head start and how annoyed he was with himself for not bringing any tools in the event of repairs. He could have easily repaired the bike himself had he had the gear.

However, once the breakdown company arrived, the bike was fixed quickly enough and finally getting on their way, they'd made short time in reaching London. But reaching their destination had not improved Zane's mood.

Erin tensed as they pulled to a stop at the side of the road in what looked to be an industrial estate. She stared through the twilight at the surroundings, unsure where they were, short of somewhere in Battersea. 'Is this it? Here?'

Zane said nothing. He got off the bike and stared at a large building at the end of the road, which looked to all intents and purposes, deserted. Maybe that was how the Morelli firm preferred things to look as cover of sorts. But judging by the waves of anger rolling off the man, Erin got the distinct impression the location was right, but *something* was not.

She was about to get off the bike and walk to where Zane stood, when he strode back towards her, the look on his face through the helmet's visor showing she'd been right with her assumptions.

As he clambered back onto the bike, Erin clutched at his leather jacket. 'What's happ…'

'We can't hang around.' Zane fired the engine. 'We're probably being watched.'

'Which is your building?' Erin pressed, her voice all but drowned out by the noisy roar of the bike.

'It *was* that one.' Zane nodded towards the large building at the end of the road. 'The one that's now empty.'

Erin blinked in confusion. *Empty?* 'You mean they've…'

'I mean, Marco's sold my fucking premises and gone elsewhere and I haven't a bastard clue where!'

Pulling back on the throttle, they roared away before Erin could ask anything else. Whatever Marco had done with Zane's business in his absence, she strongly suspected from what she'd seen on that news report a week ago, that a similar thing might have happened to his apartment.

Where this left them, she wasn't sure, but a deep-seated chill settled into her bones. Something had to be done and fast. Anthony would have reached London several hours ago, meaning Marco and the rest of Zane's firm were one step ahead, ready and waiting.

. . . .

'YOU'VE GOT TO BE JOKING?' Anthony muttered to himself as he stared through the Mercedes windscreen at the horrible tower block.

Waiting hours for Sonny Mitchell to show up was bad

enough, but when the man finally made an appearance and instructed him to tail his motor, he'd been led here? *Surely this was a mistake?*

Sensing motion to the right, Anthony glimpsed the large head of Sonny Mitchell. Contorting to press the button to open the window with his left hand, he'd lowered the glass only an inch before being interrupted.

'Don't open the fucking window! Just park your motor behind the block of flats.' Sonny motioned to a dingy backstreet.

Anthony stared in dismay at the narrow entrance, containing a cluster of suspect-looking people: possibly men, perhaps women – either, for all he could tell. What he *did* know was that it was negligible his Mercedes would still be there after half an hour, let alone overnight.

Marco had instructed he should stay here? No, no, no.

Feeling his hands begin their standard twitching, Anthony made no move to shift the car. That was until Sonny wrenched open his door.

'I said, get a fucking move on! We can't have anyone seeing you. We don't know who's watching.'

Anthony's lips set in a straight line and he started the engine, reluctantly manoeuvring the Mercedes into the backstreet leading to the rear of the tower block. He raised his chin defiantly, purposefully ignoring the nasty hooded specimens that allegedly classed as human life which clustered around his car, some pressing themselves against the blacked-out windows.

Sonny watched Flame tentatively drive through the lurking group and smiled. That bloke was as much of a tosser as he remembered. A small part of him would enjoy knowing the jumped-up twat would be trapped in that hovel of Marco's, surrounded by hookers and drug addicts, whilst being watched by one of their very own enforcers.

And, he thought with a wry smile, it hadn't taken long to fall back into an enforcer's mentality, despite the years he'd spent behind a keyboard.

However, he was dealing with Flame, not Zane.

Zane Morelli was a different kettle of fish. Waiting for the time when he had to do with *that*, wasn't the most pleasurable thing he could think of. Still, it would happen and would happen soon.

Scowling at the youths around the entrance, who rapidly backed away at his appearance, Sonny strode towards the tower block door where he would wait to show Flame into his new abode for however long Marco deemed it acceptable he would survive.

And however many days that was, Sonny didn't think it would be long.

That was the other problem... For some time, both he and Bill had questioned how long it would be before Marco's lunacy got them banged up or killed. Now, by the looks of it, Bill was already dead and Sonny was sick to the back teeth of waiting for the same thing to happen to *him*.

FORTY FIVE

IT HAD BEEN several hours since Zane had left Erin in the hotel and she was getting twitchy. For the fifth time in as many minutes, she peered from behind the navy blue curtains out into the dark night. Their room didn't offer much of a view, aside from a dimly-lit car park for hotel guests and the murky London skyline in the distance. The hotel was nice enough, but it wasn't where they should be by now.

Not that Erin knew exactly where they should be or even what they would do. All she knew, without Zane needing to utter it out loud, was that they were in danger.

Somewhere not far away, Marco and the rest of Zane's firm, or what had once been his firm, would have no doubt already been briefed of their pending arrival in the smoke, so at any given moment, trouble could land on their head. They could be ambushed; attacked. *Killed...*

It was crystal clear Marco wanted his brother dead. And although Anthony had not killed her father, like Zane had originally believed, he was still behind the complex set up. The despicable creature she'd forced herself to live with for years, had broken his promise to Zane about remaining in the Midlands and not getting in touch with Marco. Like the lying snake he was, those had been the first things Anthony had done, the minute Zane allowed him to walk away.

Erin's anger stewed further. The urge to rid the world of Anthony almost overtook the need to remove her father's murderer. *Only almost.*

But where was Zane?

This last week and a half had blown her mind on so many levels. All the things she'd held in black and white for so long had turned on their head and she couldn't think straight. But she had to. She must find a way to think clearly on what they did from here.

But how could she do that, when she wasn't sure of the other factors involved? It was all too bloody complicated and the shit could hit the fan at any time.

And Zane? There hadn't been proper time to consider how she felt about him, either.

Okay, so Erin knew she was attracted to him in a way that surpassed anything she'd felt in her life, but had she thought through what this meant for her as a person? Her life's work - everything she'd centred herself on which had kept her alive all these years since the bottom had been ripped out of her family, had been removed, shaken up and shoved back in a random order. And she didn't know which way to turn.

As well as revenge on her father's murderer, she wanted revenge on Anthony for... for *everything*. How was she supposed to do either of those things, when Zane was planning to be the one to remove his brother and Anthony?

What was left for her? Could she justify the outcome of this situation if she were allowed no hand in it? Furthermore, how much more of Zane would be destroyed once he'd taken the life of Marco? After that, would there be anything remaining in the man's heart that she had recently awakened?

Zane killing his own flesh and blood was akin to her killing her father. It was the cardinal sin and one she believed no one could recover from. Unfortunately, it was the only option Zane had. Because if he didn't, then Marco would take his life with no such qualms. Along with *hers*...

• • • •

ZANE SILENTLY FUMED, conveniently positioned in the shadows opposite the flats on Barker Street.

He hadn't felt comfortable leaving Erin alone in the hotel, but he'd had to check this out. There was no point in them *both* standing around watching and waiting.

Plus, he hadn't wanted her witnessing him seeing what he believed he already knew - that Marco had taken control of his penthouse. *His* penthouse - the only thing he personally owned.

And he'd been right, as his drive-by of the place en route here, proved.

His eyes narrowed. He'd *known* Marco must have taken his hard-earned property for himself the second the news cameras panned across his balcony during that report about that woman falling to her death.

The poor cow hadn't 'fallen to her death'. Zane knew his brother too well, and this was just his style. Marco had killed the poor wench - either because she was surplus to requirements or purely because he *felt* like it.

Zane didn't know which one was correct, but one of those scenarios were. And now, his home - or what *had* been his home was the scene of a murder. The murder of an innocent person to satiate Marco's sick mind.

Murder was one thing. It wasn't like he was averse or had clean hands on that score, but what he didn't condone - would *never* condone, was taking people out who had no part in anything. *Especially women.*

Marco didn't have the same ideals though and never had.

Zane risked sparking up a cigarette. Even thinking about what had occurred in his absence, and what still was going on, pushed him into a dangerous level of rage.

Yeah, he'd driven past his penthouse, but hadn't risked entering it. The keys he'd kept close at all times would most likely no longer work. Anyway, he didn't need to go in. Not yet.

For now, he'd seen all he needed to see.

That his expensive neutral blinds at the huge lounge windows had been replaced by garish curtains, spoke volumes. That and the pile of empty cans littering one of the balconies visible even from ground level was enough.

He'd go into the apartment. And soon. Just not now.

Zane's eyes tracked back to the dingy tower block, wishing things would start moving. He couldn't leave Erin unguarded for much longer.

He'd been gone three hours already, which was long by anyone's standards, but immeasurably long knowing Flame was inside this building. It had been excruciatingly difficult standing by whilst Sonny led that two-faced bastard inside in front of his very eyes.

Knowing Sonny Mitchell was part of Marco's plan to have him incarcerated and killed, stung. The man hadn't shown more allegiance to either of the Morelli brothers over the other in the past, so it was a surprise to find him in the driving seat. But by the looks of it, he'd taken Bill's place as Marco's wing man.

However, Marco's supposed cleverness and scheming had omitted one thing. Despite his brother clearly believing otherwise, Zane remembered their father purchasing this block of flats. *'Something for the boy to concentrate on, rather than cause trouble,'* had been his exact words.

Marco had always been problematic and a loose cannon, but his father's wish of keeping his youngest son busy by having property to oversee, hadn't worked. Marco had instead ploughed his energy into utilising the flats as stash holes for stuff he'd syphoned from the business that he thought no one knew about and forcing desperate tenants to pay through the nose for a hovel not fit for a dog.

Despite the graveness of this situation, Zane's mouth curled into a half smile.

Marco presumed he was unaware of this place, otherwise he would not believe it safe to stash his mole there.

Suddenly seeing movement at the flat's entrance, Zane

threw his cigarette to the floor and pressed himself further back into the shadows.

In the gloom he watched the unmistakable figure of Sonny exiting the horrible excuse of a building and primed himself ready to move. He'd tail Sonny back to wherever he was going. Flame could wait.

Marco wasn't so slack to not give instructions to guard Flame. And that would be another thing to deal with.

Zane secured the buckle of his crash helmet and hoped Sonny would head to wherever now acted as the firm's headquarters.

It was imperative he knew where that was, so he could get to work.

FORTY SIX

THOROUGHLY MENTALLY EXHAUSTED, Sonny walked across the car park of Luna Motion Films. He was in no rush to go inside the building, but there was stuff he needed to check before he could go home.

He wouldn't update Marco tonight with the news that Flame was successfully installed in flat number nineteen or that an enforcer was stationed outside the door to ensure he didn't leave the building.

If he called, he'd only get a round of abuse. Marco was out on the piss with Hazel, as he wouldn't see her tomorrow - the night before the wedding.

Superstitious nonsense, but never mind.

Yeah, Marco was too enamoured with Hazel's newfound urge to spend time with him, rather than her previous offhand and business-like demeanour.

'She's finally seen which side her bread's buttered on,' Marco had said earlier, taking great pleasure in droning on about the change of his betrothed's attitude.

Sonny rolled his eyes as he neared the steps leading into the studio's back entrance.

Like he gave a fuck? Hazel, or Lisa, whatever she called

herself, was as transparent a window, minus the glass. It was obvious to anyone with eyes that her marriage to Marco was down to kudos and money. But that was *her* problem. She'd soon realise her hideous mistake the second Marco got bored.

Because he would...

Despite the man's unhealthy obsession with the tart, this was *Marco*. Marco always wanted what he hadn't got and when he got it, no longer wanted it.

Yep, Hazel would meet a sticky end, like everybody else. She'd find that out for herself soon.

As for Flame...

Just thinking about the creepy weirdo made the hackles on Sonny's neck bristle. That freak of nature had bleated and whined, like a teenage girl about the location and state of the flat he'd been deposited in. What exactly did he expect? The fucking Savoy?

Knowing Flame, yes.

That man would get nowhere by laying down the law and issuing diva-like commands. Nowhere at all. In fact, *nothing* would get him anywhere, because he was fucked.

Was the bloke so blind to not notice the sand rapidly trickling out of the timer representing what remained of his life? Did he believe he'd walk away from this?

Obviously...

Tragic really, because that wouldn't happen. By this time tomorrow, Marco would have dispatched him, so Flame might as well enjoy the tiny amount of life he had left, even if that consisted of listening to glue sniffers arguing in the corridor outside that cesspit of a flat.

He could also have done without Robe playing his face about standing guard for Flame.

Sonny found himself grating his teeth again. He was sick of this. Sick of all of it. Sick of being everyone else's sounding board and sick of copping the brunt of people's displeasure over Marco's orders.

And it would only get worse.

Still, he'd installed the enforcers in the lobby of the penthouse complex to pose as security guards, as instructed. Of course, the concierge had accepted the intrusion. It wasn't like the prick had any choice, so everything Marco wanted was sorted for when Zane arrived.

Sonny sighed. He couldn't think about this any longer. It was late and he was ball-bagged. He'd have a quick whip around the studio to make sure all the shit was powered down and there were no dumbass girls hanging around hoping to be invited back to Marco's and then he'd fuck off.

He'd grab a curry on the way home, watch the box for half an hour and then hit the sack. Anything else he'd deal with in the morning. This was more than enough for one night.

Reaching the steps to the back entrance, Sonny's mind was so tied up with the unfortunate events of the evening, his guard was down just long enough to miss the figure lunging from the shadows before it was too late.

• • • •

ALTHOUGH ZANE had no specific grievances with Sonny Mitchell, he was at risk of taking his pent-up rage, disappointment and hurt over his brother, Flame and Bill, on the only man he had chance to vent it on.

He tried to constrain himself but was fast approaching the point where he would be unable to stop from unleashing everything onto Sonny, rather than on the person he *really* wanted to get his hands on.

Zane was coiled and wired. For too long he'd held back, forced to sit tight and wait for until the time was right and the window of reason for Sonny was slipping into obscurity.

Tailing Sonny back from the flats, Zane realised straight away things were worse than he'd first surmised.

Pulling into the car park of a film studio - an *adult* film studio, he'd initially thought Sonny must be making a detour, but it didn't take long for the horrible realisation to hit that this place was the Morelli firm's new headquarters.

The vast majority of what had once been a firm Zane had been proud of, now consisted of making money from sleazy films and shoehorning women, as well as men, into corners to perform in front of the cameras.

That concept alone riled Zane. Thinking about other firms who had their fingers in this kind of get-up, he knew there was lots of money in it, but his father was adamant making cash from sexual extortion was not something ever to be considered by the Morellis.

This was a view Zane shared and his plans, when taking over from his father, were to run things exactly the same way. He'd incorporated as many improvements to the firm as possible, without going down roads he didn't agree with.

And he'd done just that.

Or he had, until Marco trashed everything both he and their father had strived for.

All this had been backed up by the dirt that had immediately spilt from Sonny Mitchell's mouth, like it was a huge relief to finally give his opinion on Marco.

Zane centred his focus back to the man on the floor under him, red hot rage thundering through his veins. Panting heavily, he increased the pressure on Sonny's windpipe, feeling exhilaration as the man's scared eyes bulged from their sockets.

Sonny Mitchell was a fundamental part of all of this shit. He'd had a choice and he'd taken the wrong one. *Now he would pay.*

'Please! I...' Sonny uttered a couple of words before the air remaining in his lungs ran out. He'd expected to die in the end, but not tonight. He really hadn't thought it would happen right *now* and like this, but he should have known Zane wouldn't hang around once he was in the vicinity.

Sonny stared at the unmistakable face of Zane Morelli - savage as ever. The only difference to the last time he'd set eyes on him, was the scar on his right cheek - the only thing marring his movie star good looks.

That scar told a story of its own...

Even being close to death, guilt bloomed in the pit of Sonny's gut.

He'd been present when that instruction was issued. At the time, he'd sniggered at what was to happen, knowing no other response would have been acceptable to the man giving the orders.

Yeah, Sonny had grinned at Marco's words, even though he knew the reasoning behind what was due to befall Zane was untrue – lies manufactured as part of Marco's plan - a plan of which he, himself, had gained from.

And he *had* gained. He'd received a chunk of cash, a promotion, plus he'd been moved away from the muck and bullets of his enforcer's role. He'd also gained more besides - most of which he didn't want. Even less so as time went on. Now, never more so.

And not for the first time, Sonny accepted that he'd made a fundamental mistake and given the wrong brother his allegiance.

He'd supplied this allegiance and the lies that went with it because it was, a) easier and, b) he was a stupid, deluded, greedy cunt.

How he wished he'd backed what he knew to be right all along.

It was too late now.

If nothing else, he could apologise. Even if it achieved nothing, which in all fairness was nothing less than he deserved, it was better than saying sod all.

In the dim gloom of the nearest streetlamp, Zane watched Sonny Mitchell's memories flickering across his face. The fleeting expressions included the decisions that had helped bring his existence to such an untimely and abrupt end. But then as quickly as his rage escalated, it slowed to a stop.

The pause didn't make Zane relinquish his tight hold around Sonny's throat, but for the first time since seizing the opportunity to pounce, he weighed up his options.

Sonny Mitchell didn't need to vocalise his remorse. It was

clear. The man's self-chastisement wasn't down to being pulled up either, but it was because Sonny had *always* held misgivings over Marco's decisions.

Sonny's thoughts were not new. It was the way he'd felt for some time - most probably since the start.

Zane had initially found Sonny's involvement with Marco's twisted plan a surprise. But was it *that* much of a surprise?

Anyone worth half their salt could sense the man was terrified of his present situation. But it wasn't just that. Sonny was petrified to not agree with Marco. And what would befall him if he didn't... He always had been, but he'd had no choice if he wanted to live.

Zane's eyes narrowed in the half light. He knew that, apart from himself, and perhaps, Bill, Marco demanded *everyone* must agree with him.

Sonny was defeated, exhausted and crippled from acting on things he did not agree with. He'd been doing it for a long time now and it showed.

Killing Sonny might release some pressure, but it would be short-lived. Would it not make more sense to utilise the man's present place in Marco's life to get into the position needed to take revenge on the real culprit?

FORTY SEVEN

'YEAH, BABE, everything's good,' Marco drawled, the smug smile bright on his face even though he knew Hazel couldn't see it down the phone line.

He wasn't putting it on. In just one day from now he'd be married and so whatever Zane did after that would be too late to stop his ascension to top of the pile. Once he'd got hitched, the deal was set in stone. Trevor Grimes could whine and moan all he liked, but it made no odds.

Hazel was different. Acting like she was reluctant to wed him had disappeared. She was now a woman who couldn't *wait* to call herself Mrs Morelli.

Marco's chest puffed out with inflated grandeur as he congratulated himself on his prowess. Hazel's previous reticence to allow him to lay a finger on her beforehand had also now, well... *definitely* changed.

She couldn't keep her mitts off him and he suspected her witnessing his power in that club during her hen night was partly responsible for that.

Yeah, birds loved that kind of thing.

That and because he was cracking in the sack.

Those two things were why he'd always had a string of

chicks queuing up to get into his bed.

It was about time Hazel realised he was a catch.

Realising she was still on the other end of the line, Marco concentrated on what she was saying, even though he'd got side-lined admiring himself in the mirror. 'I've got to dash now, babe,' he said. 'I'll see you at the church tomorrow. Prepare yourself for one hell of a night!'

He ended the call, expecting Hazel would already be dripping wet in anticipation of another red-hot session with him. It would be like that *every* night from now on.

Marco's hand pressed the throbbing bulge in his crotch, the anticipation of releasing his arousal, all consuming.

That was until the penthouse intercom started buzzing and the image of his new wife in crotchless knickers, spreadeagled in the honeymoon suite evaporated.

'For fuck's sake!' he muttered, resentfully getting out of the chair.

Pulling his bathrobe around him, he moved to the door, his face thunderous. *Didn't people understand he was getting married in the morning?*

Sonny tried his best to not let Marco's expression deter him from his mission. He also had to mask the guilt prodding within him.

Guilt was unnecessary because Marco had no scruples. Look what he'd done to those women; to his own brother. What they'd *all* done to his brother, thanks to Marco... And what was planned next...

Because of this man's way of working and his need to have it all, Bill was dead and more people would follow suit - himself included, if he didn't put a stop to this.

The position Sonny found himself in last night exacerbated what he'd wanted to do for a long time, yet he'd consistently edged away from because he was too bloody scared.

Was he scared now? Of course he was, but he'd assisted Marco's greed-driven plan of destruction for long enough and when faced with the choice between the two Morellis, it was a no-brainer.

Zane scared him more than Marco. *That* brother wasn't loopy or tied up with irrelevant things. Zane was one hundred percent on the ball and totally compos mentis. His violence was methodical and executed with precise intent. No coked-up fits of madness for Zane.

And *that* made him the more dangerous one.

But the betrayal he was about to unleash wasn't just because Zane was more dangerous than Marco. It was because he was right.

Zane was right and always had been.

Sonny couldn't turn back time and change what he'd been part of, but if what he'd agreed to do went some way towards righting his part in Marco's bulldozing of the Morelli values, then a small part of him could die with a modicum of peace.

Sonny plastered on a grin as he walked down the hallway into the lounge before his confidence deserted him. 'I thought I'd bring you an update, being as I didn't want to disturb you last night.'

'Good job I'm not in the middle of something important,' Marco muttered, letting it go that Sonny had invited himself in. He wasn't about to admit that he'd been about to have a wank. They might think Hazel wasn't giving out or worse, that he couldn't get it up for her. 'I presume Flame is where I instructed him to be put? And yeah, I know I said I'd get rid of him today and I *will*, but it will be later on.'

Sonny kept his smile fixed. His whole life depended on getting this right, but it took a massive effort to look nonchalant. 'Yep. Flame's in that flat. He's most put out about it!' He laughed heartily. *That bit was genuinely funny, even if the rest of this wasn't.* 'You should have seen his face. Not a happy chap. Plus his mug's stitched up to fuck. He looks like the Elephant Man!'

Sonny realised that wasn't a wise thing to say as Marco's eyes narrowed into the horrible slitty look he wore when Zane came into his mind. Reminding him that Flame had received this latest beating, courtesy of Zane the same night Bill was killed, was stupid. An error which he needed to quickly remove. 'There's an enforcer on his door too, like you wanted, so Flame's going nowhere. Pluss, judging by his take on the flat's location, I suspect he'd rather stay inside!'

Marco's mouth twitching with a hint of a smile told Sonny that he'd successfully glossed over his error. He pressed on, hoping he could swing it.

He dared to lay his hand on Marco's wide shoulder. 'Look, I know you were dead set on taking Flame out today, but I've been thinking... I didn't make it easy yesterday by having a wobble about stepping into Bill's shoes - after all, they're big ones to fill, but I'm good with it now. 'And...' He made his eyes twinkle, like they used to in the old days before Marco ruined everything. '...I have to admit I enjoyed manhandling Flame into his final prison, so please consider what I'm about to suggest.'

He continued looking at Marco even though the serpent-like eyes made him immediately want to look away. He knew from watching Bill that this was the only way of subduing Marco's paranoia. 'It's your wedding tomorrow, so you should concentrate on that, not this. Flame can wait as long as he has to. Forever if you like! Don't get your hands dirty on a meaningless piece of shit like him, today of all days. Your concentration should be on you and Li... erm, Hazel.'

Like Marco ever thought about anyone but himself...

'Flame will still be there when you get back and everything's covered downstairs here with guards, should you have any "visitors"... So, what do you reckon?'

Marco blinked, his brain jumping between paranoia and thinking about what he could be doing instead. Before all of this kicked off, he'd planned to invite a top-class escort to the hotel he was booked into tonight. Being as he hadn't had a stag night, he owed himself a final bit of fluff before getting hitched, didn't he? This shit had threatened to use up that available time, but if Sonny had everything sorted, then perhaps...

'Cheers!' Sonny cried.

Marco stared at the large glass of whisky suddenly being shoved into his hand, having missed it even being poured.

'Relax and leave all of this until afterwards. As said, everything's in hand.' Sonny clinked his glass against Marco's. 'Here's to you and Hazel!'

Marco gulped the whisky. Sonny had undergone a complete transformation since yesterday, which was good. His pep talk about pulling shit together must have resonated. Not surprising, considering he'd always been good with words. Maybe Sonny was a fitting replacement for Bill, after all?

Yeah, why the fuck should he run around the day before his own bloody wedding, doing housekeeping like killing that twat of an ex-accountant? The man was a pointless fucker and would get nowhere if he stepped outside. Sonny had already agreed to watch out for Zane when he showed up, then keep him under lock and key until his return. What was there to stress about? 'You've made sure Flame has no way of contacting anyone?'

'No phones. No fuck all. Trust me, he's going nowhere until *you* decide. You're the boss!' Sonny knew his words - the last bit especially, would stoke Marco's ego. And being as the man was wavering enough to question Flame's ability to contact anyone, it meant he was almost there. *Come on, come on.*

Marco's face split into a grin. 'D'ya know what? You're right!' He necked the remains of his whisky. 'I *am* the boss and it's my bastard wedding, so fuck it! I'll go to that hotel, like I planned and deal with everything when I get back from honeymoon.'

Sonny grinned, trying not to act overeager. 'Good choice, boss.'

• • • •

ERIN WANTED TO CONTINUE where Zane left off last night, but since the minute she'd woken up, she'd felt more on edge and distracted than expected. It seemed she wasn't the only one.

She tracked Zane as he moved from the hotel room's en-suite bathroom to his holdall of clothes, his muscular back covered with a thin sheen of steam from the shower making his olive skin more delicious than usual.

How she'd love to pretend there was no history; that there wasn't a shared burden pushing a wedge between their attraction and instead be normal people embroiled in the giddiness of a new relationship.

It felt like that in many respects, until her mind strayed from the all-consuming power Zane's magnetic charisma and powerful body had, to expose exactly who they were and why they'd been thrown together in the first place.

It hadn't been chanced upon or a random meeting. Zane had snatched her from the street for leverage against her fiancé, whereas she'd been waiting for her chance to kill him.

The same as she'd been waiting for the opportunity to kill Anthony.

But life worked in mysterious ways and now her plans were upside down, the people on her list had shifted places.

How many *normal* people held a list of people they intended to kill, whilst waiting years for an opportunity? How many *normal* people would agree to marry someone they despised to regain what was theirs, then murder them?

And from Zane's side, how many *normal* people would stay in a hotel with a woman he'd planned to use for vengeance on the man who had set him up and was now getting ready to murder his own brother? A brother who he loved fiercely, yet who had betrayed him in the worst ways possible?

Not many people could appreciate what that involved or have a clue what it felt like, but her and Zane did.

Her and Zane...

Erin pushed away her forming smile. Was there really a 'her and Zane'? There was no doubt their attraction for each other was powerful, but was it real?

Was the intensity of her feelings true or had their odd relationship occurred because it was the only way to deflect from the terrifying prospect of what they were both facing? Were they using sex as a diversion tactic from the inevitable?

Erin bit her bottom lip, experiencing the familiar anticipatory lurch of her stomach as Zane's eyes locked on hers, seeing that twinkle that was switched off the rest of the time.

Feeling her arousal kick start, she couldn't help but return his smile. She avidly watched him slip his strong legs into a pair of black jeans.

See? She was diverting again - using lust to refrain from thinking of things she'd rather not. But those things were there regardless. And whether she liked it or not, they would remain.

But the thoroughly unexpected love she felt in the short time since she'd given into what her...

Wait! Love? Who said anything about love? It was too soon to think about that, wasn't it? Even if it wasn't, it was unlikely to be reciprocated. How could it even work?

Erin frowned. Had she finally cracked under the pressure? Has she gone a bit crazier with what she knew would come to pass?

How could there be a future for someone like her? Especially with someone like Zane?

There was no turning back, once the one thing she needed to do was taken from her. *She* had to be the one to kill Anthony, yet Zane would do it.

Not being the one to finish Anthony would finish *her*. It wasn't like, if she killed him, she'd have an issue living with it. Partaking in that act that wouldn't kill any part of her because that part was already dead.

But *not* doing it would. Nothing could be the same after that.

And Zane? Zane might believe it important to finish Anthony, but it wasn't as important as dealing with his own brother.

With those things set to push them apart, how could they have a future? They were too damaged and these things would cause even further damage.

This time, it would be beyond any form of repair.

FORTY EIGHT

ANTHONY HEARD the talking clearly enough, but still pressed himself up against the flimsy door to double check he wasn't imagining things. Considering this dump of a place was fashioned out of little more than balsa wood, he doubted it.

That gorilla man stationed outside this flea-infested dump *was* being told to stand down. Plus, he was certain the gravelly voice speaking belonged to Sonny Mitchell.

Anthony slid his face against the ill-fitting door to enable a thin view of the corridor outside through the crack. It *was* Sonny Mitchell.

Holding his breath, he squinted further. *Why was the gorilla being sent away? Were they coming in here first?*

If so, it could only mean one of two things. Sonny Mitchell was about to kill him, or he was being taken somewhere different to be dispatched.

Anthony's fingers began jerking in response to this realisation.

Shit!

He was going to be offed. *No, no, no!*

He hadn't done all this; got this far to be offloaded by these two fucking baboons. It wasn't happening. It *couldn't* happen.

What about his business? What about everything he'd worked for? He'd lose the lot, whilst that bitch, Erin, swanned around doing what she damn well liked? *She* should be the one caged in here waiting for death - the sly little whore.

All this time he'd been living with David Masters' daughter – and the tramp of a slut had played him? Actually *played* him! Her plan had always been to kill him. How dare she! How fucking *dare* she!

It was *him* who had taken the shit for those greedy Morelli bastards because of Erin's cunt of a father, yet after everything he'd done – all the changes he'd been forced to make, he was the one to die for it?

He thought not.

The urge to rip the balsa wood door from its hinges became overwhelming.

Breathing erratically, Anthony forced himself to count. *Nine, eighteen, twenty-seven...*

Keep controlled. Keep controlled. Just wait.

If he attempted something now, there wouldn't be a chance to reverse this situation. Not that there were many options to do that, but hearing something interesting, Anthony paused.

'It's what he said,' the voice continued the other side of the door. 'And that's why I'm here.'

Anthony returned to holding his breath. His lungs felt like they may burst as the voice of Sonny Mitchell continued.

'Yeah, he's decided to leave dealing with it until he gets back from honeymoon. He'll be gone at least a week.'

Anthony heard the gorilla man mumble something about not wanting to stand outside this cesspit for another seven days.

Good. That made two of them who weren't happy about this.

His heart thundered in his rib cage. They had to be talking about Marco. And if Marco was determined to finish him off himself, yet wouldn't be around for another week, it was easy.

A grin pulled at Anthony's stitches. Oh, Mitchell had thought himself clever by taking his phone and shutting him in here, hadn't he? Did the moron really think he wouldn't find a way to get out of this dump?

Within minutes of those drongos leaving, he'd be gone.

Anthony was feeling extremely pleased with himself, until he jumped back from the door as the men outside started boarding it up.

• • • •

'ERIN, DON'T FIGHT ME over what I've told you, for Christ's sake!' Zane's voice was calm yet held a clear note of warning. This was the second time she'd brushed him away when he'd gone to kiss her. Aside from disliking the cold shoulder, he needed his concentration on what lay ahead, rather than diluted by Erin's behaviour.

As much as what might be going through her head, Erin was embedded in *his* head. She had been ever since he'd laid eyes on her.

Pushing his advances away was one thing, but making things difficult because of his plans, was another. It was imperative there were no slip ups and there could be if she got under his skin in the wrong way.

Yet now she insisted on knowing everything and how it would all work?

He didn't know half the answers himself, so how could he tell her what she wanted to know? If anything, Erin's probing questions made him doubt his instinct and double think his decision.

Furthermore, he couldn't tell her *everything* because he didn't want her analysing the situation before it panned out the way he hoped. It was hard enough reaching his decision, without being given a reason to backtrack.

Zane ran his fingers through his hair. He'd never answered to anyone before and didn't want to start now, but Erin was part of his life, albeit via strange and ill-conceived ways. But there he wanted her to stay. He just hoped he hadn't got her wrong.

A bit like he hoped he hadn't made the wrong call about

Sonny Mitchell...

'How do you know this Sonny person will honour what he's promised?' Erin folded her arms across her chest. It was a defensive movement, but also to stop her from throwing this nightmare to one side and running her hands in Zane's hair, down his chest, pressing her lips to his...

'The honest answer is that I don't, for certain, but I'm confident I'm right,' Zane said. *And he was.* Sonny was angling for a way out of Marco's clutches and this plan offered him exactly that.

Yes, he could have easily taken Sonny's life last night. It was warranted via association alone. Plus, the risk was real that Sonny could already have already updated Marco and set a trap by now, but the chance had to be taken.

Whether he was right or not, would soon come to light.

'So, let me get this straight,' Erin continued, keeping her resentment at bay. 'You know where Anthony is; there's one of your enforcers guarding him until Marco arrives to kill him, but this Sonny bloke will somehow convince Marco not to bother doing the business and instead dismiss the enforcer, giving *you* the opportunity to do it instead?' *Marco killing Anthony was a worse prospect than Zane doing it...*

'In short, yes, apart from that it's not one of my enforcers,' Zane nodded. 'It seems all the men *I* employed were dismissed the day Marco took over.' *Something else to rectify once he was back in charge.* 'Sonny told me everything. Marco's got enforcers stationed at my penthouse too. He's expecting me to go there, which I would, if only to rip out those shit curtains he's put up, but that will have to wait.'

Erin's mouth dropped open. 'Shit curtains? How do you know? Have you already been there?'

'Only as a drive by last night,' Zane admitted. By rights he should have already filled Erin in about that, but returning fired up with anger, along with the new possibilities open to him, he'd diverted.

It hadn't been difficult.

Returning to find this gorgeous creature waiting, her face a mixture of worry and annoyance, sparked the powerful need to lose himself in her. The unfamiliar feeling of having someone he wanted to be with, stark relief on her beautiful face at his presence, was an experience he could get used to. *Wanted* to get used to.

Erin had succumbed to the same need, but this morning it was different.

Zane found his hands forming into fists. 'My brother has violated everything,' he snarled. 'Everything our father did - everything he stood for. A fucking porn studio? Jesus Christ! And you don't want to know how he's been treating the women who work for him...'

It was a sad fact that he hadn't been remotely surprised when Sonny confirmed Marco had chucked that bird off the balcony. *His* balcony in *his* apartment. Not that Marco had admitted the deed, but that was typical of him.

Zane had guessed who was responsible the minute he'd seen that news report, but to hear of what had also been done to other women in aid of Marco's sick sex kicks...

He shook his head with a mixture of disappointment and rage. 'And now he's getting married? I can't believe it!'

Erin could have wept for the crushing devastation she saw peeking from behind the fury on Zane's face. The whole thing was abysmal - a hell of a lot worse in so many ways than she'd contemplated. How on earth would they successfully put an end to his animal of a brother's destruction, with it being just the two of them and Sonny Mitchell - a man who may or may not be setting them up for death? Marco Morelli had an entire host of men willing to cover his back and stoke his sick mind? Where did that leave them?

And the woman who Marco was set to marry tomorrow? A business arrangement, Zane was told. What was she like? Was she sick and twisted, like Marco? Or would she be another statistic on Marco's tally of victims?

Erin couldn't help but shudder. Even thinking about any of

it made her nauseous. The whole bloody thing was so, *so* wrong. 'What will you do about his wedding? How will you play it?'

Zane slowly raised his eyes. 'I have a plan for that.'

Erin waited patiently for him to embellish on what that plan entailed, but she was wasting her time. He would say nothing until he was ready.

Holding his hand out, Zane stood up. 'Come on.'

'Come on, what?' Erin asked, her frown deepening when Zane shoved his gun into his inside pocket.

'We need to get to Flame now.'

'But...'

Grasping Erin's hand, Zane pulled her to her feet and handed her a crash helmet. 'We have to put my theory to the test. Sonny will either have done what he promised or not. If he hasn't, then we've had it within a matter of hours, but if he has, then we need to act.'

Reluctantly taking the helmet, Erin turned from Zane's searing gaze. She hadn't expected to accompany Zane whilst he undertook the task she so desperately wanted for herself. Witnessing the man who had treated her like a piece of dirt for the last six years die by someone's hands other than hers, was happening sooner than she thought.

She wasn't ready to take this, but then again, she never would be.

• • • •

THANKS TO A CROWBAR, it took Zane little effort to rip the planks of wood from the door of flat number nineteen. He could barely contain his eagerness, knowing Flame was cowering in there, like the toad he was.

And for this to happen just when the prick thought he had a chance to extricate himself from this shit situation too?

Shame...

Zane's relief that Sonny had delivered what he'd promised was huge. Now all would be good. Well, as good as this collection of situations could be. And although what he was about to give up galled him, it was the correct thing to do.

He glanced at Erin studying his progress, looking every inch like she'd prefer to be anywhere but here. *She wouldn't soon though.* 'Are you ready?'

'As much as I'll ever be,' Erin replied quietly. Yes, the end of Anthony was something she'd always factored into her solution, but the disappointment for it not being the way she'd envisaged, stung. Still, this was how it was, so she must accept it.

With a final flourish, Zane removed the last plank nailed to the door and after a quick check to make sure Erin was ready, kicked the door off its hinges with one hefty boot.

Erin followed as Zane flew into the flat, her nostrils filling with the stench of damp and rot. At least she could take solace that Anthony's last night on earth had been spent somewhere so putrid it would have thrown him into a crescendo of unbearable OCD.

She barely registered where Zane had gone he moved so fast, until she heard awkward squeaking noises coming from the mess of Anthony's mouth, his body pinned tightly underneath Zane's big frame.

Erin's veins twitched with adrenaline, her fingers closing around the knife in her jeans pocket.

It would be simple to rush over and stick this blade in Anthony's lying neck. It would mean she might partially absolve what that bastard had put her through. It would also mean that her and Zane could have some kind of future after this was over.

Maybe...

The knife became slippery in her clammy hand.

But she couldn't. What if during the chaos she was off target and got Zane instead? Her past attempts with weapons hadn't been too successful, so what made her think she would do any better, just because Anthony was the target?

Desolation filled her mind. Maybe it was time to take stock? Perhaps she just wasn't capable enough? Maybe Anthony was right all along and she was a useless bitch?

Erin's jaw set with resolve. *What was she thinking? She was not useless. She was...*

Her train of thought stalled when Zane stood up. Had he done it? Had he killed Anthony already and she'd missed it because her thoughts had taken over?

Her eyes darted towards the figure on the floor, relieved to see Anthony was still very much alive, bound like a trussed-up pig.

A wave of exhilaration flooded her. Her eyes locked with the horrible ones of Anthony, which were always devoid of emotion, yet now there was something behind them. And it was clear exactly what that was. *Pure, unadulterated fear.*

Zane had worked fast to get Anthony bound and trussed like that. There was no escape now and Anthony knew it.

Her eyes moved to Zane, wondering why he wasn't completing the job.

'Anything you want to say to this piece of shit before he descends into hell?' Zane's voice drowned out the muffled wailing seeping from behind the gag in Anthony's mouth.

'Not really,' Erin said calmly. 'Short of that I hope he rots!'

Watching Zane pull his gun from his inside pocket, she steadied herself to relinquish what she'd dreamt of doing herself for so long.

That was until she realised the gun was held out to her...

Her eyes darted from the gun to Zane. 'Wh...? I thought...'

'This job is yours, if I'm not mistaken?' Zane's eyes were immeasurably dark, speaking silent words that only Erin understood. 'That's if you still want it?'

Did she ever? Gratitude and exhilaration crashed through her as she stepped forward to take the gun. Overwhelming happiness may seem a strange emotion to experience when being given the go ahead to kill someone, but nothing about her life was normal – this being another facet. To *her*, this opportunity was one of the greatest gifts anyone could ever give her.

It might be wrong in other's opinions, but not to her. Other people didn't have to think the way she did. They hadn't had to live like she had. They'd hadn't experienced what she had.

And what she was about to do now would make all the difference.

Had her need to finish this not been so great, she would have thrown her arms around Zane and pressed her lips to his. They had a future. A future that only people like them could - something not possible with anyone else in the world.

And by the look in Zane's eyes, Erin now knew for definite that he felt the same way.

Cocking the gun, she pointed it at Anthony's head. 'Die, you fucker!' she screamed.

Tears of joy formed as the crack of the bullet resounded through the mouldy flat.

Now it was up to her to help Zane through what he would have to do next.

FORTY NINE

HAZEL WASN'T FAZED that the collection of women she'd invited to the wedding didn't look pleased the marriage had gone ahead. She'd only invited the miserable bitches to fill up the church pews. It had been impossible for the famous faces of the adult film industry, which would have looked good from her side, to get here with such short notice. But it was the same from Marco's side. The only people he'd invited, were from his firm.

Of course, it would have been preferable had he invited a selection of faces from other established London firms he was on good terms with, but there would be time for that down the line.

All that mattered now was that this deal was done.

Hazel glanced smugly at the wedding band nestled next to the Cartier engagement ring on her finger.

Now she was privy to the Morelli fortune and everything that came with it. She would be overloaded with more kudos than ever, not to mention the vast amount of extra money coming her way.

She'd already earmarked a new place for them to live when they returned from honeymoon. Although Marco's penthouse was nice, there were plenty of places in the city with a more salubrious postcode to showcase her rise in standing.

Her mega shift up the career ladder to number one adult film actress in the country would be a welcome accolade too. She expected calls to flood in from the top American porn industries, offering roles the minute the news became public.

It wouldn't be long now.

The world would be more her oyster than previously. She'd have endless money to spend on further cosmetic procedures - none of which she would have to fund herself. From now on, everything would be courtesy of Marco.

Boy, how she'd landed on her feet and it was all down to her father's negotiation skills. Hazel had always known her father would ensure she got the best deal. And he'd managed it with bells on.

She scanned the hotel's banqueting suite, finding her father looking as proud as punch, chatting amicably with a couple of Marco's men. He was as overjoyed about the upshot of this arrangement as she was. Even Marco wasn't as offensive as she'd first presumed.

Hazel took longer than usual admiring her reflection in the floor to ceiling window that looked out over the landscaped gardens. She refrained from giving her large bust a replenishing hike up to push her boobs a little further out of the jewelled corset of her skin-tight wedding dress. This tit tape worked wonders in keeping her famous assets in place, but they could still benefit from a bit of adjustment.

Pushing her full mouth into a scarlet pout instead, Hazel flicked her long tresses over her shoulder, aware of the cameras pointing in her direction. She couldn't blame the guests for grabbing the opportunity for ad-hoc pictures. Photos of her were worth a fortune. Even more so now.

Glancing over at her new husband, Hazel smiled, her victory complete when he broke away from a group to make his way over. Just as it should be and exactly how it *would* be from now on.

The man was obsessed with her, meaning everything she

demanded; everything she could wish for, would be supplied quicker than she could shake a stick at. Life would be comfortable as fuck and she intended to reap every part of that - starting with the extortionately priced honeymoon she'd booked, courtesy of Marco's bank card.

They were flying first class too and she couldn't wait.

'How are you, Mrs Morelli?' Grabbing Hazel's waist, Marco pulled against him, his lips trailing up her slender neck.

He buried his nose into her skin and inhaled the intoxicating scent of Chanel N° 5 and found his hand skimming the backless wedding dress, his fingers slipping under the material to trace the tantalising edge of her lacy G-string.

He had been tasked with hiding his semi-erection since Hazel had entered the church and now, after hours of this reception; of the torture of holding her close during the first dance and then eating the meal whilst she stroked his leg under the table, he'd been rock solid for ages. It showed no sign of abating and if he didn't stick his cock in her soon, he would burst.

'I'm doing good, husband,' Hazel whispered, her lips brushing Marco's earlobe, gloating as she felt his tell-tale hardness pressing against her stomach through her corset. 'I see you've relaxed a little now?'

Marco smiled into Hazel's hair extensions. It wasn't that he hadn't been relaxed. If anything, he was relieved the deal was firmly signed and sealed, giving him full use of the Lisa Tequila brand. A deal that for a short while he'd thought might not pull off. But he need not have stressed. Everything had panned out exactly as it should, despite a few hiccups along the way.

And he wasn't letting having to still deal with Flame and his brother, bother him.

Through the blonde mass of Hazel's fake hair, Marco grinned at Sonny standing with some enforcers over by one of the champagne bars. The man had come up trumps and done just as good a job as Bill would have. Despite the rocky start, Sonny was a perfect replacement for his previous right-hand man.

Everything was in hand - that tosser, Flame, as well as the penthouse, were guarded up to the teeth. There would be no one going AWOL and no one gaining entry. There was nothing to stress over. He could afford to kick back and relax for the next week, doing nothing but ploughing his new wife. When he returned, he would slot nicely into the life he'd cleverly manufactured and reap the immense rewards coming his way.

His brother's return, whenever that may be, no longer needed to be top of his list. Zane could scupper nothing now the wedding had gone ahead. All that was left to do now, was offload the golden brother and that could now be done at his leisure.

Marco couldn't help but smile, wondering how Zane would take it if he knew of this marriage and how he'd swung the deal of the century. Ensuring this wedding happened before Zane stuck his head over the parapet and trashed everything was the main reason he'd been happy to get it done so fast.

The way it had been arranged avoided the papers becoming involved and because few were invited, his marriage wouldn't be public knowledge. The special licence skirted around having the banns read or details printed in the local rag too.

Hazel might have preferred the publicity, but for once, being out of the public eye was the sensible option.

So, what with all these safeguards, there was no way Zane could have discovered the upcoming nuptials and what they relied upon. Even if his brother was lurking around the vicinity, unless he'd been informed by someone in the firm, then he'd be clueless.

And Marco was confident no one in his firm was stupid enough to discuss his business.

· · · ·

KEEPING A CAREFUL WATCH on Marco and seeing him fully involved with Hazel, Sonny knew from experience that his boss would remain otherwise engaged for long enough not to notice if he slipped out of the reception for a few minutes.

Even if the place was on fire, no one would dare risk incurring Marco's wrath to interrupt him from smooching with his new bride. It was common knowledge the world stopped for Marco where Hazel, or rather Lisa Tequila was concerned. They knew better than to push their luck and lose their jobs, or even their lives by spoiling his groping of the woman he put on a pedestal above all others - including, and thankfully for him, anything else, regardless of its importance.

Sonny took another quick glimpse in Marco's direction, his frown deepening at the man's hands blatantly running all over Hazel's body for all to see. His grotesque pawing was unsavoury, but Hazel had no objection. She revelled in the attention.

She'd learn...

Still, no time to waste.

Looking at his watch, Sonny casually ambled into the corridor, pretending to rummage in his suit jacket for his cigarettes.

First, he'd deal with the enforcers stationed around the front of the hotel, before nipping around the back to deal with the ones positioned in the grounds.

His heart thumped. Everything depended on timing. If this didn't run exactly on cue, the whole thing would go tits up.

It had run to clockwork so far. In fact, it couldn't have gone better. Marco had swallowed everything that had been said so far, plus no one receiving orders had overly questioned them either. In a way, that in itself was disconcerting - almost like it was *too* easy.

Fear prickled along Sonny's spine. Being so straightforward thus far made him worry it must only be a matter of time before something went wrong. It would only take one enforcer to mention the change of plans to Marco, or someone returning to their post at the wrong moment, for the whole thing to implode.

But he couldn't think like that. There was no reason why

this should go wrong. Marco was so consumed with his wedding and impending honeymoon, he was less on the ball than usual. Unless the obvious was shoved in his face or everything unravelled in front of him, there was no reason why the next part of the plan wouldn't slot into place as perfectly as the rest had.

Striding down the stone steps of the hotel's sumptuous entrance, Sonny made his way towards the nearest enforcer and checked his watch once more.

Five minutes to go.

Three minutes to get around the back to the men in the garden and deliver the message, then two minutes to return to the banqueting suite before it happened.

It was time.

'Hey!' Beckoning the enforcer over, Sonny moved towards him. 'It's time to stand down. The next shift's coming on.'

The man frowned. 'Stand down? I thought we were here for the duration? We were told th…'

'There's two shifts today. Mr Morelli doesn't want anyone exhausted on account of his wedding. He's expecting you to do normal hours on the usual routes tomorrow, so two shifts are required.'

Stop questioning things, Sonny prayed, gauging correctly that the enforcer didn't look too convinced. 'Take it that Mr Morelli's had a rare flash of generosity! It's only because he'll be in bed with Lisa Tequila tonight, whereas the rest of us won't!'

Winking, Sonny slapped the enforcer on the back for good measure. 'Round up the others here, will you and then push off. But get a move on. The boss won't be pleased if he wastes his good mood by finding out there were two shifts on at the same time.'

Watching the big man nod and promptly hurry away, Sonny sighed with relief, then rapidly made his way around the other side of the hotel. He knew the dig about Marco's generosity would swing it. Everyone knew the man possessed little, if none, the majority of the time. No one wanted to appear unappreciative by looking a gift horse in the mouth.

Then after he'd spoken to the others, he'd go back to the banqueting suite, making sure to be in place at the correct time.

• • • •

HAZEL WAS LOVING the attention Marco was smothering her with. Every pair of eyes in the room were on them. 'Shall we play to our guests and lead another dance?' she purred.

'Nah, I'd rather just cop of feel of my gorgeous wife without prancing around.' *Poncing around during the first dance was more than enough*. Grabbing Hazel's buttocks, Marco squeezed so hard a small yelp of pain escaped her luscious mouth, which turned him on further.

Jeez, he couldn't wait to get her upstairs. He might have to bin this reception off soon just so that he could. It would be no skin off his nose. With his standing, politeness and etiquette were unnecessary, so he could do what he liked.

Failing that and if Hazel didn't want to retire quite so early, they could nip into the posh grounds of this gaff and have a quickie.

Actually, that wasn't a bad idea. Neither was cutting down on the spirits going down his throat. The last thing he wanted was to be Mr Soft when the time came! Not that that had ever happened and the chances of *that* occurring whilst he was between this bird's legs was implausible.

Yeah, they'd pretend they were going for a spot of fresh air or admiring the gardens...

Feeling enthused by the prospect, Marco glanced in the direction of the large windows to scan what he could see of the grounds. *Any strategically positioned tree or a fountain he could take her up against?*

Knowing they would be at it only yards away from this lot here made the prospect more attractive.

A sudden wash of cold avalanched over Marco. *There! That person!*

Squinting harder, he tensed, his whole body primed, sure he'd just seen...

'What's the matter, babe?' Hazel asked, her talons moving along the lapel of Marco's frock coat.

Marco jerked his head away from Hazel's hand as she attempted to turn his face towards hers. He blinked hard in the hope that his less than perfect vision improved enough to deduce whether or not he was seeing things.

That man was no longer there...

'Marco?' Hazel snapped, a pout sliding onto her face. She didn't appreciate him having more interest in something else, when he'd just married her! What could be more important?

'Just give me a second.' Marco untangled himself from Hazel's arms and strode towards one of the windows. *If he was here...*

'Not off already, are you? You've forgotten your wife!' Sonny laughed, reaching Marco's side just as he neared a patio door.

He subtly scanned Marco's face, knowing what was eating him, but played out the act, like he's set out to do. He pushed on a concern frown. 'What's up? Has something happened?'

Marco turned, a rare look of confusion on his face. 'I just saw... I'm sure I just saw...'

'Who? You saw who?' Sonny looked around the room with overemphasised gusto. 'Don't tell me the press have snuck in. I...'

'No, not the press,' Marco hissed. 'It was Zane. I'm sure I've just seen my fucking brother!'

'Your *brother*?' Sonny exclaimed loudly.

'Shut it, you fucking idiot!' Marco spat, his eyes flashing. 'I'm telling you, he was there peering through the window.' He jerked his head towards the expanse of glass.

'It can't have been!' Sonny swallowed his smile. *Zane had made it and done what he'd wanted?* Now he'd finally given the second shift of enforcers the nod to take up their positions, providing they remained in sync, Zane would make sure to disappear from view. He walked towards the patio doors. 'Let me check out here.'

Marco followed Sonny out onto the big patio, feverishly scanning the grounds. His heart jumped at a man in the shadows several yards away. His hand moved towards his gun. Wedding or not, he was never unarmed. 'There! Over there!'

'That's one of *our* blokes. You know, the security I put on?' Almost tasting the adrenaline rippling off Marco in waves, Sonny called the enforcer over. 'Anybody about?'

'No one, Mr Mitchell. I've been here since the shift change. First shift reported no one either. It's all clear.' He nodded in deference at Marco. 'I hope the wedding is going well, sir?'

'Yes, yes it's fine, thank you.' Marco flapped his hand to dismiss the enforcer before turning back to Sonny. *Was he imagining things again? Hearing things? Seeing things?*

Just as Sonny was about to open the patio door to steer Marco back inside, Hazel rushed out.

'What's going on?' Hazel's eyes narrowed as she looked at Marco. 'If something's happened, then you need to let me know. I won't be happy if you're rushing off on some stupid business errand on our wedding day, Marco!'

Sonny hid his forming grin before anyone noticed. *Errand? Stupid?* Marco doing 'errands' would be a sight to behold. That Marco hadn't punched this bird in the face for such impudence underlined exactly how obsessed he was with her. Either that or seeing Zane had achieved the desired reaction.

Probably both.

Sonny was equally pleased to have pulled his side of things off well. Marco's face spelt out that he'd seen Zane. He *knew* he'd seen his own brother - it wasn't like he wouldn't recognise him, yet he was convincing himself he hadn't. It was so obvious, Sonny could hear the gears grinding inside Marco's skull as he silently fought to talk himself out of what he'd witnessed.

The best thing anyone could do to someone with Marco's state of mind, was to play on his fear that he was slowly losing it.

And now that two people - Sonny included, had reiterated that no one had been in the grounds, it would be enough to convince Marco to question his sanity. He'd talk himself into dismissing the situation, leaving only the worry that people thought he was losing his marbles.

Zane's plan was unfolding perfectly. The only thing left to do now was wait for things to start shifting. And that would happen the minute Marco disappeared with the delectable Hazel to whichever far-flung shores they were heading for the honeymoon.

Judging by the expression on Hazel's face, Sonny didn't fancy Marco's chances of getting much action, like he clearly hoped for, if he took the decision to remain here, rather than getting on the plane.

Zane had said it was a dead cert Marco would leave because he always legged it in the face of adversity - or more to the point, legged it away from anything he didn't want to face on a *personal* level. The prospect of questioning his sanity would undoubtedly send him scrambling for the airport gate, Zane had promised.

So far, so good.

'Marco! Are you not going to answer me?' Hazel spat, her previous loving demeanour having vanished at the concept of not ranking in pole position on Marco's attention scale.

'Yeah, of course I am.' Marco pulled his smile back into place. 'I just wanted to double check everything was in order before we leave.' He playfully slapped Hazel's pert backside, missing the knowing look burning in Sonny's eyes. 'Right, let's fuck off out of here and go to our room. I want you in my bed and we need to be up bright and early for the flight in the morning.'

Immediately backtracking from her sour mood, Hazel squealed with excitement. 'Okay then, babe.'

Marco steered Hazel towards the doors, turning back to give Sonny a wink. He didn't know what he'd been thinking for a minute there, by flying off the deep end. Sonny was right - there was no chance in a month of Sundays of Zane getting through his guards around the perimeter of the hotel.

Furthermore, if it *had* been Zane he'd seen, then he knew his brother better than anyone. Zane would not be content merely peering through a window, like a gatecrasher.

No way! He'd have stormed into the banqueting hall to announce his arrival, ensuring maximum damage was incurred.

Nah, no chance he'd have taken a guilty glance, then skulked off with his tail between his legs.

And, Marco realised with a smile, he wasn't seeing *or* hearing things. Not in the vein that he was losing his mind, anyway. The person at the window had been that enforcer. He'd even thought that same bloke to be Zane for a moment just now in the shadows too. That's how easy it was for the mind to play tricks.

As much as he'd tried and thought he'd succeeded in not letting his brother infiltrate his thoughts today of all days, he'd obviously been thinking about him on a subconscious level. Look at what it had caused.

Well, no more. Not another millisecond would he allow his tosser of a brother to encroach on his wedding, nor his honeymoon. And *that* he was going on, by hell or high water.

Zane was past it. Finished. A nobody.

Anything he might be thinking of and whenever he *really* rocked up to show his face on *his* turf, then he'd be forced to wait in line for attention, just like everyone else. If it turned out that Zane spent time locked in a shitty flat, courtesy of Sonny's ever-watchful alertness, that was *his* problem.

Marco's face set in a wide grin as he eagerly followed Hazel up the sweeping staircase to the honeymoon suite, his mind focused on his new bride.

And that's where his attention would stay until he got back from their holiday.

WRAPPED IN A FLUFFY white complimentary bathrobe, Erin sat on the closed toilet lid in the bathroom and stared into space.

A long soak in a bubble-filled bath should have worked wonders. It may have soothed her body, but it hadn't soothed her mind.

Being left alone whilst Zane put his plan into action was torture. She'd wanted to accompany him. *Insisted* on it.

But he'd refused.

Under normal circumstances, she'd have dug her heels in and kicked up more of a fuss before accepting defeat, but this time she'd quickly accepted his decision. It would have been wrong to push it. Furthermore, there hadn't been time to argue. With a very thin window of time to pull this off the way Zane was determined it should be done, she didn't want to do anything which could impede that.

Hearing a noise the other side of the door, Erin's stomach leapt into her mouth. *Was that someone entering the bedroom?*

Had the police come to arrest her for Anthony's murder? Or was it one of Zane's enemies, who should have been an ally, come to gloat and give her news things had gone wrong? Was

Sonny yet another traitor and Zane had walked into a trap? Or worse, was it Marco himself – his gun aimed straight for her and then – *poof* - she'd be gone.

It would all be over in a flash.

Realising it was the flaps of the bathroom extractor making the noise, Erin slumped against the cistern. It wasn't the door. No one was here. Not Zane.

Just her.

Alone.

She'd rather this be over and be dead than carry on, than remain in a world free from Anthony where for once she had a future, if Zane wasn't part of it. Life without him was not something she could consider.

Not now.

Just like she'd envisaged, there was no guilt for being the one to pull the trigger and end Anthony's miserable, spiteful life. None whatsoever.

Maybe there should have been, but there wasn't. Not a shred. What did it matter? It didn't. The only thing that mattered was that Zane returned to her.

She didn't care if he had no firm or money. She didn't care if he had nothing. None of that was important. Only him being by her side was.

However, it would matter to *him* and Erin knew just how it felt to live and breathe the need for revenge. How it ate away at the very soul if it couldn't be achieved. But because of Zane, because he'd stepped aside, she'd got her revenge. Half of it, at least.

But Zane not wanting to kill Marco at his own wedding reception seemed an odd decision, until Erin came to slowly understand the reasoning behind his logic was much better that going in all guns blazing. The outcome for Marco would be harder hitting and a lot more painful.

Of course, Zane would kill Marco in due course. His sense of honour dictated that to be the only way, but this plan would go a small way in pushing his brother to experience what it felt like to lose everything.

What was good for one, was good for the other.

Yeah, she understood that.

It went without saying that when the time came for Zane to take Marco out, she would be there to help him through - the only person who could.

Erin shuddered, despite the heat from the steaming bath she'd had to pass the time and concentrate on something other than what had or *could* have unfolded during the time she'd lay in it.

But if her world had crashed and something had gone wrong... That Zane was no more...

A lump formed in Erin's throat and hot tears burned the back of her eyes. If she had to go on without Zane, then the one and only thing she would ensure before taking the decision to join him, would be to do the one thing he hadn't been able to complete.

She would kill Marco Morelli. She would kill him both for Zane and for herself. The one remaining name on her list belonged to the man who had *really* killed her father and the one who, if her worst nightmare was realised, the one to also take the love of her life away from her.

Yes, she'd kill Marco for both those reasons and for both her and Zane.

Erin's stomach made its way into her throat once again at the sound of a slamming noise. It was definitely the door this time and not the extractor grate.

Jumping up, she flung open the door from the bathroom and dashed wide-eyed into the bedroom. Her eyes fell to Zane as he placed his gun on the side table, then casually shrugged his leather jacket from his shoulders.

Within a split second she'd inspected him for signs he'd been hurt; any hint of there having been problems. But seeing his mouth curl into a half-smile, relief fell over her. A strangled sob escaped from between her lips as she lurched forward to throw herself into his arms.

'Part one of the mission completed,' Zane murmured into the sweetness of Erin's freshly washed hair. Cupping her face in his hands, he tilted it up, his heart swelling at the relief and love in her eyes.

He never thought he'd feel this way about anyone, let alone for someone like he'd first believed she was. Or even for who she *really* was - the daughter of the man who had inadvertently sent his life into the pits of hell.

And this was the very same woman who had on several occasions tried to kill him. She'd very nearly succeeded...

But he hadn't been wrong about Erin on one thing - she was a wildcat - a headstrong, brave and outstandingly beautiful woman with the soul of a warrior. If he got to make the choice, he wouldn't let her go. Now or *ever*.

'I did as planned and Marco saw me, but convinced himself he didn't, just as I thought.' Zane explained. The quick phone call he'd received from Sonny only a few minutes ago as he parked his bike up, confirmed that his wanker of a brother had fallen for his plan, hook, line and sinker.

Zane pressed his lips to Erin's, only for her to pull away a lot quicker than he'd wished. 'I have exactly a week from tomorrow to remove all the shit Marco has caused in my absence and put the firm back to what it should be.'

And he'd very much like it if Erin remained around to share what he could then offer her. But he couldn't expect that, surely? 'I'm going to have my work cut out to pull all of this off, but I'm determined to put this right.'

Erin studied Zane intently, not believing she could ever love anyone like this. 'Don't you mean, "we" do? Unless you want me to, I'm not going *anywhere*.' She pressed her lips to his. 'We're in this together now, Zane. You and me. I want to be with you and I'll help you in any way necessary. Whatever it takes.'

A wide smile broke on Zane's face. 'Fuck, I love you, wildcat! I'll make you as proud of me as I am of you.'

Bursting with happiness at his words, Erin led Zane to the

bed, her hand on the buckle of his jeans. 'I'm already proud of you. More than you realise.'

Pushing Erin backwards, Zane wasted no time in following her onto the bed. 'I doubt others will share your view by the time I've finished and got the firm back to what it should be.'

'Ah, but like you said before, we're not like anyone else, are we?'

Zane's mouth crashed down on Erin's, knowing without a doubt, he'd met his match. That was okay because he couldn't think of anywhere else he'd rather be, than with her. Now he had even more reasons to right things.

And that was exactly what he planned to do.

Next in the Series

SCARRED #2
THE PRICE OF BETRAYAL

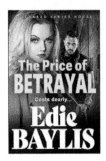

Locating previous loyal members of his firm before his brother took the reins is proving easier said than done for Zane Morelli.

He cannot afford to be spotted around his old haunts before he's ready to strike. Neither can anyone fighting Marco's corner be allowed to get wind of the plan.

Although it is difficult, Zane can wait.

But Erin can't.

Each passing day unable to take revenge on her father's murderer is a further twist of the knife – one that is threatening to slice through what she and Zane have.

And how will Marco's new wife, Hazel, react when she discovers the man she's just married isn't the true heir to the Morelli empire after all...

MORE FROM THIS AUTHOR

ALLEGIANCE SERIES:

TAKEOVER | FALLOUT | VENDETTA | PAYBACK |JUDGEMENT

Daddy's girl Samantha Reynold hadn't bargained on unexpectedly needing to step into her father's shoes and take over the family casino business.

Pampered and spoiled, Sam knows nothing about the rules of this glamorous but deadly new world. She has a lot to learn and even more to prove. But she won't let her family down, especially when it looks like they could lose everything to their biggest rivals – the Stoker family.

Eldest son Sebastian hasn't got time to pander to pretty girl Samantha as she plays at being boss. Rumours are swirling around the streets of Birmingham that have the power to rip the Stoker family apart and destroy everything they've built.

MORE FROM THIS AUTHOR

RETRIBUTION SERIES:

AN OLD SCORE | FINDERS KEEPERS | THE FINAL TAKE

Three families... One prize...

Teagan Fraser had no idea what she was getting herself into when she took on an assignment as a live-in carer for Dulcie Adams – a retired dancer from a Soho club. Dulcie has waited forty years for her lover, Michael Pointer, to return, but she's been living in hope for a time that never came and left looking after something important, which Jonah Powell and his firm want back.

In addition to the notorious Powell firm, there are others wanting to claim what they believe is rightfully theirs and they'll do anything to get it back. If only Dulcie wasn't around it would be a lot easier, but she's difficult to shift...

A lot can happen in a short space of time and Teagan might wish she'd never become involved.

More From this Author

HUNTED SERIES:

THE STATUS DEBT | THE FAMILY LEGACY | THE TARGET OF LIES

Lillian Morgan would do anything to regain the status she lost by marrying beneath her and to cover the sordid details of her husband's death. This includes blackmail and the hand of marriage of her own daughter.

Tori thought her life couldn't get much worse, but someone is not being honest and secrets have the power to rip everyone to shreds.

Especially when life is built on lies.

** This series contains written depictions of graphic violence, sex and strong language. It also contains some themes that may be uncomfortable for certain readers. **

MORE FROM THIS AUTHOR

DOWNFALL SERIES:

UNTIL THE END OF TIME | ESCAPING THE PAST | VENGEFUL PAYBACK

Dive into Seth and Jane's train wreck of a life, where drugs, alcohol and obsessional love means this downright dangerous pair will do *anything* to ensure nothing gets in their way.

They do bad things. *Very* bad things and their promise to love each until the end of time turns into a war against each other.

A war neither of them can win.

** This series contains written depictions of graphic violence, sex and strong language. It also contains some themes that may be uncomfortable for certain readers. **

ABOUT THE AUTHOR

Over the years Edie has worked all over the UK as well as in several other countries and has met a lot of interesting people - several of whom have supplied ideas for some of the characters in her books! She has now settled back in central England with her partner and children, where she is pursuing her writing.

Edie writes gritty gangland and urban fiction for Boldwood Books and Athame Press.

Edie's series so far include her latest – the *Scarred* series; the *Allegiance* series; the *Retribution* series, *Hunted* series and *Downfall* series.

When she isn't writing, Edie enjoys reading and is a self-confessed book hoarder. She also enjoys crochet and music as well as loving anything quirky or unusual.

Visit www.ediebaylis.co.uk for the latest news, information about new releases, giveaways and to subscribe to her mailing list.

gangland | crime | urban

THRILLER AUTHOR

CONNECT WITH EDIE

https://fb.me/downfallseries

https://www.goodreads.com/author/show/17153586.Edie_Baylis

https://twitter.com/ediebaylis

https://www.amazon.co.uk/Edie-Baylis/e/B075FQHWCZ/

https://www.bookbub.com/authors/edie-baylis

https://ediebaylis.co.uk/

info@ediebaylis.co.uk

https://www.fantasticfiction.com/b/edie-baylis/

https://www.instagram.com/ediebaylis/

https://www.tiktok.com/@ediebaylis

https://www.pinterest.co.uk/ediebaylis/

JOIN EDIE'S MAILING LIST

Subscribe to Edie's mailing list for the latest news on her books, special offers, new releases and competitions.

https://ediebaylis.co.uk/signup.html

CWA MEMBER

ACKNOWLEDGEMENTS

Firstly, special thanks goes to the four lovely ladies (you know who you are) - who were brave enough to allow their names to be adopted by some of the characters in this story after winning a competition on Facebook. (I must point out that these characters are in no way anything to do with, or connected to, their namesakes in real life!) Just want to get that out there!

Also, many thanks to the people that kindly read my drafts of *Mirrors Never Lie*. I appreciate your time and feedback.

As always, thanks to all of the supportive friends and readers who give me the incentive to keep on writing. And, of course, love and thanks to my family.

Thank you for reading *Mirrors Never Lie*. I hope you enjoyed reading it as much as I did writing it!

If so, would you please consider leaving a review on Amazon and/or Goodreads. Reviews from readers are SOOOO helpful and especially important to us authors and without you we would have nobody to write for!

Thank you once again and hope you enjoy the rest of my books.

Edie xx

Printed in Great Britain
by Amazon